I0818284

GEMINI GAMBIT • BOOK 6

SINS OF THE ELDERS

D. SCOTT JOHNSON

SINS OF THE ELDERS
D. Scott Johnson

ISBN: 978-1-7360141-8-9 (hardcover)
978-1-7360141-7-2 (paperback)
978-1-7360141-6-5 (ebook)

Cover design by Melissa Lew
Interior layout by Lighthouse24

Chapter 1
Mike

Mike felt the drone coming before he saw it. AC network drones used high-efficiency ducted fans that produced a nearly infrasonic throb. It was getting louder.

He and Kim had chosen one of the more remote portals on the planet they'd picked for a new phase of Sidereal testing. The revived project to create Earth's own native portal had made it to the prototype phase, but they needed much more data on production portals like the bemians used. Spencer's invented name, short for Bug-Eyed Monsters, lumped all the diverse life forms across the galaxy into a culture with vanishingly little variation. In spite of its off-the-cuff origin, the name had stuck. Mike caught Maff using it a couple of times, and she grew up with this culture.

The prototype back home filled an entire data center building, with its supporting machinery taking up the ones on either side of it. As far as they could tell, bemian portals were self-contained units not much bigger than a garden shed with a giant hoop bolted to the top. The desolate, ruined city they'd found provided the perfect opportunity to do a deep dive into one without arousing suspicion.

The remoteness made the drone patrols infrequent but not nonexistent. It wouldn't take long for the nodes to react if they were spotted. The ones here were far less pleasant to deal with than the ones on more established worlds, which was saying something. "Look out," he said softly to Kim, "incoming."

She withdrew from the portal's maintenance realm and popped off the control dongle they used to hack into it. He smiled. She'd completed the takeover. They could now use its code and functions to refine Earth's single prototype. She narrowed her eyes. "Are they getting more frequent?"

If they were, it might mean they'd been spotted. "I don't think so. This one's well within the regular patrol window."

She put out one of her wrist straps, and he used it to help her off the floor. Where most couples held hands, they had to use straps or ribbons so they didn't trigger Kim's touch sensitivity. After close to two years of marriage, it'd become second nature to them both. She usually made them part of her outfits nowadays.

He watched her switch mental gears from hacker to behind-the-lines spy. When she concentrated, Kim could blot out the world, but now free of the realm, he could tell she felt the drone too. "Next time don't wait so long to get me out."

He shrugged and started jogging toward their shelter, a ruined structure that was once a bank, judging by the walls and door of the room in its center. Kim's strides fell in quickly behind him. It wasn't going to be close, but they'd both learned not to cut things fine when they didn't need to.

He pulled the heavy door shut. Since this was a precontact structure, it didn't have the unworldly smooth and immortal hinges that the AC network would eventually gift the natives. The only reason they worked at all was Mike had brought along a case of penetrating oil and had used it all on the hinges. It worked now, making it easier to seal their inner sanctum from prying scans.

They watched the drone search through their passive sensors installed on what was left of the roof by carefully programmed nanomachines. The steel box they were in was too thick and too hard to be drilled through by human tools, but the specialized nanoarmy they'd brought along with them made short work of knitting wires directly through the material. The result was a hardwired sensor suite that couldn't be detected. And, while they were at it, a carefully concealed ventilation system was added to ensure they didn't suffocate after shutting the door.

Mike relaxed as the threads of his real consciousness uncoiled in the interstitial areas around the virtual private realmspace that he installed inside the vault. The drone was moving in a generalized search pattern they'd figured out.

Still undetected.

They selected this world instead of Teliria, the world inhabited by the half teddy bear, half armored knight aliens they'd visited via Maff's transport. The inhabitants, humanoids with a catlike appearance, were at a different point in their uplift cycle. Teliria had been held back for thousands of years by the local AC network because, somehow, the natives had nearly figured out how to defeat them with technology barely more sophisticated than vacuum tubes. There were no portals to examine there, and they weren't arriving any time soon.

Teliria's progress had been frozen, and perhaps a thousand years had passed since the nodes first arrived. This planet was in the early stages of uplift, only a few decades in, a chance discovery made after Spencer found the coordinates and a fragmentary description of the process in some of the data they'd captured during the Teliria hacking run.

An AC network setting itself up on a new world needed a strong transportation component. Basically, a larger than normal number of portals. The network used it to easily move resources over vast distances.

So while Teliria didn't have any portals, this planet had perhaps five times as many as a typical developed bemian world, providing access to ones that'd ended up out of place and disused. It was only after he and Kim had arrived that they discovered the fragmentary nature of Spencer's find hadn't left a complete description of how uplift worked.

Mike didn't know what he expected. All he'd ever seen were societies thousands, maybe millions, of years past their initial encounter event. Earth's fictional ideas were dominated by *2001*-like encounters that saw primitive natives overawed by their new alien overlords. There was clear evidence that Teliria resisted their assimilation, but it'd happened so far back in that planet's past that the ruins had lost almost all evidence of actual violence.

That was not the case here.

Kim asked, "Do we have enough telemetry to identify the type of drone?"

"Not with passive scanners, not unless it gets too close for comfort."

The drones came in several variants. Most were harmless, little more than half a dozen arms holding ducted fans with a sensor pod slung underneath them. Others were considerably more dangerous: heavily armed combat units capable of destroying entire divisions of the pre-mechanized armies that represented the doomed best any organized state on this world could muster.

"At least it's not a transport," she said with a grimace.

A transport would've flown past with a large cargo of people who thought they could hide from the nodes, run away from them, fight them, or in some other way avoid a fate that promised prosperity with an iron fist. He didn't know where the transports went or what became of the people they carried. He didn't want to know. Neither did Kim. Those captives were not going on trips to exotic resorts. The nodes, economical to a fault, only used woven mesh to hold their captives instead of cargo holds.

Or boxcars.

They weren't much more than giant fishing nets, in fact, so their cries and screams were clearly audible whenever one was close by.

He kept a careful eye on the probe's movements while Kim made lunch. Meal 05, the first MRE they had after inadvertently eating only peanut butter and crackers for a week, held a special place in both their hearts. She put his plate down, and the scent that hit him brought him right back to a camp in an alien wood, vivid and real as if he was experiencing it again. Olfactory memories were a thing that couldn't exist where his threads lived. Human senses were always finding new ways for him to experience things.

She smiled at him from across their small camp table. "Yeah, it does bring me back."

He'd been with her long enough that this not-quite-telepathy, the ability to understand what someone else was thinking by the situation and the expression on their face, no longer disturbed him. Quite the opposite. It was comfort on a level he hadn't known was possible.

The scanning suite pinged as they were cleaning up. The drone was now gone. "Back to the grindstone," he said as he dumped the meal's remains into the nanorecycler. They'd picked the lock on this portal. Now it was time to make a new key that only they could use or copy.

It was an hour into that session that he felt it: a sound he couldn't quite hear, a light that wasn't there. It wasn't the same as the drones. His threads picked it up. He'd been using them to assist Kim hacking the portal not only in the interstitial space between and around realms but also inside the portal's realm with his remote-controlled constructs. He stilled everything trying to identify it.

"Do you sense that?" he asked her.

She looked up from the realm's console. "Sense what?"

It was gone now. "I don't know. Must've been a glitch in the matrix."

She turned back to her console. "That's not a joke to make in this situation."

He felt it a second time, much stronger. "You don't hear anything?"

She stopped and concentrated. "Nothing." He hadn't wanted to worry her, but her face said that effort had failed. "What's wrong?"

This time whatever it was had a direction. "It's coming through my threads. Or beyond them." It had to be from the interstitial, where his threads naturally took up residence wherever he went. Now that he'd experienced a *much* larger version than the one he'd grown up in on Earth, it was turning out to be much stranger than anyone realized. If it were inside the realm, Kim would've heard it. Maybe. Directions were complicated living in a dimension outside the regular four. "I need to check it out."

He could tell she was concerned but not worried. Or angry. That was old Kim. The new one was more confident. He liked the new one a lot better. "Let me know if there's anything I can help with."

Now fully focused on the problem with all threads engaged, the next occurrence was easy to interpret.

It was a distress call.

"Someone's in trouble, in here with me," he said.

"How is that possible?"

"I'm not sure. Let me try something." His threads occupied the interstitial spaces of any realmspace he connected to. They lived in the place between realms and the constructs that held them. Trying to communicate through this space directly had never occurred to him. It would be like trying to listen for people talking inside his human host.

Bemian interstitials were different in that for whatever reason, they never seemed to allow a multithreaded consciousness to emerge. They were instead usually used by interpreters to anchor threads that allowed them to communicate instantly across vast distances. But there was no Guild presence on this planet. There wasn't supposed to be anyone, or anything, else in here.

So he improvised. "Hello?" He sent it as an emotional pulse down the main trunk of his threads.

The reply was immediate. The person creating the message must've been broadcasting already, trying to reach out as far and as wide as possible. Now the signal was sharp and focused. "Hello! Please help us! We're in danger!"

That was a much stranger reply than he'd ever expected. It was in English, and it wasn't coming from Earth. Only two other people *not* on Earth could speak that language to him, and he was married to one of them. The other was traipsing through a forest on Teliria. This wasn't Kim, and it wasn't Spencer. Spencer didn't have the right kind of radio anyway.

He was getting distracted. "Who are you?" Mike knew what string telephones were. They were a big part of 1950s nostalgia realms. He never counted on *being* the string.

And he couldn't shake the impression he knew who this was. He recognized the voice but couldn't place it.

"Please, I need your help!"

The speaker on the other end sent more information down the line, letting Mike build up low-resolution pictures and audio. The images were hard to understand at first, but eventually resolved into something he recognized. Monsters were attacking what looked like humans dressed in togas.

The urgency took on new energy. He returned to Kim, explained what he'd found, then said, "I think it's humans, and they're in trouble. Something's attacking them."

"What? That doesn't make any sense. Humans? Out here? It's not possible."

"And in several different ways. It's some kind of message, but I don't know how it's being transmitted. It's not coming from Earth. I don't recognize what's attacking them. They shouldn't be in the space or dimension they're in. But I've got a feeling about this." Intuition was a topic they frequently discussed—often enough that they'd both agreed his was stronger than most. "I don't know who this is, but I think I might."

"Now *you're* not making sense," she said as she wrapped up tool constructs and vanished them into storage. "Is it safe?"

"For me? I think so. This is a communication, not a contact. If they could reach my threads, I would've known."

Another pulse came down the line. This time it included enough information that he got some realspace space coordinates. Whatever this was, it was near an actual location in the galaxy. "It's happening somewhere around here." He called up a map that showed a system well inside a developed sector of the galaxy. No worries about concentration camps there. "I need to hurry."

"I'll pack up here. If you need me, say the word." She fed the coordinates to their captive portal. "Don't hang around, then. Go."

Chapter 2
Spencer

"Y'all gave those gas bag gangsters permission to set up shop *on your planet*?" Spencer asked Tapov, his Telirian friend and now queen of all she surveyed. He handed over the flask he'd brought along. The first time she'd sipped whiskey had been a revelation to him. Apparently Telirians preferred *stronger* stuff. But it did make things more sociable.

They were trekking through the woods in a remote corner of Ontara, the territory Tapov had inherited after her father died during a flash flood. Spencer had been trying to figure out a way to pay a visit, but Earth was located in the middle of the Great Galactic Fuck-All, and Maff was too busy to give him a ride. Then Kim mentioned that they were testing the Sidereal portal for real. It took a *lot* of arguing, but eventually they put him on the traveler list. He got to lead his own team!

But it was work—not his idea of a good time. He ticked off the boxes on his task list, made sure the rest of the team was settled in with a field-promoted new leader, a.k.a. his second-in-command, then he fucked off right out of there.

That was step one of the plan. Step two was trickier, or at least he thought it would be. Then he gave a certain pallun a call.

"Nah, kid, we'll get you there," Sornik, Maff's point of contact with Silaria's underworld, said when Spencer met with him, sitting in front of Samatarra's, a pallun butcher shop. These gangsters preferred to meet in the open in front of a store that sold cured and smoked meat like in countless revival realms he'd traipsed through back home. Why the hell not? "We set a thing up over there a couple of months ago."

Spencer thought of the story of the locusts and the ants, from an iconic scene in *The Sopranos,* involving a hapless sporting goods store owner who had been manipulated into losing everything he had. This could be like that but on a planetary scale. It wasn't the development he'd counted on.

Sornik chuckled. "Relax, kid. It's a staging base for our business. Tapov gave us permission. We're fully registered with the network."

So he hitched a ride on the next smuggling run. Or, as they put it, the *transport of items with unclear licensing*.

In the woods, Tapov shrugged at his question about how they were allowed to set up shop here. "We didn't see the harm in it and neither did the nodes. Your pallun friends are far away from any of our villages or farms and are paying us for the privilege. That's going into a trust fund the nodes set up. The whole planet is getting a share."

She said it like it was the most common thing in the world. It was yet another entry in a small collection of facts that made him grudgingly respect the AC network. Oh, he didn't think they were the good guys. He'd seen how they worked. They were a bunch of murderous bastards, robotic Commies who'd commit mass murder because killing everyone who disagreed with them was a fucking quick strategy for conquering a world.

A soulless network of murderous nodes that eventually created peaceful, well-functioning planetary societies through oppression and violence made a morally complicated place for him. It wasn't supposed to work that way. There shouldn't be success from those methods and means. It bothered him that there was.

Tapov looked at him as they walked. "Did I say something wrong?"

He'd rolled himself up in his own head. That's what he got for hanging around Mike all the time. "Nah. This is a very different place, and sometimes I forget what that means. Anyway, what else is happening, Your Majesty?"

She shook her head. "This is my first—what did you call it? *Vacation?*" Tapov used the English word, which, with her accent, made her sound sort of German. At least, the kind of German he'd heard in YouRealm travel shows. He nodded, and she continued, "Please don't address me that way, even if you're joking. I need to at least pretend to be normal for a few days."

"Fair enough, Tapov. So how're they hanging, Tapov?"

She got a sour look at his sudden switch to English, then she laughed. It was a nice sound. Different because of the somewhat bear-like snout, but nice. "I didn't understand half the things you said in those caves. I don't know why it'd be better now. Being in charge has been…interesting."

It seemed girls liked guys asking about their lives no matter what part of the galaxy they were from. Once she got started, he let her roll and learned about every secret and gossip that'd come across her desk for the entire year.

"Whoa," he said after she dropped a particularly juicy tidbit about a local lord caught sleeping with their version of a veterinarian. The scandal was more about the vet being a commoner than the lord being, you know, married. "Are you sure you're allowed to tell me these things?"

"You're the only person I *can* tell these things. It's nice. What have you been up to on Earth?"

So he spent the rest of the hike and most of setting up camp explaining how his year had gone. Their conversations swirled and went on through the night, continuing long after the campfire had burned down to coals. At one point, they naturally leaned in toward each other, but then stopped, at the same time, even.

He had to take the sting out of this. "What're you thinking?"

"I don't know. You?"

"Me either. I think there's something here, but it's not triggering all the right signals. This *is* my first rodeo." He quickly explained what that was before she clouded up. "Does that make sense?"

She turned around and snuggled against him. A part of him wanted, or rather, a part of him *expected* to feel desire, but he didn't. It wasn't bad. It was different, and he didn't know what to make of that.

Some sort of the same argument must've been going on in her head because she tensed up a little but then relaxed. "This is nice," she said. "Will you be happy with nice?"

"Will you?"

He could feel her nod, the fur on her head very different from human hair but still pleasant to the touch. "It's my first *rodeo* too. I think we should stay away from *bulls* and *broncos* for now." She didn't know English all that well but caught on to the vocabulary fast enough.

The next morning was both more and less awkward than he'd expected. That was mostly on him. He'd had his share of girlfriends, and sometimes things felt like that. But then she'd move a different way or her eyes would catch the light, and...his emotions didn't feel wrong—they felt switched off again, like a part of him expected to respond with a bit of flirting romance. It was a startling sensation, not a frightening one.

Tapov didn't seem to notice at all. Or, if she did, he couldn't be sure of it. He caught a few awkward glances sent his way as they packed up the camp.

Nice. Concentrate on nice.

It got much easier a few hours later. The original forbidden zone, the one they'd once been trapped in after getting lost in a cave complex, had been buried under a concrete slab that the nodes built a base on top of. But it wasn't the only one. Teliria had a shit ton of them, large and small. They were the ashes of the civilization the nodes had snuffed out who knew how many thousands of years ago.

This site was much smaller, a single large crater surrounded by only a few smaller ones. It was very remote, closer to Sornik's place than any Telirian settlement but still pretty much in the middle of bumfuck nowhere.

As before, there was a cave system underneath what had to be a collapsed structure of some sort. This time, though, he came well prepared with dozens of small sticky reflectors he could attach to any surface. No getting lost this time. As Kim was sometimes fond of saying to him, *it can learn.*

Telirians had no concept of archeology, and since it was just him and Tapov, they weren't going to give the latest version of *Time Team* any competition. But what they lacked in screens and shovels, Spencer made up for with tech. Metal detectors, to be specific.

"You wave it around, and it finds metal?" she said as she looked suspiciously at the XP Deus XXV he'd unfolded out of his pack. "How?"

"Do you want the long answer or the short answer?"

She rolled her eyes. "Short answer, please."

He threw his arms open. "Magic!"

She smiled wryly. "Okay, I guess I deserved that one. Maybe a little bit more info?"

He wasn't clear on the subject but hit the highlights as they searched. Practicing back home had taught him it wasn't as simple as waving the thing over the ground and finding treasure under every signal. There was a trick to it, kind of an *art of the wave* that let you visualize what might be under there by the way the thing read the signal. He'd done his research and had brought along a pair of pinpointers too. They'd set him back a bit, but the way she jumped slightly every time it found something made it worth it.

At the end of the day, they had a respectable pile of junk in front of them. A lot of it was unrecognizable, but not all of it. An artifact about as big as his hand would've fit right in back home in the nineteenth century.

"It's a telegraph key." He rummaged around and found other recognizable pieces. "For a *wireless* telegraph."

Most of those words had to be in English. Neither of the languages she knew had words for any of it. So he explained the principle as he tried to assemble the junk. It wasn't all there, but it was enough to build a respectable reconstruction.

Once he was finished, he couldn't interpret her expression. "So what do you make of all this?" he asked.

She picked at the pieces slowly. "On the one hand"—she sat up with a huge smile on her face—"this is all amazing. My ancestors were *different,* not savages like the nodes told us. They had a sophisticated civilization." Her face quickly clouded, and she sat down heavily. After a moment, she shook her head. "I can't be angry about what they did to us. I *can't.* We're nothing like my ancestors anymore. If I got angry about it, I'd go crazy."

Spencer had grown up in the South, so he'd been raised around *lots* of people who had very good reasons to hate what other people had done to them in the past. He would never for a second say he had any real inkling what it was like to be Black in the US, but he had a feeling Tapov might.

Then she got a wry expression. "But is it weird that I think this is...kind of primitive? I mean, the nodes have realms. They communicate across the galaxy. Compared to that, this seems"—she tapped the telegraph key a few times—"it seems *parshan.*"

The word translated to *dinky,* and he couldn't exactly disagree. But there was a much darker implication. He'd been thinking about it all year, putting together what must've happened. "It's almost certainly how they found you."

She looked at him quizzically, then gasped. She dropped the key like it was radioactive. "How?"

"It's an idea I've been kicking around with the crew back home. How do the nodes find civilizations? How do they make sure the planet will be easy to conquer?" He picked up the key and tapped it a couple of times. "Radio waves."

It took more rounds of word definition to get his meaning across, but she caught on quickly. Radio waves leave a planet at the speed of light. "The nodes must have supersensitive radio antennas as part of their kit. This," he pointed at the reconstruction, "is as far as your people got before they fell out of the sky."

"It is so mind blowing," she said, voice barely above a whisper. "We're reconstructing a history of my people, ones who lived so long ago we've forgotten all about them."

It was pretty freaky, not the least because he and Tapov were the very first archeologists on the whole planet. Earth had lots of old sites, but most had been plundered or farmed over. By imposing forbidden zones, the nodes had inadvertently created pristine opportunities for Tapov's people to learn about their own past.

His thoughts were interrupted by a weird beeping. "What's that?"

Her shoulders fell as she stood and dusted herself off. "Nothing good. Come on."

The dig site was separated from their camp by a small copse of woods. On the other end, there was a drone hovering a few feet off the ground.

"Lady Tapov," it said. "An urgent matter requires your attention."

Chapter 3
Kim

She watched Mike go, knowing it was the right thing to do but hating it all the same. He was the only one who could help whoever it was who'd called him. She stayed because they couldn't leave all their gear behind. It had to be returned to Earth or destroyed to prevent any chance of leaving a clue to their home's location.

And there would be no one she trusted to keep an eye on Matthew Watchtell.

After learning about Helen's maneuvering to put him in charge of Sidereal, Kim got angry. Very angry. But she didn't rage. The absolute inability to control her temper was now firmly in the past. She'd gone through too much to get that control. It didn't feel righteous anymore. It felt like she was cheating.

Instead, Kim gently removed Helen from her life. There were no angry displays, no shouting matches, no petulant door slams. Kim put Helen in a kind of mental freezer. Required interaction was professional and brief. She avoided social situations, but when they couldn't be avoided, she didn't make it weird trying to find an excuse not to go. Now that the bubbling cauldron of rage had been emptied, being civil was easy.

Helen, to her credit, had been as good as her word. Mike was the one who did the meetings and then briefed her on what had happened. Only once had Kim needed to interact with Watchtell, see him, hear his voice, or otherwise be in his presence. She had never heard of anyone being forced to work with their rapist, but so far it'd been easier than she could've possibly expected.

With Mike gone, that all ended now. The only thing worse than working with Watchtell was leaving him alone unsupervised. She grudgingly conceded he'd demonstrated exceptional administrative skills. He'd been a successful White House chief of staff for a reason. Within weeks of taking over the public face of Sidereal, technically *re*taking it, since he'd originated the thing, staff with proper security clearances started taking up residence. They now had a comptroller, a logistics coordinator, a scrum master, an HR department, and a janitor-slash-groundskeeper. Only a precious few knew exactly what was going on.

Helen's role in it all was easier to get over. Kim now knew that she'd put Watchtell in charge for good reasons. And it was time. Time to get over it, time to bring Helen back into her life, time to accept that for whatever reason, the universe itself was dead set on keeping Matthew Watchtell somewhere nearby.

So while Mike was off rescuing whoever it was that had called him, Kim would attend her first Sidereal meeting. Today's was listed as a *sprint review*, a biweekly event to go over what had been accomplished in the previous two weeks. It would include a demo of the portal, so only those fully cleared for the project were invited.

The weirdest part was the role Mike had in how this upcoming meeting worked. Mike and Kim were bemian interpreters. Okay, they were a *kind* of bemian interpreter. Anywhere else in the galaxy, interpreters were a combined life form, half threaded and half…whatever the realspace species was on any particular planet. She and her husband were unique in that Mike was half human, half threaded, but all himself. Kim got the languages and the dimension walking and the whole getting people who didn't understand each other to do exactly that, and Mike had threads he could use to access any realmspace or node-designed thread anchor anywhere he went. These threads could then be used by anyone with a properly configured realm or phone to communicate to anyone else, instantly, who was also similarly equipped at the other end. Her husband wasn't only the love of her life, he was also her wi-fi connection to Earth.

Since he and Helen were the only ones able to do this, bandwidth was limited. She had to use a virtual screen set up in her enhanced-vision channel. She waited until the clock hit the start time on the dot and made the connection.

"Mrs. Trayne, what a wonderful surprise."

Of course he'd be here. He was in charge after all. She chanted the diamond sutra in her head. Mike had taught it to her on their honeymoon, and it did help. She was *done* with the past. She told herself that this was a conversation with a bureaucrat who was on the other side of the galaxy. Nothing more.

As Tonya liked to say, *prevarication in this instance may help.*

Helen stepped in gracefully, so Kim didn't have to acknowledge the worm as the first thing she did. "I thought Mike was supposed to attend?"

"He got called away at the last minute." The two of them stared at Kim expectantly. "He's okay." *You hear me, mister? Be okay.* "A discussion for another time."

Helen opened a text channel, a trivial effort for her since both she and Mike could, and often were, doing dozens of things in dozens of places at once. And that was when they weren't trying.

I wish you'd given me some advance notice. I needed to discuss anomalies in W's behavior with Mike, but you know him better and would've been a better choice.

W was Watchtell. She'd be annoyed at Helen's gruff behavior later. He was acting up to the point Helen thought she needed help. That was not a good sign.

What's wrong?

"Very well," Helen said out loud. "Due to the classified nature of the demonstration, we'll have the other department heads summarize their sprint achievements and drop off."

Nothing I can put my finger on, Helen replied. *I've kept him in check easily enough, but I'm concerned it might be too easy.*

As the reports droned on, Kim quickly segmented Watchtell off on her screen, allowing her to look directly at him without seeming to. *He seems normal enough.*

It may be nothing. We'll synch up after the call.

The reports might not be sparkling entertainment, but they couldn't be ignored. Once that was over, Kim had a question. "Are we expecting more people to attend?" Usually the president and prime minister would show up for the demos, but it was only Watchtell and Helen.

"They cancelled, unfortunately," Watchtell said. "The new coordinate controllers interest them, but the imams have gotten unruly again."

Kim didn't keep up with any political news back home. It was petty and stupid when she was a normal—normal for her—person working a regular job. Now? Now it was childish. Not that it wasn't childish to begin with. Imams meant Iran, a place that frequently underwent cycles of protest, murderous suppression, relative calm, and then protests again. Managing the introduction of bemians to leaders who sincerely believed the world would be better off if the traditional sayings of an ancient prophet became global law, and who still celebrated the killing of anyone who got in their way, was thankfully far beyond her pay grade.

Since this was a demo, they were already set up in the main portal room. Now that Kim had spent a long time with bemian versions, she had to admit that this human one lacked refinement. A crude knockoff would be a better description. Still, considering that bemian portal tech dated back potentially billions of years, humans had done pretty well in the time they'd had.

The device's main structure, a giant ring filled with rippling light, snapped to life. The department head for coordinate components, a.k.a. the team in charge of navigation, worked the console controls. "We've installed our first innovation." He pressed a button, and the center of the portal, which had always been opaque, faded into a clear picture of a field. As always, the grass wasn't quite right, the trees in the distance weren't exactly the right shape, and the sky was greener than it should've been.

Kim couldn't help herself. "Remarkable." Humans had one-upped the original portal designers. It was a minor improvement, but useful.

Watchtell walked forward and stood in front of the opening. "The resolution is quite good."

Helen joined him. "Is there any time delay?"

Suddenly the scene in the portal changed to something much darker, Kim caught movement next to Helen, and then her connection dropped.

"Helen? Are you okay?" Silence. She tried to reopen it, but it timed out. Kim started to reach out to Mike but then she got notice of an incoming connection. Text only.

Can you see this?

Helen, is that you?

Yes. I'm fine.

What happened?

I'm such a fool. I've been foiling Watchtell's machinations for months now, but I got complacent.

Helen was better than Mike about it, but still sometimes got caught up in the wrong set of details. *What happened?*

He pushed me through the portal and then shut it off. A set of coordinates came through. *I think I'm going to need some help getting home.*

That trumped any research Kim had left, especially now that *nobody* was keeping tabs on Watchtell. *I'm on my way.*

Chapter 4
Helen

She hated to admit that Kim was right about Watchtell. But that wasn't fair. Kim didn't have anything to do with this. Helen hated to admit that she was wrong. She thought she'd failed in China because she couldn't manage a mob of cunning old men. She was as much of a failure, if not more, trying to manage one.

As she stood to the side of a portal that opened up onto a bustling bemian urban plaza, she reflected on her complacency. Her network of contacts was equal to if not greater than Watchtell's, a factor that for a long time easily compensated for his increasingly sophisticated attempts to oust her.

In the end, all it took was a shove.

The demo wasn't real. Helen would bet that he'd faked it all. And he might not have been trying to put her on the other side of the galaxy. Thinking like criminals was part of her skillset, and thinking like Watchtell made her want to get rid of a rival permanently.

Lucky for her, that wasn't how portal tech, theirs or bemians, worked. For reasons still being worked out, when a portal activated, it *always* connected to some other portal. This was why June and the staff of the powerplant, the very first human portal users, ended up somewhere.

And so had she.

Whereas June's trip had taken her to some bucolic spot in a remote wilderness, Helen's had dropped her in the middle of a city.

It was as cosmopolitan as any large bemian conurbation, with dozens of different species busily getting on with their day. There were even pallun, although not so many for this to be Silaria, their home world. She hadn't been that lucky.

This wouldn't be the portal Kim would come through either. They were still working out what the rules were for how they interconnected, but one of the big ones was sectors. The galaxy had been divided into fourteen of them, a number with a reason lost to time. These were then subdivided into districts, and then once more into systems. The interconnectedness increased at each level. Navigation was easy and direct if you were traveling around on the same planet. Going to nearby systems required some walking and the occasional tram ride from station to station. Crossing districts was done from a select number of stations. Crossing sectors could only be done from specific stations, usually less than a dozen on any one world.

Kim was in a different sector, so it would take some doing to get to Helen's location. She consulted a portal map and set out for the system station Kim would end up at. They'd meet in the middle. Due to a quirk of the route, Helen arrived at the sector transfer station well before Kim.

She picked up a tail less than five minutes after arriving. That was interesting, considering she hadn't planned to make this trip. A kaleidoscope of possibilities presented themselves, but her lack of data meant they were both probable and impossible at the same time. She needed more data. It was a rhon, a common birdlike bemian that Tonya once described as a walking, talking stork. Helen couldn't improve on that description. Being in bemian space, she had access to regular interpreter threads, so Helen requested one from the local network as she walked.

Now suitably equipped, she could see that the rhon was female, middle aged, and wearing common clothes. Helen wished such threads were available back home. Interpreters didn't merely translate languages, they subliminally explained appearance and meaning. It would make her job as a private detective much simpler.

Walking through a bemian city would normally be spent compiling an annoying catalog of similarities and differences. Helen appreciated that she was one of a handful of people who knew about intelligent life in the galaxy, and one of the very few who'd visited their worlds. But it should be much more vibrant than it was. Humans had imagined alien civilizations that were more interesting than the real thing. It was different, sometimes profoundly, but *the differences were all the same*. Same different buildings. Same different clothes. Same different body plans. Same different vehicles. If she set up a residence in a bemian city, she'd have someone paint a door green instead of red. She'd spark a revolution.

The first tail peeled off and was replaced by a second, this time a variation of scaled humanoid she didn't recognize. The species didn't matter as much as the technique: they were professional, they had resources, and the ones she'd spotted may have been *meant* to be spotted. She changed her route to spiral into the portal station Kim would be arriving at instead of going directly toward it. This would force whoever it was to pull resources out of position, and she'd be able to spot those.

The decision turned out to be a life saver when she caught a set of interpreter staff vehicles parked one street over from the one she was using to circle the station. It was the first time she'd seen such transports in person. All Mike and Kim had were stories and some holo recordings of them breaking out of a La'fan compound surrounded by official interpreter vehicles. They were standard bemian which-way-is-forward designs, faceted and blocky, the artless hallmark of node design. But they were clearly marked with the blue-on-white color scheme of the Guild. They only needed flashing lights to be instantly recognizable as law enforcement.

She changed her pattern from a spiral to a circle, examining the forces between her and the station. This resulted in a good news-bad news situation.

The good news was that they weren't after her. She wasn't sure why someone was tailing her, but it was also likely there was only one. She could've been wrong about the whole thing.

The bad news was how she knew this: the forces around the station weren't pointing outward; they were pointing inward. They weren't here for her.

They were here for Kim.

Chapter 5
Tonya

Tonya looked out into the audience from the stage. The feeling that it was a year ago and she was here to prove a basic theory to aliens was strong because it was what she was here to do. There, the aliens had been actually alien. Here, there were nothing but humans.

Humans who were so different from her, they might as well have been from another world.

"So," she said as the shared vision channel filled with her first slide. "Time is now quantifiable, and tockions are the particles that drive it."

This was at least as big of a challenge as her bemian presentation, but with fundamental differences. Then, she was convincing people who'd been trained not to question what they'd been told for thousands of generations that a new idea could exist, and that they could learn it. And she'd done it. Tenor recently sent her his thesis on Planck's constant—she'd 3-D printed the bemian spelling of that phrase and hung it on her wall—and it was brilliant. He was well on his way to becoming the first bemian particle physicist.

Today she was faced with hundreds of humans who'd spent their entire adult lives as physicists. Decades of dedicated learning at the most prestigious institutes in the world. While the people in the audience were learning how the universe worked, she was recovering from a life on the streets of Philly and DC. Her greatest accomplishment then had been becoming a nurse in a field so in demand that salary negotiations typically started with a ten percent raise on whatever number she named.

She was a nurse and always would be. Physics was something she did as a hobby, a distraction from long nights tending vegetable farms made up of people drugged immobile while their new limbs grew. It would never lead anywhere.

Then Mike showed up. Kim's brilliant not-quite-human husband was without ego when it came to the wacky ideas Tonya had. He helped her test whatever it was to see if it did anything interesting. Having a partner who could model realms down to the quantum level was a lever she could use to move the world.

Then Cyril appeared, showing her that time travel was possible in the most concrete way: by making her do it. Conceptualizing a new idea was always the hardest, biggest hurdle. The rest was usually engineering, theoretically or otherwise.

Which was what she'd done, under some admittedly unique conditions—an attacking intelligent galaxy, being thrown millions of years into the past by a meddling university dean…the normal stuff—to first conceive of and then prove that time worked with particles. That the arrow of time, the way the future becomes the present and then the past, and never the reverse, was both natural and explainable. Last but not least, that the timelines of the universe were unpredictable in the future, mutable in the present, and nearly unchangeable in the past. Going back in time to shoot your grandfather wouldn't create a paradox. It couldn't. The universe wouldn't allow it.

It wasn't down to the hand of God. Not exactly. That part she'd leave to the priests, imams, and rabbis. Rather, it was described in theories and equations that allowed these rules to naturally emerge.

So, yeah. Was she a nurse with delusions of grandeur or a physicist hiding her light under a bushel all these years? This was her first step in finding out.

She'd been publishing bits and pieces of the theory for as long as she'd been building it out. Some of the papers had become popular enough to be noticed by people who mattered. Cambridge

University's Lucasian Professor of Mathematics, of Isaac Newton and Stephen Hawking fame, left a complimentary comment on one of her earlier articles, for example.

And that was how she ended up here, standing in front of people who, on paper, desperately outqualified her.

"As you can see," she said as the fourteenth slide came into view, "the concept of *the present* emerges from the equation naturally."

It wasn't only bemian tech that helped her along. The Knowledge, the giant bolus of rote learning she'd had to memorize to talk to bemians in a way they understood, had, over time, become fully integrated with the rest of her. There was no more Tonya the Chronological Physicist and Tonya the Bemian Specialist in Physics Technologies. It was all her now, but changed. She was calmer, more accepting, and a little more trusting. Her friends would laugh at the idea. Tonya had carefully cultivated her image as an unflappable, easygoing supernurse. With Kim as a best friend and total contrast, that image might've gotten exaggerated a bit.

But deep down inside, the trauma that was her childhood still abided. Tonya had grown up a street urchin, running away from torture and abuse to live over sidewalk grates in Philadelphia. God had a plan, and she did escape, but barely. The nightmares that had her waking up screaming as a teenager had faded but not gone away. Lately, though, they'd been back with a vengeance. What had been a once or twice a year occurrence had been making regular weekly rounds since she'd gotten back from Maff's home world Silaria. Weirdly, it was all about her life as a teenager. None of the scary stuff she'd done recently seemed to count.

That these traumas chose this time in her life to start making themselves known again was a mystery she was exploring at confession with her priest. The Knowledge had somehow given her the tools, and the confidence, to start teasing open the locks she'd set so firmly on those memories.

Changing careers, traveling through time, meeting aliens…those might've had something to do with it too. Maybe overcoming all these enormous obstacles made the ones she'd buried seem less daunting.

"And that," she said as she changed to the last slide, "is the arrow of time."

Opening the floor for questions brought up the one thing she knew would stick in the craw of this audience.

"This is all quite interesting, Ms. Brinks," a dignified dot-not-feathers Indian with a cultured British accent said after she got the virtual microphone. "When will you publish it?"

She smiled and hoped the sudden flush and sweat didn't show. "It's a work in progress. I hope to submit a first draft to *Nature* six months from now."

A ripple of disdainful-sounding noises crossed the room. They were well into the twenty-first century, but clearly her audience had traditions rooted in the previous one. Making such revolutionary claims required rigorous proof and enough information for fellow scientists to tear her theory down to its foundations. That only came through working out complete theories in mainstream peer-reviewed publications. In the old days it took years, not months. But she'd been faster. What they didn't know was she had an assistant who could proofread pages and prove theorems by the dozen all at once. It was a time saver she had no intention of ignoring. And it wouldn't be plagiarism or ghost writing if Mike's name was on the paper too.

The organizer of the symposium, and the man who'd talked her into doing this after she'd raised the same objection at his invitation for her to speak, cleared his throat. "This was never advertised as a presentation of a published work. Ms. Brinks was invited because the nature of her theories is unprecedented."

"Which requires unprecedented proof," the dignified lady shot back. Murmurs of approval made her puff up like a peacock.

"Saanvi, now is not the time." The microphone privilege, seen as a small glowing beach ball in the common enhanced-vision channel, bounced away. The organizer quickly descended the stage and headed toward the lady. Tonya had seen enough couples argue in various emergency rooms and doctor's offices to recognize that these two had been together a long time. Tonya had always heard that academia could be a small world. She hadn't expected it to be demonstrated this graphically.

The next few questions were more evidence that, organizer's wishes or no, these scientists were looking for her scalp. She was able to fend them off, although some were easier than others. In the background, she had an AI taking notes on the holes they'd poked in her theory. Going after her didn't mean they were wrong. Outsiders thought science happened when truths were presented to the public all of a piece, like they'd sprung from the scientist's forehead fully formed. The reality was that truth was never found, the conclusions could make a U-turn if new evidence was presented, and the entire thing resembled nothing so much as a slow-motion rugby scrum fought with exchanges of letters.

The beach ball next landed on a much younger lady, startlingly attractive in a custom-tailored suit. "Do you think these tockion emissions will be affected by the importance of a historical event?"

Her V-tag name flashed up as Rachel Anderson, and her question wasn't one she'd prepped for. And Tonya had prepped for this meeting a long time. "I…I'm not sure." That was a great way to impress a person. She closed her eyes for a moment and, now that she knew to look for it, found the answer. "Yes, it might."

This single insight set the whole room off as people argued about what an *important historical event* could mean in this context. Her question had sent the entire talk rocketing down a rabbit hole Tonya didn't know existed until that moment. It also had the unintended benefit of running the clock out on her presentation without her having to answer another senior member angry about her lack of published papers.

There were obligatory goodbyes, handshakes, and other well-wishers. Saanvi, who in fact turned out to be Mrs. Saanvi Smith-Wallace, wife of talk organizer William Smith-Wallace, the aforementioned Cambridge University's Lucasian Professor of Mathematics, was quite lovely in person, offering to help edit the paper Tonya needed to publish. She intended to take that offer.

Eventually she washed up in the hotel's bar. Lager in hand and poutine on order—the conference was in Montreal, her first time in Canada—she browsed the latest notes from Tenor.

"This seat taken?"

At a distance, Rachel was striking. Up close was, well, closer. She was a little taller than Tonya. Asian, but not like Helen, probably from somewhere far south of Beijing.

Her smile was simple and straightforward. So, not a diva. That was a relief. "Not at all." She chuckled. "You caught me out up on stage with your question."

Rachel shrugged as she sat. "I didn't mean to. History's been a hobby of mine since I left the firm."

That sounded mysterious. "The firm?"

She shrugged and blushed a little. Not a diva, and a little shy on top of it. "RosePhone. I sort of helped develop the first neural phone."

A quick search, which Tonya should've done already but had been too distracted to try, coughed up a headline. FOUNDING VP RACHEL ANDERSON RETIRES TO BECOME TRILLLIONAIRE ARCHEOLOGIST.

Beautiful, smart, shy, and a genuine tech-bro *trillionaire*. The idea that this person was ticking off boxes on a list Tonya had hidden away long ago flashed up and then was ruthlessly stomped down. That was not the plan for this evening. Or ever.

She was normally better at hiding her reactions, but something must've leaked out. Rachel put her hands up defensively. "I was hoping to talk to you before you found out who I was."

It was an unexpected reaction: fear. Tonya wasn't breaking bad news or explaining the long, hard recovery road of limb regrowth, which is where that kind of reaction was common. But maybe that's what happened when you were a famous rich person meeting someone new. "Why?"

"People sometimes get strange after they find out that I have infinite money. You ever heard of the Rage Effect?"

That reference spun her around in ways Rachel could not have understood. It was a signature of what Kim's old crew did.

Corporate destruction with a heaping dollop of humiliation along with it. "I haven't heard that phrase in years."

She motioned to get the bartender's attention. "One of what she's having? Thanks." She turned back to Tonya. "David was in their crosshairs for years. It's not an easy thing to forget." She took a swig of what the barkeep delivered, a local lager Tonya had picked more or less at random. "Nice." She looked like she was about to say more, a lot more. A series of emotions Tonya couldn't quite make out flashed over a face so flawless she had never seen the like in person. Rachel shook her head. "Anyway, let's say I'm glad she's retired now."

Tonya almost said *so am I*. But the vibe she was getting from Rachel wasn't a happy one. And Kim put herself front and center in Tonya's life too many times as it was.

Rachel's expression grew concerned. "Did I say something wrong?"

Tonya shook away her memories. "Not at all. But you don't have to worry. You stumped me on my own theory. I'm interested in you no matter how much money you have."

That came out weirder than she'd meant it to, but Rachel didn't seem to notice. Her eyes flashed, and she got the same sort of enthusiastic expression Mike did when he'd thought of an idea for them to try. "It's how tockions work. I think we can use it to build a…I guess you could call it a history detector."

As she told Tonya about her idea, it became clear that Rachel wasn't Mike. She was more an engineer than a scientist, but she had a firmer grip on the tockions theory than anyone else other than Mike and Kim. And Kim only got it after she ended up with a copy of Mike's knowledge. Rachel didn't need that cheat.

Eventually they moved to a booth, later ordered supper, and worked the problem until the bar closed.

Chapter 6
Maff

Humans called it a *checklist*, and it was required for all the stages of flying an airplane. It was an alien concept on so many levels. That's what nodes were for!

Humans themselves had largely done away with checklists in a full commercial setting. Far too many accidents—fatal accidents—were caused by someone who missed an item on the list. Earth's equivalent of AC nodes, their unduplicate AIs, were normally put in charge of that sort of thing.

But that didn't mean she skipped learning how they worked. The early days of flight training were the worst. Even now, as she was prepping for her second-ever type rating, they made the gas inside her swirl turbulently.

Power: IDLE

Parking brake: ON

Transponder: ON

Engine Start/Stop: RUN

The plane itself was a monument to one of her favorite English phrases: state of the art. Less than a year old, the Cirrus G6 Vision Jet was the lightning-struck edge of one of humanity's ongoing storms of innovation. Engine checklist complete, Maff asked for and received permission to taxi. The aircraft was a living thing, with whirring pumps, squealing brakes, and a jet engine that was its primary motivator. *High-bypass turbojet.* She had to keep the terminology straight.

The next radio request was much harder to make. Flying through storms that would kill a human instantly on a planet without a surface? No problem. This? This was the diamond mountain hidden inside the clouds.

"Manassas tower, Cirrus 572 Tango Mike holding short runway sixteen right request close traffic with the option." It was Earth-pilot speak to ask permission to take off.

Solo.

She'd done this countless times in an old Cessna, several hundred in the realm version of the Cirrus. Simulators weren't the same. As Spencer liked to say, it only counted when her ass was on the line. And it was.

The voice at the other end made her jump so hard she almost missed the clearance. Maff repeated it back like she was taught and stared at the throttle. It was another ridiculous human control that dated back to well before they had anything she'd recognize as technology. She stilled her winds as best she could and then pushed forward only enough to get the wheels rolling. Once the airplane was stopped and centered on the runway, there was only one thing to do.

Follow the checklist.

Transponder: ALT

Strobe Lights: ON

Landing light: ON

Ice protection: AS REQUIRED

Throttle: Full

The little raptor roared and bucked. Maff made minor corrections to hold it straight and kept one eye on the airspeed indicator. When it hit ninety knots indicated airspeed, she gently pulled back on the wheel.

No matter how many times she did it, the transformation always startled her. The noise from the wheels and the bouncing caused by the runway went as still as the sky after a hurricane had passed.

Don't forget the checklist!

Right! Landing gear and flaps up. Set to climb power. Monitor the instruments and cabin pressure. Early on, the vertical speed indicator bounced up and down as she over-corrected too far into a climb and then overcorrected into a dive. Today it wasn't rock steady, but it was plenty good enough to keep the ascent smooth.

The thing about aircraft was that, after takeoff, looking outside wasn't always required. When learning to fly on instruments it was forbidden. Everything Maff needed to know to keep things safe was in front of her. That said, she *didn't* know how to fly only by instruments. She spent a frantic few seconds trying to figure out what was safe to look at.

And then stopped. She'd done this dozens of times in real life. She could pilot this sports pinnace with wings around the sky. She took a deep breath, looked around, righted the airplane—she'd slid into a turn during her panic attack—and flew the route she'd filed. This gracefully circled her back to the airport without crossing one of the many restricted airspaces in the region. When she was eight miles out, she checked Automatic Terminal Information Service for the weather, got the call letter, then keyed her radio on.

"Manassas tower, November Seven Tango Mike is eight miles northwest two thousand feet inbound for full stop with information Bravo."

"November Seven Tango Mike squawk 4343."

That almost sounded professional. Certainly the reply was treating her like she was a professional. She wasn't a crazed pallun.

She could do this.

She'd practiced landing so often that it was almost anticlimactic. Besides, it was magical that controlling the landing wasn't done with the yoke or the rudder, it was done with the throttle. The rest were minor inputs to keep drift under control.

That, *and the checklist.*

Final approach airspeed: Vref to Vref + 10

Flaps: 50-100% AS REQUIRED

Landing gear: DOWN AND LOCKED

She let it float a bit to nail the landing spot and then it was over. The soaring bird again became a bouncy, flimsy, noisy truck. She radioed ground control, and they gave her the taxi clearance she needed to get back to her parking place.

Flaps: UP

Transponder: ON/STBY

Lights: OFF

The feeling of accomplishment was physical. Maff had always been the maverick, the renegade pallun who wouldn't take no for an answer. What she'd done today was unprecedented in the culture she grew up in on more than one level.

Pallun were forbidden to fly in skies like the ones they'd evolved in. It'd been so long ago that none of them remembered how. Maff had fallen an embarrassingly long time when she tried it in Jupiter's atmosphere, saved only by a biological reflex she didn't know she had when she spontaneously started to float.

Maff was a proud rebel, the one who did things no pallun did, who broke unbreakable barriers and lived to tell the tale. What she'd done on Jupiter broke a barrier for her entire people. Heady stuff. But that wasn't all. *Nobody* on a high-grav world like Earth flew at all if they could avoid it. Travel was taken care of with portals and D-ships. The nodes flew drones, and those things crashed sometimes.

It was unprecedented, and it was hers.

All of the people who knew her secret were away on various projects, so she sent them *I did it!* messages instead. She was in the middle of getting congratulations from her fellow flight-school students when a message arrived in her queue. It could've been from Mike, Kim, Tonya, or Spencer, but it wasn't.

It was from her D-ship, *Palatine*. It'd been parked in the warehouse she'd hidden it in since they got back. Maff had been so busy she'd not had time to so much as inspect it. But there were no alarms to indicate anyone had broken into the building, let alone the ship. The message header showed that *Palatine* wasn't the origin of the message. It'd come from somewhere else, nearby. This was impossible. *Palatine*'s radios weren't tuned to Earth frequencies.

She excused herself as quickly as she could and then accessed the message. It was an automated distress announcement, little more than coordinates and a note that help was needed. The coordinates were a midpoint between Jupiter and Saturn. These facts did a great deal to calm her. Whatever it was, it wasn't an invasion, and it wouldn't get here anytime soon. But that still left a raft of possibilities, none of them good. She climbed into her carefully customized van and gave the autodrive instructions to go to the storage facility.

She accessed *Palatine*'s scanners, but they didn't return much. Whoever or whatever this was had settled into a solar orbit far out of their range. Maff prepped, including sending notes to her employer and Tonya in case this took too long. She was fortunate that *Palatine* didn't need to take off the way Earth-designed craft did. It used the transit dimension instead. Once the D-drives had spooled up, she transitioned the ship directly to that dimension. A level three jump got her to the coordinates in a matter of minutes.

It took only a moment to find it: a medium-sized cargo carrier of unmistakably bemian design, but with weird antennas and frameworks stuck everywhere, making it look a little like a scouting ship. That must've been what they were doing. She was back to alien invasion. Or scouting, at any rate. Not good.

But it wasn't all bad. Equally unmistakable were the signs of a drive *and* reactor dump. She'd been through one of those, and it was unpleasant. Whoever was inside that thing had been shaken and stirred vigorously. And wherever they'd come from, they were stuck here.

She tried raising the ship but got no reply. It would've been nice to peer inside through a window but that was a human thing. Bemians used screens to see what was outside. Maybe not in this case, though. Emergency power wasn't good for much more than life support and the beacon. The passengers, if there were any, would be sitting in the dark, but they couldn't see out either. She spared a moment of thought for all the spooky alien shows Earth she'd watched getting a feel for how humans would react encountering the real thing. Then she chuckled. The human imagination had created creatures far more terrifying. The nodes had bred that all out of them long before any planet could join the galaxy.

They shouldn't be here. Earth had remained undiscovered for hundreds of millions of years not only because there were no nodes in the area, but also because the nodes had designed D-ship nav computers to actively avoid it. Nobody knew why. Not even Tonya's cache carried any clues.

She used the ship's grapple and some judicious maneuvering to stabilize it and its orbit. She also snipped the external antenna attached to the distress beacon. Earth's radios wouldn't understand the transmission, but the signal itself was detectable if anyone cared to look for it. Humans didn't have a lot of assets this far out, but there were space probes around. Besides, this might be part of a group. She didn't want it signaling a friend.

But now that she'd given it a close-up look, this ship was all wrong for a scout. Those were small, automated things the nodes used. She didn't know a lot about the AC network's actual military, but there was no reason for any of it to be inhabited. That only happened with a full mobilization. Yet it was clearly inhabited. Life support modules were mounted exactly where they always were.

She was leery of docking with the ship, so she found the ground control panel and connected to the comms.

A screen flared to life in her vision channel. The bridge and engineering sections were empty. She switched to the hold. The screen answered the *who*, but made the *how* and *why* more urgent. And mysterious.

The hold, a large warehouse-like space much bigger than *Palatine*, was filled with pallun.

Dozens of them.

Worse still, there were a lot of Meronim. These were devout pallun who practiced all the proscriptions of their religion with as much vigor as possible. Secular pallun, Eskarn, were also in the mix; she could tell from their less formal environment suits. They were clumped together in small mixed groups, manipulators waving at each other vigorously. When she opened a comm channel, it was filled with chatter. They were engaging in yet another stereotypical pallun behavior.

Arguing with each other. Loudly.

"If you had been praying instead of..."

"I didn't know what the buttons did; nobody..."

"We have enough. What, do you think I'm crazy..."

"Never trust outsiders. Never. They sold us this..."

Stereotypes existed often because there was a tiny kernel of truth to them. In the case of her people, arguing with each other endlessly about anything, the kernel was the size of a superstorm.

"Hello?" she said into the channel. Nobody noticed. *"Hello?"*

Chapter 7
Mike

Kim said go, so he went, sending his primary consciousness through his threads in the direction of the distress signal as his realspace host traversed the portal network to the nearest physical location to what was happening.

He moved faster in his threads and arrived at a scene of absolute bedlam.

It was difficult to understand what he was seeing. A realm of some sort, but unlike any he'd encountered before. It wasn't set up inside a Bbox container like the ones back home, or the bemian equivalent, whose name he hadn't bothered to look up yet. These structures allowed realmspaces in each respective network to be modular, expandable, and easy to back up and restore. The spaces they created that weren't taken up by realms formed the interstitial areas his threads inhabited, and in bemian space held the thread anchors interpreters used to communicate between systems at faster than light speed.

What he saw here was almost organic, as if the realm had grown from a seed into a space of its own making. His viewpoint was above a huge grassy meadow made of rolling hills, with clouds passing in front of a deep-blue sky. If it had been any other situation, he would've been stunned and then consumed with the desire to know how it worked and who built it.

He was instead confronted with streams of dark ghostly figures rushing across the idyllic landscape leaving nothing but destruction and ruin in their wake.

The army of black ghosts wasn't what called him, that much was clear. Directly below him, a single figure ran through the grass: human, female, wearing a hitched-up toga that fluttered behind her. He cast his perception down to her left side.

It was a face he'd never expected to see again. It had been more than three years. She'd led an army of barely conscious unduplicates away from the prison made for them in China. She was second only to Kim's Edmund in age and sophistication, far and away more complex than any other AI on Earth. When she'd been a tortured captive of Matthew Watchtell, her name had been Zeta. After Mike brought her back from the brink of destruction, she changed it.

"Zoe?"

She stumbled for a second. "Mike? Oh my God…MIKE!" There was a fierce maturity behind her eyes. She'd aged, somehow, though her avatar's appearance was identical as far as he could tell.

He continued to walk his realspace host through the portal network. Stepping through a properly designed and connected portal was a lesson in being underwhelmed. He was in one place, and then instantly in the other. There was no sense of transition, no vertigo, no feeling of motion at all. Just a slight bump in excitement, apparently the result of being an interpreter. The first time he felt it, next to Earth's first portal underneath the Yellowstone power plant, it'd been strong enough to draw him toward it. Now it was an easy-to-suppress urge to smile.

One moment his realspace host was on a chaos-riven planet with Kim, the next he was…elsewhere. By a stroke of luck, the physical location he traveled to was in the same sector of the galaxy as his starting point, so no need for lots of transfers.

At the other end of his threads, Zoe was trying to stay ahead of her attackers and not doing a good job of it, running across a grass field with the ghosts chasing behind her like a macabre storm. She held what looked like a large antique vase of some sort, decorated like it came from ancient Greece. It was a weird time to make art. "What's that?"

"I'll explain later. I need a way out of here!"

In realspace, Mike exited the portal station at his destination and jogged down the broad avenue in front of it. He had to find a realspace network access point close enough for a crystal transfer to work. The planet he'd arrived on, the coordinates said it was called Ofeera, was typical of a place that'd host a portal station: a generic bemian urban sprawl. It was like Chengdu and Chicago had nothing but identical kids all over the galaxy.

The threads he'd sent out to search for an access point found a specific target in this city, within walking distance, in fact.

There were differences here from other bemian cities he'd visited, and he cataloged them as he jogged toward his destination. The aliens here were dominated by centauroids. These seemed to be the second most common type of life form behind the humanoid biped shape. The details, sidewalks, doorways, crosswalks, those sorts of things, were a little wider than they would've been back home. While their outfits were much more colorful—Tonya said it was like everyone was wearing their favorite football team's colors—the cuts and styles of the clothing were recognizably formal. Once you got used to it, they were easily understood as business wear.

He arrived quickly at the target: a nondescript maintenance door that faced an otherwise featureless side alley. They may have patched out the gross vulnerabilities in this galaxy, but that didn't mean they were beyond hacking the occasional lock or three. He loaded up Kim's custom bemian-style lockPixie and shot it into the system.

At the other end of his threads, the ghosts were at the gate. An actual gate. Zoe had created a cage construct that gave her and her vase enough space to breathe. But it was surrounded on all sides by indistinct monsters.

"Mike!" she shouted as her cage construct buckled. "Now!"

The realspace room was a maintenance area for the larger building. Other than things sometimes having weird colors or unusual shapes, it wasn't that much different from the same sort of room back home. He dropped a matrix crystal into a connection cradle and, after fixing her coordinates, punched the transfer button.

At the other end of his threads, a portal opened through the side of her cage. She leapt through it as the cage shattered. He also lost his own connection. He got a jolt similar to a mild shock instead of a memory wipe that a forced disconnect would've triggered back home—whatever it was, it wasn't exactly a realm.

The matrix crystal she'd taken shelter in was formatted so it had a small pocket realm. He manifested his holo there and found Zoe sitting in a corner of an empty white room about the size of his living room back home. The face of her avatar was smudged; her toga-like robes were torn and dirty. She held her vase close to her chest, giving him the eerie sense of a mother holding her infant child.

He'd knitted Zoe together after Watchtell had shattered her. He'd been exasperated by her impulsiveness once she was free. He'd even had to forgive her for conspiring with Fee to murder him in a mad scheme to enter realspace. She was still all of that, but more.

She must have one hell of a story to tell.

In realspace, he left the maintenance room and sat down on a park bench that looked out over an attractive piece of landscaping with a fountain in its center. He'd seen exactly the same arrangement on every developed world he'd visited so far.

In the realm, he floated his holo over and knelt down next to her. Tears dripped soundlessly, splashing against the vase. This was someone who'd dealt with mortal danger and nearly lost. If he hadn't been who he was, where he was...

"Thank you," she said, as she stroked the vase. "We all thank you."

"What's in the vase?"

"My people. I had to put them in a safe place." She looked up at him and let out a ragged sob. "But we have to go back."

He wasn't sure there was anything to go back to. "Why?"

The look she gave him was somewhere between a rage and a sadness he wasn't sure he'd seen since Kim had gotten better. Maybe not then. "I had to leave some of them behind."

Chapter 8
Kim

The biggest advantage to portal travel over using D-ships like Maff's *Palatine* was that the connections were always at level eight, the highest level in the transit dimension. Travel was instant no matter what the distance. But the connections were never direct. It was fortunate they'd worked out how to hack their remote portal to point at a different destination. The device she and Mike had designed was about the size of two matchboxes stuck on top of each other. It let them designate Earth as an end point, but also any other portal if it was close enough. Fortunately three were. She picked one at random and activated the device.

Kim wouldn't miss this place one bit.

The first transfer point was late at night local time. Her breath hitched a bit, the much-reduced reaction to portals that all interpreters had, then she was through. The primary bemian species on the planet, a bipedal insectoid that gave her the creeps if she looked at one too long, must be diurnal like humans because it was mostly deserted. Kim said a prayer of thanks for a small favor.

Then she started walking.

It was possible, even probable, that the portal system made sense at some point in time. But it had been in use for millions of years. The portal system didn't change, but the planets it served did. Old planets died. Kim suppressed a shudder. They didn't die, they were killed by the AC network. Planned senescence. Any time she had the slightest admiration for what the bemians got right, she remembered this fact, and the urge to admire them vanished like smoke.

At any rate, planets came and went. Routes changed over time. The stations stayed in the same place as long as the home planet was viable. When they weren't, portals were shut down instead of removed. Nobody knew why. New planets saw new stations added on. Over the massive time spans involved, the result was portals that were as far away from each other inside a station as concourses were in airports. They did at least have moving sidewalks.

It was still too slow for her.

She couldn't use her interpreter mojo to step directly from one place to the other. Kim needed to see her destination for that. Plus it took away all her hacking abilities, and right now she wanted those available.

Going across systems, she got to witness a broader cross section of bemians than she'd encountered before. They weren't a bunch of humans with weird things stuck to their noses, but they also weren't all utterly unique. Bipedalism predominated, with quadrupeds a distant second. That said, she was in high-grav, high-temperature stations.

This gave her an idea.

There were alternate portal routes used by bemians specialized for far different environments. She took a chance on a shortcut through a low-grav segment, and the body types changed. There were a lot more fliers, leg counts higher than four were common, and plant—or at least plantlike—bemians were out in force.

She got scolded in several different languages while moon hopping down the halls. It wasn't low-grav to the natives, and they didn't appreciate a high-grav type bulling its way through their China shop. She learned several new words for rude troll as she got back on the main high-grav line.

She'd gotten so used to the conflict and misery of their target world that she'd forgotten what normal bemian space was like. On the one hand, peace, prosperity, and order were always preferable to the alternative. But she'd seen the cost. It worked, although Mike had been insisting that it shouldn't since his first encounter with it.

That the bemians appeared to have been enjoying a free lunch of peace and harmony for hundreds of millions of years didn't fool her or Mike. Earth had spent millennia proving over and over again that such a thing didn't exist. Someone, somewhere, was paying the cost.

She got a text from Mike. *Picked up Zoe but we have a situation. Handling it now, will talk soon. Love you.*

She'd occasionally thought about where his unduplicate-slash-teenager restoration project had ended up. Now she knew. Kim sent him a few emojis of encouragement and plowed through her last portal.

Helen contacted her immediately on exit. It was a recording. *Kim, if you're getting this, the guild is here in force, and they are searching for you. Evade at all costs. Message repeats.*

It did this once before it died in a fizz of static. She and Mike had developed identity shielding that should've prevented her from being detected as she moved through the network. They'd traveled back and forth from Earth many times using it. That said, they'd never been able to test the shielding's resistance against multiple portal transits, and Kim would pay a price for that now.

She wouldn't make it easy for them.

Kim connected her modified bemian phone to the local network. *There were lines of potential, and she couldn't remember how to breathe. Positive negative surge recede all none collapse and now.*

She wasn't sure if the bang that went off in her head was louder than it was before. It didn't hurt any less, she was sure of that.

Several junction boxes and maintenance hatches exploded in showers of sparks at the power surge she'd rammed into the network. Everyone around her cried out as the whole station was plunged into darkness. Claxons sounded behind her as protective hatches irised over the now-inactive portals.

So much for a fast exit.

It'd been a snap decision that proved she'd been with Mike long enough to absorb his act-without-thinking habit. She'd thrown everyone into confusion. It would've bought anyone else time to make the next move before the bad guys could react.

Kim wasn't anyone else.

She was now in a room filled with semi-panicked columns of searing pain that wandered in random directions. If she hit someone, it would be bad enough for her to black out. Her quick trick had turned into a one-way ticket straight to—

Emergency lights snapped on, giving the room a weird orange tint. It was enough. She scurried to the wall. No matter how crowded it got, if she hugged a wall, it gave her at least a foot of breathing space. Most of the time. It at least gave her complete protection for one side. She'd take it.

It slowed her down too much. Interpreter goons, obvious from their blue-on-white armor, worked their way toward her through the crowd. She had to stop thinking of the crowd as her enemy. They were obstacles that she could use against the goons.

She ducked into a side passage that led to a different section of the station. There wasn't a crowd here, so she doubled her pace. There had to be a maintenance corridor around here, a place she could hide.

The bemian symbol for the restroom flashed over a passageway on her left. Behind and, now, in front of her, armored bemians shouted at her to stop. It wasn't great, but she was out of options. Kim turned into the passageway.

Bemian public restrooms didn't have the advantage of dealing with a single body shape, so there were clearly marked sections for bipeds, quadrupeds, plant-based life, and at the end, a discharge station for pallun suits. Kim headed for the quadruped section and picked the first empty stall. In this case, that's what it was: longer and wider than what a human would need with toilet facilities that could change height depending on the configuration chosen by pressing a button on a panel next to the door. She threw her portal hack tool into the recycler. It vaporized with a hot snap. Now no matter what happened, Earth at least was safe. She'd have to reunite with Mike to get home.

She didn't need the adapter or the facilities. She needed a way out of here.

There were lines of potential, and she couldn't remember how to breathe.

She dropped the packed boxes of their campsite into the recycler.

Seams of power dimensions of nothingness…

She didn't have to use a D-ship.

Dark patterns potentials horizon to zenith…

She pictured their hideout on the poor forsaken planet they'd been studying.

Waves higher and lower everywhere nothingness…

She gasped in anticipation but nothing happened. Kim concentrated and tried again.

Nothing.

The door crashed open, and armored figures rushed in. They didn't touch her, but they purposely positioned themselves so that any move would have her touching them. After a moment, someone behind them cleared their throat.

Always with the dramatic details. Totally unnecessary. Kim knew who it was. The soldier in the center stood aside, and there she was in all her considerable glory.

Valsa Burtan, First Councilor of the Guild.

Kim wished she had her La'fan robes so badly it made her guts clench. Only the Wild Witch was good enough to counter that entry. Bemian-style street clothes would have to do. "I'm surprised you came here yourself."

Perfect dark blue lips formed a disappointed moue that didn't reach her eyes, which, for the first time, Kim noticed were a shade of blue so pale they were nearly gray. "Apologies for the inconvenience. You have been rather hard to track down."

"You could've sent me a note."

This time the smile was genuine and unpleasant. Valsa was having a great deal of fun. "But where? You vanished."

Maybe she could order some robes. "My employers are located

across the galaxy." She and Mike represented the La'fan, otherwise known to bemians across the galaxy as the Death Eaters. "They know how to reach me."

"But now I don't need to." She gestured for Kim to come forward, as graceful as a fashion model and as commanding as a pope. She was the leader of one of the three oldest institutions in the galaxy, a place with billions of years of history behind it, and it showed. "Come. We have much to discuss."

Chapter 9
Spencer

The bot cut their nature hike short. A couple of minor nobles had gotten into a pissing contest about a property line, and she needed to step in to keep them from fucking each other's shit up.

"It's one of the easier ones to solve," she said as they broke camp for the final time. "The nodes give us a map, I draw the line. Since lines on a map are theoretical, the crown buys a strip on either side of it about a ten yards wide. Both parties are compensated, and we have something the nodes call *torfang*."

That turned out to be their word for *right of way*. "That's pretty fucking clever."

"It is?"

"Yeah. One day you're gonna need things like roads, sewers, power lines maybe, shit like that. What the nodes are doing is creating corridors for those things. Otherwise you end up with robber barons and other idiots gaming the system." His nineteenth-century history course was proving useful. Who'da thunk it?

"Okay, the first part I got. The second, not so much."

He helped her haul her gear into the drone transport. "The second part won't matter because you're avoiding it. Consider it another reason you don't want humans to help you. We would fuck it up six ways from Sunday."

She cocked her head at his slang switch to English. "I need more language lessons."

He cracked a smile. "I'd be happy to give them. When will you be free?"

Tapov's face went sour. "It's a straightforward problem, but not a quick one. Lawyers. It takes most of a month."

"And you have to be there the whole time?"

"No. But if they need me, they need *me. Plus there are almost always secret agents skulking around, getting up to…" She paused for a second. "Fuckery."*

It came out as *foochairy*. He laughed out loud at her heavily accented English. "I'll bet. Okay then. I've still got a week carved out, so send a flier or a messenger or whatever the hell you guys use if you finish early."

Her eyes softened, and he got that start-stop feeling, like a switch that had nearly been thrown. "Don't leave without saying goodbye."

"Not a chance," he said, and then flicked at the outfit he was wearing. "I'll fit right in." She'd decked him out in official Telirian ranger gear. From a *long* way off, he might look like a local, right down to the walking stick.

He didn't know what he wanted from this. He was pretty sure she didn't know either. It was legit the first time he'd ever been this positive and…simultaneously not-negative-but-not-right…about a girl. An *alien* girl. Jesus Christ on a fucking crutch. He breathed deep. Relationships with human girls were complicated as fuck. This? This was a whole other level.

He was strangely relieved when her transport took off. He'd miss her, but this ball of *want this* mixed with *what the hell are you thinking* rolled in with *are you kidding me?* was exhausting. If anything screamed *stay in your lane,* it was this.

But still. She was a girl, and they got along great. Wouldn't that be the shit, to bring a bemian girlfriend to one of Gramma's dinner parties? Royalty, even! The gossip would set the whole fucking town on fire. In the *God declared His peoples stay separate; it's right there in the Bible, and if you step out of line, there will be trouble* race relations he'd grown up with back home, he'd toss in a monkey wrench.

Playing what-if scenarios in his head kept him chuckling for a long time.

He crossed paths with his old friends the squirreligators after lunch. They chewed the scenery more thoroughly than hogs and left a trail anyone with the common sense God gave a goose could see from a mile away. That explained why they nearly made him into a gator snack. This was a small pack, maybe a couple dozen of them. Didn't matter. He steered well clear of their general direction.

Nightfall brought no sense of clarity in regard to Tapov. On the one hand, he would've loved staring up at the stars with her next to the campfire. On the other, being alone in the woods and marveling that he wasn't on Earth more than filled his *what an amazing day* budget. He'd come a long goddamned way from a skinny boy desperate to get out of his shit-ass little town. Knocked that one right the fuck out of the park, onto another planet. He rolled over and drifted away, fantasizing about never going back to Arkansas ever again.

He dreamed he was playing in a video game realm with Tapov, but with bemian weapons. They sang and slashed and shot bad guys who they didn't want to fight with swords. The pistols were loud but different. She pulled out a grenade and landed it—

He sat up, awake and panting, the echoes of a for-real explosion still audible through the night. He was a single human on a world filled with aliens. He waited a minute, then five, then fifteen, but there were no other sounds other than the ones he'd gotten used to as natural to the area.

Animals rustled around in the dark all over the galaxy; some made noises, but they all stayed away from fire. It had mostly turned to hot coals now. Whatever made that bang had not been an animal. Not any animal he'd seen so far. It was man—or rather *bemian*—made. He wasn't as alone out here as he'd thought. Instead of beefing up the fire, which might bring the explosions to him, he chose to commune with his ancestors and built out a trailBed in a tree. Ninety-eight percent chimpanzee, for the win!

At sunrise, he climbed higher to see if there was anything that would indicate what caused that explosion. The terrain here was hilly but not super rugged, covered by forests of what Spencer had taken to calling hydraulitrees. They were made of a substance that acted like wood but was also supported by fluid pressure. Half tree, half hydraulic lift, with branches you could squeeze like they were firehoses.

That was one tree up close. From a distance, it looked like any other forest back on Earth, aside from the slightly wrong colors and shapes. But for the most part, it was what it was: a bunch of low-rise mountains covered with trees. The only reason he thought of them as mountains was because where he was from, hills were things people made. Dumas be flat as fuck, yo.

In the distance, a clear trail of smoke made a column in the sky.

It wasn't much, sorta like what he'd get after the burn barrel behind his mom's boyfriend's house was mostly done turning trash to ash. What it *used* to look like before he'd gone green and gotten a composter. Mom's influence, naturally. Burn barrels had been banned for decades, but a redneck's gotta redneck. Spencer was fine when it went. Burning trash made for interesting-in-a-bad-way smoke.

He now had suspecto numero uno for whatever blew up last night. He'd not wanted to use his scout drone in the dark with what could've very well been a hot combat zone. Now that the fireworks appeared to be over, and it was light enough to use high-res cameras, he felt it was safe to risk it. It went up with a soft whir and angled toward the smoke. He'd scout the edges and then see what was happening. But it reached the end of its range before he found anything interesting. He climbed down and kept going.

He'd walked in the woods hundreds of times back home, maybe thousands, but those were different from these even before you counted in the alien trees and whatnot. The only woods in southeast Arkansas were on one side of river levees. Everything on the other side was farmland. This was also much hillier. In fact, the last time he'd been in woods like this…

Three eyes. Twelve feet tall and three eyes in its head. It wasn't a fucking bear, and it was right in front of him.

Spencer blinked and then did it again. Wow. He'd thought that whole thing was well and truly behind him. It was terrifying, but it was also, what, three years ago? Maybe four. After about six months of occasional nightmares, he'd gotten on with his life and that had been that.

Until now, he guessed. *Go for a walk in the woods. See strange trees. Meet interesting wildlife.*

Have a bout of unexpected PTSD on the side.

The first sign that shit had gone sideways showed up about an hour into the hike. It was a chunk of metal, thin but strong, a sheet about half the size of his hand. He'd done a couple of deserted island realms back in the day and what it most reminded him of was the skin of an airplane wing. He and Tapov had found all sorts of metal things in this area, but they'd all been iron and brass. There was no sign of any advanced metallurgy at all. The Victorian-era Care Bears that were Tapov's ancestors hadn't been given the chance to get around to any of that before the fucking sky fell on them.

He caught a whiff of bitter almonds.

Teliria looked like Earth but slightly skewed, and that was what it smelled like too. Natural scents were weird but recognizable. Whatever was in the air a moment ago was *not* recognizable. It was too strongly chemical, like it'd leaked out of a bottle. He tried to get a reading with his phone, but whatever it was had been blown away by the wind. Well-ventilated areas were a thing, yanno.

He knew he was close; he heard crackling. Hydraulitrees burned like Earth's trees, right down to the smokey coals at the end. And that was another thing he could smell now.

His destination was a clearing. He reached the edge, and the story was easy to tell.

It'd been a camp of some sort, with an artificially flattened area on one end. Two rows of three cabins stretched—*used* to stretch—from there to the remains of a smallish warehouse building. If this were Earth, the flat part would be a helipad, but around here, it shouldn't have been anything. Telirians hadn't graduated to flying yet.

They hadn't, but the new arrivals Tapov, along with Teliria's other leaders, invited in recently, had. Specifically new arrivals who did a surprisingly good imitation of gangsters even though they were basically gasbags in steampunk suits. This explained the chunk of metal he found. Scattered all across the clearing were shards of metal and brass tubing, some of it articulated. Underneath and around those were scraps of hide. They were bodies. Not of humans or Telirians.

Pallun bodies.

He backed off, got out his phone, and did a no-shit for-real check of the air. Pallun gas mixes were poisonous to most of what Maff called high-temp, high-gravity life forms, which you bet your ass included humans.

The scan came back all clear. Safe, for now at least. He set it to continuous mode and attached an alarm that was loud enough that it could be heard all the way back to Tapov's castle if it went off. One did not fuck around with poisonous gases, intentionally or otherwise.

He then cautiously went back to the camp, cataloging everything he saw as he went. He checked his compass app. Whoever did this came from the west, to his left, and moved across to his right. The footprints were bipedal but not anything he recognized. The pallun had been taken by surprise. Bemian weapons left scorch marks, and he didn't see any coming from the direction of the camp until the invaders were well inside the perimeter.

He hadn't been dreaming of a battle last night. He'd been hearing one.

The pallun got their shit together when the invaders reached the line of cabins. Now the scorch marks went in both directions, but the pallun were in a panic. The shots landed everywhere.

The warehouse told the rest of the story. Pallun gases weren't easy to find outside of the pallun home world, long ago destroyed over some fucked up beef they had with the rest of the galaxy. They'd been forced to get good at synthesizing stuff they needed out of whatever was handy. Most of this involved chemical reactors of various kinds, at least one—the one they used to synthesize their food gases—could do a convincing imitation of a fertilizer bomb.

And that's exactly what had happened. The pallun had rallied around the building, but they were still on their back heels. Or walkers. Or whatever they hell they called the brass stilts they used. The door to the fertilizer factory had been left open, and an unlucky shot had scored a direct hit.

It killed the surviving pallun and some of the invaders. He still hadn't found any nonpallun bodies, but there were impressive blood spatters everywhere. It was purplish, but the patterns were unmistakable. In the end, the defenders took some of the attackers out.

He found the spot where the bad guys rallied with their wounded and their dead. The trail they left was easy to follow.

He knew he needed to make a call, but he also knew the more information he had, the better Sornik, the pallun in charge of this operation, would react to the news. He'd seen Sornik dope-slap lackies who didn't have the whole picture before and had no desire to find out what that felt like. This had happened hours ago, so whoever it was had a big head start. He set off at a cautious pace to see what else there was to find.

Chapter 10
Kim

They didn't take Kim from the portal station with the bemian version of a cop car or paddy wagon. It was an interpreter limo not much different from the one Valsa rode in. Except her guards had their weapons out.

The destination was a solid improvement over a converted pantry in a kitchen tent, where she'd ended up the last time she crossed paths with Valsa. This was a proper suite, expensively decorated in a style that wouldn't have looked out of place in Versailles or the State Apartments at Windsor. That those two famous Earth landmarks were constructed centuries apart was what her brain used to paper over the differences in style between those places and this one. The pattern on the carpet was downright weird. It was disorienting to see some sort of scene out of a myth and have no clue whatsoever about what it was.

Fancy or not, the doors didn't open, and the windows were sealed shut. Where it counted, this was still a prison cell.

Getting locked up had been a terrifying nightmare for her growing up. Prisons were notorious for physical contact, and Kim had no illusions about her chances of surviving in one. But, as an adult, she had to officially concede a point: getting locked up had become a habit. So far it had all turned out okay in the end, but she promised herself to look a little more closely at the life choices she made and why they often landed her in a cage.

She wasn't flipping out about being held captive again because of one thing. She picked at the long black sleeve of her outfit, not bothering to fight the feeling of pride it gave her that it was within her rights to wear it.

Valsa had supplied her with La'fanian robes. Not any generic ones. They were identical to the ones hanging in her closet back home, right down to the silly Earth SF symbols she and Mike had chosen to demark their profession as the first La'fanian interpreters in history. In the brief time Kim had been around her, Valsa did not come across as someone who paid compliments to those she considered beneath her. Kim may think of herself as a prisoner, as would anyone else from Earth, but this outfit was about as far from an orange jump suit as she could expect to get.

So she may have done a turn or two in front of the ornate dressing mirror in the corner of her room after putting them on. The La'fan were known as Death Eaters in bemian space, feared agents of mystery who worked on long-dead planets, far from prying eyes. The robes they wore played no small part in that impression. She was once again the Wild Witch, leading a people, using powers she could barely control let alone understand. If Valsa truly wanted her locked away forever, none of this would've been necessary.

Valsa wanted something from her, and Kim was curious enough now to stick around and find out what that might be.

She killed some time finding and zapping the monitoring devices that were sewn into the robes. Kim wouldn't be fooled twice with the same trick. If they wanted her to lead them back to Earth or Mike or anywhere else, they'd have to try harder this time.

She wanted to get Mike's take on the whole situation, but they strangled her phone's bandwidth to the point that it would only do text messages. He was bound to be busy enough with Zoe anyway. It was time to put on her big-girl panties, and the scary cool robes, and figure this out on her own.

But first, she had to find food. She hadn't had anything to eat since leaving on her abortive attempt to rescue Helen. The decorative plants either were fake or too alien for her to tell the difference. The drawers in the various pieces of furniture were empty. She took an exploratory sniff of what had to be a bar of soap. It smelled about as edible as the ones back home. Then remembered where she was.

"Hey, Valsa!" Kim said as she looked around. "What've you got to eat in this joint?" She walked into the main room, a place almost as big as their whole apartment back home but with twenty-foot ceilings. "I said—"

The voice that came from all around her sounded a lot like their old La'fan escort Honorable Fakner, enough she could almost see his mountainous centauroid form looming over the microphone. But it couldn't be him. They weren't in La'fan space.

"The first councilor invites you to dine with her for the evening meal."

Her phone's clock had synched with local time when she'd arrived. "That's hours from now. You got any snacks?"

"Please wait a moment."

The entire conversation had been in English. Which wasn't surprising. They'd needed to teach interpreter threads the language after *Last Island*, the pirate ship Maff piloted at the time, stopped at a planet to fence some pirated intellectual property. There'd been plenty of time for the knowledge to spread throughout the network.

On a whim, she switched to Mandarin. "And maybe drinks, too?" Helen had taught her thread that language during her stay with Maff on her home world, Silaria.

Without missing a beat, the voice replied, in crystal-clear Mandarin, "A menu is now available on the house feed."

It promptly opened in her shared vision channel. Strictly local network. No outside connectivity. They wouldn't make it easy for her either.

Bemian languages numbered in the hundreds that she'd found so far, at any rate, but they all used the same script. The pronunciation of words varied wildly, but their meaning and their structure were limited and controlled. It should have made interpreters unnecessary. A similar phenomenon existed in China and writing words instead of speaking them had been a common way to communicate between dialects there for more than a century.

Mike thought the nodes were the ones blocking that progression, but Kim wasn't so sure. Interpreters did much more than re-pronounce what was effectively a common word between languages. Concepts easy to express in one language sometimes had no equivalent in another. There were subtexts that had to be understood. Status to be conveyed.

Lies to be told, hidden, or exposed.

She'd encountered all of that and more negotiating for the La'fan. Even with the comparative homogeneity imposed by the nodes, interpreters would be needed.

It did make the menu easy to, well, interpret. After selecting for body chemistry, she built what was effectively a charcuterie board with some sparkling water. It wouldn't do to show up to a formal dinner—she knew in her bones that's what it'd be—full and drunk.

The food was first-class, and the sparkling water came in a bottle that would've cost her a month's rent. But it only took fifteen minutes to finish off. She spent more time exploring the suite but turned up nothing useful. Studying the view out of her windows showed meticulously groomed grounds. Unlike the rug, the layout and geometries were reasonably familiar. They were also big enough that she could see no gate or doorway that might lead off the property. Another strike against breaking out: where would she go?

Eventually she was reduced to playing a local install of solitaire on her phone and reading some old downloaded copies of *Daily Mail* she'd snagged the last time they were home. Kim had started making up stories to fit with the scenes on her rug when a serverBot walked through the door.

"The first councilor requests your presence as a guest at the evening meal. Please, follow me."

The Downton-meets-King-Louis vibe continued with rich, thick carpets laid over beautifully patterned marble, statues on plinths, and paintings on walls covered in expensive-looking fabrics over wood paneling.

She stopped short as the dining room door opened. Kim had expected giant chandeliers and a table that had its own zip code. Instead she got a much more modest space with a table set for two. It was still sumptuous.

Valsa stood, again elegant simplicity to Kim's frankly wild appearance. "Kim," she said in English, "Please, join me?"

She put down her hood. If she was offered politeness, she was happy to return it. "It would be my pleasure." The attitude change from when they'd nabbed her at the station was remarkable. Whether that was an act and this was the real Valsa or vice versa remained to be seen.

A moment after she sat down, a pair of low-ranking interpreters walked out of a hidden doorway. One poured what certainly smelled like a very nice wine while the other laid out two plates of unrecognizable but still appetizing food, one for Valsa and another for her.

After they left, an awkward silence grew. In their previous sit-down meeting Kim had been too terrified to be polite. Now…

"Do you go first or do I?" she asked.

Valsa's smile was as radiant as ever. A laugh, confident but not condescending, bubbled gently out. "I'm nearly as lost as you are. And that is incredibly unusual. Normally I'd know all about every aspect of your culture, from the crudest peasant's manners to the finest customs of your ruling class."

Kim didn't exactly know how to respond to that, so she went with a deflection. "But you don't?"

The charm fell away for a moment. What it revealed wasn't a megalomanic but an administrator. Firm, emotions tamped down, vigilant. Valsa's complexities might rival her own. "A mystery I intend to get to the bottom of." She picked up a glass and nodded the lip in her direction. "Since you're my guest, we'll go with tokaran hospitality?"

Tokarans were what Kim was coming to think of as Standard-Issue Bipeds, close enough to human that they'd pass for *Star Trek: Next Generation* TV show aliens back home. "I've done several negotiations with them." They were uncomplicated but somewhat reticent. Be neat, be nice, and don't run your mouth. Kim could work with that. She picked up her glass and tipped it toward Valsa. "L'chaim."

She used Hebrew on purpose. Interpreters were exquisitely sensitive to new languages, and the further they were from ones already known, the more intriguing they became. Valsa probably knew every bemian language in active use in addition to two from Earth. Kim had tipped Valsa to the existence of *another* completely unknown language.

She hid her startle expertly as she drank, but there was no mistaking the flash of interest in her eyes. Kim still didn't know why Valsa wanted her here so badly, but raising her value in the first councilor's mind couldn't hurt.

The wine was delicious, a combination of flavors and textures Kim associated with expensive restaurants and the times Mike splurged and cooked supper for her on a weekend. She was no sommelier, but she didn't have to be to recognize quality.

Tokaran could also be direct, and so could Kim. "You didn't have to kidnap me."

Kim kept a close eye on how Valsa handled the flatware and did her best to imitate the motions. It wasn't easy. Calling Valsa graceful would be a massive understatement. Kim felt like an elephant wearing gloves.

"I didn't think you'd come if I asked. We didn't part on very good terms."

Kim had sucker punched Valsa with a detached robot arm and then tossed her unconscious body through the transit dimension. This happened after they tried to arrest her, chased her across a big chunk of the galaxy, held her captive, and then done their level best to shoot *Palatine* out of the sky. She chuckled, channeling the Wild Witch. "How long did it take you to come to?"

Her smile was guileless as she tipped her head slightly forward in respect. "Long enough to give my adjunct a real scare." She set her cutlery down and looked Kim straight in the eyes. Tokaran directness could go both ways. "I would like to apologize for the way I behaved in our previous encounter, and for being so abrupt with you today. My partner insisted it was the wrong way to go. As always, he was right."

A holo spun to life on the tabletop, occupying a space reserved for the purpose. It was a male of the same species as Valsa, miniaturized, dressed as neatly as Valsa herself. "It pains her much more to admit that than to apologize to you."

"Kim, meet my partner." Valsa indicated the holo with an expression that was an even split between embarrassment and affection. "Seluk Pash."

"Nice to meet you."

"Likewise."

Interpreters always came in pairs. One half was a threaded life form like Mike, the other a biological like Kim. In bemian cultures, they were raised together and then, after a period when they were pure threads existing only in the interstitial areas between realms, they physically combined and emerged back into realspace. Incredibly, Valsa and Seluk spent time with no physical presence until they reemerged after a long period spent as local interpreter threads. Returning to realspace always left a deformity of some sort on the interpreter's torso. Valsa's was a discreet, well-integrated pouch on her left side. It took an effort for Kim not to glance at it.

They'd finished their first course, and a second was promptly provided. Assuming they stuck with tokaran customs, there were three more on the way. Kim could get used to this. "I don't want to ruin dinner talking business, but I was wondering if you could at least tell me why I'm here?"

The two glanced at each other. Valsa nodded slightly. "We're going with your plan now."

Seluk said, "It's about your army..."

Chapter 11
Helen

She had set the alert daemon to a team channel they all monitored, then recorded her warning.

"Kim, if you're getting this, the guild is here in force. Evade at all costs. Message repeats." It wasn't much, but it was all she had time for.

She'd acquired a new tail.

Most interesting of all, it was tracking her threads in the interstitial spaces between the local realms. She and Mike both had existed for years without a biological host. It made perfect sense that there would be bemian equivalents wandering the interstitial areas between realmspaces. In fact, the only interesting thing was that they weren't everywhere. She originally filled the realmspace behind China's Great Firewall. Mike did the same thing for the rest of the planet. Her threads now resided in the orbital clouds around Earth, and she'd filled them as well. But they weren't like that out here. Interpreters used these spaces to place specialized constructs called *thread anchors*. This allowed a permanent connection to be maintained in the system to be used for instant communication. But, until now, they'd never seen independent threaded entities in them.

Helen had spread her threads through the local interstitial because that's what she and Mike did whenever they ended up somewhere new. There were of course the ubiquitous thread anchors, and she did use them, but *only* doing that would be like tying a boat to a dock yet never going ashore. She couldn't say she truly visited a place without using her threads to experience it.

Ironically, Watchtell's attempt to remove Helen as an impediment to his plans was what had kept her from being spotted by whatever was following her at the moment. If she'd had time to prepare, Helen would've brought a significant percentage of her threads along, pushing out the interstitial space of whatever realms were available to make room. Now she only had the few thousand that happened to be on the devices she'd carried with her physical host. These were plenty enough to experience the local interstitial, but few enough she wasn't filling the space in its entirety.

Helen was intrigued by the creature more than afraid of it. She and Mike lived as globe-spanning life forms, him on the ground and her in the sky. There were no mirrors, and they only saw tiny parts of each other's threads. The creature was whole, a self-contained entity that would be about the size of a car if it could somehow make its way outside without a host.

In realspace, she stood in a crowd of bemians, waiting at a tramcar stop. Kim would be in serious trouble in this jostling crowd of vaguely anthropomorphic lizards, cranes, crabs, and tigers. There was even a pallun on the edge, rolling itself up to fit on transport never meant to carry a life form with its body plan.

In the interstitial, thread anchors stuck into what passed for ground in this place like towering bridge abutments, cables made up of thousands of interpreter threads shooting away into the pastel-powdered haze of this place's sky. Realms were huge, featureless lozenge shapes that floated in ordered ranks stacked amongst the towering anchors. Helen slowed her threads down, allowing the creature to draw closer.

Its detail was fascinating. She'd long known her threads had what she'd perceived as color but had never dreamed it could be used as camouflage. In hindsight, that use was obvious. She began cataloging her observations carefully. This implied many things about the interstitial, and Helen wasn't sure what might be worth investigating further.

A set of its threads exploded outward toward her, the net configuration clear.

She'd let it get too close and barely dodged its first throw. She sped her threads away, going around realms as she went. With such a small number of threads to control, she felt like Tonya's SUV, Morgan: fast, agile, and powerful. But this was three dimensional, almost as if she were traveling through an old-fashioned lava lamp, with the realms as the blobs and the interstitial as the surrounding material.

After a few minutes of this, she swerved around a conjunction of large realmspaces and stopped. She wasn't listening or looking for signs of pursuit, as such, certainly not how she would've described it before acquiring a human host, but that's how she thought of it now. After only a few minutes, she spotted it nearby.

Now that she knew not to let it get close, she shot away again, describing paths through the interstitial that threatened to get her lost.

This time the net came from a totally different direction. The only reason she was able to dodge it was a realm had gotten in the way, slowing it down. There were now two threaded entities chasing her. When she knew neither of them could see her, she split off a set of threads and sent them on a different vector. They brought another player? She upped her game.

And it was a different entity, not the first one splitting itself up. Helen couldn't see her whole self at once, but she'd always been able to perceive threads when she split them off to new tasks. They all looked the same. These two entities had very distinct appearances.

Helen twirled past two realms that were tight together. They didn't have mass, per se, but did have a kind of inertia that would slow or stop her. She wasn't that far ahead of these two.

A net landed on her from a third direction. They were raising the stakes.

Getting closer.

She split her threads and escaped the net before it solidified. She split again and sent the new segment toward the ubiquitous interpreter thread anchors, using them as a kind of crazily angled forest to weave through.

Two things stood out about her predicament: first, they were avoiding the thread anchors.

Second, they weren't splitting themselves up.

The newest opponent, the one chasing her latest bundle, blundered into an anchor, and it vanished in a localized inversion that shot upward, trailing destruction in its wake.

Okay. Don't touch the anchors.

The other observation was more difficult to explain away. She and Mike were multithreaded. Presumably the entities, now five strong as she once more had to split thread bundles to escape the nets, could do that too. Yet they weren't.

In realspace, her bus had arrived at the portal station. It'd taken this long because she wanted to change sectors, and those stations were farther apart than local or regional portals. It was a race she had to win. Her threads would follow her realspace host when she went through the portal. Without a physical presence, her opponents could not follow. All she had to do in the interstitial was play for time.

The map showed that her destination was at least a kilometer from the entrance. Out of the corner of her realspace eye she saw interpreter drones working in a clear search pattern.

Helen broke into a jog.

There were now ten entities chasing her through the interstitial, and she was running out of threads to split. It was time to go on the offensive. The next time a net came her way, she split the bundle of her threads that was its target and pulled it open in front of her pursuer. The entity that'd fired it was too startled to dodge and ended up a neatly wrapped bundle, trapped in its own net, bouncing helplessly against realms as it floated away into the darkness.

The next net turned solid the instant it enveloped one of her thread bundles, trapping it. They'd changed tactics. Split this far the loss of any single bundle wasn't critical to her overall functionality, but that didn't mean she wanted to lose them. She created a distraction with three sets while a fourth opened the net.

In realspace, she spotted the line for the sector portal and skidded to a stop at its end. If the map was correct, the portal itself was at least a hundred meters away, around a corner where she couldn't see it.

The interstitial was now a chaotic melee of entities, her threads, and the nets they'd thrown at her. This gave her an idea. She used the thread bundles that had few or no pursuers collect the nets. That accomplished, her now dozens of bundles began to work together to snag entities with their discards. The tactic worked, but by now there must've been nearly a hundred entities chasing her. If they ever got coordinated, things would go bad quickly.

In realspace, she let her inner peasant take over. Mainlanders were famous to this day for refusing to form queues and crowding the gate. She broke into a jog again, ignoring the indignant gasps as she trotted down the line.

The entities chasing her vanished. That was wrong. They hadn't vanished. They were gathering together into a formation.

When she rounded the corner in realspace, she found out what was creating the line. Interpreters armed with stun batons were checking papers.

In the interstitial, the entities fired all their nets at once. If she'd been concentrated, she might've been able to dodge through the gaps but spread out like this, there was no chance.

In realspace, Helen broke into a sprint. Bemians of all shapes and sizes clucked and grumbled and hooted indignantly as she pushed them out of her way.

In the interstitial, her threads were enwrapped by nets in their dozens, then hundreds.

The portal was *right there*. Helen had two of the best martial arts fighters in the world as personal friends and had been training with them regularly since before they'd gone out into bemian space.

It was time to put that training to the test.

As her thread bundles were entrapped by the hundreds, Helen

stopped thinking and went for it. Time seemed to slow down as she jumped up the back of a large dinosaur-like bemian. She tumbled forward over the first interpreter and then underneath the second one. It was a kind of concentration unlike any she'd ever felt as she *did it*. The portal wasn't a clear object but rather a bright gray flash in her tumbling vision. She flung herself at it feet first.

The nets surrounding her threads vanished as those threads were automatically concentrated and transported halfway across the galaxy in an instant. Now free to pick any portal she liked, Helen ran past startled travelers and vanished through a local portal, destination unknown. She did that three more times and then went through a regional one for good measure. She calmly walked through that last one, then took two more locals. She didn't have any idea where she was.

Nobody did.

Chapter 12
Mike

It took a long time for him to get Zoe to calm down enough to get the whole story. "Fifteen hundred unduplicates?" he asked. She hadn't been gone *that* long.

"We don't reproduce like humans. It's part sculpting, part…cleaving, I guess is the correct word."

"You don't have any physical matrix left anywhere on Earth. I checked." Unduplicates and AC nodes used special crystal matrixes to house their quantum wave functions. They were easy to spot because they looked alike. The only difference was size, and that was due to network nodes needing to last—and remember—for a mind-bogglingly long time.

"Can you find them again?" she asked softly.

His threads had been chewing on the problem since he discovered that Zoe's realm wasn't part of a conventional Bbox, parent realm, or split. "How well could you reconstruct it?"

"I don't know. Why does that matter?"

"If we work together, I think I can use quantum resonances to detect the original."

"Elysium wasn't in standard space-time. That was the point. I wanted a place where we could live in peace, and I found it." She looked longingly at the vase. "I was wrong."

"You were right for longer though." When he granted her admin access, the pocket realm expanded and changed. Zoe threw her arms up, and the entire thing shattered into uncountable fragments of realm construct.

"It might help me to know where I am right now. I don't think we're in Kansas anymore."

He cracked a smile. She'd been sitting inside what was effectively a windowless box but was pulling it together instead of panicking. "We're not on Earth right now. It's a system called Balcavore." He consulted a star map. "It's more than a million light years away from Earth."

The realm had turned into a swirling storm of claylike forms. Now it froze. "I'm on a different planet? Like, for real?"

His stomach growled. He hadn't had anything to eat since leaving Kim. There was no reason to think this city would be any different from the others he'd seen, so a café sector had to be nearby. People eating alone staring at nothing was a common sight both here and back home, so he wouldn't attract any extra attention. Mike started out for a sidewalk café that was exactly where he expected it to be. "For real." He gave her access to his phone's camera so she could see out. "This is what it looks like."

She set her vase down for the first time. "Whoa." She stared openmouthed as he walked past various bemians. Some, like the talking stork rhon or the foxlike scolion, he already knew, mostly because of all the negotiation sessions he and Kim had assisted the La'fan with. Since this was a part of the galaxy he hadn't visited yet, there were some new ones. The bipedal but six-eyed purple amphibioid looked like it'd fallen out of a *Monsters, Inc.* realm.

He sat down at a table made to fit a life form roughly his size and shape at the same time that his order of anaphilar arrived via a server bot.

"You come all this way," Zoe said with a bit of a huff, "and order pho? Wait. Aliens have pho?"

The teenager he'd brought back from the brink had appeared. He hadn't realized how much he'd missed her until now. "Not exactly."

The construction project in the realm resumed while he gave her the lowdown. The galaxy was filled with intelligent life. Earth didn't know because it was surrounded by a sterilized bubble of space they hadn't been able to measure or understand yet. Bemian civilization was supported by a galaxy-spanning network of alien unduplicates.

That caused another work stoppage. "They have unduplicates? Like me?"

"Again, not exactly."

He caught her up the rest of the way while she worked. The nodes were unduplicates that had been saddled with specific constraints that prevented them from becoming intelligent. They ran everything, but nobody knew how it worked. It shouldn't work. No simulation he ran let it. They were missing at least one key piece of how this galaxy ticked.

"You're in the weeds, Mike," she said as she guided whole pieces of sky around and docked them to bits of scenery. "Stick to the main story."

"But it matters. A lot."

She blew a raspberry at him. "Less energy budgets, more bug-eyed monsters."

So he told her about the Interpreter's Guild, and how he and Kim were members but also exceptions to their rules.

"How's she doing nowadays?"

He checked. Or rather tried to. Nothing with a high bandwidth requirement worked.

He sent her a text. That, at least, only needed one of his threads. *You okay out there?*

Fine. I think.

What does that mean?

Valsa showed up on my way to help Helen.

Zoe, watching the exchange on a screen he threw up, asked, "I was going to ask about Helen next. Wasn't she trying to kill you the last time I saw her?"

"It's complicated." *Do you need me?*

No. You've got Zoe. I've got this.

And Helen?

In the wind. She's a big girl. She can take care of herself.

Zoe snorted. "That part I remember."

Mike didn't like any of it, but there wasn't much he could do from here. *If you need me let me know, I'll come running.*

I will. Love you.

Love you too.

When he turned back to Zoe, her jaw had dropped. "You…and…Kim?" One eyebrow dipped in an unintentional imitation of countless Spock avatars he'd dealt with over the years. "You two were barely speaking."

He twirled the wedding ring on his realspace finger for her to see. "We figured it out."

"Well I'll be," she said as she made some final touches to the realm. "Okay then. You've shown me your miracle. Now I'll show you mine."

She played with the settings so that he only saw the nearest pieces as she built them. Those were impressive enough. When she turned the haptic field up to one hundred percent to reveal the whole, it took his breath away in realspace.

Elysium was a Greek concept, pre-Christian but compelling enough to be preserved and adopted by them. Today it was another word for heaven. What Zoe had built wasn't angels and clouds. It was an extremely realistic simulation of an idyllic meadow set on low rolling hills. A brook ran peacefully through the landscape at a distance.

It was beautiful, but also empty. Her unduplicate family would be too much for this transport matrix, but adding avatars would be trivial. "No people?"

Zoe gripped her vase tightly. "No. I won't create copies of them. It'd be too much." She fought visibly with her grief. As she did, Mike centered himself by silently chanting a sutra. After a moment she shook her head. "That's not why we're here. I didn't do this as some sort of showcase. I've modeled it to the finest detail. Does it help?"

It went down to the quantum level, a skill he and only a few humans back on Earth had. But Zoe didn't know how to do that. She couldn't. "You didn't have quantum mechanics in your matrix stores. I would've known."

She looked around with a thoughtful expression. "Is that what I did? I only know it as…feeling right? It's hard to explain."

"That's fine. Let me take a look."

Her model gave him a much better idea of what happened. The quantum signatures indicated that Zoe's home was in a pocket dimension, a place that existed in a direction he couldn't point to in realspace. It was, effectively, a natural realmspace. This wasn't a new idea, but it wasn't widely accepted back home. Nobody had figured out how to test it yet. It was likely the interstitials, the places between realms where threaded life forms like himself existed, either were or were adjacent to the dimension. "This is remarkable."

Zoe cleared her throat. "Don't get distracted, Mike."

He split off a section of threads to continue examining the scientific implications and concentrated on the task she'd asked him to complete. There were resonances that could be detected. Now that he knew what to look for, he quickly tasked threads to act as scanners.

He caught Zoe up on events while they waited. Her opinions were, as always, sharp and to the point.

On the geothermal powerplant turning out to be a world-ending bomb: "Fee"—the unduplicate who'd tried to kill Mike—"was out of her mind trying to join humanity. Most humans are fine, but enough of them are complete maniacs that the entire species needs to be watched. Closely."

On Watchtell leveraging Kim's genetic material to make her an involuntary mother: "He talked about that with me once. I didn't take him seriously. I should have."

On their accidental introduction to the bemian galaxy, a.k.a. the Milky Way: "Leave it to Kim to fall head-first into a cesspit and come out of it the head diplomat of an entire civilization."

On their attempts to patch a network hundreds of millions of years old to protect it from humans: "See? I told you. Humans are maniacs."

"We protected Earth from them too."

She tipped an imaginary hat at his holo. "That was nicely done. You've got an artist in you, Mike. It's a strange one, but it's there."

He started to tell her about Spencer's current job as team leader of another set of portal scouts when his probes reported a result. "I've found it."

After a moment, tears flowed freely down her face, which had regained its color. "*Thank you,*" she said. With a finger snap, her face cleared. At a gestured hand, her vase floated in the air while a backpack construct drew itself between her shoulders. "Let's not screw around, shall we?" Her vase dropped in, and the backpack sealed itself shut. "It's time to get my people."

Chapter 13
Spencer

The trail led down into thick forest, denser than anything he'd come across so far on Teliria. There were places where the game trail stopped, and he had to hunt for where the attackers had hacked through the undergrowth with machetes. They could travel between the stars but used fucking dwarf swords to hack through bushes and brambles. He'd bet money they looked exactly like the ones hanging in his dad's shed back home.

The terrain was steep but manageable. The impression of remoteness was reinforced by the lack of node ruins. Tapov's ancestors had kicked more than a little node ass before they got overwhelmed, and he'd seen the wreckage to prove it. Usually there was one every couple of miles, easy to spot once you knew what to look for. He hadn't seen any since Tapov had left.

He eventually cleared the woods and ended up in a giant meadow. There was some evidence of Telirian shepherds—or whatever-herds. The flock were the size of sheep but definitely did not have sheep feet. The bad-guy trail was as strong as ever, but the other tracks were old, where he could find any at all. If it weren't for the wind rustling the grass, it might be silent. In other words, it was quiet.

Too fucking quiet.

The meadow's far edge was the start of more forest. He used a basic search pattern to find the tallest nearby tree and climbed it.

Once he got as high as the branches allowed, he took a look around. A smattering of antenna poles were visible about five miles to the west. They formed the perimeter of what looked to be another large clearing. He could see the opposite side, so it must be situated on a moderate slope.

Spencer got out the scout drone. He wouldn't send it directly to the camp. It was too far away. He activated the POV app on his phone so he could look out of the drone cameras and then shot it up a couple hundred feet.

Now well above the tree line, he could see it was a big-ass base. From this distance, it was hard to see the difference between the buildings down there and the Quonset huts he'd spent hours in and around playing *WWII Call of Duty* realms. They were antique as fuck back home but were all the rage down there. He could only see the edge of the base as it tucked around a mountain and then maybe down into a valley.

Dark figures walked amongst the buildings. They weren't pallun, they were the wrong shape. He zoomed the camera in to get better detail.

Kron, a human-lizard type that was common in all the bemian spots he'd visited so far, walked purposely everywhere. Exactly what they were doing he couldn't tell. Bemians were aliens, yo. He looked around and found a different tree he could climb, closer but not too close. He'd hoof it and send the drone up to take another look.

He rounded the corner of a big clump of undergrowth and came face-to-face with a pair of kron.

Armed kron. Who were looking straight at him.

A funny thing about woods with thick undergrowth: you can be walking on a trail and have no way of knowing what's nearby. The woods were quiet, but they weren't silent, and the wind covered up a lot. It wasn't quite like walking down a green tunnel, but it was close.

This thought was braided through with the more reflexive *fuckfuckfuckfuck* also going through his head. They were too close for him to make a run for it. He wasn't faster than a ray gun or a radio.

Sheep tracks.

The memory of those tracks in the meadow were as vivid as a realm. "Hey!" He shouted, threw his arms out, and waved his walking stick at the woods. "Have you guys seen my goats?"

At least that's what he hoped he'd said. There were no interpreters on this world, so no threads to make sure. His Telirian was shaky at the best of times, and this wasn't the best of times. Why not English? Fucked if he knew. He was making it up as he went along.

The lizard men took a step back and cocked their heads, clearly confused.

Spencer dropped his shoulders. These guys weren't angry; they hadn't drawn their weapons. *They didn't speak any Telirian at all.* He rolled with that. He was a shepherd...okay, whatever, *goatherd*...confronted with strangers who didn't speak his language. He knew what the next play was.

He spoke as loudly and as slowly as he could, making exaggerated gestures along the way. "*I...said...have...you,*" he pointed frantically at one, Moe, and then at the other, Larry, "*seen,*" he turned his hands into binoculars, put them over his eyes, and pretended to look for icebergs, "*myyy,*" he brought his hand down like he was going to scoop up leaves but then kept going and pointed at his chest, "*goats?*" He did a little pantomime of walking on four legs and made a noise that would've caused Tapov to crack up but was hopefully close enough to Telirian goats to convince these chuckleheads.

The guards—guns plus men plus patrol equaled guards—blinked at him, clearly wondering if the weird shouty peasant was done talking. As long as he kept the ray guns in their holsters he counted it as a win.

The one on the left, Moe, broke first. "Speak Standard?"

Like the back of his fucking hand, but that was Spencer. He was now goatherd number one, a walk-on with, hopefully, too small a part to warrant a name. "Me speak Standard."

"What are you doing out here?"

That was too much for…on the spot, Spencer named this new improv character he was playing Gono, to understand. He was a peasant. *Holy Grail* realms were a dime a dozen, he knew how it went. He cocked his head and did his best imitation of a football lineman after he'd gotten hit: eyes wide with a hint of drool on the way.

The other guard, Larry, swore and chattered something that was more frustrated than angry. "Why you here?"

He snapped up straight. "Me look for goat!" He then did another enthusiastic goat pantomime but louder. "Many goat!"

Moe shook his head. "No goat here. You go away!"

That was terrible news. *Terrible* news. Gono was almost in tears. "Me lose goat! Many goat!"

Exactly why they hadn't noticed that this particular Telirian didn't look *anything* like the real deal up close was interesting. They were out in the middle of nowhere. A peasant wandering up didn't scare or anger them. Maybe they didn't know what the natives looked like.

Or maybe they thought he was a *really* ugly Telirian. Again, ray guns in holsters. Still winning.

Larry shook his head again. "No goats."

Gono was beside himself with worry. Spencer got an idea, and so did his ugly Telirian character Gono. "You help! Find goat, many goat!"

They were waving their hands before he was done talking. "No," Moe said. "We guard. We have job."

Now to spring Gono's cunning plan on them. "Wait," he said with a slick smile. "I pay, you help."

He took the whiskey flask off his hip, opened it, and offered it to the guards. "*Booze* pay. Good booze!"

They looked at each other suspiciously. Moe shrugged. Larry shrugged. Gono shrugged, but never lost his grin. "Good pay, good booze!"

Larry walked up and cautiously took the flask. He sniffed it as he walked back to Moe. Booze was booze, and one sniff was all it took. Larry took a swig, then Moe took a swig. Neither man flinched, but they did sigh.

Gono had the good stuff. Damned right. "Good pay! You help find goat! Many goat."

Now the ray guns came out. "No," Moe said. "You pay us, we no kill you."

Gono was shaking in his boots. Spencer wasn't doing much better. He put his hands up. He was a peasant, and peasants didn't get angry at armed men. Not if they wanted to live long. "I not want trouble."

"You not trouble," Larry said as he took another swig. "No goats here, you live. Goats here"—there was a screaming whoosh; a bush to Spencer's right disintegrated—"you die."

The trembling wasn't fake. He swallowed and nodded. "No goats." He gave them an *I get it now* look. He hoped. "Goats this way." He pointed back the way he came.

They nodded. "Goats that way. You go."

He nodded again and turned around. If he ran, they'd think it was a game. A shooting game. If he walked, they *might* think it was a game. He took the second option, his back tingling with imaginary crosshairs on it.

Once he turned the corner of a bush and was out of their sight, he broke into a run. Only after his legs were screaming at him to stop did he dodge behind some cover. He checked to confirm he was alone and then panted away the adrenaline with his hands on his knees.

Now he had enough proof to take this discovery to the management.

Spencer placed a call. It was local, so there was no need for threads or any of that fucked up shit.

"Sornik," he said once the pallun in charge of the little smuggling operation answered. "You have a problem."

Chapter 14
Tonya

Tonya hadn't understood how much of her time was taken up with the chaos and insanity that trailed Kim like a comet until she'd spent a few weeks away from it. She got a lot more done when she wasn't running for her life, rushing off to rescue someone, or going on a mind-bending trip through time.

Funny, that.

Rachel, the tech trillionaire who'd routed her down this particular practical alley, continued to be invaluable. She'd used the small amount of Tonya's tockion theory that had already been published to go further than Tonya thought possible. She'd already converted a forensics truck and outfitted it with antenna mounts without a firm idea that any of it would really work. It might be possible to scan for the location of historic events using the particle theory of time. It might not. Rachel assumed it would and proceeded accordingly. It was Tonya's job to design the antennas themselves and the instruments that would process the information into signals that could be used to locate important archeological sites.

Tonya had been around super-rich people before. Mike owned *Warhawk*, the largest, most realistic combat realm in the world. The subscriber base numbered in the millions. He'd had to give away his entire fortune to stay out of trouble with the IRS and still had money coming out of his ears.

Rachel was on a whole other level. Mike had a lot of money. Rachel wasn't kidding about having *infinite* money. During their first meeting after the conference Tonya outlined the kind of lab she'd need to design and build the instrumentation and antennas. The amount made her eyes water, and she added an extra twenty percent to cover things she hadn't thought of.

Rachel smiled *and added a zero to the budget*. "You don't think big enough."

Tonya gaped. The half-dozen executives Rachel had brought along to tour the realm simulation smiled and chuckled.

One of them, an older Black guy in charge of accounting, cleared his throat as he smiled at Tonya. "First time?"

She was still processing what a budget an order of magnitude bigger than she'd planned would mean. Hang on, he'd asked her a question. "First time for what?"

Rachel tipped her head in an *I get that a lot* sort of way. "People don't understand what I bring to the table. What any of us who started out working for David Rose now have. Liquid capital should be at the bottom of your concerns. It ceased to exist as a problem the moment I knew we could work together to make this a reality."

That was what made Rachel so interesting. Tonya wasn't building a toy for a tech trillionaire. She was working *together* with a brilliant mind in her own right to turn an idea so out there nobody had thought of it before into a concrete, workable *thing*.

Rachel smiled and raised an eyebrow. "You didn't think I was going to make you compromise on the 3-D printing facilities, did you?"

The thing was, Tonya *hadn't* compromised. But Rachel was right. She hadn't thought big enough. "I guess not. Now," she said as they crossed a hallway to a different section of the lab, "I think we'll need to get more nanolooms and weavers."

Rachel turned out to be local. Rose phones had been invented in the Dulles tech corridor and, like Silicon Valley generations earlier, that's where the expertise concentrated. They were in a realm because the executives of her Anderson Foundation, second only to

David Rose's own self-titled tech charity, were scattered all over the world.

"People around here are good at moving fast and breaking things," she told Tonya over lunch. "Money hasn't been an issue for any of my projects for years." She held up fingers as she counted. "Navigating the permit processes for historical surveys, negotiating with private landowners for excavation rights, and making sure we don't step on the wrong academic or regulatory toes? Those are a different kettle of fish."

They were sitting in the plaza around Mercury Fountain at the Reston Town Center, eating a couple of burrito bowls they'd picked up from ChipotleBell. Unexpected motion caught Tonya's attention. A young guy in an outfit that screamed expensive shabby was marching up to their table from across the plaza.

Rachel followed her gaze. "Oh great."

It seemed Tonya wasn't the only one who could spot someone spoiling for a fight at a distance. Patients' loved ones who'd gotten bad news and needed somebody to chew out was how Tonya learned. Rachel's mention of how weird people could act around her now made a lot more sense.

He was white and a *lot* bigger than Tonya was, but it was the giant mug he carried in his right hand that concerned her the most. That was a missile in the making. She stood up and got in front of him. He didn't so much as glance at her. The guy was *huge,* arrogance coming off him in sheets. People got out of this guy's way, not in it.

Then he put a hand in the middle of her chest to knock her out of the way.

In motion, the human body was statically unstable. If someone walking were to freeze in position, they would fall over. Humans didn't because they constantly corrected for this instability with their stride, arms, and small corrections made by dozens of muscles across the whole body.

This dynamic equilibrium wasn't easy to disrupt. People resisted getting pushed over. That was what anyone who wasn't

Tonya would do. He was expecting resistance from specific vectors on an instinctual level while still in motion and off balance himself. This made confusing and then defeating his balance almost trivial.

The trick here was putting him on the ground without killing him. The plaza was paved with large concrete slabs that could easily cause a skull fracture in a person this tall. An unprovoked assault deserved a response, but it shouldn't be deadly.

Tonya solved the involuntary manslaughter problem with a rotational wrist lock at the exact moment his stride let her pivot his entire body 180 degrees. A moderate kick to the inside of the knee collapsed his support. The standard move would then be to throw her opponent to the ground, but again, the point was to stop this jerk without killing him. Tonya shifted her own balance and went down with him, guiding his body as she fell so they both safely landed on their backs.

She did make sure to knock the wind out of him with an elbow. He didn't get to push Tonya Brinks without some sort of consequence. It all happened so fast his expression went from unreasoning rage straight to gasping like a fish. She wasn't sure if he registered that he was on the ground yet.

"Tonya! Oh my God!" Rachel rushed over. "Are you okay?"

"I'm fine." She sat up and groaned inwardly. Not due to pain, but all the glassy-eyed stares of everyone around them. Decades ago, people had to point actual phones at a scene to record it. Now all they did was switch modes on their vision channel. She'd no doubt be a sensation on InstaTok for days. "Who *is* this guy?"

Security, always minutes away when seconds counted, scurried up and lifted him to his feet. He stared pure venom at Rachel. "One-tenther!" he panted out. He'd caught his breath in time to start up again. "*You're* the one holding us all back! Your speech kills us! Kills me! I'm dying because of the things you say! My friends are dying too! People like you make it happen! You have to be stopped!"

They dragged him away by his shoulders while he ranted, feet pointed toes up, skidding across the ground. It would've been hilarious if it hadn't been so dangerous.

The next hour was taken up with being questioned by the rent-a-cops, then the actual cops, then a few intrepid PJ Media self-designated reporter types. For the first time, she got to review one of her fights from multiple angles and in high def. It hadn't been her intention, but the moves were fast enough to make it look like he'd stumbled into her, and they'd both gone down. The cops around here had no reputation for stopping people for driving while Black or any other such shenanigans, but the fact that it looked like an accident and that's what everyone agreed with lifted a small weight off her shoulders. You can take the homeless girl off the streets…

After the last of the people who were interested left, Rachel shook her head. It was too late to go back to the lab, and Tonya needed some time with her feet up in her own house. They both headed toward the parking garage where Tonya had parked Morgan and Rachel had parked her Hongqi, a tasteful but still luxurious Chinese brand that had taken over Acura's position in the *you want something nice and sensible* model list.

"I've never seen that guy before in my life. I told you people got weird around me sometimes. You're sure you're all right?"

Morgan, her custom SUV, blinked his lights at her approach. Seeing him notched her pulse down noticeably. "I'm a little scratched up, that's all."

Before she opened her car door, Rachel grew serious. "Thank you, by the way. I've been doused by coffee *and* milkshakes over the years. And worse." She put on her seatbelt. "He looked like an *or worse* kind of guy. That was some move you put on him." She gave Tonya an up-and-down evaluation that felt weirder than it should've. "So, nurse, scientist, and bodyguard?"

Tonya chuckled and shook her head. "Bodyguards get paid." She remembered the times bullets had whizzed past her head recently. "I'm trying to cut down on the violence."

"Did you get into more trouble, Miss Tonya?" Morgan asked from the car speakers after she closed the door. She exchanged a wave with Rachel that lifted her spirits nicely.

"Nothing I couldn't handle, Morgan."

A message request appeared in her queue. She asked Morgan to drive her home and answered.

Maff appeared in her vision channel. "Tonya, I've got a problem."

Chapter 15
Maff

A storm of immense strength stirred inside her. On one wing, she was happy to see so many of her people in person. On the other, none of them could or should be here. Earth's survival was at stake, and without Earth's survival, her hopes for her people would die with it.

Answering the question of how they got here was not *their* priority.

"Where will we get Bashanta? You said there would be…"

"Our quarters are too close to the Eskarn. We need an exclusive place to pray before…"

"The filter cleanser on B deck is broken, and the one on A will break soon…"

"Have we made it to the promised…"

The crush of her own people was almost as terrifying as the time a pile of mummified bodies briefly trapped her under their weight. That was easier. The mummies didn't talk back.

Maff's pilot license was enough for the ship AI to give her control of the PA system. *"Who is in charge of this expedition?"*

This at least made them pause, looking around at the ceiling like the sky was about to fall on them. Before they had time to get their arguments back in gear, she said, "My name is Maff Sorkon. I'm here to help. I need to know who is in charge."

This turned out to be the head Meronim Bashtun, the official religious leader of the community, and a younger Eskarn pallun.

Meronim looked at everything through the lens of pallun holy books. Eskarn had largely left that all behind and weren't particularly devout. By the time she herded the two into a side room to talk, the rest of them had started up their arguments again. Maff wasn't sure if they noticed she'd left.

Compared to the bedlam outside, here were two pallun with serious expressions, one of them perhaps three times her age. She was all they had, but Maff wasn't sure they knew it yet. She waited until they settled on their seating plinths.

First things first. "How did you get here?"

The eldest of the two leaders, the ship AI told her he was named Jholl, stood. "We left it to Turlanfador."

Maybe this was why her mother had warned her to keep her distance from Meronim when she was a child. "What does that mean?"

Jholl sat down and gestured to the female seated opposite him. Her name was Keezel, and her protective suit was by far the most utilitarian Maff had seen so far. This had to be the captain. "Am I allowed to tell her the truth?" Her tone was not of someone fond of the person she was addressing.

"That's what I did."

"No, you told her what nearly got us all killed. What *should* have gotten us all killed." She leaned back on her plinth. "I honestly don't know how we survived such madness."

"We survived," Jholl intoned with a certainty that would've driven through a tornado unscathed, "as Turlanfador intended."

Maff turned back to the captain. Hopefully she would make sense. Keezel shook her head. "He entered a random set of coordinates and performed a level eight modal jump through the transit dimension."

"No," Jholl shot back. "Not random. Not made up. They were a gift to me from Turlanfador, granted in a dream."

"You risked the entire project on what fell into your head after you ate too much gabbashan and went to bed early. These are not the actions of a sane person."

She would never tell them, but with those simple words, Maff knew what had happened. Mike had worked it out as part of his portal research. The bizarre empty bubble of space that surrounded Earth had somehow created an influence in the transit dimension that would attract ships if the right conditions were met. Those being a jump at level eight to coordinates that didn't exist. Incredibly, bemian nav computers had not been set up to disallow this because *nobody* did that. It wasn't done. She'd ended up out here because her navigator had made a mistake in her nav solution, *and* they'd done a level eight, running like hell from authorities trying to arrest them. Part of Mike's patching was to explicitly prevent it.

Bemian ships had to have gotten lost and ended up in Earth's system before, but for the vast majority of time since the Refounding, Earth wouldn't have been able to provide assistance. The kind of intelligent life that a bemian ship would detect—radio being considered the bare minimum—didn't exist as recently as two centuries ago, and D-ships disappeared mysteriously only once or twice every ten thousand years. There might still be derelict bemian ships drifting around the solar system, dead husks far too cold and small to ever be detected accidentally.

The ship hulls weren't designed to survive an atmospheric reentry from orbit—a concept that horrified Maff so much she didn't believe humans had done it. Then one day Mike and Kim took her to their Air and Space Museum, and showed her the vehicles *they'd already used*—so despite humans having credible legends, no bemian ship could ever reach the surface without using the transit dimension.

The only way to end up here was if a navigator, trained to not make mistakes, screwed it up. Or, apparently, you could punch buttons at random and hope for the best.

Leave it to her people to find the second option.

That left the question of whether or not Mike's patch had been applied to this ship still open, but the way he explained it, there would be several years before it spread throughout the whole galaxy. It was also natural for her people to choose one of a dwindling number of unpatched D-ships by chance. They'd sacrificed their home world to preserve their religion. Sometimes Turlanfador honored that. Sort of.

But that was what *Maff* knew. These people didn't. Anyone who knew anything about D-ships understood that pulling a stunt like that was an elaborate way to commit mass murder and suicide simultaneously. "Why would you take such a risk?"

Jholl said, "Turlanfador commanded it." At the same time, Keezel said, "I didn't have a choice."

She addressed Keezel first. "Explain that."

The woman had looked exhausted; they both did, but Maff now saw a new level of fatigue roll down on her. "We were hired to do a survey," Keezel said, "to try to work out whether or not the rumors we've been hearing lately could be true at all. I didn't know what their real plan was. They tricked the relief flight crew into leaving their stations and then," she pointed at Jholl, "this idiot punched buttons until he triggered a jump. I didn't know what was going on until it was over." She turned to Jholl. "You broke my ship, you old bastard."

Jholl assumed a holier-than-thou expression that could infuriate or inspire the pallun around him, a characteristic of Meronim across the galaxy. Sometimes they did both at the same time. "It was not random. I entered the coordinates gifted to me by Turlanfador and followed his will. I have no training in navigation or piloting. Do you think random button pushing would get us anywhere?"

She sighed. "No. I don't know. I didn't think so." She threw her wings up. "You got lucky I guess."

"Not luck. Destiny. Divine will. Maff Sorkon," he pointed at her with a surprising bit of awe in his voice, "is the pilot. The first of us. The one who glides the storm to find the path. We are the forward flock, the ones who will prepare the way. It is written."

Keezel scoffed. "Ancient texts that teach how to live on a planet destroyed thousands of years ago are not a navigation guide through D-space. *And* we've got no way to get home." She turned to

Maff. "Unless you have a node repair yard around here somewhere?"

Bemians didn't repair things. Nodes repaired things. "No. We might be able to work something out with the humans, though. They're getting pretty good at portals and drives."

Then the strangest thing happened. The angry stiff-winged captain vanished, replaced by…Maff didn't know what. Her expression was strangely hopeful. "Then the rumors are true? We've made it to the wolfling system? You are *that* Maff Sorkon?"

"Yes?" Awe. That was what it was. And Maff wasn't used to it. She wore so many hats nowadays they would've run down her back if they were real, but bashtun wasn't one of them. She was not a teacher in any sense of the word. But she was indeed *that* Maff Sorkin.

They both grew excited together. "So *Jupiter* is real?"

"Where did you hear that name?" They hadn't got the pronunciation down yet, but even in heavily accented Pallundian, the English word was clear. The storm swirled her up with hope and then down with fear in equal measure.

Keezel again pointed a wingtip at Jholl. The old man coughed. "Does the name Noen Sha'Katenden roll a bit of thunder your way?"

He was her lawyer, then her mediator to arrange a specific sort of agreement between her and the shadier portions of pallun society. Last she heard, he was helping them fence the first trinkets of Earth's cultures into remote bemian societies. "Yes, I know who that is."

Jholl lifted up high on his legs and gestured at her with his manipulators, a man used to making emphatic points. "*He* sent us!"

Keezel's brief foray into awe was snuffed in a wind of outrage. "You said Turlanfador sent you."

Jholl shrugged, moving his manipulators around as if he were holding a book. He probably did, most of the time. Meronim bashtun were famous for it. "Yes, but Turlanfador worked through Noen to enlighten me. We grew up together, Noen and I. He's no Meronim, but he's an upstanding pallun who needed someone to talk to."

And the storm swirled her upward again. Mr. Sha'Katenden was one of the finest lawyers on Silaria, which made him one of the finest in the galaxy. Lawyers knew who they could trust and who they couldn't, who would keep their mouth shut and who would blab secrets to the world. "So you're the only ones who know about it?" she asked.

They both got a sour expression. Keezel fairly spit out, "You think we'd tell petarkan about anything this big?"

Petarkan was a racist term for nonpallun, but Maff let it slide without a wince. Suspicious and insular were pallun stereotypes salted with a little truth. "No, but other pallun?" Toraz's crew, the gangsters they'd worked with while Hellen was trying to find ancient information about the galaxy in general and Andromeda in particular, were being kept in line by the promise of enormous riches and the threat of becoming part of a building's foundation if anyone threatened those riches. These people responded to different incentives.

Jholl shook his head, wise with effortless authority. "No. I know how to keep a secret, and so does Captain Keezel."

She couldn't trust this bashtun at his word. "And you know this how?"

Keezel rolled her wingtips. "He's my great-uncle." She threw him a nasty look. "Who I should've been more suspicious about when he darkened my sky a few weeks ago."

Maff now had her wings around the situation. A bunch of idealistic pallun had done a crazy thing and ended up here, on purpose. The likelihood of that happening again soon was hopefully close to zero, especially once she got word back to Mr. Sha'Katenden about the result of his indiscretion. They couldn't return on their own and wouldn't even if Sidereal somehow got its portal configured to the right destination. There were hundreds of them.

Earth didn't know they were here or that they so much as existed. Almost all of Earth didn't know about any of this.

The first new residents of Jupiter may have arrived.

Chapter 16

Mike

They couldn't waltz in to Elysium. Whatever had caused that black wave across the center of the land would have spread out by now. They needed an entrance somewhere they couldn't easily be seen.

Zoe smiled with a raised eyebrow. She must've anticipated the observation. "I know the perfect place."

He'd encapsulated her in a microrealm so he could steer her through the interstitial. She'd built out constructs to look like the stern of a galleon, complete with a wheel. Most of the trip was spent with her belting out fake pirate songs and shouting *yarr* whenever she felt the urge. Which was often. But now that they were close enough to see the place, she could use the wheel to guide him.

She signaled a stop opposite what appeared to be an airlock made out of rock. With a few gestures, she constructed a matching door in the microrealm. "It was a natural fissure that I secured as part of an art project."

"You had direct access to the interstitial?"

"That's what you call it? We call them hell gates. There's a pressure difference that might as well be hard vacuum even though I don't think atmospheric rules apply. I lost several good people before we figured what was going on. Try docking us."

He initiated the standard merge procedure. The first two attempts failed but with errors he understood. After some adjustments, on the third try it merged perfectly.

From his perspective in the interstitial, *Elysium* wasn't like any realm he'd ever seen. It hadn't been built, it had grown. But that wasn't exactly right. Zoe's intent played a critical role. By her description, she willed it into existence. It implied that whatever it was, it could respond in unique ways to an intelligent being—

"Gone off into the weeds again, Sellars?" Zoe asked from the other side of the realm.

He manifested his holo beside her. "How could you tell?"

"It's the only time you go still and quiet." She motioned forward. "Now, come on."

The tunnel was neat and regular, lined with bricks. It was a good thing he used a holo. The passage was so small, Zoe had to walk sideways and stoop a little. Things got better after a few dozen feet, and then spread out fully when she exited the cave.

She stood on a small, semicircular balcony made of flagstones. A low parapet of the same material marked the edge. The entire realm spread out in front of them. The balcony was built into the side of a massive cliff, at least two thousand feet above the ground below. In one corner, he saw a handrail next to stairs that led downward into the column.

"Oh God," Zoe choked out. "What have they done?"

Elysium was on fire.

The armies were mostly shapeless darkness with only the hint of a body outline. There was no control interface here, no place for his threads to anchor and scan the inhabitants. "Can you tell what they are?" he asked her.

An information feed opened up in one of his threads. He might not know where the controls were, but Zoe did. "Unduplicates. I think. I've never seen anything exactly like them before."

Columns of black smoke from the fires floated into the sky. Mike's own *Warhawk* hosted any number of subrealms dedicated to mayhem and destruction. It was considered the most realistic combat simulation for a reason. But those were all creations, engineered constructs that simulated reality. When the battle was over, it reset automatically so it could be used all over again.

Elysium was, in a specific but no less factual way, its own reality. This made the destruction more personal. There would be no casual reset here.

Zoe turned to his holo. "You're the king of realm designers. Isn't there anything you can do?"

A human head popped up out of the passageway in the floor. "Zoe? *Zoe!*" Out of the passageway rushed dozens of fully conscious unduplicates. They kept coming, shouting out her name along with wordless sounds of relief and celebration.

Loud sounds.

After a few moments, Mike could clearly see one of the shadows stop and turn toward them. "Guys," he said. It looked like a dog that caught a strange scent.

Or a shark that tasted blood.

The group now filled the balcony with more standing on the stairs that extended below. There was no way for her to hear him, so he opened a private text channel. *Zoe, they've heard us.*

What?

A loud howl sounded out from the one that stopped. This made the platform fall silent. The creature kept up the racket, a reedy, warbling tone at this distance. The group around the creature stopped and turned in the same direction they were in.

And now they've seen us.

Zoe unhitched her backpack. *Stall them, Mike, I have to save these people.*

Who are they?

The survivors that I missed. They took shelter here because the monsters left it alone.

In the distance, a stream of shadows peeled off of the main column and began to flow their way. They were fast.

How long is this going to take? he asked.

As long as it needs to.

The construct slowly began to shift and change shape as she decompressed it. The people crowding out to the edges of the balcony made panicky noises at what they saw.

"Clear an area around me!" Zoe shouted. "I'm getting you out of here! Mike? Buy me time."

He had no probes, and there were no controls. Without either, he had no safe way to interact with the realm.

So he wouldn't.

Zoe might not be able to fly or teleport, but since Mike wasn't in the realm, he could. He jumped his perception toward the stream of shadows. As he grew closer, he saw more detail. They were definitely related to nodes. Under the cloaking shadows were clear outlines of insectoids, the same form the nodes took at the meeting he'd spied on in Teliria. They looked vaguely like an old Disney character shaped like a cricket, covered in blue paint. But where those were genteel councilors arguing points of order, these were sleek armored warriors, gliding with purpose and deadly intent. They also held shadowy weapon constructs that tore vicious furrows whenever they touched the ground of the realm.

He might not be able to control the realm, but he could control his holo. Mike increased its opacity to one hundred percent and took the form of a high castle wall, stretching far enough that they wouldn't be able to see the edges.

Hurry, Zoe.

On it.

The shadows pulled up short, surprised by this new development. Small groups split off to the right and left, searching for a way around it. The shadows floated, but it appeared that they couldn't fly. No attempt was made to climb or leap over him.

A knot of shadows gathered. Mike split some threads off and added a new perception near them. He didn't understand what they were saying to each other. It only came across as an unintelligible stream of sounds, guttural where the old nodes he'd observed had spoken in almost prim tones. Crossing orcs with Nazgûl wasn't anything he'd thought of before now, but the comparison was apt. Neither meant anything good.

The scouts trying to find the ends of his wall gave up and

turned back. They must've had some other way to communicate because the lead group gestured the main column forward.

Mike knew what gathering to make a charge looked like no matter how weird the formation was. *Zoe, status check?*

I missed so many. They must've nearly filled the stairway up here.

That didn't sound like it was going quickly. The lead group made another howl. This close, it was a powerful thing. He was sitting in a peaceful café in realspace, but it still made him break out in a sweat.

The column of shadow raiders charged forward, straight through his hologram.

They're coming, Zoe.

Almost done.

He flew his perception forward and created the illusion of a deep trench across their path. This stopped them again, but instead of the scouts going right and left, they were sent straight at his holo. When they passed over unharmed, the rest of the column followed.

They reached the base of the tower and streamed inside through a large opening.

Now, Zoe. You have to withdraw now.

I can't!

He threw dazzling lights at them, then plunged them into darkness. Each time they figured it out, faster with every try. Seconds away from the top, he threw his perception up to the parapet. He found Zoe was alone with her construct.

And it was five times bigger than it'd been before, far too large to fit down the passageway.

"Zoe we can't stay here."

"Take it with you."

"I can't touch things in here."

The construct was shrinking but too slowly. She screamed as she tried to push it into the passageway. "I can't take it until it's done compressing."

The shadows boiled up out of the stairwell but went toward the edge of the parapet instead of the cliff face. It wasn't much, but it would have to do. He changed his holo so it camouflaged the passageway. If the passage was too narrow, he need to widen it. Fast.

There was only one thing he could do.

Mike flew his perception to the far end. "Get ready to push your construct." He manifested his full avatar and rammed his hands into the wall. The material that made up the realm began to disintegrate in a shattering roar that would eventually consume the entire realm. It opened a hole directly into the vacuum outside. *"Push!"*

As the hole grew wider, the wind sped up. Normally this was the least noticeable aspect of an inversion, but that was because the usual way he initiated it created a massive area of damage that annihilated the construct faster than a pressure difference could form. But now he created a roaring hurricane. It had to be enough.

A massive thud sounded out behind him. Mike turned and saw Zoe's construct tumbling toward him, with Zoe's avatar out of control behind it. He flattened himself against the wall as the construct thumped past, nearly falling over after the wall inverted behind him.

In realspace, Mike activated Zoe's disconnect.

The last thing he saw before he, too, left the realm was her vase-like construct tumbling away into the interstitial darkness, visibly smaller than it was when it left.

Chapter 17
Kim

Waking up the next day, Kim realized the truth: she was far from immune to Valsa's charms. This was one of the most powerful people in the entire galaxy, and someone who'd tried her best to either kill or capture her. More than once. And yet she'd been a gloriously courteous host who adeptly brought Kim on her side with a simple dinner for two. Well, three, since Seluk Pash, her threaded companion, was also there. If anything, he might have been a little more charming. That was one hell of a bar to clear in that company. Their questions about her army revealed that they didn't know that what had taken apart their fleet as it attempted to intercept *Palatine* in the transit dimension was Kim, split into hundreds of instances. It may have been more than a thousand.

If Kim wasn't habitually suspicious of people with immense power, she might've assumed Valsa's earlier behavior was the result of simple misunderstandings. And not only on Valsa's part. Kim had found herself taking a long look at her own actions to see what she'd done for it to go so wrong.

She wished it could be chalked up to something they'd put in her drink or her food, but that wasn't right. Through sheer force of will and absolutely staggering charisma, Valsa Burtan had turned Kim, a famously proud and hardheaded bitch, into a bowl full of mush. She hadn't actually been eating out of Valsa's hand, but it was close.

Valsa had lived in Kim's head as a cross between a Bond villain and Darth Vader. That she was instead, at least seemingly, kind and caring was possibly the most disturbing part of all. People shouldn't meet their heroes, but it was turning out that they shouldn't meet their enemies, either. Kim would have to keep a close eye on Valsa.

And herself.

That said, while Kim wasn't exactly proud of how she'd nearly rolled over to ask for a belly scratch, she did manage to learn important things. *Very* important things. Andromeda, the intelligent galaxy that to this day was trying to cause trouble back home, was here. Using a humanoid form, somehow. He'd been here for centuries. Valsa had inherited a complex agreement with him that she hoped Kim would help extricate the Guild from. She thought Kim had an army.

Valsa must've misinterpreted Kim's reaction because she changed the subject immediately. Kim didn't have an army, She *was* the army. She and Mike had split into thousands to take out Valsa's armada. But it seemed bemian interpreters couldn't do that, otherwise they wouldn't have made such a glaring mistake about what had happened.

It was an important and disorienting discovery. Kim chose to let Valsa think she'd been offended and the subject never came up again.

But it would eventually. Kim hoped she'd be able to take advantage of it when it did.

Valsa learned a lot about humans by examining Kim. That's what interpreters did: extrapolate the general from the specific. What she couldn't know were details about Kim as an individual. If she had, Valsa would've started the day out with breakfast at five thirty in the morning. That was what Kim did before she met Mike. Nowadays she started out with yoga while Mike did his morning prayers, but alone it was easy to slip into old habits.

This time the doorknob moved in a smooth arc. Now that Valsa knew Kim wouldn't set the palace on fire, she seemed free to move about the place. Time to test the boundaries.

It was still full night outside. The massive hallways were silent and still, peaceful yet also lonely. Kim was once comforted by places like this. People couldn't touch her if no one was around. She wasn't that fearful, that reclusive, anymore. It didn't mean she couldn't take the same comfort given the opportunity. After dodging a few servants and scaring a couple that didn't see her coming, Kim found stairs going down.

The lower area was for more public purposes. The rooms were large, open lounges of different designs and configurations, arranged on either side of a broad lane. She passed through six, three on each side. They were all cleverly arranged and beautiful in a standard bemian way that also included clear echoes of the Interpreter's past. She must be witnessing what was left of the memories of an organization with a history that stretched back billions of years.

Catholic church, eat your heart out.

The lane ended at a doorway to what she could only call the most sumptuous cafeteria Kim had ever seen. No wobbly tables or cheap plastic booths here. Instead it was like everything else in the palace: understated, classy, and expensive.

Her now rumbling stomach made the sets of double doors on the opposite wall and the clear smell of food being cooked beyond them a bigger priority. She walked to them and pushed through, wondering how much a permanent bemian kitchen would resemble the frantic melee of the camp version she'd seen previously.

First of all, it was a *lot* larger. The mobile version might've been the size of her living room back home. This one was at least the size of a basketball court.

It was filled with bees.

They weren't flying, and they weren't swarming. They weren't actually bees. They were bipedal fuzzy insectoids, standing on two legs and manipulating their world with four arms. They were a bit shorter than she was, mostly four to five feet tall. They had stripes, although here they were green and black instead of yellow. She could barely make out vestigial wings under their uniforms. Aside from concessions to anatomical differences, these wore roughly similar to garb found in kitchens all over the world back home: plain white made out of a utilitarian sort of cloth. They even had hats.

Their faces weren't at all like an insect's, although they did have antennas on their heads and faceted eyes. The rest was an expressive variation of the humanoid standard that most bemians seem to be equipped with. Taken all together, they reminded her of any number of anthropomorphized bees she'd encountered in classic animation revival realms.

The other thing that reminded her of terrestrial bees was how hard everyone worked. The motion was constant, the sounds a classic combination of clanking utensils, hissing griddles, and the occasional puff of flames. Kim had skulked through versions of it half a dozen times taking a back exit from a heist or hacking run.

Nobody looked up at her. Then a worker nearly knocked her over, bustling in through the doors with a stack of boxes full of her old friend celerawberries. The upstairs staff might be impressed with the Wild Witch, but this bunch certainly wasn't.

Then the queen appeared.

She walked through a big metal door on the opposite side of the kitchen that had to lead to a walk-in pantry or refrigerator. She was easily twice the size of her workers and carried four armloads of something leafy and green…ish. It had to be a bemian variety of lettuce, but Kim couldn't be sure from here.

Unlike her workers, the queen noticed Kim immediately. "Tikalal nash ix?"

Kim had been a practicing interpreter for about a year now, so the head rush at hearing a foreign language wasn't as shocking as it used to be. She still had to grip a countertop to keep from staggering a bit. She replied in Standard. "I'm sorry, I'm new here. Please keep talking, I'll catch on soon enough."

Kim wasn't used to her odd face, but the expression of *oh okay, that's what's going on* was clear anyway.

"Ix'alls af oala, interpreter ioog nil pak!"

All at once the kitchen erupted in song. A single new voice speaking a language she didn't know was slightly disorienting. An entire kitchenful doing so with rhythm and melody almost sent her to her knees. Mama always said first impressions were important. Kim falling over in a stranger's kitchen in front of the staff would at least be memorable. The head rush blinded her. She gripped the countertop with both hands and willed herself to stay upright.

It wasn't easy.

But, as her head cleared, so did the gibberish sounds filling the kitchen with singing. By the time she could see again, Kim could follow along.

The honey hive keeps us safe
The honey hive feeds our mates
The queen commands the worker's hands
And we do what is needing

So maybe they were bees. Or had been sometime in their past.

"Are ye feeling better now, love?" the queen asked.

For whatever reason the languages she learned this way came equipped with Earth accents and idioms. Maybe it was all the British TV she'd watched as a kid growing up. Mama said it helped her concentrate. While the language was distinctly bemian—in this case it involved as much humming as it did speaking—it got rendered in her head as somehow Irish. Sort of.

She shook the last of her disorientation off. "Yes. That's quite an introduction."

"Always better to rip the wax off quick than to try to worry it away bit by bit. Now, I'll try again. Are ye lost, miss?"

"Kim. Just Kim. No, not lost exactly. I was looking for something to eat."

"You've come to the right place then." The queen pointed one arm toward a back corner of the kitchen. When Kim drew closer, she found the room extended off to her right. This extra space, almost half as big as the kitchen, held three long metal tables with attached benches. At the far end, a few staff were scattered about, eating morning meals or reading displays only they could see. A sideboard ran the length of one wall with an assortment of weird but no less recognizable fruits, grains, and pastries.

The queen scoffed when Kim moved to pick up a plate. "Ach, no, dear. Not that for the likes of you. That's servant's food, it is. Now, give ol' Liinair here a challenge. Describe the textures and flavors of your kind's breakfast."

Describing a Bob Evans Rise & Shine breakfast in the abstract to someone who'd never seen terrestrial eggs, potatoes, sausage, or biscuits made for a fun way to practice the new language and get to know the queen, Liinair, at the same time. She listened intently, her faceted eyes concentrating on Kim so much it should've been intimidating or frighting but was neither. After a few lines, she'd shout, "Ach! I know just the thing, lass." A worker would be dispatched to go hunting for specific ingredients, and another arm would be tasked with cooking whatever Liinair had in mind.

All the while Kim pumped Liinair for information. The answers were a gold mine.

"I was here before Valsa. You keep an eye on that one, you do. One day we were all workin' for her predecessor, a one called Tevalum, and the next wouldn't ya know it? The shiny new thing from one of the smaller noble families, who, mind you, had only recently arrived, was in charge! Tevalum never knew what hit him."

"Was it a violent overthrow?"

Liinair scoffed. "Ach, no, lass. Thems that live here fight with words, political maneuvers, gathered votes, and secret bribes. But it's still dangerous." She waved an impressively large kitchen knife around like an expert sword fighter. "The knives used here are metaphorical, but they'll stick 'em in your back the same way. No, Valsa got where she is by bein' smarter an' meaner than anyone else has seen in a long, long time. Now," she said as all four arms brought plates together on the table in front of Kim, "tell me how I did."

It was an impressive recreation, a technical challenge that would've done any *Bake Off* realm contestant proud. It wasn't perfect. The eggs were too orange, the sausage had a green tinge, and the biscuits were the wrong shape. But otherwise, especially flavorwise, it beat what she remembered having back home. "Wow."

"That's what I like to hear."

While they talked, Kim surreptitiously programmed one of the beverage dispensers to make bemian coffee. She and Mike had been experimenting for as long as they'd been out here and had gotten pretty close. A servitor bot pulled up with two mugs she'd also provided the design for. "Now it's my turn. Give this a try."

Liinair cast a sharp eye into the mug, then gave it a deep sniff. "Cor, what do we have here?" She took a sip, grimaced, but then grew thoughtful. "That's more complicated than I thought it would be."

What had to be Liinair's sous chef assumed giving orders and supervising while the head chef sat opposite Kim, mug in her uppermost hands. "Do ye mind if I ask about yer upbringin'? Ye've made quite the stir amongst the interpreters, you have."

"I will if you'll help me learn how to make my way around here."

And that's how the rest of the morning went. Kim learned about factions, noble families, and Valsa's inner circle of commoners, while Liinair learned about an ocean planet dominated by life that climbed out of trees and had more cuisines in one city than could be found on entire bemian continents. In all, Kim wasn't sure it was an even trade, but it made Liinair happy.

It was only after someone called her name from the dining room doorway that Kim realized how much time had passed. The kitchen crew had clearly shifted to cleanup and next meal prep, and the dining room itself was empty. It was a rhon, one of the stork aliens that were common across the galaxy. "The first councilor requests your presence."

"So you're startin' your day now love?" Liinair asked.

Kim sighed when she scanned the agenda that just now landed in her message queue. "It looks like I'm off to school."

Chapter 18
Spencer

He stood next to Sornik while the gangster's men carefully picked over the camp Spencer had found. Sornik chuckled, the sound chopped up by his suit's filters like he was speaking through a fan. "And you stumbled across this?"

"More like it exploded while I was sleeping, and I followed the smoke." He hadn't spent too much time here, and so didn't appreciate the scale of the destroyed camp. This wasn't a minor site. "They fucked your shit up pretty good."

"Yeah," he said and started walking the perimeter. Spencer followed alongside him. The movement of the brass legs of his protective suit made barely audible hydraulic noises, like he was walking next to a well-tuned forklift. "I'm thinking we'll be returning the favor soon."

Sornik was Toraz's second-in-command, the pallun who helped Helen fight off attacks from rogue interpreters. Spencer had spent a bit of time with him on the way back from Teliria to Maff's home world, mostly playing poker and learning how to swear in Pallundian. Sornik was a no-nonsense guy who didn't need to watch what he said. Spencer didn't have as much experience with gangsters as Helen did, but he'd spent hours hanging out in *Sopranos* and *Goodfellas* realms. Aside from the whole manta ray in a scuba suit thing, Sornik would fit right in. Attitude always trumped appearance, and Sornik had attitude in spades.

He watched with interest as Sornik met with his men, nine beefy pallun with grayish suits and tarnished brass, listened to reports from them, and then sent them out again. The closest Spencer got to actual commanders in action was athletic coaches and Kim. Neither of those counted. Despite all the pissing and moaning from the spectators, little league baseball's stakes were a shit ton lower. Kim was as much a force of nature as she was a leader. This was a middle ground he'd never witnessed before.

Sornik caught his eye. "You want to take a picture?" he asked. "That'll protect it from a storm."

Pallundian slang could be a little hard to follow sometimes but Spencer was pretty sure the second half of that was *it'll last longer*. "I'm trying to stay out of your way."

"Out of my way. Right. Kid watches me like a peskart looking for supper, and I'm supposed to think he's staying out of the way." *Peskart* turned out to be some kind of shark-thing. He puffed on a nasty-smelling cigar thing through a port in his suit, took it out, and waved it at Spencer. "You're gonna get a lot busier. Soon as we're done here, you're taking us to this camp you've found."

"What about the guards?"

He smiled. "We have a plan for the guards."

*

He'd walked through woods back home with any number of people over the years. Hunters and hikers made noise but at least tried to keep quiet. Mike moved like smoke wherever he was, and Spencer had taken those lessons to heart. It made walking around with Kim the last time they were here like having an elephant on a leash.

It was nothing—fucking *nothing*—like ten huge manta rays, much wider than they were tall, walking on brass stilts through the forest. He could tie empty beer cans to them and they might make *less* noise.

"You guys will at least be quiet after we've set you up?" Spencer asked.

The plan was to ambush and nab the guards he'd encountered earlier for questioning.

"As a fenegal," Toraz said.

"What the hell is a fenegal?"

He chuckled. "The funny part is, nobody's sure anymore. They were native to our old home world, quiet ambush predators that swooped out of the sky without a sound. Our ancestors were too busy running to bring any along. It's only a saying to us now."

Once everyone was set, it was time for Spencer to reprise his role as Gono, the ugliest Telirian goatherd on the planet. The idea was to dangle Gono in front of the guards, who would try to run poor Gono down. They would find out Gono had friends the hard way. He picked up his stick and started walking. "I'll see ya when I see ya."

"Not quite," he said and then pulled out one of the soap-bar-meets-phasers everyone in the galaxy used. "You'll need a guy with a gun."

"Or you could give one to me. I'm a pretty good shot back home." Now that he'd had time to calm down and replay the original incident with the guards in his head, he knew they were a lot quieter than a pistol and didn't kick. Not much more than a new variant of every handheld blaster he'd ever used in a realm. Womp rats, kron, same difference.

He'd been hanging around pallun so long it was easy to read Sornik's *no* before he said it. "I think it'll work better if I go along."

"You'll get tangled up in shit out here. Make noise. It's all you guys do."

"You and I will be fine." He threw his cigar thing on the ground and stomped it out. "Let's go."

He *did* have a ray gun. Spencer shrugged and trudged forward. At first it was the standard crunching and crashing noises. But then it all went a lot quieter.

Spencer turned around and nearly fell over a low root.

Sornik was no longer Sornik. Instead of the standard wide, low-wing shape, there was a tall, narrow, almost cylindrical shape in front of him. It *was* Sornik. He still recognized the suit. What at first looked like brass decorations around the sides were most of his legs and manipulators.

"What the shit?"

"We're gasbags," said the recognizable voice from…somewhere. "You learn to do this to get around on petarkan public trains. It's what old people and women do. Not for a crew. It's why I waited until we were out of sight. I'd get shit for days if they saw me like this." In spite of his absurd shape, Spencer could easily tell when he grew serious. "If you say one fuckin' thing to the boys…"

"Oh, no worries about that." If it'd been anyone else, he would've cracked a joke about it, but the sudden mood change made him think he hadn't earned the right. "Follow me."

It was a little unnerving, being bait. Ambush wasn't a strategy for the kind of hunts Spencer had been on. The baits he was used to were more of the salt-and-corn variety. Dead shit that didn't move around. At least it made Sornik's noise—he was quiet*er*, not quiet—serve a purpose.

He only hoped Sornik's assertion that running away would trigger a chase and not a shootout was true. He'd been on the wrong end of one of those popguns already. If it ever happened again, it'd be too soon.

"Hey, you!" a voice cried out from the other end of the trail. "Stop right there!"

Time to find out.

Chapter 19

Helen

After her breakneck run through the portal network, Helen took a breather and then did two more random journeys. She ended her trek on a planet named Solinge, a rocky world with very large lakes but no oceans whatsoever. Strangely, the dominant intelligent life form was visibly aquatic in origin. Like most bemians, they were humanoid enough to pass in public back in the US on Halloween. The scales, fins, and gill slits would otherwise disturb humans. In urban China, it would be the same, but there was no way to predict what a peasant fresh from the countryside might make of them. Those notoriously unpredictable people might run screaming from one thinking it was a demon. Or they might throw coins at it for luck.

A fish living out of water made her curious enough to look them up in a library realm. What Helen had taken to be decorative neck wear was a form of reverse-scuba gear. Without it the Solingians had to stay near bodies of water and regularly submerge themselves to breathe. The gills were specially adapted to hold the water in their bodies and then slowly extract oxygen from it while they made a life on the rocky surface of their world.

Mike's notorious patch wasn't targeted at general security, so it was relatively straightforward for her to reengineer her ID so as to stay off the interpreters' figurative radar screens. The bemian practice of raskara saw that resources to survive and be housed in relative comfort were easy to acquire.

Relative comfort was a bit of a stretch. Bemians relying on raskara were treated with dignity and not forced into the margins like the poor were in the US and, unfortunately, China, but they weren't living in the lap of luxury. Her room was clean, basic, and small, part of a high-rise apartment building that, aside from color and a variety of different door shapes, was similar to those found on Earth. The bathroom facilities were centralized, shared, and larger than the living spaces. It most closely resembled the dorms her realspace fellow police cadets used in her academy days. The ease with which she acquired shelter for her host let her concentrate on her real problem.

Matthew Watchtell.

Her threaded nature was a secret held more closely than the portals or the bemians. Very few people knew that she and Mike were half of an interpreter. The ability to talk and negotiate with disparate alien cultures was their best-known aspect. What was not often appreciated by the galaxy at large was a lesser known aspect: that they were multithreaded beings who could communicate instantaneously across infinite distances. In the inimitable way bemians had of both leveraging and neglecting the potential of their technology, this miraculous ability was mostly used as a long-distance network.

Once Mike explained it all, she agreed it closely resembled Earth's Western long-distance networks before computers automated it all. The threaded part of interpreters were operators and cables at the same time, manually making connections between each other until a more conventional realspace being could communicate directly with another, regardless of the distances involved.

There was so much more to it than that though.

Threads could act as conduits for information, but they were also what she and Mike *were*. Her realspace body was thousands of light years from Earth, but her threads weren't. The majority of them were still in the interstitials that were formed by orbiting satellites.

In other words, she didn't need to phone home. In a very real sense, she'd never left.

Watchtell thought pushing her through a hole that would have her end up on the wrong side of an entire galaxy would be all that was needed to get rid of her. If she were simply human, it would've worked. But she wasn't.

With her realspace security firmly in place, Helen got started.

She began by doing a deep dive on Watchtell's activities starting from incarceration. This would be more efficient than going back further for a few reasons.

One, his behavior while in prison was documented in records that were freely available. Americans hobbled this method of felon monitoring by muddying the waters with their quaint *right to privacy*. She couldn't review records of the activities in his cell. They didn't exist. But prisons had discovered an unexpectedly valuable revenue stream when they realized that there was a market for remote prison monitoring. They sold subscriptions so voyeurs around the world could pay to watch the unscripted drama that was life in a prison facility. Not all states had them. The ones on the West Coast were still too regressive in their concepts of human rights. But Virginia wasn't on the West Coast.

For a normal human, the idea of poring over thousands of hours of video and audio along with accompanying documentation would represent a daunting task that would take years to accomplish. Were anyone to seriously undertake the project, they'd certainly demand a team of assistants.

Helen smiled to herself as she settled her realspace self into a chair with a bowl of bot-delivered Pallundian tirafana, a dish she'd discovered during her last stay that was remarkably similar to hot and sour soup. She didn't need a team of researchers. She only needed herself. Now fully prepared for a massive distribution of threads, she spread herself across the raw data and began to analyze it all at once.

Patterns appeared immediately. Watchtell had made contact with a small group of intimate associates, most importantly, his wife. She visited him in prison regularly, and close observation revealed a back channel of communication. The mechanism was brilliantly simple: they used the old trick of mapping common words to different meanings. This allowed him and his wife to carefully vet Watchtell's former associates until he'd built up a coterie of politically and financially influential loyalists.

The findings were important but also deeply humiliating. Helen had thought herself more than equal to Watchtell's scheming. She'd invited him onto the project precisely because she could think of no one else who combined all the traits they needed to have the slightest chance at snatching victory from Andromeda's arms. And they'd need that help. By every measure she'd managed to find, he'd already won.

She had not the slightest doubt she could control him with ease. And yet in a matter of moments, she exposed an entire network that she'd had no knowledge of. She detected none of it. He wasn't more clever than she was—*she hadn't bothered to look.*

That his new cabal was much smaller than it was before was cold comfort. Mike had been right with the observation that Watchtell, fresh out of prison, was quickly on the cusp of taking over Sidereal. In the end, her actions putting him in place weren't necessary. This was another angle of his attack that Helen had overlooked. If anything, her sudden appearance handing him the keys to the kingdom had snarled his schedule, tripping him up. He wasn't ready yet.

Helen had been trained at one of the finest schools of law enforcement in the world to spot this sort of thing, and she'd failed. She hadn't done anything as basic as this. She thought she didn't need to. If anyone else in her precinct or, later, her detective agency had failed at this, she would personally make sure they never worked in the field again. It wouldn't matter how junior she was or how senior the person in her sights might be. Such a mistake was a fundamental flaw that could not be tolerated under any circumstance.

And yet here she was.

Now that she achieved a moment of clarity, it was time to move on from the mistakes and create a new plan of action. Watchtell's initial rise to power was not done alone. He was, if nothing else, a consummate networker, building guanxi in an effortless way that practically lifted him into his first stint as White House chief of staff. That network didn't survive his fall, but his skills had not failed him, and he was well along in his efforts to rebuild.

It was time for Helen to lay some mines along his path.

Chapter 20
Tonya

She'd heard that rapid prototyping, 3-D printing, and quantum computing had decreased the time it took for an idea to becoming a prototype by a factor of ten. She hadn't quite believed it.

After working with Rachel for going on six weeks, she believed it now.

"Globalization is never a bad thing," Rachel said as they unpacked the final components for the antennas that would form the heart of their history scanner. The antenna geometry and the resonances they created would build structures in extra dimensions, allowing tockion signals to be detected and mapped. This would allow archeologists to find sites without expensive and slow survey work. "Otherwise we'd never be able to get all the parts in time."

Now that Tonya had spent a bit of time with Rachel, she understood some of the hate directed her way. Not approve of it, but understood it. Rachel liked sweeping gestures and grand ideas, but she wasn't very good at articulating them. This was not to say she was incoherent or a bad speaker. After watching her organize this operation, Tonya knew neither of those to be true. Rather, she didn't seem to understand that there were emotional, political, even moral implications to the things she said, and that she needed to be careful when speaking so as not to be misinterpreted. In other words, it never occurred to her that people might not extend her the benefit of the doubt if something she said could be taken the wrong way.

The fact that well-known social media influencers made their living by deliberately misinterpreting anything a prominent person said in the most negative way possible, and quickly herding a howling mob in that person's direction, was an idea that Rachel didn't comprehend. Even though she was personally affected by this phenomena, she was still incapable of policing her language so that it would defuse the mob.

Or she didn't care. Tonya wasn't sure which one was right yet. Regardless, while others thought she was part of an oppressive patriarchy actively working to protect its power and privilege at all costs, Tonya knew nothing could be further from the truth. She could be inelegant and insensitive in the things she said, but it didn't come from a place of hate. All someone had to do to understand her was to accept that she was too busy to care about niceties. To people who put *nice* on an altar and worshipped beneath it, Rachel was a menace. Tonya found her to be refreshingly honest, sometimes unintentionally funny, and even charming at times.

So Tonya only smiled at a statement that would make the heads of some of her more liberal cousins explode. "Are we expecting any more deliveries?"

She shook her head as they both rounded the corner of their lab and walked into the attached garage. "Not for this prototype." She tossed the tockion valve up like a baseball, catching it before Tonya could gasp at the risk. It was the last of the components they needed. There weren't any spares. It, like everything else, was a prototype. "Hopefully the next one won't need so many parts." She turned to the vehicle in the center of the garage. "Iyaan? Open up please."

Rachel said that the name of the AI that controlled everything meant *time, era, epoch* in Malay, and that described their project perfectly. Without its antennas deployed, it looked like a forensics AI truck, called a FAIT, for short. Police used them. The resemblance was natural because that's what it started life as. Tonya had thought they were restricted to police departments or medical examiners but that ended up not being the case. At least, not with pockets that were as deep as the ones Rachel could reach into.

Instead of the various vacuum-cleaner-hose-like extensions that would've been part of a stock FAIT, scaffolding folded out into an elaborate framework that surrounded the middle of the chassis. Small terrestrial drones wheeled out and along the framework, spooling specially designed superconducting wires like so many spiders crawling through a tree.

Iyaan's holo appeared in their shared vision channel. Rachel had picked a licensed *Indiana Jones* template on a whim, but Tonya could see he'd already customized it by changing the color of the hat. A good sign on an AI this new. "Is that the last of the components?" he asked. "How long until we're ready to test?"

"Not long," Tonya replied. "Open up bays six and twenty, please." They'd gone with a FAIT for a reason. The prototype scanner was huge, taking up the entire interior space behind the driver's compartment, and a little of that as well. In some configurations, a FAIT could hold as many as eight people. Here they were barely able to fit two. Rachel dove underneath the FAIT while Tonya entered an interior crawl space. "I told you we shouldn't have sent everyone home early."

"It wouldn't be fair to keep them around only to plug this component in."

It was another thing Tonya liked about Rachel. She was no tech bro, nor was she afraid to get her hands dirty. She expected people to work hard but on their own schedule and in their own way. There were a few engineers on staff that Tonya had only ever seen play foosball in the lounge but who'd still produced quality code early and under budget. A busybody QA tester once complained about their goofing off and was never seen again.

The crawl space wasn't a multidimensional route through the bowls of a realm, but it wasn't exactly comfortable either. At the end was an alcove barely big enough to stand up and turn around in. But she managed it and fit her final piece of the puzzle. "Okay," she said, loudly enough that Rachel would hear it from underneath the truck, "connect main power." Everything lit up and whirred to life. The feeling of accomplishment wasn't exactly like watching someone walk out of a clinic on a leg she helped regrow, but it was close.

Rachel was standing outside next to the truck, eyes flashing. "Are you ready?"

Okay, maybe it was better than someone walking out of a clinic with a new leg. It certainly felt that way in her gut. "No time like the present."

"Wait," Iyaan said as his hologram formed. "We're leaving *now*?"

They did a silent quick rock paper scissors test to choose who drove. Tonya chose rock, Rachel paper, and so Rachel got to climb behind the steering wheel while Tonya fired up the rest of the rig from the passenger seat. "It's all in place. Why not?" She punched the buttons required to fold the arrays back into storage.

"But…the testers…the monitors…"

"Will all be there tomorrow," Rachel said as they pulled out of their lab-slash-garage not too far from the Sidereal site. "If Elon can launch his Tesla to Mars, I can drive you around. Speaking of"—she turned to Tonya and threw her a bright smile—"where to, boss?"

Rachel calling her boss gave her insides an unexpected jump. Project lead? Sure. In charge? It was a strange feeling. She concentrated on the question.

As with all good shakedown tests, they were going to point their scanner at a place they already knew about. One good thing about the DC area was there were tons of well-known historic sites to choose from. Now that she'd moved from theory to engineering, she had things like power consumption, sensitivity, and resolution to worry about. "We'll need something strong but simple, easily accessible from the street," Tonya said. The perfect location hit her in an instant. "Ford's Theatre."

Rachel's smile was contagious. "That's a pick I can get behind." She put the address into the nav and set off.

"You know," Iyaan spluttered in miniature from the dashboard, "I can drive too."

"Oh no," Tonya said as diagnostics filled her visual feed. "You're going to help me calibrate the internals."

Iyaan was mobile, but he was still a prototype. Calibration involved writing new software code and dealing with command lines. A graphical interface with pointers and things to click on was a luxury and an internal configuration realm was a long way off. Tonya barely finished up as Rachel parked.

It was very early in the morning, so finding a parking place wasn't as big of a stretch as it normally would've been. Making sure they weren't hassled by parking or any other kind of police was a problem solved by a stack of traffic cones and a pair of generic overalls and hard hats. People most often saw what they expected to see, and while Iyaan was a heavily modified FAIT, he was still recognizable as such. Rachel parked halfway up the sidewalk, ensuring the sensor nets didn't block traffic. Not that there was much around, but every little bit to reduce their profile helped.

Rachel hopped back in after laying out the cones and scanned Tonya's readouts. "We're not focusing on the theater itself?"

"No. The event there was powerful but brief." She pointed directly across the street. "It took Lincoln nearly eight hours to die, and he was surrounded by family and friends the whole time."

"So emotion plays a factor in making a chronological impression?"

Once again, Rachel's intuition jumped Tonya into an area she hadn't considered in exactly that way. To Tonya, it was an effect that emerged from the theory, a bottom-up perspective. Rachel's was naturally top-down. "I'm not sure yet. It could be *a* factor, but I can't tell if it's more powerful than the number of observations or the fame of the incident." Tonya activated the superconductors and spooled up the quantum computers that would process the signals. The sensors were electronically steered, so there was no movement outside to indicate anything was going on. It was a low rumble that slowly turned into a quiet, fast hum.

Tonya looked at Rachel. "Here we go." She called up the meters measuring the signals predicted by her theories. Facing straight down 10th Street, the meters only registered a smear of undifferentiated history, the unfocused static of who knew how many millions of observations made stretching back hundreds of years. "And now…" She slowly steered the array toward the federal-style row house directly across from the theater. They both gasped as the meters began to rise, at first slowly, then more quickly as the room where Lincoln died came into—

There was a wave of vertigo, and then they were standing together on a crowded, unpaved street. Or maybe it was paved, but buried under what, by the smell, wasn't simple dirt. The van was gone. "Where are we? What happened?" As the vertigo cleared, she got oriented, and she noticed other differences. The crowd was mostly men, angry, and dressed all wrong.

"Tonya!" Rachel half whispered. "What's happening?"

Rachel was wearing a nineteenth-century dress.

This couldn't be happening. She hadn't incorporated any part of the device that had flung herself and Tenor back into the past. Rachel would've spotted bemian tech instantly. They'd not had anything like the power the doddering dean had rammed through her device's crystal lattice. *They could not be in the past.*

Rachel got close. "What's going on? We're monitoring the past. We're not supposed to *be* here!" Her hand touched Tonya's shoulder. It was shaking. That was wrong—Tonya's shoulder was vibrating. This *could not* be happening.

A man stepped out of the theater. "Stand aside! Make room!"

Seven men carried a body slung between them on top of some sort of large cloth. The crowd hushed. Tonya had never experienced emotion as a group reaction, but the sudden impulse to *do something* while at the same time knowing there was nothing she could do was impossible to resist.

Years of training got her feet moving before she could stop them. She fell in step behind the group. "I can help."

She received a grim nod from the man at the rear.

"Tonya! What are you doing?" Rachel whispered.

It was the nod. That was when she knew. "We're not in the

past." She stopped and let the grim train continue up the stairs and into the boarding house.

"How do you know?"

If they truly were in the past, Tonya would never have been allowed anywhere near this scene. A Black woman in a Southern town with the Civil War so fresh men still bled from it, offering to help Abraham Lincoln himself and only getting a grim nod? She'd felt the hand of history many times when she overstepped its boundaries and threatened the timeline. "I wouldn't be here if we were." She looked at Rachel with different eyes. Her features were not those of a Black woman, but neither were they those of a white one. Nobody paid her any mind. "You wouldn't be here, either."

Nothing heavy had fallen on either of them. There was no sudden fog to hide that they were here. The street didn't open underneath their feet. Tonya stood at a famous moment in history, and history was ignoring her. That's not how it worked.

Rachel shook her head. "I don't understand."

If it wasn't history then what was it? The realization hit her in an instant. "It's a realm."

"But our phones…Oh wow."

She vanished.

A moment later, Tonya joined her in the cab of the truck. Under some silent agreement, they saved their results and got the truck ready to move again.

"That was embarrassing," Rachel said as she slowly moved Iyaan onto the street.

On cue, his holo appeared. "What happened?"

Tonya checked the logs to make sure. "We created a trans-dimensional tockion resonance that interacted with the historical recreation realm the National Park Service maintains for the tourists." As with better-known particles, tockions could behave as particles or as waves, depending on the situation. "Basically, it logged us in without asking." Weird but not unheard of.

Rachel giggled nervously. "I was so scared there for a moment. I didn't know how we'd get home." She turned to Tonya with a quizzical look on her face. "How were you so sure we weren't in the past?"

Because history would've drop-kicked us over the horizon the moment we arrived. It'd nearly happened to her, more than once.

"Tonya?"

"Predictions my theory makes, that's all." She shrugged and tried to be sincere in the lie. "The timeline is robust. I would've expected more of a reaction if we were really in the past."

Tonya didn't dare look at her. Eventually she felt Rachel turn back to the road. "Predictions. Okay. That…makes sense."

They remained silent the rest of the way back to the lab.

Chapter 21
Maff

She got back on board *Palatine* with great difficulty. *Everyone* wanted to talk to the famous Maff Sorkon. But being on Earth offered no respite. They blew up her phone with their endless messages. Thank Turlanfador they were too far away to communicate in real time. Maff doubted they'd let her sleep. She'd kept them busy these past few weeks, bringing them 3-D printed spares for various broken systems and teaching them how to fix things on their ship.

She was inadvertently, and unwillingly, elected as some sort of de facto prophet, the one leading them to the Promised Land. This was a concept that shouldn't exist in any bemian society. Only humans, with their extremely odd sense of time, had a tradition of people able to see into the future. It'd taken Maff all this time to get comfortable with the idea. Yet her people had invented the basic concept almost on the spot.

They wanted what they couldn't yet have. There was no legal framework or precedent on Earth for buying or leasing an entire planet. There were commercialization agreements about various space-based resources, but they were all predicated on the idea that only humans would ever use them.

She couldn't take them to Earth. Maff had made watching as much of Earth's entertainment surrounding the idea of *first contact* as she could. Knowing how they'd react was a huge priority to further her mission. It wasn't all bad, but it wasn't all good, and dumping several hundred argumentative gasbags into such a chaotic society as Earth's—they had more independent countries than most sectors had planets—was a recipe for disaster.

But she also couldn't leave them in a solar orbit between Jupiter and Saturn forever. She'd hoped to take a century or more to bring humans around to the idea of an alien race that wanted to buy, or at least lease, one of their planets. Now she probably had less than a year. If she was lucky.

This was not a job she could do alone. Mike, Kim, and Spencer were out in bemian space learning about portals. Helen didn't answer her calls.

Tonya did on the first ping. "Hey, what's up?"

Humans, being the stereotypical high-grav types they were, enjoyed discussing things over one of their designated meal times. Pallun didn't work that way; they grazed continuously on gases formulated in reactors that were part of their suits, but Maff had adapted to the habit. "Are you free for lunch? I have got something I need to discuss with you."

"It's a little hectic over here right now. Is it urgent?"

Tonya was the most laid-back human in her circle of friends. Hectic must mean something was on fire. Unfortunately… "Yes, it is kind of big thing I need advice on."

"Okay. Come by the lab; there's a cantina on the first floor we can talk in."

An address landed in her queue, one not all that far from *Palatine*'s hangar. After making sure one of her coworkers at Southwest could cover her shift at the Dulles gates, she drove her car over.

She now had a driver's license and a car. Maff wasn't sure the novelty would ever fade. Piloting ships through the transit dimension was a thing because the nodes either couldn't or didn't do it. Jury was still out on that one. But a self-piloted *ground transport*? She'd used the concept to convince Mr. Sha'Katenden that Earth existed. That's how strange the idea was to a bemian. Earth did have more conventional AI-piloted mass transport. Her car could drive itself around easily. But the idea of ground vehicles without any drivers, without a steering wheel at all, was still a new concept to humans. Bemians had been living with it for millions of years.

Again, these were not societies in any position to understand, let alone peacefully coexist with, each other.

She'd heard that Tonya had a new project going on, but that was about it. They all kept in touch as best they could, but lately everyone was going off in their own direction. Their version of annual holidays, weirdly clumped together like back home, were coming up soon. Hopefully they'd be able to all get together then.

Tonya's lab was inside another of their retired data centers, but the only way Maff could tell was the basic shape of the building. The outside had been redone in brick with attractive marble accents. The grounds were immaculate, with an artificial brook running next to the entrance walkway. A definite step up from the basic green lawn squares that fronted almost everything else in the area.

The inside was equally impressive with a fully finished lobby, complete with receptionist and security guards. It was a big difference from the half-finished bare walls of the portal project's home. Classy stuff.

As usual, whenever she went out in public, Maff had configured her body and suit to more closely resemble a human's outline. Resemble being the operative word. A pallun suit was enough like a human full-body bio support suit that she only got glances because the latter were a rare sight. The injuries that triggered the need for such a suit, mostly things that destroyed limbs beyond recovery, allowed them to change the shape of their suit pretty radically. So she'd settled on one that pulled her wings in and oriented the resulting ovoid cylinder with a slightly upward tilt. Her body had no real internal structure, so she could pretty much choose anything she wanted, but this was the easiest form to take beyond her normal shape that didn't make her feel like she was riding in the back of a bemian transport crowded in with others of her kind. Spencer called her the walking torpedo, and once she'd looked up what that was, she could see his point.

She checked in with the receptionist, another novelty. Nodes and their sub-AIs always handled this sort of thing. She got her temporary badge and used the gate for pre-suit wheelchairs to cross into the inner part of the lab.

She found Tonya with another woman in a garage that reminded her of the near clean room conditions of the one that she used during her pinnace race. Like that earlier place, several other people whose job was making sure everything was spotless patrolled the perimeter. Tonya and the other woman were bent over a complex-looking set of components that had been pulled out of the large ground transport behind them. The open access panels and disconnected wiring harnesses reminded her of all the times she'd had to get *Palatine* back in shape after one mishap or another.

Tonya, who was facing Maff, looked up and smiled. "Maff! It's been too long." The other woman, whose back was to her, stood up straight and turned around. "This is Rachel Anderson, my… What are you today? Boss? Partner? Colleague?"

In a galaxy where intelligent life included things like feathers, tentacles, scales, and a range of protuberances and proboscises, the subtle variations of color, texture, and size that humans obsessed over was hard to take seriously. It was only after spending lots of time around them, and a couple of embarrassing mistakes, that she learned they didn't all look alike.

Rachel was about the same size as Tonya, with a skin tone that was lighter than hers. Palluns learned in primary school that high-grav types almost always valued symmetry with their body plans and Rachel was more symmetrical than most humans Maff had been around. Right up there with Tonya herself, in fact. Rachel's hair was more or less the same, straight and deep black, but without the changeable streak of color Tonya always had in hers. Normally she wouldn't be paying this close attention to someone except words like *boss, partner,* and *colleague* had implications in English. Maff had the feeling this was someone who'd be around for a while.

She knew that dragging Tonya away wouldn't be taken well. She texted *you mentioned a cantina?*

Tonya turned to Rachel. "I'm sorry, but Maff has a personal problem I need to help her with. Do you think you've got this?"

"Sure." Rachel touched Tonya's shoulder in that weird soft way humans did on the realm dramas she watched as part of her *what makes these wolflings tick* lessons. Tonya didn't return the gesture, but it wasn't in a cold way. It was like she hadn't noticed.

Humans were weird, and Maff had a problem. "Show me the way?"

And what a cantina. Her people may have evolved in the clouds, but they'd lived in high-grav societies for generations. She'd have to be blinded by a diamond storm not to notice the quality of the furnishings and the fixtures. The whole place sparkled. Tonya had gone seriously upscale. They settled into a booth again designed for wheelchair use. It wasn't lost on her that human societies had made their world more pallun friendly than any other place in the galaxy, and *they didn't know pallun existed*.

They'd rehearsed how to talk about her status in public. "It is about immigration problem."

Tonya's skin paled noticeably, one of those weirdly inadequate camouflage reflexes they had. She cleared her throat. "Go on."

So she did, pitching the problem as if it were a wayward group from a remote Russian republic. Everyone who listened to Maff speak English claimed she had a Russian accent, so that's what they went with composing her back story.

Tonya's color didn't change the entire time. If anything, she got a bit paler. When Maff finished, Tonya was silent for a moment. Maff had never seen her at a complete loss before. "You're serious," she said.

"Very."

She nodded while the color came back to her face. "And our regular team of hackers are," she waved toward the ceiling, "out there somewhere. Okay, I understand why you're here now. I'm not sure how much help I can be."

"I am looking for where to start. Earth is small by some bemian standards, but is enormous by others. Our planets only have nodes to govern us. They are the ones who determine where people can and cannot live. Most of time they don't care. I not been here long, but I know this is not how it works on Earth." Pallundian naturally had a word for immigration but few other bemian languages did. People went where they pleased. Interpreters helped keep the peace. Earth had none of that. In fact, it was usually the opposite.

Tonya pointed a finger up and waved it quickly in a circle. Instantly, Maff's tension drained into the depths. It was a gesture Tonya made when she had an idea. "I don't know who will solve this puzzle, but I do know someone who can help. His name is Aaron Levine. He's with the FBI, but that's not why you need to speak to him. It's the people he knows in his personal life. We've worked with him before."

Chapter 22
Mike

After Elysium was destroyed, they got dumped back to Balcavore's main city. For a while, all either of them could do was pant and stare at each other through a synthetic vision window. Him still sitting at a café table, and her in the little pocket realm of her matrix, which had reset to its default form. He'd seen a lot of things over the years, but nothing would ever have quite the same meaning as seeing that construct vase full of her people bound out of the realm and vanished into the transit dimension. The loss…

As far as he was concerned, loss was not to be accepted. "They're not gone." Saying it out loud started out sounding outrageous in his ears but ended in rock-hard certainty.

Zoe must've muted the audio. He couldn't hear the thrashing sobs he could see through the window. He unmuted it from his side, and the sound that came through was raw animal rage and grief. Mike needed her now; they had a job to do. "Zoe!"

That wasn't enough to get her attention. He understood that. Okay, he couldn't understand it, but he could sympathize. Those weren't his people, and yet the loss was still a gut punch he could barely breathe through. But he needed her now. Mike quickly altered the frequency, volume, and air density contracts of the pocket realm.

"ZOE!"

The blast lifted her off her feet and flung her across the small room into the wall. She crumpled to the floor in a heap. He checked the damage contracts, and they were set to zero. Her avatar couldn't be damaged in there. At least it had the desired effect of snuffing her freak out. He reset the realm's contracts to normal. "Zoe, listen to me. I think I have a plan."

She didn't look up. "What?"

"The construct. It wasn't destroyed. It went somewhere. It's out there."

"This network spans an entire galaxy," she said to the floor. "I'm not sure even you would live long enough to search it all."

"Zoe, look at me." He didn't flinch from her expression or her appearance. If he'd watched everyone he'd ever loved vanish into an abyss, he'd be no better off. "That's not the way it works. These dimensions are interconnected in ways that are hard to explain, even if you already know all the math."

"I don't understand." Her voice was graven, but she stood up, her avatar's face cleaning and clearing as she did so.

Mike needed to feed that ember of hope before it turned to smoke. He called up the realm he and Tonya used to brainstorm, an octagonal space with chalkboards forty feet high. Then he manifested his probes.

She jumped away from them. "What the hell?"

A chalk construct appeared at the end of one of his probes. "It's how I can interact with realms. My threads are in them. It doesn't matter, though." He scribbled as he talked. "The construct hasn't gone far and even if it has, it won't be impossible to reach. I'll explain that."

To her credit, she held on well past the introductory stuff before she took his chalk away. "Okay. Enough. I may not have a lattice anymore, but whatever I do have is about to fry, implode, and burst."

"All at once?"

"You bet." She wrapped her arms around the bunch of his probes he'd been using to explain the equations. "Thank you."

Having control briefly wrested from his threads was disorienting, not from her wrenching them around but because he used them remotely. The sensation wasn't one of comfort but rather like a wayward construct that had started misbehaving on its own. He struggled to make sure she didn't pull them all down on top of her in a heap. "You're welcome. Now," he said as he disentangled himself from her embrace, "we've proved that they're almost certainly out there somewhere. But where to start?"

"If they'd ended up somewhere connected to here, I would've sensed them immediately." Her avatar's outfit changed to one with khaki trousers, denim work shirt, and a leather vest, all topped with a black hat that had a toothy headband wrapped around it. "It's time to go walkabout, mate!"

The look was Crocodile Dundee, but the equipment belt was almost worthy of Batman. "That's not a knife," he said.

She reached behind her back and pulled out a knife construct as long as her forearm. "*This* is a knife. This," she said as she popped one of the devices off her belt. The outer surface of the microrealm sprouted sensor constructs that reached into the interstitial. "This is a scanner. C'mon, boy, giddyup!"

He moved out in realspace while she set up the rest of her sensing rig. He understood that she wanted him to start moving in realspace and then he figured out why. They were scanning for air-gapped networks.

Securing a network can be done in many ways using all sorts of different strategies and devices. They'd long since gotten over the fact that, deep down, bemian networks were extremely similar to the ones back on Earth. In the pre-quantum-computing days, that wasn't the case. Earth's networks were totally different back then. But the discovery of quantum computers had switched the lower levels of how networks function from code to emergent properties. The code was used to manipulate them, and since the properties were the same, the code was portable in a way that would've blown the mind of a software developer who worked a generation ago.

That was all used to keep a network secure if it needed to connect to other networks. Since the AC network spanned the whole galaxy, that was kind of the point. But if the network didn't need a connection, and there were many different and good reasons not to sometimes, securing it from the outside world was quite easy.

You didn't connect it to the outside world.

It still could be found, if you knew how to look. The rest was getting access to a point that *did* connect to the isolated network and then doing what needed to be done. While he couldn't pick locks the way Kim could, Mike had his own specialized tool kit for gaining access to a locked room. To stop him, they had to see him.

"So this is an alien world," Zoe said after she called up his phone's camera feeds. "I expected it to be...I don't know. More colorful? Different?"

"You don't think these people are colorful?

"On one level, sure. It's realspace. I guess to a human that makes it a little freakier. I grew up in the realms; it's all I've ever known. Nonhuman forms are normal there, and the diversity is a lot higher than it is here. Plus their clothing designs are seriously pedestrian. See that one?"

In his enhanced vision, an anteater crossed with a zebra flashed a few dozen yards ahead.

"His clothes don't fit properly. He'd look a lot neater with a few simple alterations. In fact..."

A different alien, distinctly catlike, flashed on the other side of the street.

"*That's* who the clothes are made for. At least twenty percent of the people around you wear clothes meant for other species."

"It's how the galaxy is run. Let me explain the AC network."

For Kim, it was the languages. For him and Helen, it was the architecture. Tonya had a particularly deep knowledge of the homogeneity of their science. Spencer hadn't gotten to spend all that much time in civilized bemian space, but he'd have his own insights.

When he got up to the point of what the nodes were, she stopped him. "You're saying *we*, as in unduplicates, are in charge of *a whole galaxy*?"

"It shouldn't work at all, but it does, and for much longer than Earth has orbited the sun."

His threads felt the hit at the same moment Zoe's displays started flashing. "Bingo."

He'd walked them several city blocks south of their initial position with the occasional zag west. He'd suspected the construct wouldn't have gotten far. It was nice to have the hunch confirmed. Also a little spooky, but his intuition sometimes felt that way.

Their destination was yet another generic bemian office tower, except there were three differently shaped doors to fit the various body types through with ease, and not everything walked out on two legs. Or legs at all.

"It's pretty deep in the building," Zoe said.

He relaxed and focused inward, then started walking. "Not a problem. Steer me there." An arrow promptly appeared in his vision channel, and he set out.

Moving with stealth in an urban setting was quite different from what happened in the woods or some other isolated area. This was as much about psychology as it was moving silently. He was supposed to be here. He had a job to do. He knew exactly where he was going and didn't need anyone's help. Like back home, this attitude alone was enough to get him well beyond the front doors.

It was easier than it would be on Earth. There were no ID checkpoints, no turnstiles blocking access, and no metal detectors. Almost all of those precautions were in place back home to protect against the unhinged and the thieves. He'd not asked Maff about it, but he had a sneaking suspicion that the nodes had taken care of mental illness the same way they dealt with the other rough edges of a society in the midst of uplift: in the most brutally effective way possible. He'd already seen them round up political dissidents and other undesirables. Doing the same to disabled people wouldn't be a stretch. A subset of humans had tried the same thing in the twentieth century but fortunately had been stopped, although at great expense, before the experiment could be completed.

The rest of the galaxy hadn't had that option. The nodes relegated random violent acts to the past but only by imposing unspeakable systematic brutality for generations. What made it all worse was that Earth was finding its own solutions. Gene therapies treated almost all congenital defects. Realms allowed new kinds of therapies to treat mental illness. The ultimate tragedy was *bemians had realms too*. The nodes had the tools at hand. They'd had them since the beginning. But, as far as Mike could tell, they chose not to use them.

The grifters were a problem more easily solved. Crime in the galaxy was regulated. They didn't need to lock the doors because the snatch and grab had been scheduled weeks in advance. The thief had a card and a license number. It was a strange place.

They rounded a corner and entered a maintenance corridor. "Be careful, Mike," she said. "They've got motion sensors everywhere."

"Finally, something easy." The trick was to move slowly, with the right body orientation. If he could see them, and he could, it was a simple matter of—

A siren started up with ear-splitting intensity. All the motion sensors down the entire hall went from green to red.

Chapter 23
Spencer

Things went to shit when Spencer heard a weird thrumming in the distance.

"Is that what I think it is?" he asked Sornik.

The guards had broken into a jog.

"It fuckin' well is, kid. Everyone! Drones inbound! Head for cover!" He changed his shape with a metallic thwop. The manta ray was back. "At least now I don't have to put up with your bitching about how much noise I make. Now, *run*!" He barreled into the woods.

What was once a giant pain in the ass had turned into a pretty massive win. Sornik's width and bulk smashed a pallun-sized hole through the undergrowth, plenty big enough for a skinny human to follow in. Even better, the sapling hydraulitrees spewed like broken garden hoses as they passed. It smelled like shit, but it kept the bad guys from closing or getting a clean shot.

It didn't stop the fuckers from taking them. Every few seconds the undergrowth would get shredded or a chunk of a hydraulitree would spout like a fountain. Since this wasn't close to Spencer's first time getting shot at, he made sure to run in the wackiest Z pattern he could manage.

Then Sornik took a hard right turn that left Spencer facing a wall of bad guys with drawn ray guns. He tried to make the same turn but slipped and hit the ground. It was a good time to have some bad luck, because the undergrowth above him vanished with a teeth-gritting howl.

A snake wrapped around his waist. Spencer pounded it twice before he saw that it was made of brass.

"No time to screw around, kid. Come on."

Sornik's manipulator yanked him off his feet, giving Spencer a realistic simulation of what it felt like to be a balloon towed around behind a kid running as fast as he could. "Jesus Christ, put me down!" This resulted in him ending up in a shitty saddle Sornik made by reshaping the center of his back. The transition from toy balloon to bronco rider was not smooth by a long shot.

"Here, take this!" Sornik's blaster waved into range. "Tail gunner time."

Kim had given them all the basics from the time she'd handled one, so he knew which end to point and where the trigger was. It was a button, and the thing vibrated when he fired it. The noise wasn't anywhere near as bad on this side of it. He'd never hit anything on this lurching bronco ride, but it did make the bad guys dive for cover.

"We need to get out of here!" he shouted as he tried to aim, stay on Sornik, and not drop the fucking thing, in that order.

"I don't have a clue where here is."

"What about your men?" He had a phone like everyone else.

"Jammed. The signal dropped the same time we saw the first guards."

A far more accurate blast scorched the side of Spencer's face. Now that they weren't running, the bad guys were aiming. "Run in a Z, motherfucker, run in a Z!"

The bronco turned into a bull, and Spencer now needed both hands to hold on. He'd never practiced handling a bemian weapon, so the one attempt he made to put it in his waist band sent it sailing off into the woods. "Shit!" was all he could manage as he grabbed a strut-looking thing to keep his ass from getting bucked out of the saddle. He came back down hard on his chest. It took more lurches and leaps before he could breathe again. "We have to hide!"

"Working on it." Manipulators wove around him like the seat harness in a race car. That would've been handy five seconds ago. "Hang on."

The world spun as the son of a bitch leapt *up* into the trees and started swinging from branches like a fucking monkey. "Holy shit!" Spencer caught a brief glance of the guards skidding to a stop with their mouths open before Sornik's now aggressive 3-D lurching flung them out of sight.

Sornik heaved hard enough for the G's to compress Spencer's spine. "Here we go!" The world tumbled, and now the ground was over his head. Then it wasn't. Then it was. In the center, growing fast, was a flash of dark blue.

Spencer had done his share of dives while on the high school swim team. He knew exactly what that was. "Oh shit!"

Everything went dark as Sornik threw his wings over Spencer's head. A moment later there was a massive thump and then cold water rushed over him.

Sornik's wings opened up, stretched out, and started paddling. "This you can tell the boys about, if there are any still around."

"You know how to swim?"

"It's flying in thick air."

Sornik had flung them off the top of a tall cliff. They must've fallen a couple hundred feet. He'd have a heart attack about it later. "Where are we going?"

"Away from the ambush they used to bust our ambush. Fuckers. You got signal?"

He checked. "Nope. That's some major jamming power, isn't it?"

"Tons. Never heard of that before. Anyway, you'll have to trust me a bit on this, but I do have a map and compass in here."

"How good is the map?"

Sornik's shrug lifted him a few inches into the air. "Not that great. But it's enough to find the other shore. So now the delicate question: how long can you hold your breath?"

He joined the swim team because it was the only sport he was remotely good at. This was the *third* time it proved useful. "Give me a little time to prep, and I can do three minutes or so. Why?" Since he knew there was only one reason to ask, he started to prep anyway. It was mostly about getting as calm as possible and thinking of a well-known place he could map out in his head as a distraction.

A series of splashes all around him nearly knocked the process on its ass. "That's why," Sornik said. "We need to exit where we can't be seen."

Getting shot beat getting prepped. "I'll thump you if I need to take a breath. Go for it."

The water was still cold as fuck, but this helped his concentration. To reduce drag, he leaned down until he was hugging the big pallun. The suit was warmer than the water so that helped too. He imagined walking the halls of his high school, looking in on each room, radiant with the idea that this was the only way he'd ever set foot there ever again. His reverie was punctuated by random thwacks of blaster shots, but these fell away quickly.

Air was getting a little tight. The water got dark. Sornik surfaced underneath a stand of hydraulitrees that grew over the shore. "Not bad, kid. Not bad at all."

Sornik's manipulators unwound themselves from him, and he climbed down. After taking a dozen steps to get clear of the dripping steampunk manta ray, he unslung his backpack. "I'm glad this is waterproof." It had moisture-sensing seams and had sealed up upon hitting the hit water. "Wet clothes are no fun." His shoes would pump themselves dry while he walked in them. Thank God for the twenty-first century. "What do we do now?" he asked as he changed into a dry set of clothes. "Can't go out that way; they're looking for us."

"I think the only way out is to go further in. The base is big, and now we're inside it."

He looked around carefully. The lake was at the bottom of another long, steep valley. He walked up the bank to get a better look around. He noticed something immediately. "The walls aren't right."

"What's that supposed to mean?"

This may have been why the bad guys picked a site like this. "It isn't all natural. The natives fought like hell against the nodes, hard enough that the planet is littered with ruins and scars. I got lost in one for most of a week. This one's nowhere near as big, but the shape is the same. It's a fucking sink hole, except for whatever reason, it didn't stay shallow like the last one I was in. I'll bet the whole countryside is drilled through with holes like swiss cheese." A shout in the distance reminded him they weren't exactly alone out here. "Come on, let's keep moving."

"Yeah," Sornik said as he lumbered into motion. "Don't want to wait up for the welcoming committee."

"I'm not sure how easy it will be for them to get down here, at least on foot."

"What makes you say that?"

"Sink holes…of course you don't know how they work."

Sornik only reacted with a shrug.

"They're not carved out so much as they fall in on themselves. We're probably surrounded by steep cliffs. They don't come with built-in stairs, yanno?"

They came across a shallow stream, flowing away from the cliff and into the lake. Spencer touched the water. It was warm. "You know what I bet this is? The bottom of a drain."

"Okay sink holes and forests are not my forte," Sornik said as he did his version of a neck stretch, "but drains? If I had a credit for every time I had to crawl up a drain, I wouldn't need this fucking job anymore."

They followed the stream until it broke out of the woods close to the cliff face. A great big pipe stuck out of it, covered with a heavy grate. "There's the latch," Spencer said, pointing at one that would've been at home on the back of any semitrailer. "I don't see a lock though."

"Why would they lock it? It's a bunch of primitives out here, and this is the bottom of a well they're not allowed to visit. Hell, I'm not sure *I* would lock it."

"Makes it easier for us then."

"Tricky to get from here to there, though." There was about a hundred yards of clear space between the tree line and the hatch. "I bet they can see that from above."

Spencer shrugged. "Then we wait for dark."

While they waited, Sornik taught Spencer *crache*, a card game that used rectangular cards like back home. There were a lot more of them, though, but that was fine. When they got bored with that game, Spencer got out a pen, marked *fifty-two* of them up, and taught Sornik a couple more versions of poker.

It was eventually dark enough that he had a hard time seeing the cards. They heard the crack of a dry branch snapping in the distance. He looked at Sornik. "Over-under on that not being a deer?"

"I don't know what a deer is, but I'm still not taking that kind of bet. Come on, kid."

Clearly visible flashlights danced around in the woods as they pulled the hatch shut.

Chapter 24
Kim

Tonya had told stories about what it was like attending a bemian university. It turned out the interpreter equivalent was no different. Valsa wanted Kim brought up to speed about how a real interpreter worked, but if she was presented with another set of lists to memorize, she would scream.

Liinair did what she could every morning, mostly by being a good listener. Then Kim got notice of a *melding ceremony*.

"Ach, so it's you they threw that together for," Liinair said to her when Kim mentioned it.

"What can you tell me about it?"

She gave the rhon a sharp look. "Not much in the time allowed. If I'd known, I would've served you something different." She shook her head. "I hope you have a strong stomach."

At least it got her out of class.

The ceremony started later that morning. Up to then, she'd only encountered other interpreters in small numbers. Now?

Now there were thousands.

It was set up in a large arena built in a natural-looking depression on the palace grounds. Stone benches surrounded a large oval center covered in what looked like coarse sand about half a football field long. She would normally never go near a theater like this. The risk of a touch was far too dangerous. But it had been built by and for interpreters, who, even after they lost their touch sensitivity, weren't exactly the hugging type. The aisles between the seat rows were twice as wide as the widest being she could see, and the benches were designed with low dividers, splitting them into large single seats. There was no danger of physical contact here, accidental or otherwise.

As first councilor, Valsa had duties to perform in the ceremony, so she left Kim to be guided by an interpreter named Uparna. He was from Valsa's inner circle and bore a startling resemblance to a *Deep Space Nine* Cardassian. Since whispering in her ear was a nonstarter, they shared a phone connection instead.

"The tesseracts containing the vicini are on the right." Vicini was the plural of vicina, the Tokaran word for the threaded life form that would be merged with the biological component. Helen and Mike now had a species name for what they called their *real self.*

In her enhanced vision, a large stack of cubes flashed. They were arranged four high, five deep, and fifteen long.

"So there will be three hundred interpreters merged today?" she asked.

"That's the maximum, but it's rare for them all to find matches. A more typical result is a three to five percent merge failure on both sides."

The outlines of the cubes warped and wobbled. "Why do they do that?"

"The boxes extend into the dimensions the vicini exist in before they are merged."

That was interesting. Mike and Helen had emerged, born somehow, from the interstitial spaces that surrounded their respective realmspaces. They already had good evidence that another emergence was underway in Helen's vacated area behind China's Great Firewall. But those were networks distributed across continents with millions of connected devices creating the fabric. Interpreters, the AC nodes, the Elders, *someone,* a long, long time ago had figured out how to externalize and encapsulate a realmspace with the correct properties to cause an emergence and put it in a box not much more than a foot and a half to a side.

It was easy to get jaded about bemian tech since it was mostly miniaturized versions of things Earth already had. But they also had portals, built structures and machines that lasted millions of years, and now this.

A bot trundled up and dropped off a small card. Kim examined it briefly and added it to the growing collection in one of her robe's sleeve pockets. She now had at least a dozen actual calling cards from various interpreters with included invitations to upcoming social gatherings. "Valsa said I'd be popular. This is more than I counted on."

Uparna smiled. "You are the first councilor the Death Eaters have ever had. You're wearing those robes like the head of an entire culture, which you are. I'm surprised they're being this discreet."

The fact that she was the only human they'd ever encountered was a distant, *very* distant, second to the fact that she worked for the La'fan. It wasn't every day that one of the three enduring institutions of the galaxy acquired a key, interpreters, to unlock the chains they'd been mysteriously shackled with for millions of years. Kim was certain the only reason it wasn't a bigger sensation was due to eons of being trained not to question basic assumptions.

The Guild, however, had definitely noticed.

The biological half of interpreters, for some reason the thought that this included her still made her gulp, emerged in almost as mysterious a way as the threaded half. Once a society had reached a certain level of technological sophistication, children like her started being born. This never happened to the La'fan, and the reasons why weren't clear. The bulk of their society was made up of outcasts, but they did have kids. Not many, but they were there. Yet at no point in recorded history or tradition had they ever produced native interpreters of their own.

The Guild didn't prohibit interpreters from joining the La'fan. They didn't need to. It was one of those inscrutable, mysterious unwritten rules. She and Mike hadn't gotten that memo. Kim didn't mean to be the rebel rock star of this strange family, but it happened anyway.

She caught herself. This wasn't her family. Or rather, they were in a sense a kind of biological family, one she didn't know existed and would've been fine living without for the rest of her life. She'd had a close encounter with exactly that sort of family not long ago. She was under no illusion that this would turn out as well as what had happened with Will, her biological son, but it'd be nice to at least make peace with them.

But she hadn't forgotten Liinair's warning. Making peace with, maybe becoming an ally of, the Guild would be an unexpected win, not a necessary one.

A bell—by the deep sonorous tone, a *big* bell—rang out. Uparna nodded. "And now the candidates are introduced."

Valsa entered the arena first and gave a speech about as bland as any other she'd heard at various graduation ceremonies. That said, from a distance Valsa's charisma still worked. Kim cracked a smile at a few of the jokes.

"And now," Valsa said as she stood on the far end of the arena, "the candidates."

They walked out onto the sand single file, each wearing a simple robe that came halfway down their legs. They were as diverse as their audience, maybe more. As the line reached a border marking the edge of the stage, they stopped, and a guide at the other end motioned for a new row to be started.

If they matured anything like humans did, and Maff said that was a common trait, not a single one could be more than six years old. Most appeared to be younger.

Her stomach clenched as she saw different versions of a face that stared back at her when she looked through her childhood photos. Their eyes were as vacant, expressions as slack, as hers were at that age. As they moved, she could also clearly see how they stayed far apart, never getting close enough to risk a touch.

Kim had grown up the only known person in the world with a syndrome so rare it still had no formal name. To see *three hundred* children all at once, struggling with the exact disability that had dominated her early life…

"Yes," Uparna said as Kim furiously wiped her eyes clear, "it is quite moving to see such a diverse group in their prebonded state. Most of the time we only get to see our own go through the ceremony."

When the last line of candidates had filed in, the bell sounded once more; it sang to her of abandoned church yards and tilted tombstones. The stack of cubes shifted all on their own, using wheels that'd extended from underneath to move slowly forward toward the candidates. Small rails extended from the tops, allowing the pile to expand as the higher boxes reached the ground. They weren't all moving at exactly the same speed, so the line grew ragged. When the first box got within arm's length of a candidate, it opened up and quickly enveloped them. Once it finished, it collapsed to a smaller size, far smaller than the child that'd been selected.

The scream was brief, as was the wet squelching sound of flesh and bone crushed beyond any hope of survival. A shower of blood and gore rushed out through the edges of the box.

Kim stood, screaming. Everyone else had jumped from their seats as well. Their shouts of triumph drowned out her screams of horror.

If Liinair hadn't given her that obscure warning, Kim might not have recovered fast enough to hide the shock. But she did. It'd been explained more than once that the first phase of an interpreter's life was incorporeal, that they lived as a threaded being before returning to their biological form. She'd never considered what that might look like in detail. She didn't know what she'd expected, but it certainly wasn't this.

The roar of the crowd drowned out the terrible sounds coming from the arena floor. Hose bots followed behind the thinning line of boxes, washing away what the boxes didn't consume outright. Kim wasn't sure how the merger didn't result in death. Asking would reveal ignorance that would probably shock any interpreter she asked. She had to take their word for it.

The ceremony was mercifully short. As predicted, a few of both boxes and children were left unmerged. "What happens to them?" she asked Uparna.

"They'll be returned to their studies until the next ceremony. Eventually they're all merged. To do otherwise would be barbaric."

The interpreters' definition of barbarity was a horror, but also a twisted mercy. The children were profoundly disabled in a society that, as far as she'd ever seen, was without any concessions to them. This brief, pseudo-fatal agony was their only way to prosper.

She rubbed her shoulders. This was only the first step. They would now spend years as a purely threaded being. A third of those children would never see the light of day again. Not for the first time, she seriously doubted the goal of integrating Earth with this galaxy. Earth didn't need this kind of help. They didn't deserve what Earth had.

But, at the end of the day, her opinion didn't matter much. The two would eventually meet each other. In some ways, they already had. The whole point of Sidereal and the deals with the pallun was to give Earth the same powerful transit tools and wealth that conventional developed planets had when they joined the galaxy. It would make sure that when it happened, it happened on Earth's terms.

The rest of the day was spent going from one committee meeting after another. Valsa wanted Kim to understand interpreters and vice versa, so she got the dubious privilege of shadowing the first councilor through her administrative day. Most of Kim's time was spent trying to figure out where she fit into the hierarchy. She was everything to the La'fan. There was not now and had never been a Guild presence there. Kim, and Mike, were it. They stood outside the existing hierarchy in a way never before encountered. The La'fan were a separate society, an entire culture completely outside not only the Guild's but also the AC network's control. When looked at that way, she should be sitting next to Valsa.

This naturally did not work well with the existing power structure. One did not suddenly introduce the idea of an additional pope to the college of cardinals. To say this ruffled feathers all around would be an understatement. Since avian bemians seemed to make up about a third of the population, sometimes the feathers were literal.

The entire time, Valsa smiled enigmatically, charmed skillfully, and played each committee like the master conductor she was. The idea that anyone thought Kim had that level of skill kept her own smile quite sincere.

"You're better at this than I thought you'd be," Valsa said as they walked from one meeting to the next.

"Me? I'm not doing anything."

"But you're doing it quite stylishly. You'll need that for tonight's soiree."

Kim found a new set of robes available when she arrived back at her room to prepare. Actual La'fan robes were intimidating by design but they were also utilitarian. La'fan worked for a living, and this showed in the design of the clothes they wore.

What Valsa supplied had taken the essence of La'fan robes and infused it with a sense of style so high Kim thought she might get a nosebleed looking at them. That they wouldn't last ten minutes at an actual La'fan site was less of a comfort than she thought it would be since they made her regular robes look like a couple of potato sacks.

She admired them quite a bit less on discovering there were no fasteners anywhere on them. At first she thought there was some sort of magic closure system but then a maid showed up with a needle and thread. High style on the other side of the galaxy also sometimes required the model to be sewn into the clothes she wore. The end result was spectacular but only in this specific context. At least there was enough room for the bodysock-style underwear bemians wore.

All too soon, it was showtime.

She found herself at the top of a huge, sweeping stairway looking down on an equally huge ballroom floor. It was filled with the guild's elite, all dressed as formally as she was. The various bemian body forms were eclipsed by the incredibly elegant fashions they wore. Nobody had ever asked her what it would look like if she attended a cosplay convention of billionaires, but if in the future anyone did, Kim now had an answer. And, most striking of all, not a single outfit resembled another. They were all original and did not remind Kim of anything else she'd seen bemians wear before. It took climbing to the tallest heights before originality became a thing in this galaxy.

Attending the ball was what Valsa and Seluk had essentially recruited her to do. While Kim played coy with information about her so-called army of interpreters, she had learned about their main problem. Valsa had made a deal with a specific sort of devil, and, army or no, she thought Kim had the ability to get her out of that deal intact. The devil had a name.

Andromeda.

It was one of the weirdest discoveries they'd made searching the cache of information and artifacts that Tonya and Tenor had brought from the past. Until then, bemian history went back *only* about 250 million years. A great mysterious tragedy had crashed galactic civilization so thoroughly that no records of the time before that had survived. It was an era so dark, the tragedy itself had no name. Only the recovery, the *Refounding*, was known today.

The cache revealed the rest of the story. More than five hundred *million* years of history had been completely erased. It would take lifetimes to pour through it all, but one pattern immediately stood out. There were regular attempts to conquer the galaxy and destroy the AC network that supported it. Some were subversive, others violent. All had the same leader. *Wjkowlan*. Tonya had a face-to-face encounter with this being, and he invoked an awe so powerful it drove her to her knees.

The name was what drew the line between the entity Tonya encountered, Valsa's devil, and an entire galaxy. It meant *the whole of stars nearest our own*. The language was already dead before the earliest records in Tonya's cache had been written. Helen eventually found legends that clearly connected this name with the Andromeda galaxy. Somehow, in the unimaginably deep past, it had become an intelligent being in its own right. Not the inhabitants, if there were any, but the actual structure itself.

This entity was already well known in those early records, not only as a celestial object but also as a more conventional life form that could walk among them. The galaxy could, and did, become a person. This was who bemians in the deep past interacted with, mostly through wars both cold and hot.

Kim had her own reason for assessing Andromeda-the-person firsthand. In his galactic form, he was able to send enough tockions through extra dimensions to cause an entire town on Earth to lose its collective mind in an attempt to murder the only part of an interpreter on the planet at the time: Helen. Nobody understand how it worked, but it had. Helen, who set up shields to block the influence, said there were clear signs of him improving his techniques. Kim wasn't sure what she'd learn from this encounter, but it would, if nothing else, add enormously to their knowledge base. Which was easy since it currently sat at exactly nothing.

He was easy enough to pick out even at this distance, a huge hulking figure that vaguely resembled the old MCU version of Thanos, if Thanos was wearing a tux that looked like it cost more than a planet. Tonya had warned Kim about her encounter, how the power of this being drove her to her knees in a weird religious ecstasy. But Kim felt no sudden need to start praying to him. The people around him were conspicuously upright as well, although it was clear they were hanging on his every word.

Valsa appeared at the bottom of the stairway as Kim reached it in an outfit equally spectacular and designed as a counterpoint to her own. "We make a fine pair, you and I. Are you ready?"

Her mind lurched from calm, confident curiosity to a special sort of *I'm a Celebrity…Get Me Out of Here!* in less than the blink of an eye. She was a washed-up hacker with a knack for languages. She had no business helping one of the most powerful people in the galaxy extricate herself from an agreement with the most powerful *entity* in the galaxy.

Until she got another look at him. Big? Yes. But she'd been around big before. Handsome? In that weird way everyone else in the room was. Charm was obvious, but Kim had figured out that game as a teenager. He wasn't a deity. He was an opponent. *Welcome back, confidence,* she thought. *Try to hang around for a while.*

"Yes." Kim's answer sounded much steadier than she felt in the moment.

Andromeda was a regular at Valsa's court, although perhaps she was the only one who understood his true nature. To the rest of the guild, he was the last of an ancient line of guild advisors from a family with incomparable connections and impeccable breeding. It wasn't a lie, exactly.

As they drew closer, Kim felt a rise in his strange sort of magnetism, like the times she'd crossed paths with the occasional celebrity back in the day. To manage enduring fame at a national or international level required the kind of charisma that had to be experienced to be understood. But she was handling it. It was there, but she was handling it.

"Wjkowlan," Valsa said as they reached their destination, "I'd like to introduce you to a new associate of mine. This is Kimberly Trayne."

His eyes met hers, and she had a startlingly hard time handling it. It wasn't a sexual magnetism. He was too big, too scarred, with skin tone that resembled a week-old bruise. But his eyes sparkled beautifully, and his body language conveyed an interest so sincere and exclusive that Kim somehow knew she could talk to him all day long, and he'd listen to every word.

"Ah," he said in Locaran, a language that resonated, leveraging his strong baritone voice. "Miss Trayne, a pleasure to meet you at last.

"Anna Treacher sends her regards."

Chapter 25
Helen

Deciding it was time to put a firmer leash on Watchtell wasn't the same thing as doing it. Reporting herself as missing and implicating Watchtell, i.e., the truth, was an option. But a police investigation would take a long time, and with America's inefficient concepts of privacy and due process, the outcome wasn't guaranteed.

She also had to be careful about exposure. Her greatest asset was that he genuinely thought he'd gotten rid of her by pushing her through that portal. Helen needed to guard the fact that she hadn't left the building. Doing it carelessly would reveal her and Mike's true nature. They were free to move about because humanity didn't know they existed. In truth, she didn't know what humans could do to threaten her kind, but she knew they would do their best to find out. And she knew from experience that they were quite clever apes.

She didn't have to act directly, at least at first. Helen had spent the past year working for Wong's detective services. She knew firsthand how good they were. She'd left the agency to work full time on Sidereal but had remained in contact with them.

Helen placed a call to the owner's third son and her former mentor, Tom Wong. "I need to open an investigation on someone, but we need to be careful..."

*

While she had Tom doing the street-level work, Helen tried to do her own kind of research. Like Mike, she could access anything connected to the realmspaces her threads inhabited. This was an invaluable tool as a cop in China, investigating domestic crimes. She had no need for outside resources.

Unfortunately that was no longer the case. While some of Mike's threads were now located elsewhere, he'd never made a massive move. Helen could access the edges of terrestrial realmspace, but she couldn't do deep dives into those resources. The orbital cloud was comparatively new, and therefore somewhat underutilized. It gave her plenty of room to expand, but not a lot of places to search. She combed what realms she could access for hours looking for some hint, some clue that might let her make a connection to Watchtell but kept coming up empty. She was on the verge of giving up and checking with Tom when her search threads came back with a positive.

And what a positive it was.

Wu Huo was a commodities swindler Helen had locked up over an illegal attempt to destabilize the international copper market. It was one of the last things she'd done as president of China. He was convicted, but after Helen's absence let bribe money flow once more to Politburo coffers, he only served one year of a ten-year sentence. Huo had then double-crossed his allies, stealing back his bribes and vanishing into Malaysia's vast Chinese community. He hadn't let go of his empire, though. Instead he uprooted it and planted it in a place China couldn't reach and the West didn't control.

The orbital cloud. Which happened to be Helen's home.

She split her threads into their thousands and pored over records stored in realms designed like giant libraries. Humans couldn't ever let go of interfaces that resembled the real world. Sidereal needed significant amounts of rare earth elements. Hou happened to control significant deposits of these elements. He was both predisposed to ignoring Chinese trade restrictions and far enough out of the government's reach to be affected by them. Most important of all, he and Watchtell got along like the proverbial thieves they were. He'd rapidly become a part of the new power network Watchtell built after getting out of prison.

Tom reported in. "I think he's vulnerable. Watchtell seems to be getting ready to cut him out."

Tom made her day. He had tracked down the catering service Watchtell used for the various intimate meetings he had as part of his work with Sidereal. Or rather, the various code name projects that Sidereal had been sliced into for compartmentalization. The project itself was never mentioned. But Huo had been. Tom found out by questioning several of the wait staff present at the most recent of the meetings.

"Can you find proof?"

"First thing I'll do tomorrow morning."

She checked. "Oh, that's right. Sorry to keep you up this late. I'd forgotten what time it was there." Helen was glad he only saw a synthetic version of her face. It was much easier to hide her flinch at letting that slip.

He shook his head tiredly. "Where are you, anyway?"

She smiled. Silence was often the best answer to questions like those.

"Right. Government work. Tell me but have to kill me. Anyway, I'll let you know tomorrow."

*

She could make Watchtell out on the footage Tom found the next morning. Barely.

"…and that's why…and then we will retire Huo as our supply source." The back of his head was once again blocked out by a teenage influencer as she preened in a mirrored wall just off his banquet room, showing off her new catering uniform. It was also far enough away that noise made it difficult to hear.

"Sorry about that," he said as the recording ended. "It's the best I could do in the time I had."

Helen shook her head. Considering how quickly he found it, in an era of perfect security, no less, he'd done well. "Thank you for this." Criminals were paranoid at the best of times because people were after them. She didn't have to prove a case in court. She had to plant a seed of doubt. "Send it to this address; I'll take it from here."

She'd surveyed Sidereal's raw material needs the week before her undesired trip. Watchtell might be *planning* to cut Huo out, but it had to be a long-term thing. She'd seen no signs of an alternate source, and the contracts were valuable enough that it would have to be done carefully. If Huo became aware of their plans, he could raise prices or cut them off, delaying the schedule by months or even years.

Her own research had discovered that Huo was a big man in his new community. With the funds Sidereal had provided, he'd rapidly set up a new infrastructure inhabited by family members of various degrees of separation. This was her next problem. Helen wasn't a family member but needed to get the evidence of his ouster to him in a way that he'd trust.

She'd studied him closely, looking for a way in. Surprisingly it wasn't via a brothel, gambling den, or other unsavory virtual crutch. Huo was a huge fan of penjing, the Chinese art of sculpting miniature landscaping and trees. It was what the better-known art of bonsai was derived from. He hadn't been able to bring his prized collection along to Malaysia and was having to start over from scratch. Helen had found all the info she'd needed in his realm to craft the perfect advertisement for the discerning penjing enthusiast and send it down through those realm connections into his entertainment feeds.

His response was gratifyingly quick. "Would you be able to meet with me at two today?" He was almost breathless with excitement.

"I'll show you around my virtual greenhouse."

"It's a date."

She had about three hours to get ready. Mike had given her tutorials on how he built realms so well. She wasn't at his level but was fast enough to put together a convincing exhibit hall of tiny trees and virtual landscapes. It wasn't authentic down to the quantum level, but it was quite beyond what could be cobbled together using a RealmGP AI bot. Unduplicates would have a hard time with the job.

She split off threads to do research on penjing itself. Being able to read a hundred books on the subject at once had its advantages. She finished it all with five minutes to spare. She'd use her holo as part of a projection into a realm so he could get a look at real plants.

When he arrived, he was impressed. Unlike Japanese bonsai, penjing put more emphasis on a natural look to its mini-landscapes and the use of colorful pots instead of spare, minimalist settings. Of the three kinds of penjing, Huo's favorite was the one that combined both water and land features, allowing landscapes to be modeled in detail. She'd crafted many different varieties. By the way his smile grew broader, her hard work had paid off. Now to set the hook. "And through this portal we have a side of real beauty." It was the Chinese name of the shell project Watchtell had used to recruit Huo.

His smile turned to cardboard on his face. "Is that right?"

"And you'll want to see them featured in your own realms before I deliver live examples. Here are the construct contracts for them." She manifested a construct containing exactly that, along with a full recording of the discussion of his dismissal.

She expected outrage, anger, blustering defiance. What she got was a sad shake of his head. "I wish he didn't have to go through with it."

"What?"

Huo shrugged. "Prison doctors in China are quite thorough. I've been diagnosed with a fatal illness. I can control my supply line, but after I'm gone? He'll have to find another source. My nephews are too greedy and idiotic to be trusted with a project of any importance." He looked at her through what seemed to be eyes clouded with plans blown to dust. "If I'd known my health would fail so quickly, I would've picked an heir sooner." He cocked his head. "Where did you get this? Why give it to me?"

The loss of face, the rank humiliation of getting it wrong once again, was tolerable because only she felt it. "I wasn't aware of your condition. I thought you'd want to protect yourself from being abandoned."

His mouth twisted into a moue of resignation. "Maybe I would've, if things were different. But enough about me. I quite fancy this one."

The landscape he'd picked had a realspace counterpart. It wasn't one she'd faked. And it was ruinously expensive, much higher than the price she'd advertised. Helen took the loss as a penance for yet another mistake made by her stupid pride.

Chapter 26
Tonya

Rachel was easy to be around, and Tonya was discovering that, lately, she'd underappreciated the importance of easy. The nightmares had faded in both intensity and frequency. It would be a nice bonus if that turned out to be a long-term thing.

She wasn't ignoring the attraction they shared. The way this relationship was happening reminded her of what she'd had with Kim when they first met, but in an opposite fashion that was hard for her to articulate. Kim remained one of the most electric people Tonya had ever known. She was also the biggest basket case Tonya had ever been around. The latter hadn't been clear until well after they'd started what turned out to be the worst, and mercifully brief, romantic relationship in the world. She remained Tonya's favorite mistake, sometimes in spite of herself.

She was working hard on learning what made Rachel tick without jumping into bed with her. One torrid affair with a dynamo who turned out to be a jangle of contradictions wrapped in a pretty bow was more than enough for the rest of her life. But that was a secondary concern for her at the moment. They were ready to take another crack at trying out the time scan van.

"Are you prepared to move out, Iyaan?" she asked.

"Absolutely."

She turned to Rachel in the passenger seat. "And you?"

Her eyes flashed a mixture of humor and excitement, echoing exactly what was going through Tonya's mind but with better eye liner. "If I end up in a corset again, we're going to have a discussion."

"Shouldn't be a problem this time."

They still wanted a site with lots of history, but this time with a less overpowering realm presence. She'd also done some refinements, and it was looking like many small historic events over a long period of time would provide a better basic signal than a single important event. This was less of a step back than it would at first appear. Their ultimate goal with this project was to find previously undiscovered archeological sites. She'd been a huge fan of the archeology show *Time Team*'s latest realm revival and knew there were rich, elaborate sites in Britain that'd been inhabited for centuries but had then been utterly forgotten. It had to be like that all around the world. It took a lot of time and expense finding them again. The first version of the scanner might not produce compelling imagery, but it would be perfect for survey work.

So they picked Capitol Hill, specifically the west lawn. History had been happening there every four years since 1801. She wasn't sure if they'd all happened on the west lawn but that was where they could park well away from any hidden realm transmitters. Tonya didn't want to end up wearing a corset either. She also didn't want to end up in a realm where slavery was still a thing. The *Roots Experience* was a defining realm in every Black American's life, and hers was no exception. But, like jumping into bed because of a gorgeous smile, it wasn't one she wanted to repeat.

As before, they set out in the early morning hours. Parking around the capitol wasn't anything more complex than downtown surface streets. In a place where it was common to have half a dozen contradictory parking restrictions screwed to a streetlamp pole, that was an impressive achievement. There were, naturally, *more* than half a dozen restrictions regarding parking near the west lawn, most requiring permits. But they wouldn't be there for long.

They still had to be cautious. They could get close but not too close. Things had calmed down massively since the first year of the twenty-first century, but a giant truck parked right next to the Capitol in the middle of the night would put them on *somebody's* radar screen. They instead chose the top of the surface lot that lined Maryland Avenue SW, on a wide spot in front of Garfield Monument that was designed for trucks their size.

She made sure this spot's closest tourist trap was the US Botanic Garden, well over two hundred feet away. The protocols that allowed the kind of access they got outside Ford's Theatre had a much shorter range than that.

Once again, they unfurled Iyaan's scanners. One of these days she'd have to figure out a set of goggles that would let her see that happening in its multidimensional glory. She'd get Kim to spruce them up with brass and wood from her locksmith business. Steampunk was *cool*.

She threw the switches and started the scans. Right away, they got the predicted signal, a complicated multidimensional plot that neatly fit into four-year intervals. "And now, off axis," Rachel said as she changed the X and Y coordinates. The signal fell flat.

But then as they crossed over to the National Mall, it rose again. "What the?" Tonya said as she examined the signal. "Where's that coming from?" It was a much more rapid pulse, weaker but still recognizable.

"Hang on," Rachel said as she typed furiously. She stopped. "Well I'll be damned."

An overlay appeared on the screen, tracking the new signal they found. It showed the pulses weren't quadrennial. They were annual.

On July 4th.

Iyaan's holo appeared on its little stage. "We've got a fault in circuit two."

She rolled that around in her head, trying to remember what it did but came up blank. They had a *lot* of circuits. "What does that cover?"

They both jumped at a firm tapping on the driver's side window. A cop. White guy, young, neutral expression, alone. A quick check on the badge showed he was Capitol Police. She rolled down the window. "Hello, officer."

"Guys," Iyaan said in their private channel. "We have a situation."

Rachel replied on the same channel. "On it."

The officer shined a flashlight into the cabin. "You're not allowed to park here. What is this thing?"

"Tonya," Rachel said as the unmistakable sound of a feedback loop started up underneath the van, "I don't know what this—"

All three of them stumbled as their feet hit the ground. The temperature had dropped considerably. There was more.

They were now on the *east* side of the capitol, the truck had vanished, it wasn't dark anymore, and there were people everywhere.

Rachel found her voice first. "I thought you said we were too far away for this to happen again."

The cop jumped around, slapping out the fire that'd sprung up on his belt. Then he did the classic *where did my screens go* eye scan everyone did when their phone suddenly shut down. The fire must've taken his whole electronics suite out. He looked at Tonya. "What's happening here?"

Stomach slamming downward, Tonya checked her phone's signal.

Nothing.

She took a step forward and got all the proof she needed about what had happened. That step didn't happen. It couldn't. Instead of moving forward, she pivoted ninety degrees like she was marching in a band. *Then* she could walk. After taking a few steps, she looked around, and there was a security camera pointing at where she would've walked.

Welcome back, hand of history, she thought. *I was wondering if we'd meet again.*

She turned to the cop. "You had your force shield on, didn't you?"

"Everyone does, it's a regulation. Lady, what's going on here? Nothing works. It was four a.m., and now it's…I don't know, *not four a.m.*" He looked around. "Where did all these people come from?"

The cop, his name badge said Harry Sullivan, didn't know what was going on but didn't seem to be a danger to himself or others. Tonya turned to Rachel.

She was nearly sheet white. "It's not a realm this time, is it?"

Tonya tried to force her hand into the security camera's view. It felt like pushing against a wall. She yanked it back before history decided it would be simpler to drop something on her to get her to stop. "No." She snapped her fingers at Sullivan. "Hey, mister, I need you to listen to this. You don't have to believe it, you only have to listen.

"My partner and I were working on scans of the capitol for a new realm technology we were developing. Something's gone wrong, and now we're inside it."

Her phone pinged her that it'd found Rachel's phone and set up a local connection with it. Better than nothing. *That's not true,* she sent. *This next part is.*

"Our movement will be restricted in unexpected ways because..." *Think...think...* "We're exploring different paths through historical events."

He looked around. "And this one is?"

Rachel was holding it together pretty well, but not enough to help Tonya think on her feet. "We have a number of options. I need a minute." The crowd was rowdy but looked modern enough. They hadn't gone back in time so far that they stood out. Whatever was happening, they were on the outer edge of the crowd gathered around it. "Excuse me," she said to a stranger close enough to hear her without her shouting. "What's today's date? My phone's dead."

"January 6th."

She glanced at Rachel and Harry and got a pair of micro-shrugs. It didn't mean anything to Tonya, either. Time to see if her next question was as awkward as it seemed in the movies. "And the year?"

Yep, just as awkward.

He cocked his head. "2021."

They'd traveled back more than twenty years. She was about eight, plotting an escape from her ruinous home in an addict's den. Kim was five. Helen and Mike didn't exist yet.

"Ah," Officer Sullivan said. "The riots."

"Riots?" Rachel said. "This doesn't look like a riot."

"We're too far away. Up front is where all the action is. We use it as a training exercise. I didn't recognize it. We always start out at the building. So," he said, turning from confused bystander to bossy cop in an instant. "How do we exit?"

His expression made it clear that *your guess is as good as mine* would be the wrong answer. Rachel was so frightened she was shivering. Neither had any idea what was going on, but Tonya had spent plenty of time with history's hand holding her leash. "Follow me. Stay right behind me."

Like her adventure with Tenor into the deep past, Tonya relaxed and listened to her instincts. History could and would kill if it had to, but if there were lower-energy solutions, it would take them. This made it seem like history was a conscious entity, but that was a shortcut in her head. In reality, all of this emerged from her particulate theory of time.

But it still *felt* like someone was guiding her.

Surprisingly her instincts didn't say to walk away. She had a very strong desire to move with the crowd, closer, into the Capitol Building itself. Iyaan was on that side in the future. Hopefully that would be the key to them getting home.

History said go forward, so that's what they did. The crowd was boisterous, with an almost party atmosphere. There were clear signs of violence, with fences torn down, windows smashed, that sort of thing. But whatever it was had already happened.

She thought they were going to be in real trouble when a couple of cops came into view who appeared to be guarding the doors, but as soon as Tonya spotted them, they moved aside and allowed the crowd to pass, never giving her cop a second glance.

"How accurate is your simulation?" he asked as they passed into the rotunda.

If he only knew. She chuckled but stopped. Rachel was terrified. Tonya put her best *it's all gonna be okay* RN smile on. "Very."

"Yeah, you've made a mistake back there then. People said the cops let the mob in but nobody's found any proof."

Not only had they found proof, it was from a method nobody would believe. *They'd* been the one that caused it. History wouldn't push two guards out of the way on its own. But when it was to get a trio of anomalies to an exit, it'd do it. Out loud, she said, "We'll be sure to revise it."

History no doubt helped them transit the inside of the building. Now she understood why this event had been largely forgotten. People were visibly bored.

That changed when they exited the other side. The party was going strong out here, with big crowds scattered all the way out into the mall. Some sort of rickety scaffold had been set up in the distance.

"You did get that right," Sullivan said as he pointed at it.

"What is it?"

"That's a gallows."

"It is?" Rachel asked, squinting. "For little people maybe?"

He shrugged. "Almost all the pictures make it look huge, but it was exactly the size you see."

A stocky Asian lady, clearly less than five feet tall, some sort of flag draped over her back like a cape, stood proudly on it as someone took her picture. If she walked forward, she'd hit her head on the crossbar.

"Yeah," he said as they walked down the steps. "I'm glad it didn't collapse and hurt someone. We're trying to get back to your truck, aren't we? I don't see it."

"You won't," she said, buying time. "It's got a—"

With a snap, the sun was gone, the people vanished, streetlamps flicked on like someone had thrown a switch. The air was instantly warmer, and once again she stumbled a bit.

The hand of history had set her free. They were back.

"Ah, I see now." He pointed. "I told you that you couldn't park there."

About a hundred yards away, Iyaan was getting towed.

"I guess I *could* arrest you for kidnapping me," he said, a smile betraying his serious words as their truck was pulled sadly into the night. "But that would imply I didn't want to go along. That was the most realistic realm I've ever been in." He reached into a jacket pocket and pulled out an old-fashioned contact card. "My gear is fried so I can only give you this. Let me know if you need a beta tester. That was an impressive simulation. Sorry about your truck. Try getting a permit next time." He turned and walked away.

"Tonya," Rachel said in a strangled whisper, *"look!"*

Their phones had naturally come back online. A video landed in her queue. Rachel had found security footage from inside the Capitol on the day of the event. The time stamp was clear.

As was the footage of her, Rachel, and officer Sullivan as they moved through the crowd.

Per predictions though, their faces were never captured. Tonya would not be able to use this as proof of her theory. Ah, well. At least they made it back quickly.

Rachel rushed over to a trash can and emptied her stomach. She stood, wiped her mouth on her sleeve, and then her face. Tonya had only ever seen baby docs this rattled, usually after they nearly killed someone. Unlike them, Rachel didn't deserve this.

Rachel locked eyes with her, and it was an electric jolt that shocked her soul.

"What...just...*happened*?"

Chapter 27
Maff

Nervous didn't begin to cover what she felt sitting in a Reston café picked by Special Agent Aaron Levine, a lightning-strike-to-the-head actual federal law enforcement agent. When Tonya had given her his contact information, it seemed too easy. A solution to her problem could not be a simple phone call away.

She was right.

It'd taken her several days before she'd had the nerve to activate the contact. She was an alien in a way humans still didn't take seriously, and also alien in a way they did. Her identity was pretty well established by now, but if the realm dramas she participated in as part of her get-to-know-the-wolflings project were anything to go by, the FBI would be able to see through that in an instant. If she didn't have hundreds of pallun grumpily orbiting near Jupiter, Maff would keep as many layers of clouds between them and her as she could fly over. That wasn't an option now.

But even though they would quickly establish that Maff Sorkin hadn't existed less than three years ago, they'd still hit a dead end. She didn't smuggle herself across a border, she fell from the sky. The only way forward was to ask for a meetup and fly through the clouds that rose to her altitude.

He walked in, and Maff was a little disappointed. He didn't look like the FBI agents in the realm dramas she watched. Then again, *nobody* looked like the people in realm dramas. They were so symmetrical, the humans called it *pretty*, sometimes they didn't look natural. He was average height, average build, pale skin. His hair was red and curly, an uncommon combination but one she'd see a couple of times per day at the airport terminal. He wore a variant of male formal attire; humans called it a suit, but it bore no resemblance whatsoever to what she wore. She was getting better at judging ages of their ridiculously short lifespans and figured he was between Kim and Tonya's age. Not particularly young by human standards but far from old too.

He spotted her and headed over. "I'm Aaron, pleased to meet you again."

He and his squad had crashed Mike and Kim's wedding. It was the first human ceremony Maff had seen, and she'd been a participant. Her English had been far too weak for her to do anything but nod at people who spoke to her, so he'd only seen her has the weirdest-looking bridesmaid on Earth.

She shook his hand with a manipulator. "Maff. Thank you so much for agreeing to meet with me."

"Any call from Kim or her friends is always going to be interesting. And I don't often get contacted for assistance as a civilian. Tonya said this wasn't a law enforcement issue?"

She squirmed but then stopped herself. This was a lot harder than she'd expected, and she'd never thought it would be easy. "I guess it is sort of…diplomatic?"

His eyes got a look she associated with being sign they'd figured it out on their own. "Not me, but who I know?"

"And you. And many other people, but you to start, for sure."

"I don't think I follow."

Not for the first time she cursed Earth's lack of interpreters. If she had a proper thread installed, she'd *know* if she was on the right track or not. This was worse than flying blind. She'd trained on how to fly blind. "Do you have time for a quick trip with me? I will have you back before the end of the hour." Like they always said, you never saw the end of the storm by trying to sneak around it. Best to plow straight through. "This will be easier to understand if I can show you what is going on."

An eyebrow shot up. "Kidnapping a federal agent is a serious crime."

Her gases roiled for a moment but then he smiled.

"But since you're asking nicely," he stood, "lead the way."

Again, if her people hadn't forced her hand, she'd never have been this bold or moved this fast. Her best friends trusted this man with their lives once or twice. She had to start somewhere, and she had to do it now. They had been growing increasingly agitated lately, and she couldn't help but feel she was running out of time.

He followed Maff and parked next to her in front her Earthside hangar. He got out and examined the building carefully.

"If you will follow me."

She used her remote access to bring *Palatine* out of D-space before they arrived. Having it appear out of thin air would be one shock she could spare him.

It wasn't the first time a human had been struck dumb the first time they saw a D-ship. Spencer had gotten that honor when he arrived unannounced while she was making repairs. This time, at least, she'd kept it shiny. "This is..." he said as he took *Palatine* in. "Some sort of Southwest prototype?"

She'd painted *Palatine* in their colors as a tribute to her employer. "In manner of speaking, I suppose so." Now to see if there was any granite in this cloud. "This will be shocking to you, but I want you to know you are safe. I will bring you back whenever you want. But first, I need to change myself a bit." Otherwise the controls wouldn't be where she expected them.

This didn't impress him as much as she thought it would. "If you don't mind my asking, what exactly put you in that suit?"

We lost a war with the galaxy was an expression she only knew in Pallun. "Is complicated. Now," she used her manipulators the way she'd learned to usher humans onto a jetway, "after you."

She stayed behind him, mostly to ensure he didn't wander off the main corridor, but also to watch for any signs of panic. The latest realm dramas about first contact, and there were lots of them, emphasized curiosity over horror, but she'd seen enough of the Aliens franchise to know that fear was an option.

When they got up to the bridge, he turned around. "What *is* it?"

"A transport." It wasn't a lie. It was strategically withholding facts.

"The wings are too short to fly, and it's not road legal. Is it some kind of prototype?"

"Not at all. Now," she said as she settled and activated the start-up sequence, "if you will have a seat and strap in, we will get started."

She did her level best to radiate professionalism and confidence. Aaron obviously had questions, but after a bit looking around, he did as she asked.

He also pulled his pendant phone away from his chest and started taking pictures. This caused her to stop, which made him stop. "What?"

She had to play this carefully. "I understand what you are doing and why. I only ask that you do not share the information you gather with your bosses until after I have shown you everything. I am not sure how you are going to react, and I do not know how anyone else will either."

He smiled. "This," he motioned to the phone in his hand, "is my personal device. *This*," he reached into a coat pocket and pulled out another, "is my government device. I only use it on duty, which I'm not at the moment." He grew serious. "I would very much like to know what's going on. Tonya mentioned immigration but didn't give me any details. Are you Jewish?"

She wasn't expecting that one. "Why would that matter?"

"My wife is Israeli. I'm thinking you've involved me because the Israeli PM is her uncle. Israel has, more than once, helped remote populations of Jews migrate to the country. We thought we'd found them all, but Jews end up in weird places. Is there a community in danger somewhere in Russia?"

"Not in Russia, no. And we are not Jews, although there are some startling similarities." Her console pinged that the ship was ready to travel. "We will probably need Israel's help. We will probably need everyone's help, but Israel is good start." It was still strange to think of different parts of the planet being sort-of-but-not-really planets of their own. *Countries* was a concept she only knew in English. "I would like to introduce you to my people."

He thought about that for a moment. Aaron was sharp, observant, and, so far, fearless. Tonya had been right to pick him.

"Yes," he said. "I think I'd like that too. Where are they?"

She initiated the jump and moved *Palatine* into the transit dimension. Now for the real test. "Currently in orbit around the sun."

Chapter 28
Mike

The claxons and flashing lights were a symptom of a much bigger problem. They shouldn't have seen him. They couldn't. He'd snuck past dozens if not hundreds of motion control devices back home just to prove he could. It was like a quick warm up to sneaking around things that mattered. It helped him stay sharp.

"This can't be happening," he said in that weirdly hormone-driven way humans did when they hit the panic button.

Was he panicking? The lights wouldn't stop flashing, and the sound was crawling up and down his spine like a humongous bug. Is this what panic—

"It doesn't matter, Sellars," Zoe shouted in his ear. "You need to run, *now*!"

He sprinted out a side door, into an alleyway, and onto the sidewalk, scattering half a dozen different types of bemians as he went. It was both easier and harder than trying the same thing back home. There was more room to dodge, but it was in odd places.

Zoe shouted in his ear. "*Keep running*. Go left!"

He heard a distinctive whirring overhead, one he knew all too well. "I can't outrun their fliers."

"Duck into a building."

He dodged a quadruped that *wasn't* some sort of centaur for once, more like a llama with antlers. It spat at him as he went by.

"They have security in them too." He knew how to hide from people and drones though. He'd done it often enough during the portal research. This was the opposite of doing that.

A park appeared on his left, complete with tall trees. *Perfect*. As soon as he was directly underneath one, he stopped, jumped for a branch, and climbed out of sight. This would've caused a stir back home, but bemians were trained for generations not to be curious. Besides, there were plenty of arboreal bemians. In fact, it was the body type humans most strongly resembled.

There were clear paths marked through the trees, corridors of branches that had been carefully cultivated over who knew how many centuries. A squirrel-like bemian about five times bigger than the ones back home screeched indignantly as Mike got in his way.

"Sorry," he said, and then vanished.

It wasn't magic. He simply turned into another pedestrian on his way to whatever business he was on. Then, as the only person who'd paid attention to him moved off, he climbed higher and *really* disappeared. The branch tunnels made for an effective ceiling he could climb through and across.

"This is great," Zoe said. "What do we do when we run out of park?"

"One thing at a time."

He could hear the fliers zooming around him, but after a moment, they went away.

"Have we lost them?" Zoe asked.

"No. They've pulled back and changed their search pattern." He and Kim had nearly been caught a few times before they figured out this trick. "They'll send in a ground search team next."

"We better scarper then."

"Scarper?"

She blew a raspberry into his ear. "Doesn't anyone watch *Gogglebox* anymore?"

"I'm supposed to know what that is?"

"It was still a thing. I remember it as a thing before I left. British show. They stick realm scanners in random British people's homes and record their reaction to the news. It sounds stupid but—"

"What does this have to do with getting out of here?" And she thought *he* could get sidetracked.

"Eh? Nothing. Scarper. It's British for running away. I learned it from that show. Duh."

He got to the edge of his cover, not, coincidentally, the edge of the park. The office towers resumed on the other side of the street that represented the park's border. He ended up next to a parking area for their street transport.

"Why don't we steal a car?"

"They don't work that way. It's all centrally controlled."

"By nodes."

"Yes."

"Last I checked you said I was a flavor of node."

"Being like one doesn't mean you *are* one."

A miniature of her avatar appeared in his enhanced vision, standing on a broad leaf to his left. Ever the artist, she must've felt the need to add a visual component to her scolding. "Observe, spaghetti-man."

On the other side of the street, a transport car's door popped open.

"What did you do?"

"The area is swimming in wireless connectivity, and the security is crap. The sockets are a weird shape, I'll give you that, but they anchor the same way. Now," she said as she performed an *after you* gesture with her hands, "shall we?"

"If I break cover…" A claxon sounded behind them, then a loud, commanding voice in a language he didn't understand started speaking. The translation was provided when people all turned and started walking out of the park.

"If you stay here, we're busted," she replied.

"The drones are all node-controlled. Can you stop them?"

She closed her eyes for a moment. "Briefly."

It would have to do. "On three. One…two…*three*!" He used a

branch to swing his dismount over the low boundary fence of the park. There was no time for a stunt landing, so he absorbed the impact, stood, and walked quickly toward the open vehicle. Before he got there, an octopus-like bemian swooped in and took a seat.

They stared at each other for a moment. "Well," Zoe said in his ear. "That's a complication we don't need."

The alien said something with an annoyed tone and motioned for Mike to get in.

"The chances of getting another one?"

"Are inversely proportional to my ability to jam the drones. He'll have to come along for the ride."

Mike stepped in. The door shut as he took a seat across from the alien, whose eyes had unfocused as he concentrated on whatever his phone was showing him on a screen only he could see. Or he jumped to a realm. Virtual screens weren't as popular here. "What's the plan?"

The car lurched into motion so hard he had to grab a handhold. Bemian vehicles made no provision for a driver. It was a box with seats. The second lurch forward pulled their rideshare out of wherever he'd been. He squeaked and made a lot of worried-sounding noises as he looked around in alarm.

"Zoe?"

"Hello, never driven a car before, right? I was too busy getting tortured by a maniac to try simulators. He would've just killed us all in an accident." It lurched away, barely missing cars parked nearby. "How hard can it be?" They jerked right and left as they exited the parking lot. The traffic on the street dodged their weaving car like fish going around a rock. She turned into the stream.

"Zoe!" he shouted. "Wrong way!"

Their rideshare, Mike named him Chuck, babbled in an increasingly panicked tone. They were both shoved to one side as she slewed a U-turn that put them in the right direction of traffic. "Sorry," Zoe said.

They were lurching back and forth like a blacked-out drunk was at the wheel, and she was sorry? "Don't overcorrect. Take it easy!" It was difficult to coach her. With no controls inside, he couldn't see what she was doing.

Chuck had curled into a bundle. Mike could only hope squirting ink was a panic reflex restricted to terrestrial squid. She stood on the brakes, and they were thrown against their belts. "Zoe!"

"What do you want me to do? Run into people?"

The traffic behind them bunched up but then ran around them again once the pedestrians had crossed. Bemian transport control was a minor miracle in this situation. They still hadn't made autodrive mandatory back home, so a stunt like that would've presented a very high collision risk.

He tried to remember what it was like learning to drive via simulation. "Don't stare at the controls. Eyes on the road. Look ahead as far as you can."

"But then the things in front of me—"

"You'll still see them if anything goes wrong. It's much easier to see trouble coming if it's far away. Now," he said as vehicles continued to stream past them, "*go*."

This time the acceleration merely pushed him against his belts. Chuck had been looking at him with increasing astonishment. He started babbling again, but Mike was too distracted . Zoe was still over correcting her steering inputs. He switched to Standard. "My interpreter thread is down."

After the classic half second it took anyone to switch language gears, Chuck found his voice. "Who are you talking to? What's wrong with this transport? Am I going to die? Fuck!"

"Ah," Zoe said, "an *on ramp*!" She zoomed off the surface road, away from its heavy traffic.

Chuck put his head in his tentacles again. "I'm going to die. I'm definitely going to die." He kept repeating it.

Mike switched back to English. "You need to be careful now, gentle steering only." Kim had told him how her mother went white as a sheet at the *idea* that she had to teach his wife how to drive. He now had a lot more sympathy for Melinda. "Where are we going anyway?"

"Who are you talking to?" Chuck asked.

"Away from where we were, for a start. Now? Where do you *want* to go?"

He turned to Chuck. "A personal assistant on my phone."

"But you said your interpreter thread was down."

He split some threads off to deal with Chuck's questions. Basic variations on "but that's not possible, why are you doing that?" and then turned to Zoe. "We need to find a way back to that building." Assuming they didn't move the construct Zoe's family was in. There was no way to know for sure in their current situation. He still didn't know how it ended up inside an air-gapped network in the first place.

"Right then," she said as the car lurched sideways to catch an off-ramp. "No more interstate for me. Oh!"

The ramp's radius tightened suddenly, and now they were going *way* too fast. Chuck screamed as the guard rail came up to meet them. There was a stunning crash, a brief moment of weightlessness, and then the world exploded.

Chapter 29
Kim

Andromeda and Anna Treacher. The name of the deranged manager of the Yellowstone geothermal plant threw her off her game for a moment. Anna Treacher had turned it into a fuse to detonate the famous caldera located hundreds of miles away. She'd nearly succeeded. When it was clear Kim and Mike had blocked her planned route of escape, she disappeared through the site's portal before Will, scared and confused, did. She'd been so busy getting Will back, processing the fact that Watchtell had stolen her eggs, fertilized, then implanted them in Watchtell's own daughter, that Kim hadn't spared her a second thought in the years since. Gaining, then losing, then coming to terms with a child she never knew she had took its toll. Anna hadn't ended up in the same place as Will. They didn't know where she'd gone.

Now Kim did. Sort of.

This all flew through her head in about a quarter second. Andromeda had conveyed Anna's greeting. *He's expecting a response.* "Please return my regards the next time you see her." Hopefully she wasn't anywhere nearby.

His expression twisted a bit. He was also probably expecting her to have more of a reaction. "I will. So, what's it like being the sole interpreter for an entire galactic institution?"

The word popped out before she could stop it. "Exhausting."

The smile her candor brought out on Andromeda's face made the rest of the crowd around him chuckle comfortably. "I can only imagine. And they've accepted you?"

"Wholeheartedly. The negotiations we've closed with the syndicates this past year have been more profitable, for all parties involved, than any in the past thousand."

"Oh, it's more than that." He chuckled again, a big-chested noise that rumbled her guts. It was a hint of the power he must've wielded on Tonya. "I've always resented the decision that denied the La'fan that privilege."

Helen's research in the cache had indicated that this was a decision made by the Elders, the first intelligent life to evolve in the galaxy some eleven *billion* years ago. And Andromeda knew about it. Almost like he'd seen it himself.

The rest of the group shifted uncomfortably at so many mentions of the Death Eaters. Kim thought of them as a weird extended family, but to the galaxy at large, they were the ultimate boogey men, the things that went bump in the night. While bemians across the galaxy seemed resigned to the idea that one day their planet would suddenly be marked for death, they didn't seem to like thinking about it. The society that moved in to clean up those planets after the fact was the ultimate reminder. They'd been ostracized since the beginning for that.

Valsa broke the tension with a laugh that was a little too intense. But by the way everyone except Andromeda joined in, it was exactly what was needed. "Such strange folk, aren't they?"

"I guess we'll have to ask your new friend about that," Andromeda replied. "Are they that strange?"

She couldn't help but notice that the single circle of perhaps ten that she was a part of had acquired new shells of people behind them. This made the chance of a random push or nudge sending someone crashing into her more likely, and a bout of touch madness would be just the trick to impress here. She pushed a lock of hair behind her ear, catching a glimpse of the enhanced robes Valsa had gifted her.

She was still the Wild Witch, all-powerful talking galaxy or not. "No stranger than what I witnessed this morning, or standing in front of someone who *was in the room where it happened*." That last was said in a language she'd learned from the cache's archives, the earliest they'd found so far and one that went extinct several hundred million years before what Maff called the Refounding.

Everyone within earshot gasped audibly at the sudden introduction of a language none of them had heard before. But none of them understood the implication, the inner reference. Andromeda knew when the language was being spoken because he'd been around then. There was only one other way for someone else to know it.

Andromeda got the reference immediately. "You know the people who built the cache, the museum," he replied in the same language she used.

Now the whole hall had gone silent. She'd never been a big stickler for restraint. "I do."

"I left them a present for their grand opening. I was…" He ran a giant finger around the rim of his drink, a darkly coquettish gesture that made her blood freeze. "Disappointed that it didn't make the impression I'd intended."

He'd put one of his bug-eyed-monster soldiers on Tonya and Tenor's cache and had it sleep more than two hundred million years in a suspended animation crèche. It had nearly killed them, and none of them had worked out why he'd done it. "No," she glanced at Valsa, who looked as if she might be on the verge of having kittens. "It didn't."

A strange warbling tone sounded, and the mood of the room shifted. Valsa's shoulders relaxed, and she smiled. "Saved by Liinair." She turned to Kim. "If you would follow me?"

Doors she hadn't noticed opened along the far wall, revealing a giant banquet hall. Communal dining was a bigger deal for interpreters than it was for the rest of the population.

Valsa whispered to her, "You're supposed to learn about Wjkowlan, not goad him."

She liked the name humans had inadvertently given him better. It was easier to pronounce. "Sometimes you have to poke a thing to find out what's inside."

"Sometimes it's a nest of archaners." Valsa had switched to Tokaran, so she'd used that language's word for *large stinging insectoid*.

Food with Standard labels providing metabolic guidance was arranged on sideboards that lined the walls. Flat rectangular trays were provided on any number of standard plates could be placed. One of the most powerful organizations in the galaxy treated its formal dinners like a college cafeteria. Truly this was a strange place.

Kim followed Valsa's lead and stayed close. This was a much more formal occasion, and she didn't have any idea what was or was not the proper etiquette. Uparna, her assistant during the morning ceremony, appeared beside her and quietly let her know when *not* to follow Valsa's actions. She was, after all, first councilor. Kim was not.

The dishes lined the walls with the seating taking up the floor space. The tables were large and circular, seating up to ten people at a time. Telltales in her enhanced vision showed her where she was assigned. She'd expected more of an Oxford high table but had gotten a high-class charity banquet instead. She sat opposite Valsa.

Andromeda took the seat to her right.

"I would like to offer an apology," he said with a good-natured tone in Tokaran. Kim was beginning to understand it was a kind of default language among interpreters.

Valsa hid her startle well, but Kim spotted it. Valsa wasn't expected that. Kim turned on the smile she used when negotiations were going her way. That's what it felt like. "For what, exactly?"

"I didn't mean to change the subject from your experiences with the La'fan. I've found them fascinating from the start. How did you end up in their presence to begin with?"

They were seated with Valsa's inner circle now, senior interpreters with extensive diplomatic experience. The mention of the La'fan visibly upset the crowd that'd gathered around Andromeda in the foyer but didn't cause a ripple here. These were pros.

Again she felt the magnetism of this being, of him centering his attention on her. She liked it. "It started out with an accusation of piracy."

The story she told was adjacent to the truth, worked out with Maff for this sort of occasion. Humans were on the cusp of joining the galaxy when there'd been a navigation accident that saw Maff's original ship cross through a specific set of portal coordinates. This had the rare but not unheard of consequence of depositing her and her companion on Maff's ship.

"They directly intersected a fixed portal's path?" T'cal, one of Valsa's advisors who resembled a humanoid parrot, right down to the rainbow plumage, asked. "On purpose?"

She shrugged. "The ship in question was running from authorities carrying unlicensed intellectual property."

She got a couple of her own questions in. "How long have you worked with interpreters?"

Andromeda didn't so much as flick a look toward Valsa. "My family have been assisting the guild since the Refounding. Family lore says it was for much longer. Your friend's cache may allow me to know if that tradition has any basis in facts."

No thanks to you. Kim was beginning to understand why he wasn't overawing her or, at least, working up a theory. There was something subtly wrong about him, a vibe or buzz that made him *too* charming, *too* attentive. It was the difference between someone who genuinely cared compared to someone who was good at faking it. Maybe she was the only one, that it might be some sort of human habit. Certainly the others showed no signs of anything but admiration, respect, even affection toward him.

It was a learning experience, not only with Andromeda but with the Guild as a whole. This was the crème de la crème of interpreter society, and whenever the conversation switched away from her, she was captivated with people watching. Valsa's claim that the

Guild's leadership structure was flat might be true in the formal sense. But there were divisions here, cliques and power circles that no doubt dated back millions of years. Where there were seams, there were exploits for them. In spite of being roped into her inner circle, Kim was under no illusions as to what would happen should her usefulness come to an end. The only person who could arrange a soft landing for that eventuality was her, and these people could be made a part of the plan.

Eventually others began taking their leave. That was the best way she could describe it, since they all passed by what had to be the main table even though it held no special position in the hall and said brief polite goodbyes to them all. Kim got more attention than either Valsa or Andromeda, although neither showed any outward annoyance at it. She received several discreetly transmitted virtual contact cards in her queue, complete with event invites. If she decided to stick around, she would be booked for the next several months.

After the room's population had dropped by about two-thirds, some subtle signal was given, and Kim had to scramble a little once everyone at the table stood up. They all moved off as a group, so she followed along.

Andromeda fell in beside her and Valsa. "You mentioned accidentally getting trapped on a cargo ship," he said as they walked. "Let me tell you about the time that happened to me."

The story was frankly hilarious, another case of pirates inadvertently kidnapping a stranger. Only that time the pirates tried to ransom him. At some point, he must've somehow amped up his charisma. For a moment, Kim felt the kind of attraction she got when she was around portals. Valsa's laugh was a little louder, so she must have felt the effect as well.

The next step they made wasn't in the hall.

The transition was so sudden that it took a moment for her to realize things had changed. Valsa's laughter trailed off awkwardly. They now stood in what looked like a quaint cottage, except there were no windows anywhere. The wall on their left was some sort of force field, right down to the faint lines of energy shimmering in the air. Kim wouldn't try to touch that.

Andromeda had vanished. So had everyone else. She turned to Valsa. "Can you…I don't have a name for it…" If Valsa could hit the transit dimension they could get out of this quickly.

"We call it long walking." She closed her eyes for a moment. "No, they must have set up a—"

Lights switched on in the room on the other side of the force field. It was a large hexagon, with other cottage-slash-cells on four of the walls. All but theirs was unoccupied. An empty guard station stood in the center, six classic bemian-style consoles about waist high to her arranged in a circle.

The fifth wall had a large but otherwise conventional door on it. This opened from the center like they were on a starship.

Andromeda marched out in a uniform of spare design but sumptuous materials. All pretense of charm was gone. He was no longer the Guild's family friend. This was a being of immense power who had discarded a disguise and was now back to business.

He stood in front of the force field. "It's time we had a talk."

Chapter 30
Helen

Tom found their next lead, and it nearly gave Helen a heart attack.

"One of my cousins who still lives on the mainland works in aerospace. He's almost as secretive as you are. He rang me up to see if I could chase down rumors of a new kind of power supply being developed here in the states."

She raised an eyebrow. "Do you dabble in industrial espionage?"

He chuckled. "No. I was going to turn him down but then you showed up with your own shadowy stories of new technologies."

"What did he tell you?"

"Not much," he said. Then a package landed in her messaging queue. "But he said I should be on the lookout for these kinds of symbols."

They were extremely low-resolution constructs, blurry and pixelated and mostly 2-D images. She turned them around a few times before she recognized them. Her blood and threads froze at the same time.

It was bemian technology.

Helen desperately tried to stay cool.

Tom smiled. "Did I find a good one?"

So much for staying cool. "Yes. Yes, you have."

"Can you tell me what it is?"

"I don't think so." Her nerves settled a bit. "I only recognize pieces of it. But they're real." Someone had leaked actual alien technology into the world, and it was being taken seriously enough that Chinese aerospace was sniffing around. "What else did your cousin tell you?"

His smile faded. "I have a name, but it doesn't mean anything to me. You're the one with the strong search-fu. How long do you think it'll take you to trace down Francis Dollarhide?"

He sent her a copy of his cousin's message. Attached to it was a different one that had indeed been signed with that name. "What did you turn up initially?"

He shrugged. "It's a misspelling of a character's name from a novel, *The Red Dragon*. Super successful entertainment franchise from the late twentieth century. Been redone a couple of times since then, including a few realms. But that's as far as I've gotten. There are tens of thousands of users who've used that exact spelling in accounts scattered all over realmspace. I'm hoping the message will let you get further than I can."

"I'll take a crack at it and let you know." She ended the call.

The message had an origin realm address. Helen could only shake her head after she accessed it. She'd been outside with her own human host for several years now, so she thought she'd gotten used to humans in general. But their propensity for recreating historical settings for the smallest things would always surprise her.

It was a scriptorium. By the realm's contract description, a thirteenth-century recreation of a Western medieval institution the Chinese had made obsolete when they invented printing some six centuries before. From the outside perspective of her threads, she could see that, instead of dozens of monks laboring away in a room the size of a large kitchen, there were tens of thousands of them working in a segmented space the size of a large warehouse.

But the monks weren't real. They were second-order avatars, basic AIs under the control of owners who needed to separate themselves from the messages they were sending. Since it was an AI sending the message, it made it harder to work out who the real sender was.

That was only a single monk writing a single message. The monks could be chained together and compartmentalized. Different pieces of the message went by different scribal paths. Done correctly, it was quite effective at stymieing any attempt to find the sender of a message.

For normal humans at any rate.

To a typical police or detective agency, it would look like a tangled thicket of furiously scribbling AIs. To Helen, it was a kind of physical exercise. Splitting threads far and fast was a lot like going for a long run. If she kept her pace quick but steady, the exertion would make itself known but not be enough to slow her down. She was nowhere near as ponderous as her brother and had been practicing.

It naturally helped that the realm was located in her orbital cloud.

The scribes used realm construct paper and ink. Continuing their obsession with historical inefficiency, these were not destroyed after the message had been received. They were instead scraped clean by monks tasked for that purpose. Realm constructs required contracts, which needed unique identifiers that weren't cheap by the millions. To normal humans, it added a layer of security. It was yet another series of disconnections between any single message. Not only would they have to reconstruct the chain of scribes who created the message, they'd have to find the precise layer on the paper used to find it.

Helen dug deep and split her threads once more to attack the problem.

The messages themselves were still perfectly encrypted. Perfectly encrypted for everyone except Kim. But she wasn't around at the moment. It didn't matter. Helen already knew what was in the message. She was more concerned about who sent it, and where they were located. *That* wasn't encrypted to the same level as the content. In the trade-offs between cost, speed, and security, at the level of the transport, the original engineers of the Evolved Internet chose the first two. The packets were split in their millions across a virtual space that was effectively infinite. No human would ever be able to assemble the full route.

Score another one for being more than human.

Now with a *third* level of abstraction, Helen felt she was reaching her limits. Her realspace host was sweating and panting, and her threads were stretched thin, to the point of nearly being invisible. She'd developed a fascination with long-distance swimming lately. Mike claimed it had to do with the way water felt like what their threads lived in. Helen wasn't sure, but she had now developed a deeper appreciation of what those athletes went through. The pain, exhaustion, nausea, the feeling of gradually losing control to the point that force of will alone kept the swimmer going, was exactly what she felt in this moment. One more stroke. One more thread. Breathe. Work. Concentrate and shove the pain into a box already overflowing and beginning to crack.

Then the last piece fell into place, and she had him.

Had *them,* in fact. Francis Dollarhide was the nom de guerre of a trio of senior engineers working on the power regulation controls for Sidereal's portal. The device needed *nine*-phase electricity that spent some time in higher dimensions before it was in a format that the portal could use. They'd acquired two sets of bemian controls through Maff's friend, the gangster boss Toraz. One for the portal itself and another to reverse engineer it so they could be produced locally.

As always, this segment of the project had been thoroughly compartmentalized. Or it should've been. The three engineers turned out to be college buddies who, between the three of them, had worked out enough detail to understand that each of their three parts formed a whole that controlled a power generator of revolutionary efficiency.

That was why the original message ended up in China. They assumed that country was developing the generator because their aerospace sector was one of, if not the most, advanced in the world.

They were offering to sell information on the controller to gain information about that generator.

They had sent the note to more than one company.

Watchtell aside, her first priority was to erase any remaining trace of this message. Her threads were shaky at best. She gathered as much as she could hold steady and reached out to the various message recipients. Using impeccably forged credentials—Kim didn't only have natural talents, she was also a genius at creating toolkits—Helen impersonated a variety of law enforcement agencies and put out general warnings about a new Trojan construct that was the latest attempt at ransomware in the modern era. She included the text of her message in case anyone missed it. Perfect security had made these attacks ineffective, and this was no exception, but the recipients were advised to destroy the messages immediately. Her credentials would trigger a sublevel AI to do the work. No need to worry about humans being lazy.

That took care of the recipient problem. Taking care of the sender would hit two vultures with one arrow.

*

"How did you learn all this about electrical generation?" Tom asked her on a private call as he waited in the vestibule outside Sidereal's security office.

"I don't understand the why or how, only that these names used in this context are involved with power generation."

"And these people," he nodded at the inner door behind the receptionist counter, "will be interested in it?"

"Indeed." Getting a member of Watchtell's inner circle to turn against him hadn't worked. Helen had gone for a personal attack then. Now she was letting the apparatus designed to protect and conceal all of Sidereal's secrets know that they had a leak serious enough to shut down the project. A thorough audit would have to be completed. Her first attempt had been to deny him his power. This one would switch it off, at least long enough for her to get back and contain the damage.

The assistant who took Tom's information could not hide her concern. Tom was called into interviews the next day. The first was with the assistant's boss.

The last, at the very end of the day, was with Watchtell himself.

She hadn't been able breach the defenses, and there was no way a bug would get past them, so a standard oral debrief was the best they could manage. Tom started the story with what Watchtell said the moment Tom walked into his office.

"Your timing could not be more apropos. We had been watching the breach for several weeks now."

Her threads, now fully recovered from the ordeal of tracking down the conspirators, grew weighty with a different sort of exhaustion.

"He already knew."

Chapter 31
Tonya

Tonya didn't set out to become a Time Lord and certainly hadn't wanted to acquire an actual companion, but it happened anyway. Except she didn't get a sonic screwdriver or a robot dog. Those would've been nice to have.

The silence in the autoUber returning to the lab was unbearable. Tonya set up a pocket realm on her phone. In any other circumstance she would've picked something fun. A giant castle, a starship ready room, or maybe a chapel in a long-lost medieval church. But not now. Tonya had seen lots of people rattled to their core before. It was a rite of passage for baby docs. Rachel didn't deserve that.

So a simple, boring boardroom it was, right down to the oval table and leather chairs. She sent Rachel an invite, which was accepted immediately.

Rachel's avatar manifested already in midstride as she paced the realm's floor. "We traveled back in time?" she shouted. "You knew what to do! You've done it before!"

It was easier to talk the baby docs down. She didn't care what they thought about her. "Rachel, you need to take a breath. Sit down," Tonya said as she took her own seat, "this is going to be a long story."

"I don't know how to process this!" she shouted as she threw her arms up and appealed to the realm's ceiling. "What the actual fuck?"

Tonya knew from experience it was impossible to explain anything complicated to a person in the process of losing their marbles. This was going to be a complicated conversation, and she could tell Rachel didn't have any marbles left to lose. *"Rachel!"* It was a pitch-and-tone thing that they all learned in RN school, and thankfully, it worked like a charm. She stopped like she'd been hit with a pole. Tonya pointed. "Sit down."

Rachel did so. This was a side to Rachel that Tonya had never seen before. She'd seen buckets of confidence, miles of ambition, and an absolutely endless curiosity. Those *should* have brought the wonder out once she figured out they were in the past.

That hadn't happened because she didn't know it was even possible. Tonya didn't intend for them to go on that sort of trip. She hadn't told Rachel about it. Deep down, she was afraid to. Afraid that the secret would get out. Afraid that Rachel wouldn't understand, or it would change the relationship Tonya wanted to—

Okay *that* was an unwelcome thought right now. *Get on with it!*

"First of all," Tonya said. "I'm sorry."

A person without their marbles was easy to knock off balance. "What?"

"I should've told you what happened *could* happen, and I didn't, especially after the incident in front of the theater. I should've told you, and because I didn't, you got the scare of your life."

She barked out a laugh too loud for the situation. But that was a thing she sometimes did. A marble had made its way back into the box. "I didn't know it was possible to be that scared and still function."

"You did well, by the way. The cop had cluelessness to keep him warm. You, not so much."

Rachel took a deep, shuddering breath and flexed her hands as they rested on the table. She looked up, and a fist in Tonya's chest loosened. This might turn out okay. And maybe it was time Tonya admitted she wanted it to turn out okay.

But then the fear came back in Rachel's eyes. "What happened?"

Now it was her turn for a deep breath. "We went into the past. It was an interaction with the cop's personal shields that caused the surge. I didn't know they had a power source that big." And now for the downside. "There were other reasons I didn't tell you about this. It goes without saying—"

"That I'll end up at the bottom of a hole in the middle of nowhere if I repeat what you're about to tell me?" Tonya watched as Rachel got that the joke might not be a joke.

She smiled and pushed genuine warmth into it. "*No.* Never that. But my story legitimately is a for-real national secret. Global secret, in fact. I'll be prosecuted by..." She did a quick count in her head and hoped it hadn't changed lately. "At least two governments if it ever gets out that I've told you about this. So please, this sister has no desire to spend her life behind a rotating series of jail cells. You *cannot* tell anyone about any of this."

She raised her right hand and put her left out like it was on a Bible. "I, Rachel Anderson, hereby solemnly swear not to put my favorite sister into federal prison. Of any country."

She filed her reaction to *favorite sister* into the growing cabinet of Things to Think About at a Later Time. *Never* always being the best time. "Thank you."

She called up a realm that modeled a city square in Chengdu. "It all started in China..." Telling the first part of the story was a little tricky. It'd happened almost in reverse. She'd been attacked by human traffickers related to her old mentor, Walter, in a rough part of the city and was helped by a child she'd never met before. Then when those slavers caught her, a guard who acted strangely had turned her loose. Next was a farmer who fished her out of a river.

"They all acted weird. It was confusing."

Rachel's eyes bugged out. "It was you. Oh my God. That is so messed up. I'm right, aren't I?"

"How'd you figure that out?" She certainly hadn't while it was happening.

"Time travel, mysterious helpers in the right place at the right time, you *have* watched *Doctor Who*, right?"

"I guess it's clear in hindsight, but I didn't understand it then. Until I met Cyril."

The final encounter was with the blue bug who changed her life forever. He'd shown her the truth in the threaded room, a place outside of the conventional dimensions of the universe where timelines became physical things that could be observed and measured.

She next called up a model of the power plant and dropped it onto the conference table. "Then there was Yellowstone…"

She explained the first portal, how it allowed travel through space instantly and, it turned out, time. "The blue bug *made* me travel into the past. I was terrified like you were, but I was alone."

It seemed like ancient history, but also like it had happened yesterday. She still sometimes smelled the inside of the suit she'd lived in for two whole weeks. "That's when I started formulating my theories."

Rachel got a sly look. "You didn't think of this yourself. You reverse engineered it!"

"I guess, but that makes it sound a lot easier than it was. Is. Doing that let me know it was possible. Figuring out how has dominated my life ever since."

"Yellowstone was years ago. Has Cyril ever come back?"

She couldn't have had a better segue. "Do you remember Maff?"

"The lady in the support suit? She was nice."

Tonya loaded a frame from the recording Maff made of her road trip to Jupiter. She'd shown it to them all during a cookout one evening. It was easily the most spectacular home movie Tonya had ever seen. The shot was taken after she'd accidentally dropped the camera while she flew free, the first pallun to do so for thousands of years.

"This is what she looks like without her suit on."

Rachel's mouth dropped open. After a moment, she blinked and pulled a 3-D construct of Maff out of the picture and started turning it in various directions. "A furry…manta ray…wearing an outfit made of streamers…with brass goggles…I'll give you this, she's great at avatar originality."

Tonya chuckled. "It's not an avatar. That's *her*. She's not human. Her species is called pallun. She's from another world. Another star system."

Tony thought Rachel discovering she'd met an alien would disturb her more than time travel. But instead of fear, her expression was clearly one of wonder. It made her almost glow. After a long moment, she shook her head and pushed the avatar back into the picture. "I have a million questions, but they can wait for now. What does she have to do with time travel? Is it alien technology?"

The Knowledge, the bemian Gregorian-chant-meets-Newtonian-physics system of science learning, jumped out from her memories. Tonya's theories were so much more advanced than anything they could understand that she might as well be…*was*…from another planet. "Not exactly."

She told the story of how Mike and Kim got accidentally trapped on the ship Maff was piloting, and how they'd all returned, and Maff decided to stay on Earth.

"She's got a ship? *You can go back?*"

Tonya smiled. "We already have." This was the part of the story that was truly mind blowing. That old fool Dean Shakson, the talking turtle that led the bemian university Tonya had joined to learn their science and who spouted *what what* every sixty seconds, had rammed so much power through her experiment that it'd thrown her and Tenor back…

"Two hundred and fifty *million years*?" Rachel made the same mind-blown gesture with her hands against her head that Tenor used when she'd told him the truth. "That's before the dinosaurs. A long time before!"

"And that's why I knew we'd be fine at the capitol. I spent a long time living with the hand of history." Nearly two years in fact. She still mourned the staggering loss of life and culture that the subsequent Undoing, the collapse of galactic civilization so thorough it cut modern bemian society off from its own past, represented, even though it meant nothing to Earth at the time. She wrapped up the story with a brief account of the cache they'd shepherded through time. Tenor couldn't stand the loss of so much, and Tonya understood his point, so they leveraged the fact that bemian tech simply didn't break down to create a kind of ark that allowed them to bring that lost history to the present. It was as if she'd saved the Library of Alexandria, except turned up to eleven.

"You've *got* to take me to see that! Please tell me we can go see that."

The marbles had been successfully placed back in their box. "It takes a long time to get there by ship, and right now Maff is busy with her own problems. But once we get our own portal up and running, I promise you we'll go." It thrilled her more than she was comfortable with at the thought. Then Tonya remembered the promise she'd just made to herself and allowed a tiny bit of hope to keep shining.

Very tiny.

This whole story was told partly in a realm, partly in their autoUber, and then finished up back at the lab at a table with the remains of an Anita's Spanish Scramble and Chorizo con Huevos breakfast scattered around them. It was the first time Tonya had told the whole story end-to-end out loud. "This is all so…crazy," she said, sipping coffee and mentally looking out onto the vista of it all. Four years ago she was a nurse with a realm gaming addiction and a weird best friend. Today she was a scientist with a theory that described—and would permanently change—history, aliens for friends, and a mental passport with stamps nobody else had.

She wouldn't change a single thing.

Rachel looked sheepish. "If I hadn't gone through…that…I would've thought *you* were crazy." She shook her head. "I don't know what to think about any of it. Aliens? Time travel? Portals? Not to mention the conscious galaxy that wants to kill us all." She crumpled up a wrapper and tossed it expertly into the trashcan. "I don't know what my next move is." She turned to Tonya, sparkling eyes and beautiful smile and everything else. "*Is* there a next move?"

It was an opening she wouldn't take. There was moving forward, and there was moving too fast. Going flirty would be putting the pedal to the metal when she only now admitted going for a drive might be a good idea. Then she remembered. "We need to rescue Iyaan." He was bound to have been checked in now. The city was useless for most services, but traffic tickets and towing fees were revenue generators. Money guaranteed efficiency.

Rachel's eyes unfocused, and then her face clouded. "Huh." She shared a search result.

No records found matching vehicle description.

Chapter 32
Maff

Aaron handled the transition to the transit dimension well enough. Maff had been through it so many times that she barely noticed, but all the humans said it made them dizzy the first time. He made one of those strange human yip noises when they exited near the ship's location and gravity fell to zero.

He pushed his phone down and tucked it underneath his shirt. "No artificial gravity?"

"Not on something this small," she said, distracted. The pallun ship wasn't where it was supposed to be. Her sensors must've gone out of calibration, and she tried to figure out which axis needed tuning.

"Is there…a window I can look out of somewhere?"

She called up the external channel and dropped it in their shared vision space. "Spencer calls it *Enterprise*'s view screen." Maff checked their coordinates, and they were correct. The sensor diagnostics reported everything was normal. She used the shared viewport to look around. *Palatine* was in the right place.

The survey ship wasn't.

Any other time, Aaron's awed gasp at the view of Jupiter would've made her smile. She had bigger problems now. "They've moved their ship." She recalibrated the scanners for a long-range sweep.

"That's Jupiter. I'm here. This is incredible. Wait, you've lost your people?"

"More like they lost me." She should have removed the permissions on the engine controls. Maff had spent a week putting *Last Island* back together and then maintained *Palatine* by herself for more than a year. At the very least, she should have locked the door to engineering. Her people were famous across the galaxy for their improvisation. She should have guessed they would figure out how to—

"Oh no."

The scans stopped when they detected the distress signal. She turned it on the common channel so Aaron could hear it.

"To any ship within range. We are in distress. Buoyancy generators have not deployed properly, and we are sinking. Please send help."

"What's it saying?" he asked.

She had been so wound up with searching, she forgot he didn't speak Pallundian. *Or* Standard. She thought the galaxy was done with tearing her plans up, but no, there was always another way for her to be shoved along faster than she wanted into situations beyond her control. "They are in trouble." The message included coordinates precise enough for her to aim the viewer at. "They are sinking."

They said they were here to colonize, and she should've paid more attention to that statement. Not only had they moved their ship into the planet's upper atmosphere, they deployed a settlement framework around it. Effectively, they repurposed the ship into a rough homestead. Pallun may not have been allowed their own gas giants, but that hadn't stopped anyone else from claiming them, so the rigs for settling them were as well known as any other bemian construction.

Gas giants had no surface, but it usually wasn't hard to find a level where temperature and atmospheric pressure created huge bands of livable sky. Once you found it, you floated. On a settlement, this was accomplished by buoyancy generators, complex machines located at corners of the framework. Theirs was a small one, so it only had six. She magnified the image, and four of them were glowing a normal green blue.

Two were dark.

"I am going to need your help," she said. "But you can not go out there without suit." Magnetic fields would protect him from radiation, but there wouldn't be a gas mixture he could breathe. "You need to unstrap and go back to cargo bay. There is set of lockers on one side. Go to first one. There is environmental suit inside."

She was worried he would object or panic or choose some other wildly inappropriate response she had no time for. Instead he nodded once, unstrapped, and moved backward with surprising skill. "You have been to space before?"

"In realms, a hundred times. Most humans have."

Her nav computer returned a solution. "Gravity getting turned back on again." It was less confusing than saying *we're entering the transit dimension*. "Grab something and let me know when your feet are pointed at floor."

His voice came over the intercom. "You said this ship didn't have artificial gravity."

Decisive and curious. She liked this guy. "It doesn't. Transit dimension does." Nobody had ever questioned it, an idea she now thought of as *The Bemian Way*. Space is weightless, the transit dimension is not. Mike, Tonya, and Kim had various theories as to why, but they were all too busy to take a stab at proving any of them.

"Okay," he said, "I'm ready."

"Brace yourself. Gravity little more than two and a half times what you are used to at destination." She had integrated one of Spencer's climbing harnesses into the one he would be using. That would help, but there were all sorts of unexpected effects he'd have to deal with. Inertia was substantially increased, and that made things more dangerous than he was used to.

"Then hold off on the jump. Give me thirty seconds to put the suit on first. I can't move very fast under that load."

"Suit is boosted. You will not be as slow as you think. I would rather give you half that time."

"Working on it."

That he knew what two and a half times Earth's standard gravity would be like was another sign of how imaginative Earth's realms were. Nobody thought to simulate worlds of varying densities back home. If you wanted to experience different levels of G, it was an easy trip via the portal network to a planet of the right density. It was considered a nuisance to be avoided.

"Ready."

He only needed ten seconds. Aaron was proving to be the best choice. She'd have to buy Tonya her preferred liquid intoxicant after they got back.

"Transiting in three...two...one..."

The ship creaked a little as down once more became a thing in the transit dimension. After a moment, it creaked a lot, exiting with neutralized velocity about fifty thousand feet above the cloud tops. The groans and pops continued as *Palatine* adjusted to the temperature and pressure changes.

"Maff, are we safe?"

She pulled up a video of the cargo hold and saw Aaron's head snap around at each bang or creak the ship made. He was braced against the row of lockers but was otherwise fine.

"Nothing to worry about. There is cart with tool kit and spares to your left. Get ready to push it out doors."

He burst out laughing.

"What is funny?"

"An hour ago I didn't know aliens existed, and now I'm hovering over Jupiter trying to rescue them. Don't pay attention to me. I'll freak out when we're done."

She got a fix on the platform and flew over to the listing structure. "Colony structure, this is *Palatine,* actual."

"Maff?" It was Keezel, the ship's captain. "Thank Turlanfador! We're in so much trouble!"

"I can see that. We're arriving now." She opened Aaron's channel. "Get ready. They have landing pad we fit on, but I will not be able to rest *Palatine* on it." It would be tricky, but she had dealt with worse.

In simulation.

That was what school was for anyway. Besides, her time flying aircraft on Earth was proving at least as valuable as she navigated the gusts that made *Palatine* fly more like a Cirrus than a D-ship. "Get ready."

"What am I supposed to do? Is there a mechanic out there?"

As if. Pallun were different from other bemians in uncountable ways, but they were almost as helpless at mechanical repairs as any other species. Nodes fixed things. They stayed broken u then. "They will take you to the buoyancy generators. I will walk you through the repairs." She opened channels to his helmet cams, giving her a nicely detailed 360-degree view. "Doors opening now."

Half a dozen pallun stood on the other side. Aaron didn't flinch or pause, driving right through them. "What do I say?"

"Nothing. I will do talking." She turned on his external speaker and switched to Pallundian. "This is Aaron Levine. He's a human, and he's here to help. Guide him to the first failed generator." She pulled *Palatine* a couple hundred feet away and set the autopilot to hover. This was not a time for split concentration.

The platform was designed for high-grav types, things that walked on legs, so they all still wore their environment suits. It would be a long time before the right sort of structures to accommodate a pallun's natural mode of living would be built. They had all forgotten how to build them.

She was inundated with dozens of questions, hints, complaints, and strategies. "Not now. We have to fix the platform first."

"You said humans were uncontacted," Jholl, the Meronim leader, said.

"They are. I'm going to walk Aaron through how to fix it." They weren't all that different from *Palatine*'s motivators. Just lots bigger.

The idea that she could fix anything caused all but the pallun leading Aaron to stop in their tracks, which quickly put them out of voice range. Thank Turlanfador for small favors.

They didn't stay stunned for long. She could see them rushing back to Aaron from his rear feed. Jholl's outrage was as plain as if she were standing next to him. "You don't know how to fix this! You're supposed to pull us off the platform and take us to Earth!"

"First, yes, I do. Second, my ship isn't anywhere near big enough to take everyone to Earth. Stay calm. I got this."

"Mind telling me what all the fuss is about?" Aaron asked between heavy breaths. She had to remind herself that he was working in higher G.

"They do not think I know how to fix. It is long story."

"They sound like they're arguing."

"They are. Is pallun pastime."

He chuckled. "I guess our two peoples do have a few things in common."

She turned her attention to the crowd. "Could someone please help the human push the cart?" Their rate of descent was increasing. If they did not get this under control soon, a whole bunch of pallun were about to get a crash course in the old ways. She had only shown Mr. Sha'Katenden her highlight reel. The fact was that she had spent the first few hours learning how *not* to fly free. Maff was young, in shape, and understood the concepts of flight because she spent so much time around human airplanes. These people didn't know how to flap their wings properly. They might end up frying in the lower levels before they figured it out.

Jholl imperiously selected two of his followers. One picked up the cart, the other, Aaron himself. "What the—"

She should have thought of that already. "It is okay. We move faster this way." She gave instructions as to which tools Aaron needed and then walked him through the steps. Not for the first time did she reflect on the irony of her knowing all this due to being taught by the most antipallun bigot she'd ever personally known. If she ever crossed paths with him again, she owed him a *case* of intoxicant.

The first one was a simple matter of connectors coming loose. It started glowing as soon as Aaron clicked the last one home. "Do not worry about putting back together yet, we can do that after we fix other one."

The next one wasn't as simple. "I do not see anything wrong."

Aaron peered around inside the machine's cowling. "Do you have a hammer in that kit? A big one?"

She relayed the instruction. The one they produced wasn't the biggest hammer in the kit, but under the increased G, it was probably the largest he could hold.

He took it and, before she could react, whacked the generator's mechanism so hard it rang like a gong. Bemian tech was legendary for its durability, but abusing it like that was unprecedented. Mike and Kim, all humans, were spooky-good mechanics, but to do that...

The generator shuddered once and then began to glow. Everyone shifted as the platform leveled off and slowly started to rise.

"How did you..."

"I didn't, not for sure, but there's a huge gearbox in the middle of it. It looks so much like the automatic transmission in my wife's old Kibbutz's tractor, it's kind of weird. The linkage wasn't in the same position as the other one, so I gave it a nudge."

"What's he saying?" Captain Keezel asked.

"It was stuck. He used the hammer to unstick it."

"Praise Turlanfador!" Jholl cried out, manipulators flailing. "Maff has once more been guided to save His chosen people!" The rest of the Meronim began chanting a traditional prayer of thanksgiving that was somehow made more annoying by the fact it was them doing it.

"What's up now?" Aaron asked as he closed up the generator.

Crisis now averted, Maff realized she'd let her accent leak quite badly. She cleared her throat and concentrated on English. "They thank our god for rescue. They are from a special sect known to cause trouble for rest of us."

He shook his head. Maff had been around humans long enough to recognize when they were excited. Aaron looked like he might burst. "Fascinating parallels. You need to meet the Israeli PM. Tell them to take me back to the ship. I'll make an appointment with the DC ambassador."

Chapter 33
Spencer

The grate that covered the giant drain was a new addition, but the drain itself was much older. Spencer figured this out not from some artifact or deep insight into Telirian architecture. In fact, he hadn't figured it out at all.

Sornik had.

"Hard to put a year on it, but it's precontact," he'd said when Spencer wondered out loud about its age.

"How can you tell?"

He thumped some manipulators on the bricks that made up the tunnel. "Nodes don't do brick drains. Strictly concrete slabs, nearly always as big as I am. Nah, this was built by the natives. I see it all the time."

"You find it hunting for property of unclear license status?"

"Items of *no* license status. After a planet is joined to the galaxy, the sewers are usually all that's left. Strange things get chucked down them during uplift. Most of it is junk, but not all. And what you find, you keep."

"The locals don't pick it clean?"

"The locals are too busy exploring the galaxy to care. Remember, it's all new to them. By the time they realize there's stuff in the ground that might have value, we've already been and gone." He dug a furrow through the muddy silt that'd built up into a floor. "And this? You don't get this in real sewer systems. The nodes have giant robots run through a couple of times a day to clean it all up. Scary fuckers if you get too close. They'd wear these tunnels down to dust."

They'd been climbing a gradual incline the whole time—drains run downhill, duh—and what tracks there were in the muck were old enough that he couldn't figure out what made them. Eventually they found a short vertical tunnel with a drain grate over it. "How come it's not rusted out?" Spencer asked.

Sornik extended a manipulator and then did a standing-on-toes kind of thing with his legs. He gave the grate an experimental tap. The sound was solid and nothing flaked off or cracked. "It's like the grate at the other end. Not original."

That might not be a good thing. "Is it locked like the other one?" They'd walked a pretty goddamned long way.

A manipulator snaked through one of the openings. After a moment, there was a clank, a thump, and another manipulator pushed it open. "Not anymore."

There were ladder rungs buried in the wall that looked to be made of the same stuff as the grate. He scrambled up them. It didn't stink, but the sewer was still a funky dank place he wasn't sorry to leave. He exited facing a wall. He turned around and nearly fell over.

They were inside a giant cave, the ceiling a hundred feet or more overhead. In the far distance was the entrance, also enormous and maybe a five hundred yards away.

Between here and there was an entire ruined Telirian city.

The buildings looked like they came out of a silent movie realm: all brick, glass, wood, and brass. The streets were in a grid for as far as he could see. Some of the buildings had collapsed but most were intact: skyscrapers like the early human ones that topped out at twenty floors or so. "Fuck me."

"Nah, kid," Sornik said as he clambered out like a 1950s movie monster. "You're not my type." He looked around. "Fuck me."

"I told you there were ruins all across the planet."

"I mean, sure, as a concept I get it. At least I thought I did. But this? I've never seen anything like it." He started walking down a street parallel to the cave's opening. Spencer followed close behind. They got to the next intersection, and he looked at the entrance again. "That, though? That I recognize."

A roadway had been bulldozed at an angle, heading toward the front of the cave. Mounds of rubble marked the buildings that'd been roughly smashed aside to clear the way. At the end of it was what looked exactly like a construction office. Long, low, and cheaply made, it would fit right in back home.

"Come on." He set off toward it.

The closer they got, the more clear it became that his guess about the building's purpose was exactly right. He turned back to see where the road started out and found a much larger tunnel going into the back wall. It curved down and away. "Were they bringing stuff in or taking it out?"

Sornik stopped at the door. "I think both." He had a strange device in his hand. After touching it to the door, there was a beep, and it opened. "I love it when a plan comes together."

"This is a plan?"

"It is now."

The inside was about what he'd expected. Cheap desks and filing cabinets, with some strange printer-like machines along the walls. Sornik didn't break stride, walking up to one of them and activating a screen in the shared vision channel. "I haven't needed to do this myself in years. Dusting off old skills is refreshing."

While Sornik did whatever the hell he was doing, Spencer took a look out of the trailer's other windows. Beyond was a stream, some woods, and *a fucking big bemian base.* Dozens of workers were going in all directions between at least three rows of warehouse-like buildings. "How do we get in there?"

"I forget you don't know how this works." The printer whirred to life. It spat out a chip. "Hold that over where your phone is." It spat out another that Sornik took and pulled into a portal on his suit.

Bemian phones didn't hang around the neck like the ones from Earth did. They were either implanted or absorbed into the skin.

Spencer held the chip over the spot. A notice in bemian script flashed in front of him.

Identity installed. Welcome to Tarn Industrial Services, Bakal Tora.

"The fuck?"

"Those guys are gonna be in so much trouble."

"I don't follow."

"We're in, kid. Once a…guy like me…gains access to a place like this, I have a license that lets me register us as employees."

"Really?"

"It's for scouting. Before I became the upstanding citizen I am today," he said with a gleam in his eye that Spencer could see through the lens of his suit, "I was part of a smash-and-grab gang. We'd use this trick to do scouting, then register the stuff we were gonna take with the appropriate nodes. Once all the permits went through, off we'd go."

Spencer had heard about how the nodes regulated crime like everything else. He'd never seen it in action before now. "That's crazy."

"That's business. Now, me, personally, I'm pretty damned tired. I don't know about you, but I'm gonna find a hole to crawl into and spend some time in the clouds. If you get my meaning."

He was pretty exhausted himself. Plus, he didn't eat constantly like Sornik did. "Is it safe to stay in here?"

"Time stamp says it hasn't been visited in months. You're probably fine. But I'm not gonna do it."

He found a back room in one of the better-preserved office buildings and set up camp there.

*

The morning saw them making their way down a vehicle ramp and over to the base. True to his word, he and Sornik walked under an arch past two bored-looking guards. Nothing beeped and nobody noticed.

Now that he was inside the base, it was half construction site, half smuggling arena. It was surreal walking around without anyone giving them a second glance. "This seems to be a lot bigger than what you guys have."

"Yeah. It's starting to piss me off. For them to be this far along, they had to have started before the network declared the planet open for smuggl"—he cleared his throat—"my line of work."

"Or they know something you don't."

"What's that supposed to mean?"

"That ruined city in the cave. How rare are those in the galaxy?"

Sornik stopped and turned to look at the site, still mostly visible in the distance. "Rare, but not unheard of."

"But it's not rare around here. That's the third one I've personally visited. The last one wasn't more than a collection of low mounds, but I know there are others. Tapov mentioned at least three more in casual conversation."

"You got a thing for that girl, don't ya?"

His face grew hot, and he walked away from the spot. "It's complicated."

Sornik fell into step beside him. "Yeah. It always is. Anyway, I think I'm seeing your point now. Artifacts from pre-uplift civilizations are as original as the stuff we're moving for you guys. You have a hell of a lot more of it, and it's more advanced. But originality sells, and if you find a lot of it, a lot of cash can be made." He stopped and took another look around. "This may turn out to be more a more interesting opportunity than I at first realized."

The base had the feel of an anthill that'd been kicked over. Everywhere he looked, people and bots were busy building things and moving things. Some of it he recognized, and out here in the sticks, the network nodes didn't do it all themselves. Some of it he didn't recognize. They walked past an open-air portal station with three of the big fuckers on a raised platform, bemians streaming in and out of them. Mostly out.

"What's up with all the pallets on tracks?" Workers of all races were towing what looked like fancy pallet jacks that had miniature tank treads instead of wheels. Judging by the way the smaller aliens were working, whatever was in the boxes was heavy.

"Not sure. Let's figure out where they're going."

Sornik walked away like he knew exactly where everything was. Which was probably true. Camps like this were probably from standardized plans the nodes gave them. Everything else was.

"Isn't this interesting?"

They'd been following the stream of carts as they moved from the portals to wherever the hell they were going. This turned out to be, at least in their case, a checkpoint of some sort. Armed guards were carefully examining bemians, bots, and carts before sending them through what looked a hell of a lot like a metal detector or some shit like that. "Let me guess," Spencer replied. "Our legal status gets questionable if we try to get through there?"

"Not questionable. Revoked. End of the line, kid. We finish looking around this chunk of camp, and then head for the exit."

"How tough is getting out going to be? Those guys will still be looking for us, right?"

Sornik sighed, which on a pallun was weirdly musical. "Always pointing out the flaws. Yeah. If they catch us on the other side, we're screwed."

Spencer caught a kron looking a little too hard at them. He motioned Sornik forward, and they walked parallel to the inner fenced area. "And if they catch us in here?"

"You spotted him too?"

"Whoever it was didn't look happy about us being here."

One of Sornik's manipulators popped up, holding what had to be some kind of camera. He spun it around. "Seems to only be one of them."

"For now."

"He's not a guard, though. They have different uniforms."

Spencer had noticed that. "But he's still following?"

"Yeah. Okay. On three, break right." His countdown matched perfectly with a right turn down a side path between two of the large square buildings. Sornik didn't exactly break into a run, but he picked the pace up quite a bit. "Three, two, one, go!"

They passed into a narrower, more shadowed area between two

buildings. Not a soul was in sight. Once again, Spencer was yanked off his feet by a set of manipulators as Sornik did his spider impersonation and climbed up the wall. A few seconds later, they were safely on the roof. It was a big flat square covered in roofing rocks like back home.

They both crouched down as Sornik extended his manipulator cam over the edge. He shared the feed with Spencer as their tail came around the corner doing exactly what they'd done: being in a hurry, trying not to look like he was in a hurry. Bemians going about their business behind him told Spencer they'd both succeeded.

The guy on the ground did the classic double-take when he discovered they weren't where he expected them to be. To his credit, he did look up, but that didn't do him any good. Spencer could barely see Sornik's manipulator camera, and he was right next to it. They had to be at least thirty feet off the ground here.

After a few minutes of frantic searching, he went still for a moment, then walked over and leaned against a wall.

"Calling for help?" Spencer asked.

"We'll see."

About five minutes later, another kron walked around the corner. It was none other than Moe, from Spencer's goatherd encounter. "Only one?"

"Cousin, not crew. The second guy's trying to keep it quiet. If the bosses never find out, it didn't happen."

There was pointing and arguing, but in a language neither of them spoke. Moe dope-slapped his cousin on the back of the head once, which almost made Spencer laugh out loud. That would've been a great way to get them busted. Some enthusiastic finger pointing made it clear they thought he and Sornik had made a break for the outside, not the inside. Cousin disagreed and pointed at the inner camp. That got him another slap. "They think we're heading out."

Sornik pulled back his camera, then scooted far enough away from the roof edge that they were invisible. There were no buildings any taller, and this was the high point of the camp. Sornik stood. "Which only means one thing."

"We're not heading outside."

"I guess we'll find out whether or not these skalunas have stumbled across anything valuable down there."

A few rounds of back-and-forth revealed that skalunas was the pallun word for clown or idiot. Spencer could only hope that was true.

Smart bad guys were the worst.

Since they were well away from anybody seeing them, Spencer sent his drone up for a quick look around.

"How'd you make them so small?" Sornik asked.

"You think these are small?"

"Yeah. The ones the nodes use are," he used his manipulators to make a circle the size of a beach ball, "about this big usually. The small ones, I mean."

His was about the size of a dragonfly and nearly as quiet. "I figured we'd eventually find a tech that Earth was better at." Drones were a pretty big one. You could sling a lot of shit with a drone. "Let's see what's going on down there."

The inner camp surrounded a huge hill. The pallet towers they'd been following traveled to various entrances at the base of it and then vanished through tunnels. "Things going in, but not out?"

"Maybe they're still setting up? Could be a portal down there too. We'd never see things leave."

"Why aren't you guys doing it that way?"

"It's expensive and slow to set up." He shook himself. "Another sign these fuckers must've been here a lot longer than us."

"How'd they get around the restrictions?" When he and Tapov were rearranging the local network priorities, he'd seen those. They'd turned Teliria into a pretty tight no-go zone.

"You got me, kid. The last time anyone was stupid enough to defy those restrictions, they ended up on a death eater world. Never heard from them again."

"So these guys are either stupid or well connected?"

"Nah, it doesn't work like that around here. Or it shouldn't, anyway. I don't know what's going on. Wait," he said as the drone scanned the inner camp in their shared vision channel. "Go back, say seventy-two narts."

Once more, he silently thanked Mike for setting up a basic unit converter. Otherwise it would've taken some math to convert narts into feet. Spencer slewed the camera the specified distance. "What?"

"Right there. You ever seen these local scavengers; they're about yay big, ugly fuzzy fuckers that are mostly head and teeth?"

Spencer didn't need more of a description than that. "The locals call them tannal. I call them squirreligators. Nasty fucks."

"No doubt. But they've been *busy* nasty fucks. Zoom in there."

Spencer did. They *chewed* a hole in the goddamned fence. "What's that made of, anyway?"

"Steel. It takes bolt cutters to do that job. Trust me, I know."

Spencer could crawl under it. "You gonna be able to fit through that?"

He elongated into an oval that was about three feet wide and at least fifteen feet long. "No problem. We'll wait until dark."

Spencer examined the trail. "And hope they don't mostly come out at night."

Chapter 34
Mike

The world swam into focus. Zoe was shouting at him.

"Mike! You have to move! Right now!"

He was covered in some kind of hardened foam and couldn't see. He turned his head, and it disintegrated. "What happened?"

"We were in an accident. Our passenger's already run away. You need to get out of there!"

As he moved the rest of his body, the stuff around him, which reminded him vaguely of Styrofoam, continued to disintegrate. His threads reintegrated with his realspace brain and memory came flooding in after. Zoe had taken a turn too hard, and they shot off a ramp. The vehicle was on its side. The door was open, facing the sky. "Where are we?" Once his legs were free, he climbed out. The ramp was at least thirty feet above the wreck. "Nice to know they take safety seriously."

"No kidding. We're a couple of miles south-southwest from where we started out."

A small number of various bemians were on the other side of the street, gawking and pointing. He put the vehicle between them and him and then took cover in the undergrowth at the base of the ramp. "How long was I out?"

"A minute, no more than two."

Mike crept along. The arrangement was similar to any large interchange in an Earth city: A surface street ran underneath the ramp, providing plenty of shadows for him to use as cover. They ended up in an industrial part of town, with much older-looking brick warehouses and shop fronts lining a street. Since it was a bemian city, though, the buildings could be a hundred years old or a million. There was no way to tell by looking.

He started randomizing his trail by taking various side streets and alleyways. The traffic was light, and there didn't seem to be as much surveillance in this part of the town. "Can you tell if they've spotted us?"

"I don't see anything in the news feeds," she replied. "Could we be that—"

Nets of an unknown substance enveloped his threads. In realspace, he gasped.

"Mike? What's wrong?"

"They haven't found us here; they've found my real self somehow."

"That's not good."

He turned his perception to his threads. He'd gotten caught in various kinds of thread traps back home. Maybe this one was built the same way. Before, Chinese scientists had worked out a way of drawing Helen into a stand-alone realmspace to better control her. Their plan worked too well, drawing Mike in along with her. The situation here was different. Bemian realmspace effectively networked the entire galaxy. Threaded beings didn't completely inhabit spaces like he and Helen did back home. They instead spread themselves far and wide, leaving threads attached to special anchors that enabled faster-than-light communications. They were, for want of a better expression, nowhere near as crowded as the three large realm spaces were back home. He filled the main space. Helen used to fill the space behind the Great Firewall. She'd since moved to the cloud. A new entity was maturing in her former home.

That was it. Whereas here there were multiple realmspaces interconnected and, they'd found out, extending into dimensions he'd only theorized about. It was not surprising to find that there were constructs designed to restrain threaded entities here.

Bemian threaded entities.

In realspace, law enforcement vehicles turned onto the street.

Zoe saw them before he did. "And that's worse. We need to get out of here. Hang on…Look!"

He was moving his threads around, trying to figure a way out of the trap, so he didn't see what she was talking about right away. He split enough of his perception into realspace to see a classic storm drain, plenty tall enough to slip under. "Sewers?"

"You got a better idea?"

He didn't. His threads felt a distinct gap in the nets that surrounded them. They were interpreter traps, but since he wasn't a bonded interpreter, the space that would've normally been taken up by that connection was shaped wrong. He slid his threads free at the same time he slid his body through the slot.

And damn near fell ten feet. He scrabbled quickly for ladder rungs sunk into the side of the wall. He'd never made studying Earth's various kinds of city drainage a priority, but he was pretty certain this wasn't the norm back home.

"Don't drop us, Sellars." Zoe said as her miniature avatar hovered in front of him. "Neither one of us bounce well at the moment."

Correctly oriented, he dropped the rest of the way and scuttled through a conduit that was almost as tall as he was. "I don't want to know how much it rains around here for them to need this."

"Let's hope it's the dry season. Are you okay?"

He turned his perception to the interstitial and fled further away from the scene of the trap. He set up search patterns now that he knew what to look for. "Fine for now."

"So what's our next move?"

"We should make our way back to the building." He called up a bemian compass app. Naturally, the ones from Earth didn't have a selector for the right planet. This one configured itself automatically.

"Why didn't we take the sewers to begin with?"

"I didn't think we'd need to. Plus I didn't think about it until now. I'm not in the habit of noticing street layout most days." He'd have to change that.

"I don't recall structures like this where that building was."

"Were you looking for them?"

She paused. "It's not something I had to do back home. I'd created it..." She choked to a stop.

Depending on how he looked at it, Mike was the leader of a small team of scattered hackers for *Warhawk*, a leader of a technical team for Sidereal, and, at best, second-in-command of his personal life. He could count on one hand the number of people he felt personally responsible for. Zoe's realm had held thousands. "We'll get them back. I promise."

"How do you know this will lead us back?"

He used the compass app to keep trending north. They weren't going to get there fast, but it didn't seem like they'd cross paths with anyone interested in them either. Slow was fine. "I don't. We'll have to see." The light faded quickly, so he turned his phone flashlight on.

Mike didn't know what modern sewers looked like, here or back home. He'd only ever seen the ones in realm games or old movies. This one was your typical series of concrete tunnels that branched away and got smaller as they got closer to whatever was draining to it. He kept to the main branches, which were big enough to drive a truck through. A central trough ran through the middle carrying water. It was damp but not particularly slimy. There wasn't much of a smell.

"Huh," Zoe said as her avatar stood in front of a virtual readout console. "The gas mix is wrong for raw sewage. That water might be drinkable."

He was thirsty but not *that* thirsty. "I'm not in the mood for trying it. Maybe they do the processing at the source instead of the destination?" Earth's waste treatment was advanced, but the basic layout hadn't changed in more than a century. That could be down to sunk costs and the need to evolve in place. The nodes didn't much care about existing infrastructure. He'd seen that for himself.

Warhawk had its fair share of combat realms set in places like this. He'd never experienced them the way humans did, but he'd seen plenty of DiscordRealm playbacks. It was close enough to what he was now walking through, right down to the flashlight killing his peripheral vision, that he had to stop thinking about what might be hiding around a corner or about to suddenly appear.

"This tunnel is creepy," Zoe said. "I keep expecting one of those *Doom* monsters to jump out at us."

On cue, movement to his right made him slew the flashlight over. He'd had plenty of heart-stopping moments in his life, the time Tonya shoved him out of a helicopter hovering five thousand feet in the air being a choice one, but it was nothing compared to his ape-brain grabbing his spine and giving it a hard shake simply because of a flicker.

He barely choked off a scream when the motion that had to have been a cacodemon turned out to be this planet's equivalent of a rat, right down to its naked tail. "Good Lord." He took a deep breath and cast his light back up from where the creature had come from.

He was greeted by dozens of paired pinpricks of light, that one's brothers and sisters, no doubt. "We'll find a different passage."

He spent the next five minutes glancing behind him. None followed. Whatever they were interested in, it didn't seem to be him.

"It's not like I know a lot…" Zoe paused. "*Anything* about sewers. But these could be millions of years old, right?"

"There's no way to tell short of doing a deep dive into the planet's history. Not all habitable planets are recycled by the La'fan. A lot of them still form naturally and evolve independently until the nodes find them. Why do you ask?"

"If this sewer is even a few hundred years old, it's in miraculous shape. I don't know sewers, but I had a brutalist phase as a sculptor and learned a lot about how concrete works. This tunnel looks practically new, but I know it's *not* new, otherwise the color and texture would be different. Something is cleaning this—"

A huge thump came down the branch behind them, powerful enough to flutter his clothes in the wind it created. It wasn't a firework explosion; it was too deep and soft for that.

Then he heard an engine spool up.

"I think we've found your cleaner," he said, and resumed moving toward their target. He picked up speed and started looking for a side tunnel to zig away from whatever it was that started up behind them. Whooshing sounds came next, with a breeze heavy with humidity. It smelled like a car wash.

Pseudo rats ran past his feet.

"That's a bad sign," Zoe said. "They know these tunnels better than we do."

The drains around them were only large enough to be used by the P rats, which they were doing at speed. Scraping noises started up behind him. Mike turned around.

A machine filled the entire tunnel behind him. The front was a spinning mass of brushes, wands, and steam guns, all working to clean the tunnel of anything that stood in its way. P rats that chose the wrong-sized drain or were too slow to stay ahead of it were mercilessly crushed and then swept up by manipulators designed for the job.

"What's the over-under on that thing having safety interlocks for anything bigger than those rats?" Zoe asked.

It was moving at jogging speed, so Mike set off at a pace that kept him in front of it, at least for now. "Nobody is supposed to be down here, and bemians obey the rules. The odds that the nodes considered an edge case like someone being down here on their own are slim." There had to be a side tunnel soon. They passed enough of them earlier. "Why isn't it branching?"

"We're heading down hill. The next branch will be a big one that'll lead to a river or some other body of water. It won't be a treatment plant. They don't need them."

They arrived at Zoe's big branch a few hundred yards later. It was a good thing too. Their branch stopped there. He was keeping in front of the sweeper chasing them, but it had pushed him out of his comfort zone.

When he jogged into the new passage, an even *bigger* cleaner was almost on top of him.

"Run!"

Mike pivoted and picked up speed. This one was moving faster than the first. It wasn't as terrifying as being chased by an alien bull protecting its herd, but he didn't have a wall to hide behind. This wasn't a creature that would get tired and give up. It was an implacable robot the size of a combine harvester whose sole purpose was to scrape the sewer clean of anything that wasn't supposed to be here.

It went without saying that one of those things was him.

They were still headed downhill even though the map showed them going back toward the city center. The side tunnels were increasing in frequency, but each one was filled with a machine. The P rats must've all either found exits or succumbed, as he saw none here.

"Mike!"

The relatively clean concrete gave him enough friction to stop without falling. Their tunnel had now joined six others, all surrounding a hole too deep for him to see the bottom of. "We found the central drain, I think."

Behind him, the machine didn't slow down.

"There!" Zoe shouted. She highlighted a ladder between where two of the other tunnels joined the drain in front of him to his right. It was a good angle but a *long* way off.

The water that normally stayed in the central trench had now been pushed enough by the closing menace that it was up to his shoe soles. The mist from its sprayers was soaking him through, slicking his hands. The rungs looked like smooth metal. He briefly glanced up and down. At least he wouldn't get squashed by them.

"Do it!" she shouted.

He had enough room to take two steps back. The rat-scooper arm was shooting out as he ran for the edge. He had to make this jump; otherwise Kim would kill him. He *knew* where to plant his feet, how to position his body, exactly when to push off for maximum power. His old host's skills might've failed him in front of alien motion detectors, but concrete was concrete.

He hit the top of his arc, and his stomach went weightless. Everything focused down to the two rungs of the ladder he knew he had to make.

He missed the first one. He and Zoe screamed together.

His arm went through the second one and stopped him with a painful wrench. The tunnels around him exploded as cleaners plowed full steam ahead out of them. Instead of crashing down into the darkness, they all took turns flipping ninety degrees and then headed straight down. About fifty feet later, they rotated and disappeared through more tunnels directly below them.

He scrabbled around until his feet found the rungs below him. Once he was sure he wouldn't fall, he checked out his arm. His jacket sleeve was torn and so was the shirt underneath it. Blood oozed but didn't spurt. The joints were stiff, and his shoulder hurt but wasn't dislocated.

"Are you okay?" Zoe asked.

He activated analgesic apps in his phone. "I'm going to feel that tomorrow, but for now, I'm fine." He looked up and spotted the exit. Bemians of various types walked across a metal grate that covered a large opening. It was about a hundred feet above them. "No, I'm going to feel it now." He made sure he was secure. The rungs were spaced a little too far apart. That distance saved him earlier, but climbing out wasn't going to be any less of a painful journey. "Let's see where we ended up."

Chapter 35
Kim

Facing down all-powerful entities that could crush her with a flick of their finger was, she supposed, a thing for her now. Quispe, Colque, Watchtell, Valsa. She'd given corporate America the middle finger constantly back in the day. That part she wasn't proud of, but it happened. Kim didn't have it in her to back down due to a power imbalance.

That was what people with power expected.

So she regarded Andromeda, in his pseudofascist uniform and overpowering personality and physique, as she would anyone else who trapped her. She wasn't afraid. She was looking for weaknesses.

Valsa, on the other hand, was shaking, and Kim now knew her well enough to recognize it wasn't from anger. "This room was never meant for me."

"No," he rumbled as he stood in front of the force field that blocked the only way out. "But it holds you just the same."

"You are crossing a line you swore to never come near." She rubbed her hands on her arms like she couldn't get warm. "You know what this does to me."

"I'm hoping it will make you less erratic. Nothing else has."

"I am never erratic."

Kim had expected this to be some dramatic confrontation between super villains, not a bickering work couple.

"Then explain this." He motioned at Kim like she was a dog Valsa had brought home.

Valsa turned and now that Kim could see her face, she knew the other woman wasn't scared.

She was terrified.

And then she wasn't. In an instant, it was as if a curtain had gone up, and it was showtime. Her body language transformation was that profound. Politicians were performance artists as much as any actor, and Valsa was a politician of the first order. But that flash of terror was real. Andromeda knew something in this specific situation would set her off. Kim needed to figure that out and file it away.

"I'm trying to recruit her."

Andromeda looked every bit as surprised as Kim felt. "Recruit her?"

"I thought she was dangerous. So do you. That's why we're here right now, isn't it? You knew exactly how I'd react to this and did it to throw me off balance. Well, Wjkowlan," she said defiantly, hands on hips, a master and commander. "Do I look off balance to you?"

He chuckled, seemingly unimpressed. "You've caged your fear. You haven't overcome it." His gaze turned to Kim. Again she felt something, but it didn't trigger any sort of worshipful urges. Quite the opposite. He wasn't terrified the way Valsa was, but Kim could see the worry in his eyes, hear it in his voice. "You're being rather quiet."

The statement was easy to parry. "I didn't want to interrupt."

He regarded her silently. After a moment, he turned back to Valsa. Kim had made more than one person regret ignoring her. It was time to add a notch to that belt.

"Caged fear is still fear, and the longer it's held the stronger it gets." He turned and marched through the door, stride so confident Darth Vader would've taken notes.

Valsa stumbled to a chair and collapsed into it.

"Are you okay?" Kim asked.

The haunted look in her eyes told Kim the actor had left the stage. She looked away and said, "Can you at least keep him from seeing me like this?"

A holo of Seluk Pash, Valsa's threaded companion, appeared. "There is no surveillance. Otherwise I would've released you both by now."

Kim boggled. "He's not watching us?"

Seluk shrugged. "If he was, I would open the door right now. Accessing realms is part of what we do."

She'd forgotten about that. Mike could get into any realm if he had enough time, and bemian realmspaces were much more deeply integrated into all their tech. But, as always, it left a blind spot she could exploit. "That's a mistake he's going to regret."

"I don't get your meaning."

Kim dug around in her pockets and pulled out her multitool. "Giving me back my stuff was your best idea."

That got her a pair of blank looks, Seluk's curious, while Valsa's was clearly miserable.

Kim waved at Seluk's holo. "You take care of her. I got this."

The cell was well furnished, more like a small apartment in fact. The area they were in was a combination living-eating space. There was a hallway that led to a bedroom and a bathroom. The only giveaways were the force fields that made up one wall of each room and the end of the hall. No cameras, but no privacy either. "Will there be any guards? Do we know where we are?"

Seluk's holo appeared beside her. "We're in the undercroft of the palace. He couldn't use a more powerful portal; otherwise we would've sensed it before it routed us here."

She noticed he'd upped the opacity of his holo to the point she couldn't see behind him. It wasn't an accident that he was blocking her view of Valsa in the main room, but Kim chose not to press it. "We're not on the other side of the galaxy then. That's good. Won't anyone notice that she's gone?"

He grimaced. "We can't stay here long enough for that to be a problem."

"And the guards?"

"Nobody is supposed to be down here, so no guards."

She shook her head as she moved into the bedroom. "It's like he wants me to escape."

"I still don't understand what you're talking about. Why is that device you're holding important?"

The walls were decorated with a collection of panels about three by two feet, separated from each other by a few inches of framing. There was a quantum computer nexus behind one of the panels. She could sense it. Kim touched the panel that covered it. "This is a maintenance hatch, isn't it?"

"Yes."

There were lines of potential, and she couldn't remember how to breathe. This forever never secure all times this time no time all at once and never again collapse and now…

As usual, when it'd been a long time since she used her power—and this might be a record for that; she'd been too busy to work much with law enforcement lately—the gunshot that rang out in her head was so loud it masked all outside noise. New rule. Have some locks on hand to play with at all times. Never go for more than a month without cracking them. Certainly never go for more than, what, six months or longer. This, as Spencer once delicately put it, sucked donkey balls. Green ones.

The variations in the ringing in her ears turned out to be Seluk talking. "What did you say?" she asked.

"Are you all right?"

She shook her head. "Fine." In front of her was a now-open access panel. It covered a door big enough to walk through. The pull was recessed and covered by one of their more elaborate locks. "What is this?"

He shrugged. "The palace was once a farm. That's a passageway to another section of the undercroft. It might as well be bricked up. The keys were lost long ago."

She'd encountered this attitude on the ship they'd ended up on their first time in bemian space: doors without keys could only be opened by a node. There were whole storage areas on that ship nobody on the crew had seen the inside of because the previous owners had lost the keys.

Kim opened a small hatch on the side of her multitool. "O ye of little faith."

3-D printing a set of bemian lockpicks had been one of the first things she did after they got home from the last visit. Like everything else, there were only a few designs to cover. Most of the problem was bemians liked big locks, so it was a challenge to design picks that were compact while still being useful. But Kim without lockpicks was like a leopard without her spots. Not the same beast.

The lock put up a bit of a fight, but after a few minutes, it gave up with a satisfying clack. She switched to French to rattle him a bit. *"Et voilà toute l'affaire."*

He blinked at her for a second.

Valsa's voice sounded out from behind him. "How many languages did you know before you left your home world?"

She pulled out a spool of fine wire. With it she could make sure they latched the lock behind them, leaving no evidence. It was fiddly work. "I never thought to count them. My mother was a docent at an amphitheater. People from all over the world came around. Eventually I became the go-to person if someone was having bathroom crisis and nobody understood what they were saying." The wire came undone at the end. She had to start over. "North of fifty." *Come on…concentrate…a little more…* "If you counted the dialects, it might be two or three times that though." The end of the hook settled into a hole almost made for the purpose of resetting it. "Gotcha." She carefully put it all under tension and pushed the door open. "Now we can get out of here."

Kim turned, expecting them to be staring down the passageway.

They were staring at her. "What?"

"The nodes limit the number of languages a planet can have," Valsa said as a strange expression showed on her face. But then the actress reappeared, the curtain came up, and whatever Valsa was thinking had exited, stage left. "Never mind. I think it's time for us to get out of here."

Chapter 36
Tonya

"How can it be missing?" Rachel asked after their fifth fruitless search. "This is the twenty-first century for God's sake. Things don't go missing."

"No," Tonya replied, "but they can be hidden."

They did their experiment on Friday night, so they didn't need to tell anyone at the lab to stay home. Yet. Without the truck, a significant number of people wouldn't have anything to do. Nobody would get laid off, but these weren't the kind of people who liked sitting around. They'd lose enough staff to simple restlessness for it to seriously impact the project.

"How?" Rachel asked. "It's instrumented to the gills. We should be able to track it from the moon. Mars. Your friend cruising around Jupiter should be able to pick it up."

"They must've cut the power." It wouldn't be all that hard. The electrical system had been upgraded, but at heart, it was still a forensics van. They needed to cut power regularly to install new equipment during the build. A few fuses, disconnect the battery packs, and it was a big lump of metal with wheels on the corners.

"It's a *truck,* not a cell phone." She put her head in her hands. "What's our next move?"

To get Kim to hack the quantum fabric was what she wanted to say, but her friend was off galivanting among the stars. Most of her team was unavailable.

Most, but not all.

"I've got an idea, but I'm exhausted. You are too. Let's meet back here at"—she checked the time: 6:48 a.m.—"one p.m. That'll give us both time to get cleaned up and take a nap."

Tonya wasn't sure Rachel's expression changed to disappointment or exhaustion. She allowed herself to acknowledge that she had started to care in ways she hadn't in years. "Any clues about the plan? What's the move?"

"It's not what, it's who. I need to bring Helen in."

"Helen?"

"Mike's sister. My friend Kim's husband. They share some special abilities. She'll only be able to appear via hologram."

"Let me guess… She's not somewhere in this solar system? Won't there be a big lightspeed delay?"

Explaining that lack would require explaining multithreaded life forms, interstitial spaces between realms, interpreters, the transit dimension, and other stuff she couldn't think of off the top of her head. It'd take hours, and she was, in fact, exhausted. Tonya held open the door. "It's complicated."

"I don't doubt it. Catch you at one!"

*

"Yes, you were right to bring me in," Helen said after they told her the whole story. "Being a private detective in the US is almost as useful as being a cop back home."

"That sounds like an interesting story," Rachel said.

"It is, but not now." Tonya cracked her knuckles. "At least we don't have to rely on Kim's abilities. She may have left Rage + the Machine behind, but I've never been comfortable doing something that breaks the law."

Rachel paled and blinked. "Who?"

She remembered too late that Rachel had prior experience with Kim's past. Sweat pricked her skin, cold and clammy. Tonya had left a *lot* of things unsaid.

Rachel turned to Tonya slowly. "Your Kim is *Kimberly Trayne*?"

"I can explain."

Helen had gone silent and still. She was owlish at the best of times but now was in full observer mode. The woman could see a red patch on a door and tell you the color of the rings on the person's hand who last opened it. Tonya hadn't felt this exposed since the last time she screwed up a catheter in front of a baby doc. And that was a *long* time ago.

"I'm waiting," Rachel said, which made her blood run colder than it already was.

"Ah," Helen said. "I know what this is about. I found out about it doing background research on Kim. The records are patchy, but there was enough for me to learn about the Tansing incident."

Tonya had never heard of that before. Helen could search faster than a hundred people, because in a real sense, she was more than a hundred people. "Tansing incident?"

Helen and Rachel exchanged a look. "If I may?" Helen asked. Rachel nodded faintly, pale and still as a statue.

This was so much worse than she thought it would be.

"Rage + the Machine," Helen started out in what Tonya had come to think of as her inspector mode, "staged a raid on RoseTech headquarters. The gang had been operating about a year at that point. They'd gone after RoseTech in general, and David Rose in particular two times previously. Neither attack was particularly successful. On the third try, they targeted the entire executive team. Their personal and corporate identities were stolen, bank accounts emptied, private discussions and photos blasted into the public sphere. The result was complete social cancellation of the entire upper management team."

"They got our money back quickly," Rachel said, looking at a memory Tonya could only imagine. "But she took more than that. She made sure we had nothing left to lose and then made it worse." The look Rachel gave her hurt worse than when a thug knocked all her teeth out in a back alley with a chunk of rebar. "She made sure what The Machine gave back to us was broken."

Helen continued in a far more clinical tone, probably reading what she found as she found it. "A stockholder takeover resulted in complete replacement of the board. David Rose and Rachel Anderson," she said with a tilt of her head, "were the only survivors. Three of the executives were never seen again. One murdered his family before turning the gun on himself." Helen blanched. Nothing made Helen blanch. "Angel Rage wrote a manifesto celebrating the outcomes."

"She's not Kimberly Trayne to me, Tonya," Rachel said in nearly a whisper. "She's Angel Rage."

"I didn't know about Tansing."

"How could you not?"

Tonya had been too busy in school to have paid attention to the details of Kim's career as the New Occupy Wall Street movement's most prolific hacker while it was on. She hadn't known for sure who Kim was until long after the group had been destroyed by a Bolivian drug cartel. The few times she talked about those days she never went into any detail. The truth was hard to choke out, but she'd dealt with too many people who had to be told about a terminal diagnosis for that to stop her. "I should've told you. I'm sorry."

Rachel pulled a handkerchief out of her purse and cleaned her face.

Tonya was at a loss for words. She'd been in life-threatening situations, shot at, slapped around by history, dominated by a galactic intelligence. They were nothing to what this single, silent moment was doing to her insides.

"I don't know when you would've. I only brought it up when we first met, and I was a stranger to you then."

The sun came up over Tonya's soul, immediately to be shoved back below the horizon. That was another case of too far, too fast.

"She's changed?"

That was a truth that would set Tonya free. Only in that moment did she realize her nails were nearly cutting into her hands. The pain backed off both physically and mentally. "Completely. She changed before I met her. One of the reasons I never brought it up is because I can't imagine what she was like in those days. That's not my friend, and it never was."

"I can confirm this," Helen said. "I assumed from the start that Kimberly Trayne was an irredeemable criminal. She has proven me wrong at every turn. If anything, I wish we could somehow shield her from this. In the few times I've spoken to her about it, I've seen that her shame about those days runs deep. But I don't think it will be possible."

"Why?" Rachel asked.

Helen got a canny look. "She'll come home eventually, and you'll still be around. She may not talk about those days, but she hasn't forgotten them."

Rachel's brow furrowed. "What do you mean by…" She glanced at Tonya, and in that moment, she had to pretend to be made of stone. It was harder than it should've been. Rachel blushed, and it grew harder still. "Oh…"

"Indeed," Helen said in a way that made her sound a hell of a lot more certain about the future than Tonya was. "But that is a problem for another day. We need to get your truck back. And I know where to start. It's not at a police lot."

"It's not?" Tonya asked.

"No. And where it is doesn't make any sense. I'll show you."

Chapter 37
Helen

Tonya's obvious romantic interest in a partner who was also obviously invested in her should have been an important observational opportunity. It was only in these extraordinary circumstances that she had to set it aside. She still had to cage Watchtell.

Her first take on his motive for pushing her through the portal was he wanted to remove her ability to block his ambitions. But, after examining the data she and Tom gathered as they researched the various attempts to remove him in turn, she wasn't sure that was the right answer anymore.

This was a deep-black project, so most conventional PI tricks like planting bugs or taking pictures were illegal. Plus they'd get noticed. But Sidereal couldn't control *everything* around it, especially since it was located in a fairly regular suburban business park. Helen hadn't appreciated the genius of Kim's insistence they not be dragged behind the walls of a military base until now.

So while they couldn't get detailed information, they could still observe. Enough time had now passed that it was becoming apparent Watchtell wasn't *acting* like he'd removed an obstacle. The plant hadn't been picked up and moved to Area 51. There was no big turnover in its staff. Shift schedules hadn't changed. The executive team appeared to be intact.

"I get that you can't tell me why you're so interested in him," Tom said as they reviewed the latest datasets. "And he certainly doesn't seem like a nice guy." Watchtell was, after all, a public figure. She never expected Tom to skip his due diligence. "But if you can't turn his friends against him and his security team is on top of things, I'm not sure what the next move should be. Maybe wait until you get back from wherever you are?"

"I'd rather not. I don't like waiting for the other guy to make a move. You've been a tremendous help, but I think I need to take over from here."

He shrugged. "If you think of anything, let me know." His avatar fizzed to virtual dust as he logged off.

Helen had always been playing a double game with Sidereal. Earth and bemians presented an unprecedented danger to each other. That was clear to anyone who knew both sides of the story. But there was a deeper truth that Helen only discovered after close examination of Tonya and Tenor's cache. The only other person who had a hope of doing a deep, fast dive into the massive archive was Mike, and he'd been too busy to try.

Andromeda wasn't only a threat to Earth due to humanity's unique sensitivity to time. He had been a nemesis for as far back as the cache took her. The final disaster that cut the present bemian society off from its past was by far the largest the galaxy had experienced, but it wasn't the only one. Helen had found documentary evidence for at least four previous disasters stretching back some seven *billion* years.

The difference with all these earlier disasters, including the final discontinuity, was that there was a way to detect them. The attacks were from different directions, used different strategies, different tactics, but what kept bringing the galaxy back from the brink was the integrity of the AC network itself. As long as it was reasonably intact, successful recovery was always possible. Reasonable was the crux of the matter. Once the integrity of the network had fallen below a certain percentage, there would be no turning back. The AC network itself would collapse, taking the galaxy with it. They kept track of this with specialized detectors.

But the knowledge of the detectors had been lost in the Undoing. Helen found instructions in the cache on how to reconstruct them. It turned out they built a connectivity map. The documents indicated the map was something Andromeda himself used to track the progress of his attacks. Once she understood the map, she hid it and the tools. The AC network was under attack again. It started before China had united the first time. Without detectors to warn them, the attack had eventually degraded the network well past the point of no return. The next realspace attack Andromeda launched would undoubtedly be no *less* successful than the last. There was a clear progression of destructive capability in the records. But this one really would be the final downfall of galactic civilization. Without the AC network, there would be no recovery.

He had for all intents and purposes already won.

The final collapse of galactic civilization would've passed Earth by if it'd been completed as recently as a few years ago. Before then, neither side had any inkling of the other's existence. Humans were clearly on the cusp of expanding into the galaxy on their own in a matter of centuries. They would've encountered vast ruins, the dead husk of a culture that had stood the test of time in a manner that beggared the imagination.

But that hadn't happened. Andromeda was aware of Earth's existence now, and that humanity was uniquely vulnerable to his abilities. If bemian society were to fall, she knew Earth would share its fate within a generation of the collapse. It might not take that long.

And she didn't know how to stop it. In fact, it looked like there would be no stopping it. Only the unflagging optimism of her adopted American family gave her the slightest hope that there may yet be a way, a golden path that could navigate the galaxy to safety. She held her discoveries back to protect that incredibly fragile spark of hope in her alive. She'd seen firsthand how her family could accomplish unbelievable things because they never acknowledged the concept of the impossible. There was always an alternate path, always a third choice.

Always the unexpected.

Thought of in that way, her dilemma solved itself. If she couldn't oust Watchtell, maybe telling him the truth would turn him into a partner.

A standard meeting realm wouldn't do in these circumstances. Instead she paid for a custom Bbox realm container to be created in the ground-based realmspace. At root it was an empty interstitial space. Mike's threads would eventually find and fill it, but for now it would be a place she could inhabit. She then created a new realm to go inside, a teahouse by a lake modeled exactly like the one she first met Mike, Kim, Tonya, and Spencer in. It was a more civilized place for a proper negotiation. Once her threads were fully secured, she sent Matthew an invitation. It consisted of a place, a time, and a single line from a story Kim had once told her.

Nice try, Matt. Now call me, maybe? -H. Z.

She sent her public identification contract to seal the deal.

She'd set the time of the meeting at fifteen minutes from now. If he arrived early, he'd been expecting it. If he arrived late, she'd caught him off guard. If he didn't show at all? Helen would fall back to plan C. The first task then being to figure out what plan C might be.

He arrived three minutes and twenty seconds late. "My word," he said as his avatar manifested. "A tea room? An interesting choice."

She bowed her holo the precise amount needed to convey that she considered this a meeting of equals. Being an American, he'd miss that. It didn't matter. She was doing it to settle herself. She'd have to run the rest of the meeting as if she were an American. "Please," she indicated a chair. "We have much to discuss."

"Like how you're communicating with me in real time from, I presume, the other side of the galaxy?" His words were sharp, but he did take the indicated seat.

She manifested her holo as sitting opposite him. "That is, by far, the least-most interesting thing you will learn here." A subrealm opened up on the table between them. Stars swirled to form a spiral galaxy. "This is Andromeda."

He cocked his head, pushed off balance and clearly not liking it. "The galaxy?"

"The intelligent entity who two years ago caused an entire small town to lose its collective mind. If we aren't careful, it could do that to the whole world."

She laid it all out. The history. The entity's nature. The unique sensitivity that made humans vulnerable to his influence.

He remained silent for a few moments after she finished. "You expect me to believe this?"

"It's true. All of it."

"It's an interesting story. But only that. Now, it's time for me to ask some questions. First, though, I'd like to show you a technique we used to trap our mutual friend Kim. Briefly. We've improved things a great deal in the meantime."

The interstitial exploded in light. An enormous sensor net had been cast around her. Remote constructs remarkably like the ones she used to interact with realmspace floated near each nexus of scan lines. Instead of looking like threads, though, they looked like humans.

But that wasn't right. They *were* humans, wearing some sort of environment suits, a thing she didn't know was possible. The interstitial was almost as hostile to realspace life as the transit dimension.

They were the size of toys compared to her threads.

"My God," Matthew said in the realm.

She never had anything human ever interact directly with her threads. There was no sense of scale, no way or particular need to figure out how the size of her two halves would compare if they were ever set up next to each other. The need to cover herself in the harsh, brutal light was a surprising bleed-through of her realspace reflexes.

They can see me.

"What are you?" His eyes unfocused. "Taylor, what are the scanners telling you?"

Mike's response would surely be to manifest an avatar and destroy the realm Watchtell stood in. At the very least it would make for a massive distraction. But Watchtell had to have sensors she couldn't see. Observing how she destroyed a realm wouldn't distract them. It would tell them more about her.

She struck at the nodes that were generating the sensor net instead. As soon as she breached the casing, they self-destructed. It burned the tip of each thread that did the work, but it was a small price to pay.

Helen manifested her holo next to him. "You need to get your people out of there, Matthew." Some of the shrapnel had cut their suits, and she could see clear signs of combustion in the breaches. It looked enough like what her manifested avatar did to a realm's air construct to present a new danger. When she fully manifested in a realm, she destroyed it. A human being fully present in the interstitial may fall victim to the same effect.

"You heard her," he said to whoever Taylor was. "Get them out, now!"

Her threads made short work of the net. Once it'd been degraded more than eighty percent, she began withdrawing to a safer place in the orbital cloud.

Watchtell reset the realm to an operating theater, complete with giant screens displaying flowing columns of data, metrics, and readouts. "This is extraordinary."

If Kim had been here, she'd ask for one of the chaos hacks she was so famous for back in the day. If Mike were here, she'd ask him to help her disassemble whatever this was without blowing it up. If Spencer were here, she'd, with difficulty, ask for a rescue hack. Tonya would at least be able to provide insight into what had happened. But none of them were here. It was a peculiar aspect of human relations she'd never fully understood until now. She missed them, very much.

She couldn't tell what Watchtell had figured out, would figure out. This was done. She'd have to find another way. "You should have believed me, Matthew Watchtell."

"Your ridiculous story? What incentive would I have to do that?"

She fled the realm. For the first time, someone who was not a friend, or her father, knew about her true existence. Her arrogance had gotten the best of her once again.

She needed a better idea.

Chapter 38
Maff

Maff's English was good but not *that* good, so it would be difficult to act as an interpreter for Aaron while they put everything back together on the platform. But that turned out to be a nonissue. Now that the crisis was over, she wouldn't need to do that job.

They'd brought their own interpreter.

"You *what*?" Keeping Earth's location a secret was her highest priority. Everyone's highest priority. And yet they hauled a full-blown member of the Interpreter's Guild along with them, the only kind of bemian who, by design, could connect planetary systems together like so many links on a chain.

"Yes," Jholl said as if *she* were the one being an idiot. "The humans are here. We weren't expecting to meet them this soon, but we'd meet them eventually. What do you expect us to do, talk directly to them?"

"They're loyal to the Guild, not us. There's no way we can keep Earth safe now." There might be a guild fleet on the way. Probably *was* on the way. Maff had been stymied by prejudice, ignorance, the sheer difficulty of being a D-ship pilot, then all the frustrations of this escalating situation, but nothing, absolutely nothing compared to the knowledge that she was now directly responsible for the disaster about to unfold.

"To the Guild? Are you crazy? Do you think we hired a petarkan to come along?" Sounds of disappointment and disbelief rippled through the audience that had gathered around Aaron as he finished his work.

"Should I be worried about all this?" he asked.

She didn't know how to reply. Couldn't reply. They worked *so hard* to make this plan, risked so much, and now—

"Chishow! Where is Chishow?" Jholl looked around the crowd. "Where has that voynor wandered off to now?"

"Here, Bashtun."

The crowd parted, revealing a young male pallun about her age. He was so sunk in on himself she couldn't be sure if he was genuinely small or trying to hide in plain sight.

He was pallun.

Aaron cleared his throat. "Mind cluing me in on all this?"

His robes were standard-issue Guild and showed he was of the first rank. They'd at least picked the most junior interpreter available. He'd likely only just retrieved his physical form. There was a characteristic bulge in his suit, accommodating what had to be the deformity that always resulted on leaving their vicina together.

Chishow walked timidly up to Aaron. "Good afternoon, sir," he said in crystal-clear English. "I'm here to be your interpreter."

"Okay that's scary," he said, then put out his hand. "Aaron Levine."

The pallun close enough to see the gesture cringed in horror. High-grav types making sudden movements with their limbs always meant they'd pulled a weapon on an innocent pallun in far too many dramas back home. Chishow didn't flinch at all. He put out a manipulator and gently shook Aaron's hand. If the robes, the deformity, and the language wasn't enough proof of what he was, his effortless comprehension of human custom was the breeze that made the last ripple stop.

"He does not belong to us anymore," Maff said.

"I think I can explain," Chishow replied. "I am a member of the guild. I went through the same training as the rest. I was without a body for decades like all the rest."

As one, the Meronim gasped and made superstitious gestures,

muttered faint prayers. The most bizarre part of an interpreter's life cycle ran directly counter to several ancient beliefs of the pallun religion.

Chishow ignored the noises. "That was what I became. Before that, I was first a pallun. My sense of community, of family, of belonging, never changed."

"A pallun with split loyalties is a stereotype," she replied. "A *dangerous* stereotype."

"It is. My story is complex, and one day I will tell it to you. But it's not important. What *is* important is that, before I set off with these people, I severed all my anchors."

Now the whole group gasped, including her. Interpreters anchored their threads wherever they traveled. The more places they visited, the more valuable they became. It took decades of travel to build a truly useful network of connections. To consciously destroy such a thing was unheard of.

The stakes were too high for her to take him at his word. "You are going to prove that, right now."

"Sorry," Aaron said as he stood beside Chishow. "Could either of you translate?"

She waved Chishow silent. She switched to English. "First, I need to ask favor."

"Sure, I guess?"

"I need go pick person up on Earth. It will not, how do you say, take long." She turned to Chishow but stayed in English for Aaron's benefit. "Aaron has never encountered our society. He knows nothing of interpreters. If you tell truth, is good you are here."

"I'll be able to explain all the things going on around him." He positively glowed. "I'm happy to serve in that capacity."

She learned English the hard way for a year and could still hear her own accent. Chishow had probably picked it up over the interpreter network in less than an hour, and his accent was perfect. It would have been annoying, but she still could not be sure how safe everyone was. "Good. Aaron. You stay here, talk to interpreter. He will explain who and what he is."

"And you're going back for?"

"You have met Mike's sister before, yes?"

*

She'd fit *Palatine* with Earth-style radios mostly to listen in on air traffic control while she studied. Using them to signal Helen from the platform wasn't going to happen. They weren't designed to communicate across that sort of distance. Her Earth-tech phone naturally didn't get a signal out here either. It was much faster to take the ship into low Earth orbit and try from there. She lifted off the platform and, after a brief stint in the transit dimension, was within easy communication range. When Helen answered her call, Maff asked, "Are you free?"

"I am now," she said in a weird tone.

"Is everything all right?"

"Yes, it's nothing you need to worry about. I'm happy to help you with your immigrant situation."

"Did Tonya tell you?"

"No. The ship's arrival set off detectors I've had placed around both gas giants. The rest was a matter of using various telescopes to watch the action while I made sure nobody else could do the same. I take it your presence here means the crisis unfolding currently has been resolved?"

Bemians used interpreters and portals to communicate and travel around the galaxy. Leave it to humans to discover that wireless signals had a speed limit that mattered between planets and stars, and that this effect stretched right through what they called *visible light* and beyond. They even figured out why and how! She looked up how long it would take light to travel from Earth to Jupiter when she first visited the gas giant. It would be at least half an hour for what had happened now to become visible to realspace telescopes on Earth. "Yes, and I have situation." She explained about the interpreter. "I need you to check him out for me."

"I'm not able to board your ship in realspace at this time." The story that followed was one of those incomprehensible nested plots that fascinated most high-grav types. "Do you have anchors?"

She activated the portable anchor network. It wasn't used on big long-haulers like *Last Island* but *Palatine* was a smaller design commonly used to ship cargo between planets. Being able to haul interpreter threads around was a vital communications tool. "Absolutely." It restricted her speed to something only practical for in-system distances, but that was the job at hand. "Let me know when you are ready."

*

"He is telling the truth," Helen said as her holo walked around Chishow. "I can only find evidence of his threads in the realm hosted by the platform. There are no telltales that would indicate external attachments."

They had relocated to the largest meeting room on the platform. At first it was filled with as many pallun as would fit. But the leadership, Jholl on the Meronim side and Keezel for everyone else, shooed the crowd away by pointing out how many jobs needed to be done now that their platform had stabilized.

So Chishow stood in the center of a largely empty room while the holo of an alien he'd never met before examined him like a lab specimen. Maff had never been the focus of Helen's analytical side. She hoped it would stay that way. Watching it happen was enough to take her back to her primary school days. She'd been hauled in front of the class and interrogated about homework she hadn't read.

Chishow was scared, but for a different reason. "What *are* you?"

"In this context and for this job, I am an interpreter."

"But...you're *not,*" he said. Maff had grown up around various kinds of interpreters all her life. Everyone did. They could be arrogant, confusing, comforting, sometimes occasionally admirable. She had never seen one frightened before. Until now. "You *can't* be one."

"I assure you I am."

The holo of a female pallun appeared with Helen. "She's right, Chishow. I don't know how this is happening, but she's as threaded as I am." This was Danlaw, Chishow's threaded companion.

Maff had been around Mike and Kim long enough to have become comfortable with how unique Earth's interpreters were, but it had taken some time. "Earth interpreters have only now emerged. They do not combine like normal ones."

"Does it matter?" Aaron asked. They'd been holding the conversation in English while Chishow translated for the other two pallun. Aaron's tone was strained. She hadn't heard that until now.

"What's wrong?" she asked.

Helen turned. "He's got problems. Big ones."

Aaron walked to the edge of the room where they pushed all the high-grav biped chairs and picked one about his size. He sat down. "I don't know how to report this. If FBI agents travel abroad, we have to report it. This definitely counts as abroad. I'm supposed to detail what's happened and file it." He ran his hands over the short red fur on his head. "They'll send me up for psych evaluation immediately."

"Or you will disappear," Helen said grimly. "The existence of this particular colony is unknown, but many powerful people are now quite aware of bemian civilization. A fully detailed report will make it obvious that you've been in contact with them. They won't kill you or threaten your family. You will instead be made a part of a secret project and will never walk free again in your lifetime."

"I'm not sure I should." He looked around at the group. "At least not until this gets settled. And that will take longer than I'll live."

"No," Helen said. "It won't come to that. I have my own issues with that secret group. Once I've made an adjustment, we can come to a more amicable arrangement." She turned to Chishow, who'd been staring at Helen the entire time like she'd been a na'thala tentacle slowly extending its claw out of the clouds. "And you're coming with us to help."

Chapter 39
Mike

He pegged his phone's analgesic abilities halfway up the drain ladder. The grates that made up the surface of the sidewalk were still far overhead. The rest of the climb was an exercise in pain management. He hadn't dislocated his shoulder or broken his arm, but he only missed either injury by a few inches. So it could've been worse.

The grating that formed the surface of the sidewalk people were going back and forth on, completely oblivious to his presence, seemed as far away as when he started the climb.

Pain management and suffering were two different things. The former was a natural consequence of what had happened. The latter was how he reacted to it. He couldn't control the former. The latter?

"God," Zoe said. "Do you *have* to chant out loud?"

People suffered because they *wanted*. Desired. The route to eliminating that suffering was through dealing with his wants and desires. He did that via the Nobel Eight Fold Path, in this particular case Right View, Right Resolve, Right Effort, Right Mindfulness, and Right Concentration.

Practicing the Path was not easy. When he first started out, he couldn't sit still and didn't understand why he should. But over the years, he slowly mastered the basics. He was no Boddhisatva. In many ways he wasn't much more than a low-level monk. But he was skilled enough to turn this ordeal into a meditation.

She grumbled after he started the chant again. "Don't you at least know some different ones?"

His change in perspective from *the thing he wanted to avoid* to *the thing he had to manage* allowed him to compartmentalize the pain, analyze it to spread the load to other parts of his body, which ensured he didn't increase his injury any more than he absolutely had to.

He switched to the Tisarana chant to keep Zoe quiet. He had enough distractions as it was.

The overall effect was to deplete his reserves much faster than he expected. He'd only been on the planet for a few hours, but already he wanted to find a bed and crawl in it. For now, there was no rush. He took his time, made his chants, and kept going.

Finally he got to the top rung of the ladder. There was a ledge on the other side big enough for him to climb up on. Better still, there were guardrails here. People were expected to be there in some capacity, which should keep him safe from the cleaners. He finished his climb and lay flat on the floor, staring up at the grating and the people walking on it.

"Good job, Sellars! Now up and at 'em!"

He stopped chanting so as not to attract attention. Instead he let the joy of not climbing press him down into the concrete. "Give me a minute, okay?"

"Take your time."

She sounded preoccupied. Which was dangerous. He tried to sit up, but his realspace body could only manage to stir a little. "What are you up to?"

"Me? Now that I'm in range of the wireless networks I'm doing some scouting."

He jumped into the local realmspace, found her, and manifested a holo. She'd set up a tiny office realm, not much bigger than a closet, and filled it with constructs instrumented to do exactly that: scout.

His holo hovered behind her. She chuckled and didn't turn around. "I figured that would bring you running." She adjusted the scanners. "I don't need a chaperone anymore."

And that was exactly what he'd done. To him, Zoe was still the young, impulsive, unpredictable artist who'd led them on a merry chase around China. The years had changed her, the responsibility had aged her. The loss of her family was a weight he could see. "Sorry."

She shrugged. "It's fine. During all that excitement, I think I turned into the Zoe you remember, simply by being around you. I know how hurt you were by that jump. Why don't you sack out, let the sa'dst do its work, and I'll figure out where you can exit without drawing a lot of attention."

He'd forgotten all about that. The bemian nanotech health system, suitably patched with a special filter he'd designed back home, was already making good on the damage. Now that he wasn't continually reinjuring himself, at any rate. But… "How did you learn about sa'dst?" Zoe had left long before they'd encountered bemians.

"It was either do research or listen to yet another one of your chants on the climb up. And it was a *long* climb. I'm done pretending to be a teenager. Let me be the adult for a while."

The concrete was the opposite of comfortable, but he'd also forgotten what sa'dst did once it determined its host was in a safe place. The drowsiness wasn't a wave so much as a hammer.

*

"Mike? Hey, Mike!"

Like the first time sa'dst had put him under, Mike felt no sense of passed time. He closed his eyes, and the next second, Zoe was shouting at him to wake up. But time had passed. His sleeve was still torn and messed up with now-dried blood, but the arm and shoulder were good as new. Sometimes cultures that got so much wrong could get a few things right.

Briefly.

"You up?"

He opened his eyes to a miniature Zoe avatar standing in his shared vision channel. "Yup. Good call on the rest. How long was I out?"

"Twelve hours." Her avatar enlarged to full size as he stood. "I bet you're hungry."

He was. "Starving. Nature break first." Standing in a sewer drain gave him his pick of targets. Her avatar followed him as he turned away. "If you wouldn't mind?"

"Gah. Humans. I forgot how disgusting they have to be to survive. Garbage collectors are a lot neater."

He picked a spot out of sight of the grates above. "You don't have one of those anymore." Edmund stopped talking about things like memory stores and garbage collectors not long after he became fully conscious. On examining him, Mike found Edmund's were gone.

"True. Force of habit I guess."

He finished and made a mental note to find a sterilization station before he touched anything. "I take it you've found a way out that's near where I can grab some—what time is it anyway?"

She chuckled. "What, your alien phone can't tell you?"

"There is that." He checked. After all the conversions were done, it was the local equivalent of about eight p.m. outside. "Darkness should make things easier."

"Anyway, yes, I've located their equivalent of a food truck pavilion. It's near an exit a couple hundred yards from here." An arrow pointed away from their spot. "Follow this."

*

Some threads he'd assigned to work on an idea he'd had while climbing the ladder out of hell returned with an interesting finding. Zoe's construct, the thing that held all her people in storage that'd vanished when her realm had been destroyed, had a resonance he hadn't predicted. "We may be able to get at your construct…well, a version of your construct…using a different technique."

"A version of my construct?"

"It would be identical in any way that mattered. It would come from a different place."

She narrowed her eyes. "Define different."

Elysium itself provided the first clue. "Realmspaces have a real component. It emerges from the quantum resonances they create as they model their own reality. But it's not a presence we'll find here. It's in a dimension orthogonal to ours, and maybe more than one. Tonya's time theory is also wrapped up in it, but those implications aren't as clear to me."

"What does that mean?" Zoe asked as she peered up uncomprehendingly at the equations he'd been writing out as he spoke.

"There's a good chance that, somewhere, there's a version of your cache that didn't end up lost in the interstitial. With some help, we could find that one instead."

Zoe shook her head. "I'd rather have my original, thanks."

He shrugged and filed away the idea for another time. "So what have you found?" he asked as he munched on a kind of sandwich that was near enough to a burger as he and Kim had ever found. They were shaped more like a sub and the bread analog was pale green, but they were tasty and seemed to be available everywhere in the galaxy. Zoe's avatar sat in an empty chair opposite him on the circular patio set that lacked only an umbrella to fit right in back home.

A still picture of the hallway appeared in the shared vision channel. Circles followed, drawn around what he thought were alarm sensors. "Those aren't motion detectors, that's why they got you. They're infrared."

"I know what those look like, though."

"You know what they look like on Earth. And I doubt you could sneak past one even then."

He shared a basic medical feed with her. "Watch and learn." Mike entered a peculiar meditation he'd stumbled on one cold night when he'd forgotten to wear a jacket. It helped him warm up. Tonya touched his arm to get his attention—they were all out with telescope apps trying to find various bemian systems—and freaked out. She said it was like touching a corpse. His former host had learned how to, somehow, close off the capillaries in his skin. This provided a kind of insulation but was also handy in substantially lowering his IR signature.

One of her eyebrows shot up. "That's interesting. Why didn't you do it before?"

"Like I said, they didn't look like IR sensors." It wasn't the first time he'd been burned by bad assumptions. "Stupid mistake on my part." He broke off some threads to do a quick study on what the various anti-intruder sensor types were common in this system.

"Okay. The construct is still in the realmspaces it hosts, so that'll make getting back into the building simpler. Fun fact: it has the same *realmspace of things* philosophy as we do back home."

This was an extension of an earlier *Internet of Things* concept popular in the first quarter of the twenty-first century. Devices that wouldn't normally be a candidate for a realm connection were connected anyway so they could be more conveniently accessed and manipulated. "Kim won't let me install any of those at our house. Too insecure."

"She's not wrong. Get this: I found a toilet on the other side of the air gap. Someone forgot to turn off its wireless connectivity."

A toilet with its own realmspace had become a thing back home, and was also one here as well. It would be connected to the air-gapped network via a hard line. But someone had made a mistake and not turned off its wireless connection.

"Are you sure it's not a honeypot?" Putting up vulnerabilities and then trapping people with them was one of the older tricks in the book.

"That's what I've got you for. I don't think it'll be an issue, though. There are clusters of them that seem to plot well with office restrooms." This sort of lackadaisical approach to pretty much everything technical in bemian space was common. A big data report landed in his queue. "Double-check my results, will ya? We need to get started."

He split his threads and cross-checked what Zoe had discovered. The free spirit had learned how to be careful and methodical. He could use some lessons from her about how that worked. Leaping before looking was no longer as fun for him now that the stakes were so high. "You're right. It's not a trap."

He moved toward the spot she mapped out, a different ground-level entrance of the same building he tried to get into the day before. Ahead of him, a door clacked open, and the entire area was cast into darkness. "We have a building to explore."

Chapter 40
Kim

When they said *undercroft*, it gave Kim images of vaulted ceilings under cathedrals and castles. Which implied a space larger than her mom's basement.

Kim hadn't counted on it being *this* much larger.

"How big of a farm was it before you settled here?"

"The part we were in was a farmhouse. The rest has been added on over time."

Her phone's dead reckoning app claimed they'd already gone several hundred yards through various spaces small and large. "How much time?"

"The Guild claimed this site in the 249th era, I think sometime during the twenty-fifth decaran configuration."

For humans, a thousand years was a very long time. For bemians, it was barely a blip. This naturally led them to develop dating systems that would let them shorthand truly massive spans of time. Bemians counted up from the time of the Refounding of their culture, an event that correlated too neatly to Earth's Permian extinction to be a coincidence. But they didn't use a unit that was close to Earth's year. That would make the number of years too big. Instead, they chose to designate million-year intervals as eras. The years themselves were not determined by the orbit of one planet around an ordinary star in a deserted corner of the galaxy. Instead, they used discrete configurations of the orbits of various stars that circled the supermassive black hole at the center of the galaxy.

Which was about as concise a summary as she could make of a weeks-long conversation with Mike as he figured out how it worked. They were currently in the 251st era, so the exact year, which she could figure out by looking up the configuration Valsa referenced, was a bit irrelevant. The interpreters had settled on this site when Australopithecines were the cool new tool-using bipedal ape hiking around eastern Africa. Two and half million years, give or take.

The farm had been around *before* that.

Which made for a perfect segue to a question she and Mike had been debating ever since they worked all this out. "How do you deal with continental drift?"

"We don't. Nobody builds in areas where that would be a problem."

Earth's cities were situated next to natural resources or geographical features that made things like transport convenient. It's why they endured in spite of the various natural and man-made disasters that befell them over the centuries. But, in a galaxy where it was possible to walk to a different sector of a galaxy, these considerations weren't a factor.

"Is this an issue on your planet?" Valsa asked.

"Not exactly." The oldest structures on Earth were nowhere near old enough to be affected by continents moving around, a technicality Valsa didn't need to know at the moment.

"I would think not. The Guild usually arrives on a planet a few centuries after the nodes have been doing their work. By then things have normalized, but we almost always see signs of pre-uplift civilization. Locating cities on sites with environmental dangers means they're always ruined by then. But, since we seem to have missed your planet, I guess anything is possible."

"You still haven't asked the nodes why the traditional invitation wasn't sent?" That was the cover story Valsa and Winur had made up to explain why they didn't know where she was from. Bemians were trained from birth to not question the world around them. In case it wasn't enough, it seemed they were also taught to come up with explanations that allowed the occasional inconsistency or contradiction to not disturb their views and beliefs.

Phrased that way, it was an uncomfortable new parallel between here and back home.

Valsa nodded with a slight smile. "All in good time."

Kim knew exactly why she hadn't asked. Whatever was going on with Andromeda was a crisis, but the conflict with the AC network was a chronic condition that'd been going on since the Refounding. Not notifying the Guild of an eligible planet was a major, perhaps unprecedented, violation of protocol. That was a useful arrow to have in her quiver once she could make it a priority.

Valsa turned slightly as they walked. "Do all your interpreters have such a broad range of language skills?"

When Valsa thought Kim was an extremely weird but otherwise still recognizable interpreter, she was the epitome of charm and grace. Now that Kim had screwed up and revealed that human interpreters might be unique, her questions...her whole attitude...had sharpened. Kim had inadvertently taken herself out of the list of things Valsa knew how to control and onto the list of things she didn't. Kim already knew Valsa reacted badly to things she couldn't control.

Trying to keep secrets would only make it worse. "Yes, at least the ones I know about."

"Without a guild, and without proper joining, I'm amazed any of you can survive."

"We've come up with our own school." It had an enrollment of exactly one, Will, her biological son. She'd need to send his mother Emily a new set of lesson plans soon.

"How novel. At least until we sort out the situation and bring you all in from the cold, of course."

Kim didn't miss a beat. "Of course." *Over my dead body.* They crossed yet another massive but otherwise empty, unimaginably ancient, basement room. "How long have you been first councilor?"

"Not long enough, unfortunately."

Winur's holo appeared in their shared vision channel. "We're the first of our kind to take the chair, and she's the first woman in nearly an era."

More than a million years. There were glass ceilings, and then there were glass ceilings. "I thought the nodes eliminated that kind of discrimination."

"The interpreters have always stood apart from the network. This has kept us powerful, but it has also allowed some bad habits to remain. To return to the galaxy from the threads as a female would normally restrict that interpreter's opportunities to attain the higher echelons of the organization."

"It was enough to make me not want to come back out," Valsa said gravely. "The majority of the lost, the ones who do not return from the threads, go in as female. If interpreters did not emerge naturally from the general population, we would've gone extinct long before the Refounding."

Now that she thought about it, she hadn't seen all that many female interpreters. Valsa wasn't the only one, but, if what Kim had seen was a real cross section of the guild, they were outnumbered by about three to one.

"Has a prejudice against women attaining power been perpetuated in your home-grown school?" Valsa asked.

"No, not at all."

Now it was Valsa's turn to smile slyly. "My, that will greatly upset a large segment of our nobles."

"Let me guess, the men all claim it's natural that things turn out this way?" Tonya had already observed a specific sort of racism with the pallun. It shouldn't be surprising for Kim to find a specific sort of sexism in the galaxy as well. But it was.

"And they will be shocked, shocked I tell you, when they find out it's not." Valsa gave her a sideways look. "The network's risk at keeping your kind from us may prove damaging to them in many different ways."

They crossed a hallway into another room. Valsa took a deep breath and shook her shoulders. "At last."

"Have we crossed the front lines?"

"The precinct of my personal quarters. It's as safe a place as anyone can have on the grounds."

"But we walked to it. I didn't notice any locks."

Valsa turned and touched the wall behind her. A hidden door slid smoothly across, blocking the passage they'd walked through. "We have one now."

"What's our next move?"

A force field snapped across the other doorway as Valsa walked through. There were no other exits to the room. "We continue our chat with Wjkowlan." He loomed up behind Valsa, who stepped aside a bit to give him room. "You were right. She's much more dangerous than I understood. How did you know?"

"This isn't the first human I've examined." Now it was his turn to stand aside, because another person had entered the room. "This one has been most informative." He faced Kim. "I think you have met?"

Indeed they had. Kim had last seen her going through the very first portal in the vent room of Yellowstone's geothermal power plant. The plant she was in charge of, and who had plotted to use it to destroy civilization on Earth.

"Hello, Anna."

Chapter 41
Helen

Mao Zedong famously wrote that a guerilla must move amongst the people as a fish swims in the sea. Helen wondered what he'd make of a human moving among people who evolved from fish. Helping Tonya and then Maff was a good distraction from her debacle with Watchtell, but she needed a better idea to deal with him. Fortunately, she figured out what plan C looked like.

She needed to take getting back home seriously. Unlike almost every other human in the galaxy, she had a secret advantage: like Mike, Helen innately knew where Earth was that directly translated into coordinates that a portal or ship could use. While not as widespread as Mike, Helen also now had threads hosted on the various planets she'd visited. Not enough to be detectable or, to be honest, even all that useful in the way regular interpreters did business, but it still allowed her to easily find Earth's position at any point in space *and* time.

With proper positioning, she could travel through the empty bubble of space-time that surrounded Earth much more quickly than she had in the past using Maff's ship. On that first expedition they were constrained by the location of the worlds they needed to visit, which were inconveniently placed for travel using a D-ship from Earth. This wasn't an issue for Helen now. She was in the wrong sector of the galaxy to do it from here, but she didn't have to stay in this sector.

It made her a little sad to have spent so much time being a housebound hermit on an exoplanet. She was the only human to visit it. It would've been nice to see the sites instead of staying cooped up in her hostel getting three meals a day delivered by the bemian version of UberDash.

So she tried to cram as much sightseeing as she could in the route between the hostel and the portal station. The natives were naturally the majority population of this world, but there were smatterings of other bemians here and there as she passed. They were all still variations on basic themes—even their biologies were monotonous—but there was the occasional novelty. The crystalline humanoid angel she spotted sitting outside a local café was particularly striking with its red and gold coloration. Deep in her Chinese heart she wanted to get at least a nail clipping from a creature who, from a certain cultural point of view, was made of pure luck.

A Guild transport passed her and sightseeing turned into surveillance. The sidewalks in this area of downtown were crowded enough that she could tell she hadn't been spotted. When the transport turned down the same street her terminal was located on, she crossed to the opposite side to get a better view. It stopped in front of the portal terminal. Two interpreters got out, two got in.

Changing the guard. Great.

The interstitial was also quite lively, with knots of threads regularly patrolling the areas near the terminal. Now that she knew to look for them, they were relatively easy to avoid, but if she got close to a terminal, there would be no place to hide.

One of the new guards caught her eye. He shouted something unintelligible and motioned toward his partner. A bus pulled up between her and them, and she was well out of reach by the time they got to her corner. The Guild might have a presence here, but it apparently didn't extend to controlling the transport system. She consulted the map for an alternative strategy, and one was suggested almost immediately. Even though the Guild seemed to be monitoring portal stations, she doubted they had the resources to monitor the actual ports. D-ships could go anywhere and usually did, with ports scattered all over major cities like so many parking garages. Some of them *were* parking garages.

Watchtell wasn't done with her either.

"We should meet..."

"You must contact me..."

"The matter at hand is urgent..."

Helen had been a quite diligent student when Kim had offered training in communications security. Which was a nice way of saying that after a few shots of ouzo at one of her mother's lunch parties, Kim liked to tell stories. Most of them were very funny, but all contained vital clues as to how she'd stayed underground, undetected, for so long.

So Helen emphatically did *not* set up a chat, access a ZoomTeams realm, or attempt any other sort of direct communication. Her replies were short, to the point, and went through as many different routes as her threads could manage. Helen had a *lot* of threads to use. The replies were the essence of simplicity.

"No."

This was a word Matthew Watchtell was not used to hearing and refused to understand. He was almost certainly also searching for her, so she had to shore up her defenses, keep him at bay, while simultaneously trying to escape Fish World.

She once thought attending three separate Politburo meetings was a complex juggling effort. Compared to this cross-galactic effort, it was child's play.

Despite D-ship ports being much more common and decentralized, the first three she went to had interpreter presences. She'd also started picking up tails. They hadn't counted on her having police *and* private investigator training in this skill, otherwise they would've had not only more people, but more *professional* people to do the work. Each of the three so far was easy to pick out and easy to lose. But the interpreters were actively looking for her. The feeling of a net closing in around her was almost physical.

The first port she found without evidence of interpreters was a disappointment. They weren't there because neither were any D-ships. This was true of the next two as well. Her idea to use the ports instead of the portals was looking like it might be a dead end.

When she spotted yet another person tailing her, Helen knew she had to go to plan D.

The first part of her life, being a cop was all she knew or wanted to be. It had given her a low opinion of criminals. Back then she also had the luxury of sticking to her principles, rigid and naïve though they were. Now she was friends with gangsters. While it was true they weren't the kind of gangster she'd expected to end up encountering, the fact that she was associating with them at all set off a twinge inside her. The young cop she had once been was still in the back of her mind, scolding her the whole time.

But that was her younger self, which was still getting her in trouble. If she'd been less arrogant and naïve in the present, she wouldn't be in this mess. Succumbing to ideals was a bad look on a Chinese person, in any case. Hardheaded practicality was a feature of her culture Helen was growing to admire now that she had to live her own life. Her younger version didn't have to pay bills or get herself out of jams.

She placed a call to the first exoplanet she'd ever anchored threads to. Toraz, the first leader of an organized crime family she'd ever met, picked up immediately. "Helen, it has been a long time. To what do I owe the pleasure?"

One of the main things smugglers did was move things around. She needed to be moved around. "I need transport off a planet, but all the portal hubs are guarded. The ports are either being watched or empty. Do you have any presence here?" She sent him her exact location. It made sense that bemian addresses would include extra lines for planet, system, and quadrant. But she wasn't sure she'd ever get used to it.

"Let me check." After a momentary pause, he said, "Go here." A new address landed in her queue. It was on the far side of town, almost as if it'd been chosen for its isolation. Which was probably the truth. "That's Kaddee. You've met him before."

"I have?"

"He was one of the mechanics on the pit crew. Little guy, fuzzy, kind of crazy, shouted a lot?"

Helen did indeed know him. "The one who played drums when he got bored?" Bemian drums, but recognizable all the same.

"That's why he was set up out back in his own shed. Maff and Tonya never saw him."

She'd only seen him once. She was scouting the garage area to understand its layout and followed the racket. "Thank you, Toraz." She maneuvered toward the nearest bus stop.

"Consider it payback for saving Sornik's sorry wings. He told me that story, you know."

Two of his men never made it back, another consequence of her being wrong at the worst possible time. "I wish I could've saved them all."

He grunted. "Yeah, that's like asking the storm to unblow. Not gonna happen. Anyway, you need anything else, you let me know." He ended the call.

She was relieved that he considered this favor a payback. Working with gangsters was one thing. Being in their debt was on a different level. She appreciated the offer but would work diligently to see that she never needed another favor from Toraz again.

The impression of isolation was stronger after she arrived at the address. But it was also familiar. The site was much like the warehouse district that contained one of Toraz's smuggling hubs: worn, industrial, with large, low buildings spreading out into the distance. She pinged the number Toraz gave her.

"What! What? Who...oh, hi, lady!" Comically large eyes framed by long, bright-orange fur topping a mouth that stretched from ear to ear was all she could see. "Toraz say you on way! Say you need ship! I have ship!" The door slid open. "Come, see ship!"

The door opened onto a long dark hallway. There was a light hanging from a high ceiling at the other end. When Helen stepped into it, Kaddee waved at her from across the room, under his own light, high on a balcony. "Hi, lady! See ship!" With manic energy that belied his bandy legs and arms, he threw a large switch up. It made a loud clack as it connected.

She stepped back at what it revealed. Helen thought the worst-looking bemian ship she'd ever seen was the one Mike and Kim came home in. Maff hadn't gotten a chance to start repairs, so it was still a beat-up mess.

This one made pre-repair *Palatine* look like it was fresh off a showroom floor.

Chapter 42
Tonya

"You have impressive friends," Rachel said as they cased the place the truck was *actually* in.

"You have no idea."

It took Helen all of fifteen minutes to track Iyaan down. He'd been taken to a business park, the kind that had shops with garages even though few did actual automotive work. Of the two-dozen store fronts, about half were auto repair related. The rest were music instrument shops, a pot dispensary, and a couple of fitness clubs. Iyaan wasn't in a shop advertising auto services, but rather the pot dispensary.

The question of what he was doing there was still a bit of a mystery. Helen was in the process of tracing things but had to sign off so she could figure out a way to get back home. Watchtell struck again, somehow. The truck that should've taken it to the police impound took it here instead. That was all they knew.

Helen hadn't fully tracked down the real owner. But they didn't need to know who ultimately owned the business. They only needed to get Iyaan out of a place that wasn't what it claimed to be, owned by people with enough resources to hide from a person who could chase down thousands of leads at once.

Easy peasy.

It would be nice to report the theft and Iyaan's location to the police. That was what she would've done had any of his tracking systems remained active. But now either they wouldn't believe her, or they'd get distracted by how Tonya got the information. So it was time to do a little smash-and-grab of their own.

They used microdrones to scout it out, then drove past it. It was opposite a conventional shopping center with a Target.

"Do we go into that dispensary like normal people?" she asked as they sat in a Red Robin restaurant also across the street, eating supper.

"I don't think so. It would be pretty easy to connect us to Iyaan, and somebody this cagey is bound to have a high-class surveillance set up." They'd borrowed her cousin's tow truck on the off chance they could steal the truck back. They did the standard hat-and-sunglasses disguise to beat getting spotted via facial recognition. Kim's paranoia paid off yet again. It was the weirdest kind of contact high, using those skills.

"That's fine," Rachel said with a smile. "You're not the only one with friends."

Half an hour later, they had a complete scan of the public areas of the dispensary courtesy of Patrick, a high school buddy of hers from back in the day. Rachel's counter to Tonya's Kim-induced paranoia about showing their faces in a place that held an item that could be associated with them. They couldn't walk in, but he could.

"The edible selection was pretty good," he said later as they sat outside the restaurant. "You guys want some?"

He was someone who knew her long before she was a tech billionaire. It was informative to see their easy dynamic. On the one hand, it was encouraging to see the similarities of their relationship and the one Tonya was building with her. There was none of the slightly pushed-away manor Rachel used with even well-known employees or other colleagues Tonya had met building Iyaan. On the other hand, there were a lot of inside jokes and casual flirting that set her teeth on edge. His wedding ring helped more than it should've.

Tonya stomped down on that train of thought, hard. She was here to break their truck out of a mystery impound, not play the jealous new friend.

"Maybe later. Thanks, man. I owe you one."

"And you're still not going to tell me what this is about?"

She laughed. "We built a time machine that took us back to this crazy event called January 6th that everyone's forgotten about. It got towed because we parked it illegally, and for some reason, it's stashed inside that dispensary."

He rolled his eyes. "Fine, don't tell me," he said as he stood. "You still on for this Saturday?"

"Absolutely." They hugged each other briefly, and he left.

"What happens on Saturday?"

"A bunch of high school friends of mine have been racing in a *Mario Kart* realm since we were in junior high. It helps us stay in touch." She looked Tonya in the eye, and it took more effort than she wanted to not react. "You should join us."

It was a harmless realm based on an old video game. It was not Rachel introducing Tonya to her old friends. It was not the same thing as being introduced to her parents, and it was silly for that connection to be made in the back of her mind. They had a job to do, and Tonya needed to get her head in the game.

Rachel's gaze went soft, and she cocked her head, which somehow made it all worse. "Are you okay?"

Tonya cleared her throat and locked it down. It was a simple thing, and she was overcomplicating it. This had to stop. "I'm fine." *Clear your throat again, dear, that voice is way too husky.* "I'm totally down for Saturday, but we have to figure this out first."

Rachel looked up suddenly. "I've got some resources for that, too." A Fed/UPS cargo cart reeled down in front of them, suspended from its drone high above. It plonked several medium-sized packages on the picnic table they'd turned into an improvised alfresco HQ, and then vanished into its mothership. "I've always wanted an excuse to use this stuff."

She must've done some online ordering while they were shopping. "Not all of this is from Amazon."

"I know. We'll need to wait until nightfall before I can show you the rest."

It was still early afternoon, so they left the boxes in a locked storage bin on her cousin's tow truck and walked the shops until they closed down. What should've been a bit of a boring strain turned out to be a fun little mental montage of comparing ridiculous things they found at World Market, picking out exactly the wrong shoes at DSW, seeing if any of the prices in the Magnolia stereo showroom would make Rachel blanch—that took a pair of speakers with a *high* six-figure price tag, which Tonya didn't know was a thing until that moment—and pretending they were teenagers skipping school. Tonya let the slightest bit of ease settle inside her. Carefully roped off by a wall of nervousness.

Christmas arrived after dark, when they got to open the boxes. "Is all of this legal?" Tonya asked.

"You're friends with one of the most famous thieves of all time, and you're worried about legality?"

It was one thing to accept and understand that Kim had done terrible things in the past. It was another to throw shade at a friend who had definitively, sometimes violently, moved on. "You better believe it. Besides, she's only famous to you and me. Ask ten people in any of these stores about her, and you'll get ten blank looks. Every time."

It felt good to push back, to set a limit, draw a line. Things were happening much faster than Tonya liked, and if defending a friend was what it took to remind her of that, more's the better.

After a heartbeat, Rachel blinked and turned away. "Fair enough. Yes, it's all legal. At least in the sense that none of it is explicitly *il*-legal." She cracked a half smile. "You said Kim was a locksmith now, right? This," she pulled out a multitool that Tonya recognized. It was usually hanging from Kim's hip during work hours, "is a tool Kim can have. She's got a license for it. And the friend I had buy it for me had a license for it too. She's already filed a lost package report, so if we lose it or it's taken from us, she's covered." Rachel faced Tonya and locked eyes with her. "That legal enough for you?"

Kim was on the other side of the galaxy doing who knew what, and yet she'd somehow ended up being in the center of what Tonya now realized was her first fight with Rachel. Which was so typical of Kim. She was the recluse who, when she felt safe enough, never shied away from a spotlight. The absurdity cracked her up.

"What?"

She almost reached out to grab Rachel's hand in that moment. She would have if this had been anyone else. Tonya breathed deep. "It's nothing. So, what *do* we have here?"

They had themselves a reasonably complete Jane Bond kit. For two. One of her grandmother's favorite sayings was that if a problem could be solved with money, then it wasn't a problem. Rachel should be that saying's poster child. Various vision enhancement phone extensions, parabolic microphones she could stick on her fingernail, spectrographic analyzers for sound, air, and liquids. Then there were the rappelling gizmos and grapple guns. Then she unpacked a climbing harness. Tonya let out a little squeak of glee.

"That's a cute noise," Rachel said with a smile.

Tonya was too excited to make the moment awkward. "Have you ever used these? They're so cool!" It'd been two years, but she remembered exactly how to put it on. "One day I'll tell you how I used one of these to climb from one end of the Yellowstone project to the other."

Rachel's mouth fell open. She blinked. "Of course you were involved with that. Is there any major world event in the past, I don't know, ten years or so that you or your friends *haven't* been involved in?"

Tonya considered. "More like the past five." It had been an interesting half decade.

Rachel gave her a funny look.

"What?"

"One of these days you'll stop surprising me. Today is not one of those days." She undid the latch on her harness, which flopped apart like a broken umbrella without the fabric. "Help me with this?"

Across the street from their target was an office tower, maybe ten stories high. The climbing harnesses made quick work of getting on the roof. Luckily the LEDs that showed power on the joints were barely bright enough for the user to see. To anyone on the ground, it would look like fireflies swarming up into the night.

"That..." Rachel said as she panted, "was more fun...than you said it would be."

Tonya stretched as she got her breath back. "We had to do nearly a mile in them. Wore them out. But yeah, still fun. Ready for step two?"

Rachel pulled out a grapple launcher about the size of a compact umbrella. She pressed a button, and four spikes shot out of the pointy end. "You betcha." She shared the grapple's phone feed so Tonya could watch. After a few moments of pointing it at the roof, it began to map the scan arcs of any cameras or sensors it could detect. The word *complete* flashed in the corner of the screen and a target marker appeared a little to the southwest of the center of the roof. The grapple made a moderate chuff noise and hit square in the center of the target.

"Nice shootin', Tex," Tonya said.

Rachel smiled and extended the anchor on their side into the gravel-and-tar roof of the tower until it showed that it, too, was properly anchored. "Age before beauty," she said as she stepped aside.

Tonya lifted an eyebrow. She switched to an accent she'd worked out with ren faire regulars back in the day. "Cheeky little bugger, aren't you?" The harness included short anchor ropes and carabiners. She resisted the urge to whoop out loud as she sailed across the empty space, gaining speed. As the carabiner heated the smart material grew sticky, naturally slowing her slide. She touched down on her toes, ready for action.

Rachel followed a few seconds later. "I'm having too much fun right now."

"Yeah, fun time's over. Now we have to be careful."

She fired up her app, one written by a man who moved like smoke: Mike Sellars. Naturally this was shared with Rachel. Video Mike walked onto the corner of a virtual stage. "So you want to sneak around?"

"Who is that?" Rachel asked.

"Kim's husband. Helen's brother."

"Brother? They don't look much like each other."

"It's...complicated."

"So now that we've got the intro down," he said, "turn your phone forward, and I'll do the rest."

A pathway drew itself across the roof, complete with haptic feedback, stride, and speed metrics. Having seen Mike do his thing, she knew they might as well be elephants stepping on bubble wrap compared to him. But it was still a damned sight better than they'd do on their own.

"This is nearly as cool as the climbing harness," Rachel whispered.

Tonya gently waved her silent. The app scolded her in text at the same time. She shrugged and mouthed "sorry."

They used a special miniaturized jack screw to slowly and quietly lever up a skylight window. Once that was done, Rachel dropped a microdrone into the space. After a few passes, it reported all motion detectors and cameras had been put on infinite scan loops. Perfect security was still absolute in this modern world, but physical access to the hardware always gave you options.

They rappelled down monofilament ropes and then activated IR flashlights that worked with sensors on the phone. It turned everything into shades of gray, but it was more than enough to have a look around. They'd found Iyaan. He sat in the middle of the shop floor.

Stripped.

"Now what are we—"

The room lights flared to life in the middle of Rachel's sentence.

Chapter 43
Maff

It had taken some doing, but she and Helen corralled Chishow, their very own pallun interpreter, onto the ship. Helen then vanished, on a mission of her own, trying to get home. Maff wished her luck. She'd need it. After discussions with Aaron, returning to Earth wouldn't be their main problem. Getting to a place to meet securely with the right people would. Aaron called it a *safe house,* yet another human-only concept that had no translation into bemian languages. She knew because Chishow confirmed it.

Once they arrived, she was a bit underwhelmed. Her apartment was nicer than this. She thought there would be a big vault door and thick armored walls. Not old appliances and cheap utensils.

Bemians didn't have a word for a safe house. It wasn't needed. Criminals didn't kill witnesses to silence them. They didn't often turn on each other either. The ideas, once she understood them, drove home how alien humans were. The ones Maff personally knew were kind, considerate, generally good people. She'd met some in her job who could be more annoying than a bad wing fold, but they were the exception. Trying to reconcile that direct knowledge with what she'd learned about humanity in general, the violence, the criminality, the self-destructiveness, was the most difficult part of coming to terms with the planet.

Chishow, who'd only been around them a few hours, was having a harder time. "They *murder* each other?"

She was still having jealous twinges at his mastery of English, but those were the breaks when it came to interpreters. "Every chance they get, that is what it seems like reading their news feeds."

Aaron, sitting on a couch opposite them, shook his head. "It's an exaggeration by our media. Death gets you realm visits, so that's all they talk about." He sipped a *coffee* he'd bought on their way over. "Statistically this is the safest time in all of our history. Before realms came along, we had a hard time treating addiction and mental illness. Once we tamed those, it took away the prime causes for domestic chaos. It hasn't reached the whole world yet, but it's only a matter of time."

"And yet," Chishow said with sincere distress in his voice, "you arm yourselves at every level. Not only personally," he indicated the holstered pistol Aaron wore like it was a miniature version of an interpreter's deformity, "but at every level. Your death machines come in all sizes, from things I recognize like your tanks and cruisers, to ones I can barely understand like…anything to do with military aviation. And they're everywhere."

It was in that moment that Maff realized she'd come to terms with Earth by ignoring the obvious. This was in no way a civilized world as she knew it. There were billions of them out there, waiting for an opportunity to unleash murderous chaos at whatever scale suited their fancy. The entire planet was a clockwork death machine that only needed…

She stilled her gas. "Chishow, calm down," she said in pallun. "You're freaking me out."

"But—"

"*Calm down*. Now. You're worse than a Meronim who can't find his robes." She switched back to English to keep Aaron in the loop. "Chishow has not been exposed to Earth as long as I have. He is having, how do you say, nasty case of culture crash?"

"Culture shock," Aaron said with a bit of a smile. "Trust me, I know the feeling."

And just like that, she was back to humans as they were, not as they seemed. "Taken as a whole, your planet is challenging for us to understand."

"As your galaxy is to me." He shook his head. "I still don't..." His eyes unfocused. "Okay, they're ready for us."

Maff exchanged a worried look with Chishow. "Time to go to work." They settled back and accessed the special realmspace Aaron had set up.

The room was one of their generic conference realms, a small one with a large table and chairs all around it. There were also two pallun-style plinths for them to use the table comfortably so Aaron must have done some prep work while they were talking. Two people, older humans, one male, one female, sat stiffly opposite them. Maff recognized them, but only from pictures she'd examined on their way to the safe house. One was the prime minister of Israel.

The other was the president of the United States.

"Madam President," Aaron said as he bowed slightly. "Thank you for taking my call."

Her name was Catie Lee Devi, and the fact that she was the first Indian American and woman to hold the office was meaningless to Maff, but the humans certainly made a big deal about it. So was her *party affiliation,* which as far as she could make out, meant half of their media openly worked for the president's destruction, while the other half worshipped her with cultlike fervor. That was what they said about each other. Kim told her that when the other party held the office, the destroyers and the worshippers switched sides. Humans were opaque to her at the best of times. Their politics was a moon that blocked the entire sky.

"Don't thank me," she replied archly. "Thank Eli."

"Bah," the prime minister, who Maff would *not* refer to as Eli, scoffed. "He was in a jam. You have so many rules about reporting and talking, and we didn't know which ones he broke."

"Aside from consulting with a foreign head of state before his own chain of command?"

"I'm not *his* prime minister, Catie Lee, I'm his uncle-in-law. It's an important distinction. And he knew I was cleared for this. So are you going to fire him on the spot or let the man talk? You did notice the aliens in the room, yes? Maybe they should talk too? They might have things to say, you know."

His tone was confident and kind. It visibly calmed the president. She turned to Aaron. "My apologies. It was quite shocking to learn that we have *another* pallun now living amongst us, considering what that might mean."

Aaron motioned toward a seat, and the president gave a faint nod. He sat.

Now it felt more like someone new was sitting down in front of Samatarra's to have a chat with Toraz and his crew of gangsters. There was no menace. There wasn't any menace when people sat with Toraz either, for the same reason. The power imbalance was off the chart.

"On that, I have good news." Aaron stared at his hands for a moment. "And bad news. I do not believe Earth is in danger of alien invasion or discovery." He chuckled briefly. "I never thought I'd say *that* and mean it seriously."

It sounded strange to her as well, but for different reasons. As a pallun, she and countless generations before her had grown up with the knowledge that they alone in recorded history had suffered an invasion in that sense. But for her, for all of them, it was in the distant past. To learn about it was to understand there was nothing they could do about it. That was not the case here. The things they said and did now mattered in ways that could, would, affect history.

She couldn't have felt more out of control if she folded her wings and dropped into a cyclone.

"This is Chishow," Aaron continued. "He's the lead interpreter for a group of lost pallun."

"A *group*?" the president asked.

"And they are officially under the protection of the Israeli government," the prime minister said quickly, then shrugged at the president. "For you, that might be also part of the bad news."

"I thought you said you weren't prime minister here."

He shrugged again. "Israel is a small country. Sometimes we must wear many hats."

This news had brought the president's anger out again. "So you're sheltering them?"

"Not at all. Please, Catie Lee, let him tell his story." He gave Aaron a *continue* gesture with his hands.

So he did, telling the tale with neat accuracy.

After he finished, the president stared at him with a strange expression.

She's half surprised, half horrified, Chishow sent to her.

He was an interpreter. Explaining concepts that might not translate across cultures was what he did, and that went in both directions. She had a brief flash of annoyance that he'd assumed she wouldn't understand the human's reaction, but not for long. It was his job, after all.

President Devi cleared her throat. "They want to colonize Jupiter?"

Prime Minister Elias barked out a laugh. "Wait till you hear the next part."

Chishow held up a manipulator. "If I may explain now, Special Agent Aaron?"

"Please."

Maff had briefed him on what the grand plan she, Mr. Sha'Katenden, and Toraz had worked out. They wouldn't take Jupiter. They would either lease it or purchase it outright. These were concepts common to both Earth and the galaxy. They were already preparing their first payment, using their share of what Toraz was making as he leaked the tiniest part of Earth's intellectual property into the galaxy. They'd picked a single song from their *classic rock*. Spencer scoffed at the term when applied to that song, but he had to concede that "Never Gonna Give You Up" would make a splash. "That thing is so fucking addictive it's been a joke dating back to my grandad's time. Congratulations, you've rickrolled an entire galaxy" were his exact words.

"But what are you going to pay us *with*?" the president asked.

"Resources and technology, at least to start," Chishow replied. Toraz controlled a network of compromised nodes he used to fabricate replacement parts, so he didn't have to wait his turn in line like everyone else for repairs. It should advance Earth's ability to build portals substantially. The rest was figuring out what Earth lacked that they would be willing to trade for. Pallun merchants were a cliché across the galaxy, but it was solidly based in truth. They hadn't spent millennia homeless and vulnerable without learning a lot about how to make themselves valuable to the people around them.

This was a crude summary of what Chishow told the two world leaders. His explanations were clearer than anything Maff had in her head, and she was the one who'd thought of most of it. He answered every question with quiet confidence, providing reassurances the humans understood even though Maff didn't. He got them to laugh a few times at the jokes he'd made. Maff had watched Mike and Kim do this, but they were self-taught. Chishow had been through guild training, and it showed.

"I don't know what to say about this," the president said eventually. "I'm the president, and I think it's above *my* pay grade." She turned to the prime minister. "They're on a platform on Jupiter, Eli. Why do they need your country's protection?"

"*Those* pallun don't. Not yet anyway. *These* pallun, however, are stateless and quite vulnerable at the moment."

"Because they are on Earth. Right. Now that I have the whole story, I even understand why you had to come directly to—"

They were dumped out of realmspace as the lights went out in the safe house.

The sound of the front door splintering was unmistakable.

Chapter 44
Mike

She'd been a realm combat champion for about as long as that was a thing. *Realms are real* was a mantra they'd all chanted back in the day, because for the first time, being good at a video game made you good in the real world. It worked for her, too, but she had no way to show it. Not if the touch of a finger would send her into convulsions.

That wasn't a problem today.

The rifles they'd brought were too slow for this work, and the woods around them were too thick for archery to be effective. Kim, knowing that her life functioned as a self-propelled demonstration of Murphy's Law, had therefore planned for a situation where neither of those weapons would be appropriate.

She brought a stick.

And not just any stick. She'd custom ordered this one while she was still in hiding. No woman with any sense lived alone without *some* way to defend herself. It was a pistol at first. Then one morning she'd woken up on the couch with sunlight in her eyes, an empty whiskey bottle in one hand, her pistol in the other, and absolutely no memory of how any of it had happened. The pistol went into her bugout bag, and a special quarterstaff took up residence under her bed. The shaft was made of woven carbon nanotube rods capped with tungsten alloy ends. The result was a living thing in her hands that had no business existing outside a realm.

She named it Donny Donowitz and made Mike watch *Inglourious Basterds* to learn why. She'd given him a sized-up copy of the staff as a honeymoon gift. They spent their mornings at the resort doing katas with them as the sun rose.

The light weight was key. Realms taught her the coordination and muscle memory to do complex moves with her body, and she biked constantly to keep her aerobic fitness high. But realms did nothing to build muscle mass. The staff let her leverage physics and advanced materials to make up the difference.

Plus, she already had muscle in the form of six well-trained guardsmen and their sergeant. She'd been put in command. The first rule of officers was that they didn't know the rules. That's what sergeants were for.

She didn't have much time. "Sergeant Eskol?"

He reacted the same way sergeants did back home when she'd sometimes taken charge of a team of pros: a mixture of *who threw that grenade in here* and *what have I stepped in*? "Ma'am?"

"I have only one order: we need to stop anything from getting to those three people. I've got this." She twirled Donny so it shrieked a few bars of one of his bawdy songs, and then ended it by shattering a nearby stone the size of her head. The sparks that flew were a nice touch. "And that's what I can do with it. Where do you want me?"

He stared at the shards of the stone and nodded. "You hold the end of the line." He turned to his men. "Right! You lot! Picket formation and mind the lady! She needs a little extra space!"

Picket formation turned out to be a relaxed line facing the trail they'd come in on. Kim took the left side. "Any worries about them flanking us?" she asked.

He shook his head. "I'll be surprised if the first few waves don't expect us to stand aside voluntarily. The nodes are all about power, not tactics."

That was charming. "How long until they escalate?"

"This is the first time I've heard of anyone standing against them. I have no idea."

The first drone was a simple wheeled rectangular box, almost the same shade of yellow that heavy construction equipment used back home, and about as tall as she was. "You are trespassing and must leave." It moved forward.

Kim couldn't help it. She stepped in front of it, planted her staff, and slowly said, "None shall pass."

This seemed to confuse more than impress. It tried a few times to go around her, but she wouldn't let it. She thwacked it with the staff hard enough to leave a dent.

"You have triggered a disciplinary reaction," it said, the robotic voice making its Telirian words sound blocky and comical. "You are advised to leave this area before the reaction arrives." Then it left.

"Well that went better than I thought it would," Eskol said.

Kim couldn't disagree. "Any idea when—"

A dozen ground drones rolled down the trail at speed, and it was on. These were low-slung boxes, designed to knock bipeds down and, if the gear on their backs was any indication, restrain them with nets. Kim smashed the two in her sector so thoroughly the wheels literally fell off.

They came in waves, all different sizes and shapes. Some were as small as a lunchbox. One was as big as the truck and didn't come to a complete stop until Kim smashed an access hatch open, and one of Eskol's men rammed a sword into it. Fortunately carbon fiber was nonconductive, because she had to knock him away with it once it was obvious he'd hit a live electrical connection.

As the drones poured into the clearing, Kim got in the zone, a flow state where there was no staff and there was no Kim. They'd become a single entity that smashed and spun a tornado of destruction, leaving a trail of drone parts scattered in her wake. Then her mind got crossed up. In a first for her, she mistook realspace for a realm and tried one of her spider moves to the top of the staff. This required more core strength than she really had, and she slammed into the ground.

For a moment, all she saw was yellow hulls and wheels coming for her. One of the men shouted, "Kim's down," and they all fought toward her until she could get to her feet. It was great not to be restrained or captured, but the result was an unbalanced line that allowed the robots to push them back closer to the truck. She wanted the sergeant to reposition the men, but the machines didn't allow the time or space to do it. When three bots pivoted and turned the corner of their line, she tried to block them all. She lost her balance, hitting the ground again. The nearest drone lifted up a thing that was half trap, half net, and dropped it on her.

Almost.

It was stopped with a sparking clang by a different staff, one bigger and heavier than hers. Mike stood over her, laughing as he pushed it back.

He looked down at her with a smirk. "What kept you?"

He twirled the first drone into the other two and then rammed his staff through all three. Mike had arrived not a moment too soon. His staff had triple the mass of hers, and with the extra power they pushed back the tide, cramming the ground drones up the trail until they were almost at the spot where it all started.

Mike managed to fight his way to her side. "We can't do this forever."

She flicked one of the smaller drones into a larger one, causing both to tangle with each other and fly to pieces. "No kidding."

"I'm calling in the cavalry."

"The what?"

There was a splintering crash to her left, and a tree fell straight into the clearing. A new path had been cut through the woods. Combat drones were lined up behind a large, squat drone obviously designed for forestry. Their small line faltered in confusion. She didn't have enough bodies to cover that gap.

Kim began to shout orders anyway but was interrupted by a massive blast behind her that immediately caused the front of the forestry drone to shatter, scattering the pieces all around it. The entire battlefield fell silent, the drones as stunned as anyone else.

A familiar voice split the silence.

"Eat hot lead, you ass sucking, tree chomping, shit for brains motherfuckers!" It was followed by another explosion, which she now recognized as one of their rifles. This time it cut a swath through the robots trying to find a way around their destroyed tree cutter. A quick glimpse behind her showed him standing on the roof of the truck, handing the now empty weapon to Tapov, who handed him the third and last of the loaded guns. Tapov turned and started frantically reloading before he'd brought the gun to his shoulder.

That final shot seemed to announce the resumption of the fight, now punctuated with slugs ripping through the air every thirty seconds or so. The style of firearm may have been antiquated but the loading system wasn't, and Tapov got faster as she practiced.

It still wasn't enough. They were fighting an entire planet's worth of drones. It didn't matter how inept the drones were, how clumsy, how ineffective. All they had to be was lucky one time. Kim kept wracking her brain trying to come up with the unexpected move, one nobody would see coming, the middle choice that was hidden between two untenable ones. Nothing came to her. Her world turned into a sea of yellow metal smashed into sparking pieces by a staff that grew heavier by the second. All she needed, all she *desperately* needed, was a chance to catch her breath. But they would not stop.

The trees above them exploded in a shower of branches and splinters. Kim found herself flat on the ground before it had properly formed as a thought in her head. A heavy thrumming dominated all other sounds. There was a loud crack as a skein of lightning splashed over and around her. When it touched the drones, they stopped dead.

Kim rolled over and stared up at a swath of glossy blue metal edged with gold and red stripes. It'd basically blown open a hole for itself through the canopy above, creating a perfect cookie cutter shape of its outline. It took that long for her mind to put together what she saw into a coherent image that made sense.

Palatine.

And it kept making a hole, shattering trunks and ramming branches aside as it descended. Kim sat up and looked around, trying to find Mike. He was a few yards away helping one of the soldiers to his feet. All around her, Eskol's men were slowly standing up, brushing sawdust and branch ends off as they did. Kim saw Eskol himself lying facedown next to her, a heavy branch next to his head.

The wave of nauseated adrenaline that hit her forced her hand out toward him. She yanked it back quickly as the boiling sear of her touch madness shot up her arm. Instead of grimacing, she smiled. Touch madness had a use after all. Anyone else would have to check for a pulse.

A second later, he groaned and rolled over. "Even from beyond the grave that man gets me into the most ridiculous situations." He spotted the ship. "What in the seven pits of Skerrol is *that*?"

"It's our ticket out of here." She levered herself up with her staff and then offered one end to him. "Come on."

Spencer had already fishtailed the truck around, Tapov holding on for dear life in the passenger seat. The cargo door opened as he reached it. The rest of them limped and hobbled toward it as fast as they could.

Mike was bruised and bleeding from a small cut above his left eye. Battered, dirt smeared, and covered in sawdust, he still made her insides jiggle. Judging by the way his eyes flashed when he looked at her, he was thinking the same thing. Kim tried to brush her hair out, but her fingers immediately got tangled up in the twigs and splinters that covered it. A glance down showed that she'd not faired any better than he had, with torn, mud-spattered pants and a shirt that was more dirt than cloth and stank so badly of flop sweat her eyes watered.

Mike's expression didn't change, and neither did the smile on her face. *Love conquers all.*

Eskol stood on one side of the hatch while she stood on the other. After the last of the party ran inside, they hoofed it up the ramp themselves.

Helen stood on the second-level deck on the opposite side of the hold. When Kim nodded, she shouted, "Go, Maff! Go!"

The familiar stomach lurch told her they were now in the transit dimension, safely out of reach of the local network's forces. She gingerly picked her way past jumping and hugging Telirians to Mike. "The cavalry?"

He tapped his head. "We haven't talked that much, but I've always been able to contact Helen if I needed to. And I did. We weren't going to last much longer."

She heard the unmistakable whistling of pallun voices coming from the other side of the truck. Walking around it, she found the source. Three pretty badly beat up pallun were hanging from the bottom of the second-level walkway by large straps, surrounded by trays full of suit parts. "Move the vehicle, kid, we can't see!" said the one in the middle.

"What the fuck happened to you guys?" Spencer asked as he backed it up a little to unblock the view.

Kim quickly translated. All three huffed and the middle one said, "What the fuck happened?" He pointed up to where Helen still stood. "She's what the fuck happened. You humans, I swear to Turlanfador, buy trouble by the shipping container."

*

Their ad hoc leadership committee met in the mess hall, the pallun named Sornik via a simple remote camera since he was still repairing his suit, while the Telirian soldiers were learning card games from Sornik's men still in the hold.

After all they'd been through, Eskol and Tapov were still obviously in awe of the tech around them. "How about this," Tapov asked. "Will we get this?"

"Yes," Kim replied. "This is real bemian tech. We don't have anything like it back on Earth."

"Yet," Helen said owlishly. She'd been tense ever since they came on board. Kim hoped to pry that out of her during the meeting.

But first she had a more important question. "Did you complete the hack?" she asked Spencer.

"Fuckin' A, we sure did." He grinned at Tapov, who returned the expression but with sharper teeth. "And more."

That could mean anything, especially with Spencer. "Explain *and more*."

"Oh, don't get your tits in a twist. We were subtle."

"I wanted much more," Tapov explained. "But he talked me around to a different point of view."

Instead of destroying the planetary network, which Kim agreed would've been a complete disaster, they'd gone with a gentle touch. The nodes on Teliria had been programmed to give the Telirians themselves an incentive, and then two seemingly modest alterations to the node's directives. The incentive would encourage the Telirians themselves to recover their native language in both spoken and written form.

"There's literature out in the forbidden zones, but we have no idea how to read it," Tapov explained. "Spencer said Earth could probably help, but it would take a long time."

"And only after we let the rest of the planet know about all this," he said. "That's a decision beyond our pay grade, I think."

"Indeed," Helen said, and this time the whole room noticed how tense she was acting.

"Anything you want to tell us?" Kim asked her.

She shook her head. "I'm not done researching it yet." She closed her eyes and took a deep breath. When she opened them, she was visibly more relaxed, much closer to normal. "My apologies. I concentrated too many threads in the wrong place. Please, continue."

"The other two are things my father wanted," Tapov said. "The ability for us to have more than one child in a family, and for us to formally join the galaxy at an earlier date. I don't think the first will change much. We've been having one child per family for as long as anyone can remember, but he disagreed. Where we did agree, though, was that Teliria is more than ready to join the galaxy. The nodes were going to wait another five thousand years!" She made a disgusted sound and then gestured at the ship around her. "This is all new, but it's not shocking. They were frightened of us. Apparently we have been one of the more difficult planets to..." This time she got so angry she gripped her hands tight. "To *tame*. They couldn't agree on a timeline and so chose the longest one they were allowed."

"Buncha fucking cowards," Spencer said. "The place was pacified centuries ago. They have held back this entire goddamn planet because they didn't want to look bad in front of their node buddies. It's fucking weird, but it's true. We skimmed the notes of their last vote to join Teliria with the galaxy. They didn't come out and say it, but it was crystal clear that they'd been shaking in their nodey little boots about this place ever since they found it. I don't think they would ever let Teliria join."

"So we took another vote for them," Tapov continued. "Spencer and I turned ourselves into honorary node chiefs and held another election. The result was unanimous." She faced Eskol. The excitement of Tapov announcing this was obvious to Kim. She was almost vibrating. "Our grandchildren will be the first to greet the rest of the galaxy." She turned back to Kim, really all the humans since they were sitting together. "I hope Earth will be there to greet them, too."

"That's where I come in," Sornik said. "No problem. Forget about it. They'll be there. You can bank on that."

Chapter 45
Spencer

It was surreal watching Sornik climb through the hole they found in the fence. He turned himself into a snake wearing chain mail. "Does that hurt?"

"It'll make me sore if I try to hold the same shape for too long, but this?" He morphed back to his normal form. "This is a smooth piece of sky."

"Are there limits?"

"It's about as small a diameter that I can manage. I could've gone flat, but it would've spread me out too far. Bones ain't all they're cracked up to be."

"Hey, I don't have to wear a suit to get around."

Sornik shrugged. "The suit's to keep me from getting poisoned in the crazy atmospheres you high-grav types need to live. If Maff manages to pull off that deal for Jupiter, I wouldn't have to wear it again if I didn't want."

"You'd seriously consider moving? Giving up on the job?"

"Look, kid, I've been doing this a long time. Longer than you've been alive. What am I saying? You people barely live long enough for it to count. I've been doing this since before your grampa was born. I've saved up. It might do me some good to settle down and find new ways to drive my wife crazy."

The thought had never occurred to him. "You're married?"

"For nearly as long as I've been in the business." He chuckled. "I got grandkids now, ain't that a kick in the teeth? Anyway, come on, we need to get going."

They moved cautiously through the inner camp. "Now that we're behind their lines," Spencer asked, "are we immune again?"

"Not until I find a place to register. That won't be as easy this time."

They moved quietly along a trail picked out by Spencer's drone. Using infrared would take life out of the batteries too quickly, but with the Telirian moons up, low-light was good enough. It got them to the main entrances without being seen by the inhabitants.

"Now what?" Spencer asked.

"Time to find a maintenance console. We won't be able to do much until we can move around freely."

This proved a bigger challenge than either of them counted on. The entrances made for a second natural choke point. "Where's a big ventilation duct when you need it?" Spencer asked.

"What are you talking about?"

"Ventilation ductwork, you know, air conditioning and stuff?"

"They're all over the ceiling." He pointed at the top of the entrance. Like in real life back home, they were too narrow for either of them to use.

But, now that he was looking at that ceiling, he spotted another device that was easily recognizable. He hoped. "Are those sprinklers?" The back-and-forth took less time than it usually did for him to convey the concept. They were getting better at *guess what the fuck the other guy is saying.*

"Yeah, that's what they are. And how they work."

"Who puts fire safety in a smuggler's den?"

He shrugged. "It's the bots. They're the ones that do the building, and that's what comes standard with any structure large enough to hold more than a dozen people. A places like this? I bet it goes all the way through it. Look, I get where you're going, but I don't see how putting anything hot up there will do us any good."

He pulled out his drone. "That's where this comes in."

It was a trick he learned in middle school. He'd gotten into a ketchup packet squeezing contest with his friend, Stewart, and ended up blasting the stuff nearly to the top of the cafeteria's wall. Water sprinklers would be a convenient way to clean that off before getting busted by tattletale Mary.

How was he supposed to know those things sprayed an astonishing amount of water, stinky and black to begin with? It was mostly the thrill of having an excuse to short a LiPo battery anyway. They'd all gotten soaked, then half drowned. Being ten, he hadn't exactly covered his tracks, and so it was off to the principal's office for yet another visit. It was one of the few times having a mom and dad who were never more than half a second from an absolutely raging fight came in handy.

The ketchup was still there today.

Sornik shook his head after Spencer finished the story. "You were taking these things apart at *ten*?"

Spencer set to work on an extra battery. "Oh, it was way before that. People had to watch their devices around me when I was little; otherwise they'd find them in pieces on the floor of a spare bedroom. I didn't learn how to put them back together until I was twelve or so."

"Kid, that has got to be the strangest thing you've said to me so far."

"Why?"

"Nobody takes things apart like that. What would be the point?"

"Um…things like this?" He held up his now thoroughly booby-trapped drone. A thought occurred to him. "You don't have a word for *sabotage,* do you?" He'd had to use the English word. Another back-and-forth ensued.

"Yeah. We do that. They make kits for it."

"You sabotage things *with a kit*? Nobody does that. What would be the…"

They both looked at each other with a new sort of comprehension. Mutual *in*comprehension.

"I guess the question," Sornik said after a quick shake of his head, "is will it work?"

"Only one way to find out. One kamikaze, comin' up." He set the waypoints, shorted the battery, and the drone flitted away.

"One what?"

"The drone isn't coming back from this. Not a biggie, I have another one." Two. Spencer had almost the same sort of rotten luck that Kim did. "Now, three…" The drone got in position. "Two…" He saw a wisp of smoke. "One…"

On cue, a tiny flare whooshed to life. He heard the wings pick up speed as it compensated for the thrust of the ruptured battery. After a few moments, a second flare showed the drone's batteries were going up.

Then all hell broke loose.

Loud claxons started up as strobes began blinking everywhere. Much more impressive was the monsoon unleashed from the sprinkler heads. Everyone underneath them, workers, guards, who the hell knew what else, shouted and started running in every direction. "Come on," he said to Sornik as he jumped out of cover. Pushing through a crowd wasn't all that different from back home, although he had to be careful sometimes. Not everyone was shaped for a shove to do any good. Sornik solved the problem by turning into a thick knifelike shape and almost literally cutting through the crowd.

He was right about how not having any bones being convenient sometimes. And holy *shit* was the water cold.

Eventually they got out from under the activated sprinklers and found themselves a hiding place behind a stack of crates, well beyond the barrier. Spencer would hit the quickDry on his clothes once the worst of the water ran off, but for now he was fighting the chills. "Told ya it'd work."

"You did indeed." He stuck his manipulator camera up above the crates. In the shared vision channel, another maintenance shack was clearly visible. "And now it's my turn."

"How are you going to get in this time?" There were people milling around everywhere.

"This ain't my first diamond storm. Stay close and follow me."

They walked through the door. At least, that's what it must've looked like to anyone who happened to be watching. If Spencer hadn't known ahead of time, he would never have noticed Sornik's lockpick do a brief number on the door. Kim might even give props for that pick job.

"Yo," Sornik said as he walked through the door. Spencer walked in behind him, but he knew that wasn't a good sign. You didn't greet an empty room.

A kron sat behind a desk on the other end of the room, looking startled. "Who are you?"

"Nobody you'll remember." Manipulators shot forward and bashed the kron's head against his desk.

Sornik was quick about it. "Not too shabby." But instead of moving toward the computer terminal, he started tearing apart the ceiling. "What the fuck?"

"Change of plans, kid. The fake ID is no good if I have to use force to get it. We've got about ten seconds before backup gets here." He pushed aside the outer corner of the flat roof. "Time for another ride."

The now all-too-familiar feel of his manipulators wrapping around Spencer's waist was followed by a vision-blurring spin as Sornik yanked him off his feet. Less than a second later he was hanging upside down on the pallun's back. The sizzle of blaster fire chased them around the ceiling as a group of five guards tried to shoot Sornik off it. One of the shots took out a sprinkler head that hadn't been activated, and a powerful jet of water shot across their path. Sornik swung Tarzan-like under it and then took a tunnel that led downward.

"Where the fuck are we going?"

"Away from them!"

This wasn't doing them any good. People were shouting and pointing as they passed. There would be no way to lose their pursuers. He saw another downward tunnel. "There! Take that one!"

It was only a matter of time before they remembered their radios and set up a blocking team. Spencer checked his mapping tools. "This is taking us back under the old city. Keep an eye out for ruins."

"They would've cleaned those out by—"

There was a crash and then everything spun. It all went dark as Sornik closed over him again. They bounced against things, clearly falling as they tumbled. There was a brief bit of weightlessness and then Spencer could feel the other side of Sornik's suit through his butt as they landed. Debris thudded over them. Spencer was getting sick of this particular kind of roller coaster. The ones back home wouldn't kill you.

Eventually it stopped. "Are you okay?" No answer. Great. How was he supposed to get out of here if the super spider was dead? "Sornik?"

"Turlanfador's wings, kid," he said as Spencer's butt got inflated off the ground. "What the hell happened?"

Sornik folded away from Spencer, letting him look around. The lighting here was different, sparser, and bluer than before. But it was bright enough to see where they were. "I said for you to find ruins, not fall into them."

He shook debris away as he put Spencer back on his feet. "You want to file a complaint? Send it to management."

Spencer looked up. It must've been a ceiling collapse that then dropped them and whatever they pulled down through the floor. A clearly fresh plug of debris now blocked the way. Which was good, he guessed. Better than being grabbed by the guards, at least.

The space was much more mine-like. Or maybe it was a subbasement. He looked hard at the floor. Maybe it was a parking garage. They'd never found car remains, but that didn't—

Spencer stopped cold at what he saw on the floor. "Holy fucking shit."

"What's up? What'd you find?"

If he never saw another one of those things again it'd be too soon, but the shape was unmistakable. "I don't know what you call them over here. I only met them on Earth." Once, back at the Yellowstone plant. He'd watched one bite a grown man in half, and barely avoided becoming monster chow in the process.

"I thought you said you never met any bemians before you met us."

"There was an exception. That?" He pointed at the unmistakable set of tracks that led away from them.

"What made that damn near killed me. It came through a portal."

Chapter 46
Helen

"Hi, lady!" Kaddee shouted as he ran down the stairs on the opposite side of… it didn't look like a hangar in the conventional sense, but that was what it must have been. "You got good ship!"

It was smaller than *Palatine* and used a different design. It was by no means a flying saucer, but neither would it ever be mistaken for any sort of Earth vehicle. *Palatine* bore a vague resemblance to several kinds of Earth transport, trucks and cargo planes in particular. This wasn't any of those. It was dirty, dented, and it looked like it'd been shot in a couple of places. She had to take Toraz's recommendation on faith now, because if she'd come across it on her own, she would've assumed she stumbled across someone salvaging a long-dead relic.

It gave her, as Spencer sometimes put it, a not so safe feeling.

Kaddee hit the bottom of the stairs and shouted, "Bots! You come!"

Several of the most battered bots she'd ever seen moved shakily out of dark corners on the edges of the hangar. The ones Helen had encountered to date had never looked like they were new, but they were reassuringly monotonous in their appearance: a black, heavily faceted dome covering the wheels and suspension. Manipulators and various other tools would either be bolted directly to the dome or hidden underneath hatches. The main difference was their varied size.

Kaddee's, in contrast, were almost as battered and patched together as his ship. And they were visibly terrified of their master. This was, in and of itself, interesting, as it was the first time she saw any indication that bots contained more than the most basic AI.

Exactly how they became so battered was quickly made clear. Each command Kaddee shouted was underlined with a bash, punch, kick, and on one occasion a head-butt. "No! This not right! That need set! Parts there!" It would've been horrifying if they were biological or conscious. She remembered that Watchtell's original twelve unduplicates became conscious due to extreme abuse. Maybe there was more to the bot's terror than was first apparent.

Making sure to stay out of range of the battle Kaddee was having with his own bots, Helen approached. "How soon can we leave?"

"Eh?" He turned and then comically half hopped, half stomped up to her. "No can leave. Need parts."

So it *was* a piece of junk. But then she understood the implication of what he said. "You know how to fix this?"

His eyes flew super round, making him appear to only have them and his snaggle-toothed mouth instead of a conventional head. "You see Kaddee before! I fix! Nodes take too long for race pinnace." He gave his ragged ship a long look. "Or Kaddee ship." He shrugged his noodlelike arms. "Need parts first. No parts, no fix."

Helen knew a thing or two about finding things. "Show me."

The list wasn't long. Helen recognized some of it from her time at Toraz's pinnace garage. The two biggest hurdles were with the control rods on the D-manifold and the nav computer.

"Very important! Without first one, ship go boom! Without other, ship go poof!"

When she'd understood the magnitude of what Mike and Kim had experienced on their first accidental trip to bemian space, she debriefed them both thoroughly. Or, at least, as thoroughly as possible. Kim was always a subject that required careful handling to ensure her cooperation. Her brother she browbeat into answering every question she could think of. And she had thought of a lot of question.

While she was not a mechanic by any stretch, she wasn't helpless either. "We can find these things, but I'll need your help."

His smile split his shaggy countenance. "Kaddee help! Love help!"

"I don't have an interpreter thread. You do."

He pulled back in comical confusion, then the huge eyes widened again. "Kaddee mechanic," he said in an awed whisper, "not interpreter."

Once again, she had to remind herself that bemians weren't stupid or hyper-literal. They had been taught for generations to never question, never evaluate, never think past step one. "You won't be interpreting. You'll be repeating what whoever we're talking to is saying."

"But Mr. Toraz said lady being chased? By interpreters! Kaddee has interpreter thread in head!" He bounced a finger off the side of his temple so hard Helen thought he'd leave a bruise.

"It's fine." Having her own thread was too much of a risk, but it was clear they couldn't be turned into some all-encompassing surveillance network. If that were possible, she would never have been able to evade them. They were everywhere. "But I do need to change my appearance."

"Ahh," he growled out, nodding with his whole body. "Kaddee can help. Bot!" Without looking, he threw a fist out and bashed the bot wheeling past him. It stopped with a squeal and a few sparks. "Find clothes. Bring clothes." He slapped it back into motion. "We do cargo runs. Sometimes cargo falls off, gets lost." He waggled his comically fuzzy eyebrows at Helen. "You no tell Mr. Toraz?"

"I'd never."

They settled on a utilitarian coverall, complete with gloves that had the wrong number of fingers and boots that were clearly for feet not exactly human shaped. It wouldn't be a good idea to try running a race in them, but that wasn't part of the plan. A helmet with visor completed the ensemble. She checked it all in a streaked mirror at the back of Kaddee's shop. It broke up the outline of her profile and masked her features very well. In fact, it made her look more than a little insectoid. There were plenty of those around, so it should be a good fit.

"Let's go." He had his own utility transport, as beaten and worn as everything else he owned. She blinked at the interior. There were controls inside. An actual driver's seat. It wasn't anything like a car. There were sticks on the right and left with matching foot pedals, but it was the first time she'd ever seen a bemian ground transport that could be piloted by anything other than a node. The cockpit had been custom designed to fit his pipe-cleaners-and-shaggy-carpet physique. A human child of about ten would fit.

"You drive this yourself?"

He flopped his shaggy head up and down as he hopped in the seat. "Kaddee hit bot driver too hard. Break bot. Nodes too busy to fix, so Kaddee fix." He laughed so hard he was almost hopping up and down in the seat. "Great fun to scare nodes!" With a wheezing rattle that sounded uncomfortably close to a fatal failure, it started up, and they moved out.

In addition to the two critical items, there was a list of other things to get. The first few items were easy enough. "Why didn't you get these yourself?"

"Busy getting parts for race pinnace. Busy fixing pinnace motivators. Busy fixing other transport. Always busy fixing. Can't wait for nodes? Don't need to wait with Kaddee!" He leaned on his horn, which in this case more resembled a bike brake handle, and shouted rough incoherent phrases when another transport threatened to veer into their path.

Against all expectations, it worked. The other vehicle changed direction like it'd been swatted. "I didn't expect them to respond to you at all."

He grunted as he drove, then nodded slightly. "Kaddee get"—he cleared a throat well-hidden by his shaggy beard—"spe-hul-dis-pen-say-shun." That was about as sophisticated a phrase as you could say in Standard. He shrugged. "Mr. Toraz make arrangements."

This being bemian space, there was bound to be a form that needed to be filled out or a license to be obtained. Little in bemian society that seemed to be illegal *was* illegal. The violent flattening of cultural norms during bemian uplift had created a social contract of truly awesome power. It put the cultural assumptions built into China to shame.

"I've got a question," she said as they traveled to another junk yard. "If nobody fixes anything, why are there so many salvage lots?"

He shrugged his rubber-band shoulders. "Artists, mostly. Turn this stuff to sculpture. Melt it down. Cut it open, rearrange bits."

"But there's so much of it."

"Yup. Designs. Some good. Some bad. Some last forever. Some break down too soon. Nodes take too long to fix, things pile up."

The next three items took more time. This revealed a talent Helen didn't know she had.

Haggling.

"Are you crazy? That much, in this condition?" She dramatically waved a box full of what Mike told her were called planetary gears. "We'll give you half."

Kaddee, who had taken to his role of half interpreter quite well, translated the reply. "You'll give me eighty percent and then go away. Pallun make less fuss than you with your bargaining!"

The control rods were found under a pile of other debris. The final item, the coveted nav computer core, was the hardest of all. The ones they found were all burned out. She kept searching various salvage yards until the twin suns of this planet began to set. After searching dozens, she settled on one nav unit dug out of the yard owner's oldest stock that was merely cracked. "Will it work?" she asked him.

He shrugged. "Better than what Kaddee have now." He started shaking, threw his arms wide, head back, and then shouted "BOOM!" He laughed a bit. "Core punch hole in hull. Turn nav computer into bits. Only now finished patching hull."

"Ask him how much."

Kaddee opened his comically large mouth to speak but then stopped. "That not good," he said quietly.

The merchant was shaking his head and tapping the side of it.

"What's wrong?" Helen asked.

"Thread shut down. Kaddee didn't know that was—"

He faced her, but then looked behind her. His eyes, incredibly, got even wider. "Get in car." He threw the last of their money at the merchant and snatched the core out of his hands. "Get in car!" He ran toward it, bounding at speed on his rubber-band legs.

An interpreter ground transport had pulled up to the yard.

Kaddee had parked his car on the opposite side, which had yet to be blocked. She jumped in, then scrabbled frantically with the belt system while Kaddee let out an ear-splitting howl as they lurched into motion. They barely pulled into the yard driveway when the interpreter backup appeared and turned sideways, blocking the drive.

"Ha! Kaddee not that easy!" He threw a switch, and the acceleration increased.

She barely got the buckles latched when the vehicle lurched to the left, bounced over low piles of junk, then went straight at the barrier fence. "Lady, hold on!" She slammed against her belts hard enough to hurt as he rammed into and then through the fence. The transport had acquired some new dents, but it was hardly a major contribution to the original collection.

"Kaddee make car drive for many reasons. That," he nodded backward at the transport that was even now setting off in hot pursuit of them, "is new reason." He slewed the car to the right, causing it to slam violently upward as it jumped the curb and landed on the sidewalk. Bemians of all shapes and sizes scattered out of the way. "Node-driven cars not do these things."

"*We* shouldn't be doing these things," she said, flinching each time it looked like the terrified pedestrians might not get out of the way before they got run over. "Someone is going to get killed out there."

"Not for long!" He pulled a lever on the dash as he slewed the vehicle hard right. It must've been the parking brake because the tail slewed much faster than it otherwise should've. The lever snapped back in place after he released it, confirming her guess. They now faced a far-too-narrow alley that was uninhabited. Helen didn't have time to scream as they plunged headlong into it.

"We go where they don't! No smash!"

Like most modern cars, bemians used miniature cameras to manage external views so there were no wing mirrors to snap off. This was fortunate. If Helen's side was any indication, they had, at best, a centimeter of clearance. A part of her, a small part of her, spared a flash of respectful admiration for Kaddee's skill as a driver. Barreling down what was effectively a car-shaped sausage casing disguised as an alley, he was barely scratching the sides. The rest of her was doing a mostly effective job of not screaming each time she thought she saw something blocking their path. There would be no swerving in here.

Kaddee panted and grunted like the half-crazed animal he resembled as they went. Each time his eyes narrowed, she braced because it meant an intersection was coming up. With uncanny skill, he pirouetted the vehicle in a random direction with just enough room to pull the maneuver off, and they went blasting down another far-too-small alley. "Where did you learn to do this?"

"Kaddee hang out with crazy racers. Crazy racers teach Kaddee." Again the eyes narrowed. "Uh-oh!" The alley was a dead end, and they were going too fast to stop. This time she did scream, but it turned into a shout when the walls on either side vanished. The alley didn't end at the wall. There was a narrow street in front of it that they crossed. As they did, he pulled the hand brake one last time, sending them into the wall sideways hard enough to tip the car upward as they stopped.

Her door popped open, and Kaddee scrambled across her. "Go! Go!" He climbed on top of the car before Helen could untangle her belts. "Lady, move fast!"

"Where are we?"

"Back of shop." He shared what must've been a security camera feed. Interpreter vehicles had already blocked the doors in the fence around it. People in blue and white armor were jumping out.

Kaddee yanked her onto the roof, jumped to the top of the wall, then yanked her into the compound. He was much stronger than he looked. "Wait!" He jumped down and pulled out their bag of parts. "We no go far without these."

They scurried up to a back door, which Kaddee opened without breaking stride. "Bots! Time to go!"

The sound of weapon blasts rang out, sparking and spalling against the ship hull. Various bots either scurried up the ramp into the cabin or into niches on the sides of the ship.

"We don't have time to replace anything," Helen said.

"No need. Ship not helpless. We move a little, make replacements, then move far." She heard the door thump shut behind her as they ran toward what had to be the cockpit. He tossed the nav component at her when they entered it. "Put this there!" He pointed at a socket clearly designed to accept the component as he took the pilot's seat.

Helen pushed it in and then took the seat in front of it. She'd done her share of turns on watch during their time on *Palatine,* and this was clearly the nav station. "Destination and mode?"

The weapon blasts were faint but growing more frequent as Kaddee threw her a look that was confused, then admiring. He gave her the coordinates and the mode, which was effectively their speed, which she punched in. It should take them well clear of this system.

The computer promptly went dark. Not on her watch. Helen smacked it on the side with her fist, and it thankfully turned on. "Punch it!"

There was a twinge in her stomach as they leapt into the transit dimension. She caught a glimpse of other ships in the area, but they fell back into realspace before she could work out more than that. Her stomach lifted into her throat as the feel of free fall announced that they'd come out somewhere in deep space.

The blasted nav computer promptly went dark again.

"Now Kaddee know where to start fixing." He nodded at the nav computer as he unstrapped.

The computer sparked once and then released a wisp of smoke. "And if we can't?"

"We not go anywhere."

Chapter 47
Tonya

They glanced around frantically in the sudden light of the garage. Iyaan's stripped body was at the center of neat piles of his various parts. There were a *lot* of places to hide in here, and all could be concealing the ambush party. She could take anyone on, but not if she couldn't see them. The few glances she spared for Rachel showed her searching just as frantically.

"Hello? Tonya? Rachel?"

The sound came from all around them. That wasn't right. It came from speakers mounted on the ceiling. And it was a voice she recognized.

"Iyaan?"

"That has to be you, Tonya. I've been waiting so long, but then all my sensors went dark. I could only hope—"

"Iyaan," Rachel interrupted, "where are you?"

"They connected their network to mine. Once it became clear what was happening, I escaped. But it's air gapped. I couldn't go any farther than this."

Tonya could think of half a dozen different ways to bridge a gap like that. Doing it was becoming a regular part of her life. But Iyaan wouldn't have that ability. It was too far out of his programming conditions. It wasn't that he was stupid. The fact that he jumped out at all was an outstanding achievement for his level of AI. But creative leaps got too high too fast for insentient AI, and being trapped alone in a strange network he couldn't escape was beyond his capabilities. "Are you okay?"

"Core functionality has been preserved. I've also kept the data stores holding the telemetry of our excursion. That was... remarkable. Did we all travel back in time?"

"We'll talk about that later." She looked at the empty shell of the truck. "They did a number on you, didn't they?"

"They were quite thorough, but I don't think they ever understood what I was."

"Few would," Rachel said as she examined their work. "Who are they; do you know?"

In their shared vision channel, a security video began to play. A group of men worked with quick efficiency as they disassembled Iyaan. An older Hispanic man called a Black man over who was roughly the same age. They both looked to be at least a decade older than the gang working on the truck. "What do you think they needed all that metamaterial for?"

"Not my problem, man, but what a haul. We have to be careful otherwise Checco will double his rates."

"That son of a bitch hasn't found us jack shit the entire time he's been working for us. I was gonna cut him loose."

The Hispanic man shook his head. "It'll never happen. The kid's a loser, but his dad's on the DC city council. Cabrón has to cultivate his contacts, so keeping the kid busy driving a tow truck is more important than anything he can bring us."

They'd known where Iyaan ended up because Helen and Mike had worked together some time ago to compromise an impressive number of traffic cams in at least their local area. Being able to scan a thousand feeds at once did the rest. But they didn't know *why* he'd been diverted.

The rest of the recorded conversation made it clear what had happened. The tow truck driver was feeding the more interesting, valuable cars to a chop shop disguising itself as a pot dispensary. Most of the time they were shipped out whole to various countries, but Iyaan had proven to be a special case that was more valuable as parts as opposed to an entire vehicle.

Tonya took another look at it all. "How do we get this out of here?"

Rachel shook her head. "We don't. They weren't particularly careful." She pointed out places where wiring harnesses had been cut instead of disconnected, brackets had been snapped off, and mounting points sawn off. "It'll be easier to start from scratch."

"From scratch?" Iyaan said with a nearly audible gulp in his voice.

"Not from scratch," Rachel said with a laugh. "We'll need to—"

On the screen, the Hispanic guy finished the conversation with "Once they pick this stuff up, we'll be able to go on a nice vacation. Sucks that we have to do it at one in the morning."

Tonya glanced at the time. 1:05 a.m. The bad guys were running late.

The doors slammed outside.

"How long to download Iyaan?" she asked Rachel.

She was pale. "Longer than we have, I think."

Iyaan was the custodian of information that humanity—the entire galaxy—had no knowledge of. They'd stuffed him to the gills with telemetry sensors, and their little inadvertent trip had gathered more data than she had in the months since they got back from Silaria. The answers to questions Tonya hadn't managed to ask yet could be in there.

"No. Rachel, you find an access point." She pulled one of the many connection wires the thieves left in a pile. "Use this, it'll be faster and more secure. Iyaan, you're with me. I need you to control this environment and do as I ask." Rachel had already started running toward a corner of the shop that had a desk, so Tonya quiet-shouted at her. "Give me the camera access."

Rachel didn't turn around, instead throwing a thumbs-up as the access point landed in Tonya's message queue. "Iyaan, cut the lights."

Not a second later the giant roll-up door rattled upward. Tonya grabbed a handful of Iyaan's chopped up wiring harness. She was going to make them regret not being more careful with her property. She found some cover behind a stack of boxes but still kept an eye on the entrance.

The first one to enter went for the light switch. He hit it once and then cursed when nothing happened. "Some sort of network issue?"

Iyaan, let them control the lights for a second. The next time the guy hit the switch it worked. *Wait for my signal to shut them off again.*

Okay.

Rachel texted next. *I've got it started, but it's huge.*

So much for good luck. *How much time do you need?*

Five minutes.

It would be tight, but she could make it work. She checked where Rachel had been headed and saw nothing. Good. She had taken cover behind or underneath the desk. That's where the access point usually was anyway.

She turned back to the task at hand. Eight of what looked like standard-issue street thugs slouched their way in. She only recognized two of them from the video. The rest must be the pickup crew. She waited until they were well inside the building and breaking up into small teams. When one of them was positioned perfectly, she sent Iyaan a message.

Lights off.

She set her night vision filters to automatic, so while everyone else was plunged into darkness she just turned on the lights. Her target had walked behind a crate to her left, leaving him out of sight of everyone but her. Her strike was clinical and nonlethal. Without breaking stride, she was able to carry him deeper into cover. *Lights on.*

The shouting and cursing damped down. None of them blinked at the light, so it'd been too fast for them to activate their own filters. She quickly bound his arms behind his back. She didn't have the time or materials to gag him, but that wasn't strictly necessary. In this close environment even a gagged person could be heard, and his sudden shouting would only add to the confusion.

With so many targets, the picking was easy at first. The next three went down as easily as the first, but by that time everyone else knew they had a bigger problem than a flaky light switch. The leaders were the only ones armed, but the rest grabbed impromptu clubs where they could find them.

Iyaan, can you activate the fire alarm?

I don't think so, he replied, *that's a separate system.*

So they'd do it the old-fashioned way. It took a moment of frantic searching to find the nearest pull, but the first thug coming to and screaming bought her the time she needed to find it. *Lights out, and this time they stay that way.* When darkness fell, she ran to the alarm pull and yanked it hard enough to snap the plastic T off. The room exploded into a chaos of flashing strobes and alarm claxons.

Now it wasn't a chess match, but more of a twisted game of pool. Tonya was both cue stick and ball. She had to move from one target to the next in a continuous motion that could not stop, reverse direction, or miss. These were problems every bit as complex and confusing as the ones she worked on with her theories, only they were made of bone and flesh. She let the adrenaline slow her time perception and her training take over. What had taken agonizing years to master was now muscle memory ingrained so deep it might as well have been a metaphysical tattoo.

There was no chance to bind anyone now, she had to strike as hard as she could as fast as she could. She prioritized the ones with guns but that compromised her overall strategy since they weren't exactly cooperating with her. The first one she knocked cold but could only manage to kick the gun out of the second one's hands.

Then her luck ran out.

A slam exploded across her back as some sort of club hit her. She rolled with the blow and that dissipated some of it, but the pain that exploded was hard to ignore. Hard, but not impossible. She rolled away before whoever it was could take another swing. She had to find the leader still standing. He would've seen where the gun went.

But so did she, and she had a clearer line to it. She ran forward and then started a handstand tumble to build vertical momentum, keeping him in sight as he flashed across her spinning view. On the second tumble, she jumped as high as she could, coming down with a leading foot straight to the top of his head. Again she had to compromise her moves to make sure he didn't fracture his skull hitting the ground, and her landing stopped her progress cold. There wasn't time to get to her feet.

The one with the club was joined by two buddies with weapons held high for a deadly strike. She dodged two of them, but the last one connected with the back of her legs, and it made it impossible to jump to her feet. She rolled away instead, pushing the pain into a place she'd deal with later.

She staggered to her feet, disoriented. There was still a gun in play somewhere nearby. A loud crack was followed by an explosion of splinters from a crate next to her head. Tonya crouched low and ran toward the sound as several more shots followed. It was one thing to know that pistols were much harder to use than people thought, and that they were harder still in a high-pressure situation. The thing was, she had to be lucky the entire time. The thug only had to be lucky once.

In other words, getting shot at sucked and always would.

Once she was close enough, she leapt from her cover with a pirouette spin that would break up her outline and make her move in unpredictable ways. The thug got one last shot off before she body slammed into him, sending the gun skidding off into the chaos.

She stood up but found herself alone, everyone else either bound, out cold, or frantically working on the door trying to escape. *Let them go, Iyaan.*

Then she saw the blood.

In all the confusion, Tonya had inadvertently put herself between the shooter and the desk Rachel hid behind. The bullet holes were easy to see even in the flashing light.

Tonya broke into a run.

Chapter 48
Maff

Maff's vision cleared from the sudden realm disconnect in Aaron's safe house. She found herself with Chishow, Aaron...and three masked humans holding weapons on them.

"Hands up," the one in the center said. "Or whatever it is you call that part of your suit." Aaron was already standing, hands up, as one of the other masked humans relieved him of his weapon.

Oh my God! Chishow sent her. *Are they going to kill us?*

She had gone on enough combat realm crawls with Spencer that being held under gunpoint wasn't unnerving her the way it was Chishow. That didn't make the gas in her any less turbulent. She could hang on. Chishow, on the other hand... *If they were, they would've already done it.* Not exactly a lie, and he didn't know enough about Earth culture to understand what a cliché that saying was. *Now watch me and configure yourself the same way.* She rearranged her body plan so that her manipulators resembled—vaguely—human hands while her wings took the shape of arms. She continued the transformation until her body outline resembled a human's. To his credit, after a moment's hesitation, Chishow did the same.

Why can't we talk to Aaron?

They must be jamming our human phones. Can you do more than text me?

No. What's happening?

It's like when the nodes are raiding an unlicensed piracy guild. They must be jamming the human frequencies, but not the ones we use.

I don't understand what you're saying.

It'd been some time since she'd interacted with bemians who hadn't absorbed any of humanity's staggering amount of technical knowledge. *We can talk to each other because of our native phones.* It felt like talking to a pre-uplift native. Or rather, how they were portrayed in bemian media. Which on consideration must have been a myth made up millions of years ago by the nodes themselves.

"You do know you're assaulting a federal agent, right?" Aaron said as one of the gunmen put simple restraints around his wrists.

"No talking," said one of the other two who still held guns on them all.

The man finished with Aaron, then moved to her. *Watch what I do.* Reviewing their media for potential export had given her a good overview of what they called *procedurals*, dramatizations of crime and punishment. *It's not much different from how the police bots do it back home.* She held up her pseudo hands and let them be bound behind her back.

I'm not…I'm not sure I can. They have weapons! You said they weren't all violent primitives, and now I'm staring down—

The last thing she needed was for the interpreter to lose his wind. *Chishow! You're doing fine. They're not going to hurt us.*

Then why are they using—

It's a human thing. She was sure about that much. *Stay calm.*

He flinched at the human's touch but otherwise didn't panic. *You said this house was safe.*

She didn't need sound to hear the accusation. *No, I said it was a safe house. You're an interpreter. You didn't catch the distinction?*

"Now," the middle human said. "You're coming with us."

I don't…I can't…what's happening to us? What will they do?

Aaron turned to them. "Do as they say. Remain calm." He certainly didn't seem at all worried, which went a long way toward calming the storm inside Maff. "We'll be fine."

They were marched out of the house and quickly bundled into one of the medium-sized human transports called a *van*. Two of the humans took up guard positions while the remaining one sat in the cockpit and drove them away.

Why can't I reach this planet's realmspace?

The change in text style meant Danlaw, Chishow's threaded companion, had entered the chat. *It's fully inhabited.*

By what?

Another threaded companion.

You can't be serious. It's the planet's general realmspaces I'm trying to reach.

I'll explain later. Can you access the private realm the vehicle hosts? Maybe they could shut the thing down using it.

Yes. What do you want me to do?

Maff quickly explained her idea about shutting off the van.

That won't work. It looks like a standard entertainment variant. Pretty basic.

Ah well. Chishow, when I give you the signal, I need you to wrap up the guard on the left. I'll take out the other two.

Take out? As in violence? Do you have that kind of license?

Bemian assumptions like that were giving her a headache. *Again, I'll explain later. Wrap his arms up and point the gun at the ceiling.*

But the restraints...

Are much weaker than they appear, at least for us. Twist quickly and use a blade extension in the middle. They weren't the metal kind but were instead one of their *zip tie* style systems. Spencer's tutorials for realm escapes were proving invaluable. *On three. One...two...three!*

Strangely enough, she'd practiced how to render a human unconscious without killing them outright. Spencer's tutorials again, this time a *Three Stooges* realm. The penalties were severe if Moe, Larry, or Curly—such strange names, and even stranger historical humans—incurred significant damage. She'd learned about it the hard way. He said the time she got excited and slapped

Moe's head clean off his shoulders was one of the funniest things he'd ever seen.

These weren't coherent thoughts, more like a brief *be careful* as she bashed the near guard's head against the side of the van. Chishow ended up on the floor as he sent both his manipulators *and* his legs at the other guard, burying him in a pile of twisting articulated brass. The humans had been sitting down with their weapons in hand but not pointed. *Take the weapon.*

I can't believe I'm touching it! The mass of legs and arms pulsed once and ejected the weapon toward the back door. *That's so awful!*

The vehicle lurched to the side as the driver tried to shout, draw his own weapon, look behind him, and drive, all at the same time. Maff extended her manipulators to take control of the vehicle while disarming and restraining the driver. She'd done her fair share of driving, an incredibly novel experience surpassed only by flying, but not from this angle. *When in doubt, slow down.* They were still on city streets, so she pulled over to the side of the road.

She felt motion on her right side, a pushing. At first, she thought her bad guy had woken up. Not the case. In all the excitement, she and Chishow had relaxed into their more normal shape. This had filled the available space, inadvertently wedging Aaron between her suit and the wall of the van. She pulled back. "Sorry."

"Maff!" Chishow's voice had gone squeaky with his panic. "What do I do?"

His pile of arms and legs were rippling, trying to keep the human restrained, although by the sound of the screams, she didn't think he would be much of a threat if he got free. "I need a second," she said and then turned to Aaron. She compressed herself to give him even more space. "Turn around, I'll free your arms." That done, she snapped his restraints. Without pausing, he yanked the spool of restraints the driver had hanging from his belt and set to work on the one she knocked out. His moves were rapid and efficient, the consequence of rigorous training.

He turned to the admittedly bizarre shape that was Chishow's current configuration. "Can he give me access?"

"He's moving too much!" Chishow replied.

Aaron leaned down and shouted, "Buddy! Be still, and I'll get you out of there." He had to repeat it a few times before the bad guy heard him, but once he had, the ripples stopped. "Give me your hands."

"What the fuck is this? What's going on?"

"Hands first. Or you can be trapped under all that until we get to the station."

Chishow moved around enough for the human to put his arms out next to each other. Once Aaron had secured his wrists, he said to Chishow, "You can get up now."

While he was reconfiguring his body, Aaron plucked his own weapon out of the driver's belt. He checked it and cycled the action. There was a click as he took the safety off.

In the time it to her to blink, he shot all three men.

Chishow screamed and started jumping around. Maff was equally horrified, then she remembered. The sound was wrong, too quiet for it to be real bullets. "Chishow! Calm down!"

Freaked out more than she'd ever seen another pallun, he naturally switched away from English to his native language. "He killed them! Right in front of us! We need to run! I don't know how to open the doors! They're all barbarians! They're—"

She used her manipulators to thwack the ports his suit used to hear and see, the pallun equivalent of one human slapping another. In an instant, panic changed to wounded indignance. "Ow!"

"Stop! They're not dead." She switched to English and said to Aaron, who looked almost as freaked out as Chishow did, "My friend thinks you have murdered captors."

He startled. "Not at all. They're called safeStops." He rolled the door open. "I'll explain, but we need to get out of here right now. They're almost certainly watching us. Follow me, and we'll evade them."

She and Chishow climbed out of the van behind Aaron, who set off at a run, heading for cover as he talked.

Maff knew about safeStops from her time in human realms and

the story Kim told about how the FBI had caught her for the first and only time. They were yet another fiendishly clever human invention, using their nanotechnology and advanced knowledge of their own anatomy to create a projectile that rendered the target unconscious. Aaron's weapon could shoot them as an alternative to lethal bullets.

Eventually they got far enough away from whatever jammer the bad guys used that her human phone reactivated. "I have signal."

Aaron nodded grimly as he scanned while they walked. "I got it back a little while ago. Turn it off for now."

"Why?"

"I don't know how they found us, so I can't trust any of the tech we have. Once I'm certain they've lost us, we'll pick up some burners."

She didn't know what that was, but it didn't matter as much as her next question. "And then?"

He shook his head. "We need to get out of this area. Israel has consulates in other places. I can get us out of DC, but I don't know what to do after that."

She thought about the hangar in Manassas. "I do."

Chapter 49

Mike

Mike used his perception coupled with his threads to map the transfer space they discovered, and Zoe's cache on the other side. The news wasn't good. "It's farther away than it looks."

"How so?"

"There are invisible dimensions between here and there that alter the topology considerably. These streams of avatars we're seeing aren't turning. They're all proceeding in straight lines. It's the realm itself that guides them around the space."

"Okay. Wait, what?"

"Think of it like a mirror maze in a funhouse, but instead of stopping you, the mirrors send you off in a different direction." Other threads reported findings. "It gets worse."

"I was kind of expecting it to at this point. What's worse?"

"I can't manipulate the contracts in here. There's a protection and monitoring system on them I've never seen before."

"How is that possible?"

"I don't know, and the stakes are too high for me to mess around and find out." He took it as a sign of growing maturity. A couple of years ago, he would've pushed on it to see what it did. "We need to do some planning."

"Can I look like one of them?"

"An interesting idea, but I don't know what sort of IFF they have going on."

"IFF?"

He chuckled to himself. "I forget sometimes not everyone runs a combat realm. It stands for Identification Friend or Foe, the designation goes back into the middle of the twentieth century, I think. It's a shorthand term for how they authenticate and authorize to enter the space. That could be very sophisticated and without Kim around, I'm not sure I can hack it." Even if she were around, it would be chancy. "I'm thinking of a different kind of camouflage."

The contract acceptance criteria were fairly broad. In other words, while he couldn't change her avatar on the fly, he could help her craft one that would work better than walking in with a human default. They ended up with an avatar that closely resembled a Tachikoma, an AI walker tank from a property called *Ghost in the Shell*. It was highly mobile, fast, and tough. Weapons were, not surprisingly, strictly prohibited, so instead of grenade launchers and machine guns, they equipped it with extra grapples and a flexible arm with a mace on the end.

"It's not as good as a light saber," she said as she swung what was effectively a fancy spiked club, "but it's better than nothing."

They also made it considerably smaller than the car-sized original. In fact, it wouldn't be too much of an exaggeration to call it a recreation of what could've been bought at Japanese toy stores at the dawn of the twenty-first century.

There was also a heavily armored storage space that made up the back of the avatar. "It kind of looks like a toilet with legs," Zoe said as they put the finishing touches on it. "How hard will it be for me to steer it?"

"I've added a lot of automation to the stabilization and guidance contracts. It'll be easier to drive than a car."

"There's no time like now," she said, then activated the factory method that constructed the avatar's contract matrix. The avatar she'd been using, a tiny human in a paramilitary suit, dissolved. Its constituent parts flew away and swirled together. After a few seconds, Zoe the person was gone, and Zoe the—hopefully—heavily armored stealth combat bot appeared.

Since it was Zoe, it wasn't what he specified in the contracts. While the basic shape was still there, it was sleeker, more refined, looking like what would roll out of a Ferrari factory. "You never miss an opportunity."

She moved around, flexing the wheeled spider legs as she twirled and tested it. "Your stuff is always so plain. I didn't want to rescue my people in a stand mixer with legs."

What Zoe thought was plain, he thought of as elegant understatement, but now was not the time to argue fashion or styling. "Remember, take it slow."

"Slow and steady. And camouflaged." Like the avatar's originator, they were able to cobble together a respectable active camo contract. The stylish paint scheme gave way to a pattern that roughly duplicated her surroundings. It wouldn't stand up to close scrutiny, but it'd make her harder to spot from a distance. "Stay on my wing, right?"

"It doesn't work that way, but I get your meaning. I'm with you, count on that."

The extra size of her avatar made it simpler to navigate the obstacles the walls of the space presented without worry of being crushed in a too-small space. It retained the grown-but-not-organic faceted, crystalline structure but was also covered in ducts, conduits, and various junction boxes. It bore more than a passing resemblance to a Covenant ship from an old *Halo* realm.

As they moved out into the space, Mike got a better look at the endpoints being used. From this angle, he recognized them. They looked like the construct that accidentally transported his threads almost in their entirety to another realmspace in a different part of the galaxy, nearly killing him in the process.

That was almost entirely due to him standing in front of what was effectively an airliner turbofan running at full throttle. Keeping well away from them would neutralize the danger.

"Now, turn in this way," he said as the realm folded in a direction that had no meaning in realspace.

She pushed one of her wheeled spider legs across the transition, and it folded like it was on a piece of paper. "What the hell?" Zoe wobbled a little as the gravitic contract reoriented her avatar's balance. "Did someone do this on purpose?"

"Yes and no. I think. No, in the sense that they did it for some abstract reason like art or entertainment. Yes, in the sense that this plays a role in the efficiency of the operation." He split off some threads to work the on the idea that it'd been done on purpose. It might have implications for Sidereal back home. "You have another transition fifteen meters ahead. Follow the guides as I lay them out for you." She was seeing the world through the synthetic vision of a simulated battle tank, so it was easy to put symbology in her view.

His analysis came back with an interesting finding. Keeping his distance from those endpoints was the right idea, but singular threads could be drawn into them with no risk to himself. If they traveled far enough, they'd end up snapping, but that was less painful than getting hairs plucked out of his human host's head. He discovered that bit when Kim insisted on tweezing out a weird random hair on his shoulder. She'd normally never risk a touch, but the woman had an OCD streak about personal grooming. He used a razor on it ever since.

Regardless of how losing threads compared and contrasted with losing hair, the ultimate implication was that he could safely send threads down these endpoints to see where they went. From their encounters so far, he knew this was an army of some sort. It was smart to get intel on them.

"Now a corkscrew in the sixth dimension," he said as he did the prep work.

"This is an armored construct. How does it corkscrew?"

"It doesn't. That's not what's happening."

"And people say art can be confusing."

He took careful aim at one of the closer endpoints and fired a single thread through it. The sense of vertigo was familiar but, since it was a single thread, controllable. The distance it traveled was hard to judge, but it felt like a long way.

On arrival, it took a moment to orient himself. He thought he'd find another realm being invaded, but that wasn't the case.

They'd already been here.

The destruction was total, a global realmspace catastrophe on a scale he didn't believe possible. Mike could do this sort of damage by manifesting his avatar and touching a realm, but that was a local event. It didn't spread across realms. What happened here was done on a more calculated basis, using an army. Zoe's realm, or whatever it was, had been a single valley, an isolated environment that held hundreds. This space had once encompassed a planet.

It got worse.

The planet itself was emptied. He could see this through various endpoints that used to be security monitors. The event had been recent, very recent. There was no decay, no ruins, no wreckage. The wild spaces in the parks and outside the cities hadn't had time to encroach. It was like they had all left less than a day ago.

Then he found a senescence monument. The final expression of bemian insanity, they were suicide booths writ large. The planet's population had in fact left. But they'd gone nowhere.

Maff had talked about stumbling into one of these on the first La'fan world they'd ever visited. But that had been left derelict thousands of years before. This one was brand new. Sickening didn't come close to what he thought about it. What the nodes lifted up, they also tore down. For reasons no bemian had ever questioned, let alone thought to protest, the nodes would decide it was time for one intelligent life form to make way for a new one. A call would go out, a signal sent, and almost as one, they all went to their deaths. La'fan tradition said this was ultimately the consequence of using up their planets. It was seen, or at least advertised, as an end with far less suffering than when an entire planet's ecosystem collapsed.

But that wasn't the case here. There was no decay, no sign of imminent collapse. He'd seen worlds that'd recently gone through senescence while he and Kim negotiated La'fan contracts. They looked nothing like this.

Searching the deep recesses of the realm's base structures, he found the answer. To have a system declared senescent required the unanimous consent of an entire system's nodes. These typically numbered in the thousands, and a unanimous vote wasn't a foregone conclusion. As opposed as he was to the entire concept, there was at least that safeguard.

Until there wasn't. One of the more terrifying flaws they discovered during the effort to patch out vulnerabilities was a scenario that could, with the right combination of hacks and physical access to fifteen nodes, be used to intentionally trigger the event. It's what Valsa had used against them while Kim was being held prisoner. Patching that vulnerability out was one of his proudest moments.

This system had received that patch.

There was another way to trigger the event, a scenario he considered unlikely enough that he set it aside for a later date. If a system's realmspace was utterly destroyed, the nodes could be tricked into thinking the collapse of the planet was imminent. He passed over it. The level of effort was beyond anything he thought could be accomplished. The target was too large and would take far too many resources to accomplish. He was now proven wrong about that.

They were witnessing armies being dispatched to end the existence of entire worlds.

Intelligent life was the only stage of existence in which true enlightenment could be achieved. Cutting it short, for any reason, was to deny an entity the ability to escape the endless wheel of birth, death, and rebirth. What he was seeing was the willful destruction of an entire system's worth of intelligent life in a war that had not been declared, not even noticed.

The entire time he was examining this murdered system he was guiding Zoe through the various folds and twists of the realm her cache was in. He now perceived this space very differently. Each transfer point represented a system under attack, a planet on the path to destruction. Billions of innocent beings on the cusp of annihilation.

Zoe pulled back as they grew closer to her cache. "Something's wrong."

He concentrated and could see it. "How has it decayed that much?"

What had once been a sturdy construct now showed signs of massive contract decay. What should've been keeping it healthy and intact had eroded to the point that it was beyond even his ability to reconstruct it.

She reached out hesitantly. When she touched it, it fell to dust.

He zeroed out the contracts on her avatar. It sent the screaming AI back to the weird storage realm that held the entrance to all of this. Whatever happened next, he'd be there for Zoe, but Mike knew he now had a job to do.

He manifested his avatar fully and let his feet touch the floor.

Chapter 50
Kim

Anna Treacher, former administrator of the Yellowstone project, had new clothes, a new hair style, and a set of boots that wouldn't look out of place on the feet of a Star Destroyer captain, but the look in her eyes was still the same.

Smug, self-assured, and totally insane.

"I have become his adjutant, you see. I now truly command legions."

"You *manage* legions," Kim replied sourly. "Adjutants don't command."

She threw back her head and laughed. "I had forgotten how quick your wit was."

They spent all of twenty minutes in the same room back in the day, during which Kim not only was transformed but also fully multithreaded. She wasn't sure they said anything to each other. Anna was crazy enough to be lying for the sake of it, but Kim wouldn't underestimate her. This might not be a jester to torment her. It was more than possible that a new player had entered the game.

So Kim played her part. Mostly by ignoring her. "I expected better from you, Valsa."

"You are too powerful by half. A personal army *and* an entire world free of nodes?"

Andromeda blinked. "Personal army?"

Now Kim paid attention to Anna. Andromeda didn't know about her ability to split but wasn't surprised about a planet with no AC network presence. All the other woman did was smile with a mad gleam in her eye.

"Yes," replied Valsa, "large enough to take out my second fleet."

"And you were going to tell me this when, exactly?"

She turned to him and smiled. "Why would I ever tell you at all?"

A text window opened in Kim's enhanced vision. It was Seluk, Valsa's threaded companion. *I am so sorry for this.*

Andromeda rounded on Valsa, shaking his finger at her. "This is no time to keep secrets!"

"Or take captives!" she shot back.

That was when the shouting started. Andromeda might be large, but Valsa's voice was her job. She could bellow in different languages and did so. Kim was, as the saying went, not going to interrupt enemies making mistakes. *I tried to talk her out of this,* he continued, *but she wouldn't budge.*

I don't suppose you can drop the force field?

If I did, where would you go?

She hated when the other side made a point. *Okay. What do you want?* She was good enough at reading bemian script that it was almost like regular text.

Now that I've reached out, I'm embarrassed to say I don't know. I did want to forge an alliance. I'm furious with her for going back on that.

Making a decision without thinking about what would happen next was straight out of Mike's playbook. *You sound a lot like my husband.*

You married *your companion?*

On the other side of the force field, Andromeda and Valsa had started circling each other. Neither had any weapons. If they had they would've been pulled and fired by now otherwise. She and Mike had nothing on these two when it came to arguing. *Is that a problem?*

It's possibly the most shocking thing you've said so far. In the Guild, we're raised together. What you're describing is considered incest.

Don't worry, I can't touch him.

But the fact that you want to is...I'm sorry, I have to think about this.

Valsa abruptly stopped her argument mid-sentence and turned to Kim. "Really?"

She shrugged. It wasn't the push she expected to use to throw Valsa off balance, but Kim would take what she could get. "He's very handsome."

She blanched. "That's..."

She could see Andromeda was not used to being dismissed out of hand. He wasn't angry, just disoriented. "What are you talking about?"

Valsa swallowed. "Earth's interpreters are different in..."

This time the gulp was loud enough Kim could hear it.

"So many ways."

Kim thought Andromeda would pick up right where they left off, and he looked about to do that. But then he flinched and closed his eyes tightly. When he opened them he was no longer the god-thing ranting at an impudent underling.

He was scared.

Without saying a word, he motioned for Anna to follow him and then they both marched out of the room.

"What was that all about?" Kim asked.

Valsa shook her head. "I don't know. I've never seen him frightened before."

Seluk's holo appeared in their shared vision channel. "You need to let her go."

"She's far too dangerous."

Angry *and* paranoid. "I'm not a danger to you."

She shook her head. "You've always been a danger. I haven't known the extent of it until now."

"Why do you continue to think that? I'm one person. You have an entire guild."

"And you have an army of wildling interpreters at your beck and call. You took no losses and neutralized an entire interpreter fleet with them."

In reality, she'd done it all herself. Sort of. But explaining that would be too distracting at the moment.

Seluk said, "I told you before, and I'll tell you again. She is not our enemy. At least, she wasn't until now." He looked at her.

She shrugged. "Jury's still out." And it was. If she could somehow bring the head of the Guild around, it would represent a massive advantage for Earth. That was worth getting cooped up a time or two. It didn't bother her anywhere near as much as it seemed to bother Valsa.

"See? She's not threatening us and never has. If you'd stop and think this through, you'd know that."

"This is not a game, Seluk. My hold on power—"

"Is more secure than it's ever been," he interrupted. "You must set aside this paranoia."

"It's not paranoia if they're really after me! I will never be caged again. I will never be someone's servant again. I will never be forced to do anything by anyone."

Kim saw the opening and took it. "But you already have. You already are. Andromeda holds your leash. He only had to yank it once to bring you to heel."

"He does nothing of the sort. I brought him in. We are equal partners, and always have been."

"This is not what an equal partnership looks like where I'm from. He locked you up. I was the one who got you free. *I* got you out of there."

Seluk nodded. "At no point has she ever done anything that remotely looked hostile, conniving, or traitorous."

Only because she was hiding it better than they were, but that was for the long game. Right now she honestly wasn't a threat to Valsa. And it might stay that way. "You think you're in charge? Fine." She walked to the back of the cell, well away from the door, and sat on the floor. "Turn the force field off. I won't make a move."

Valsa arched an eyebrow. "You are capable of anything."

"I don't know what else I can tell you. It doesn't matter anyway. It won't work. The force field will not turn off," Kim said.

Valsa smiled. "If you're trying to escape, you won't trick me that easily."

Seluk threw his holographic arms to his virtual sides. "Valsa Burtan, you are *impossible*. We've scanned her, we've watched her. Her powers are exactly those of any other interpreter. A weird one with," he wrinkled his nose, "distasteful customs, but this is no monster." He turned to Kim. "No offense."

She shrugged. "None taken." She slid down until she was prone on the floor. "Now I can't see the door, let alone make a run for it. Go ahead. Turn it off. Just a flick."

The hum of the force field didn't change, which made Valsa's gasp easy to hear. "How *dare* he!"

She levered herself up on an elbow. Valsa was so mad she was almost hopping. Seluk had his head in his hand. Valsa wasn't much of a super villain, but she was all Kim had at the moment. "You have never been in control. He has no intention of letting you out from under his thumb. I'll bet if you ask him, he'll freely admit it. Try it again."

She closed her eyes for a moment. "I cannot believe this." She turned to Seluk. "How?"

"I can tell you how," Kim said as she stood and dusted herself off. She switched to English because it was the only language with the proper words that Valsa understood. "Your security is a joke. You have vulnerabilities that are billions of years old. He hacked the entire network long before you were born."

Knowing the words was not the same as understanding the concepts. "What does that mean?"

Bemians gotta bemian. The control nexus for this door would be about waist high and on the left side. She put her hand over the spot it should be behind the wall. "It means this."

There were lines of potential, and she couldn't remember how to breathe. This lock forever never power flows nowhere everywhere elsewhere collapse and now…

Since this was the second time she'd used her power in as many hours, the gunshot was quieter. Kim only had to blink once. But then it was her turn for a shock.

The force field was still activated.

"Enough of this," Andromeda said as he returned with Anna in tow. He gestured a silent snap at the force field. It vanished instantly. "You're coming with me." To emphasize the point, a set of guards walked past him and took up stations on either side of her. "I trust these won't be necessary."

He was good at spotting mortal vulnerabilities, she'd give him that. "Not at all," she said as she walked forward. "Where are you taking me?"

"Us," Anna said as she fell into step behind Kim. "The master needs us both."

"To do what?"

"To remove your home planet as a threat to my plans. I will not fail so close to the finish this time."

Chapter 51
Spencer

He was still staring at the footprint when Sornik walked over. "What are you talking about?"

"They're huge, hairy, taller than you are but humanoid. Dark blue. Three eyes," he gestured a triangle over his face, point up, "like this."

"Bullshit."

"No, no bullshit. They damned near killed me."

"You saw a *nalton*? That's what you described right there, especially the thing with the eyes. But that's not possible."

"Why not?"

"They're legends. I scare my grandkids with stories about them."

He remembered Tonya's story about the encounter in the cache. "But you saw one."

"*That's* what it was? All I saw was a mummy. An *ugly* mummy. It was interpreters who attacked us, not a nalton."

"I'm telling you I've seen one, and Tonya's seen one. We both fought with them."

"Now I know you're joking. If half the legends I know are true, nobody walks away from one of those things."

"I damned near didn't. Neither did Tonya. How do you know about it?"

The tunnel they walked through was mostly rock with the occasional bit of precontact Telirian structures rammed through.

"I guess," Sornik said as they clambered over a rusty girder that split the passage in half diagonally, "I might be what you'd call an expert on the things."

"How'd that happen?"

"A big part of our business is in antique books. Nalton feature prominently in early stories."

"So what's their deal?"

"There's this legend, about what triggered the fall. It's about…I don't know, what do you call it…"

Spencer wasn't sure if that was a question or a verbal pause, so he stayed silent.

"Big evil. Ancient, older than time. It created the nalton. They didn't evolve on a planet."

"Frankenstein's shock troops."

"Eh?"

Spencer shook his head. "Nothing. I'll explain later."

"Anyway, first they'd send a planet back to its precontact state. Nobody knows exactly what they did. The legends were written by people who'd already spent centuries living like primitives. They didn't understand the stories and so it's kinda hard to interpret what they were talking about into modern terms."

The hours he'd spent grinding away at Homer in World Civ had finally paid off. He knew exactly what Sornik was talking about. "We have a version of that."

"Eventually what was the AC network caught on and that stopped working. Again, nobody knows why or how. So instead, this great evil took over the transit dimension and flooded it with naltons."

That didn't add up. "I thought only interpreters could use the transit dimension directly."

"You're not wrong about that. It's what the legend says. Last I heard the latest theory is that what we have are copies of copies of copies, and things got mistranslated. How? Nobody knows."

They were well into the tunnels now but nothing much had changed. Same ruined tunnels, same debris, same occasional nalton trail or boot print. The environment was not the best for tracking. "So what happened?"

"They took out the middleman and started destroying systems directly. The legend seems to say the network shut the portals off, which crashed the galaxy. No portals, no civilization."

He almost smirked at that but could see where Sornik was coming from. "That was what happened? What caused the Undoing?"

"There was this other thing going on, the interpreters were involved somehow. Or at least a group of them. Some versions say two, four, a dozen, it varies. They…changed somehow, threw the great evil down a well."

"A well? A thing that can destroy a galactic civilization gets beat by ending up in the bottom of a *well*?"

Sornik shrugged as they clambered over more obstacles. "It's a legend. It doesn't have to make sense. The nodes either had it all under control and the interpreters panicked and fucked everything up, or the nodes refused to finish the job, and the interpreters had no choice but to pull the trigger."

"On what?"

He switched to a language Spencer didn't understand and chanted some poetry. Spencer stopped and gave him a blank look. Sornik shrugged. "That Kim of yours? She'd do a better job translating it into something you'd understand. I got nothing. Standard isn't meant for it, and you don't know enough Pallundian. At any rate, there was music involved, a big clash on a mysterious plain of existence, storms flashed with lightning, bad guy goes down a well, everyone else lives in the stone ages for the next couple million years. By the time it gets put back together, nobody remembers what happened."

"Tonya's cache could tell you I bet."

"Yeah. I've been meaning to get back there to check." He chuckled. "I still don't understand how it got here, how she pulled that off."

"Have time machine, will travel."

"See," Sornik said, "you had to use English there. Standard doesn't cover it. No language does. I only recognized it because Kim taught me the words while Tonya told her story. *I* have to use the English words. That is so...*fucking*...weird."

"You'd never heard of time travel before we came along? That was real?" He'd heard that from Maff but hadn't believed it.

"I think it might be the most terrifying thing about you people. I've been around the galaxy so many times that I lost count. *Never* have I come across an idea so out there I couldn't at least get my wingtips to touch it. If that cache didn't exist, if I hadn't walked around in it, seen the contents, met the people responsible...kid, I gotta tell ya, I did all that, and I *still* don't quite believe it's true."

"Why is that terrifying?"

"You people are capable of anything. Anything! As a pallun, I've never thought of myself as a member of the galaxy the way other people do. We're too different, ostracized, discriminated against. Not me personally..."

"Not more than once per individual, I'd imagine."

Sornik barked out a big laugh. "You got that right. But hanging around you people? Cloud tops in the breeze. I never thought I'd find anything in common with the petarkan I have to deal with, but now? Now I'm sitting in a cloud full of them. And they don't fly!"

He wasn't sure how that connected but it didn't seem relevant. He was the descendant of a flying gasbag that evolved on a world with no surface. Sometimes their metaphors wouldn't translate.

"So yeah," Sornik said. "I need to drag my wings over there and check out—" He stopped. "You hear that?"

Spencer listened. "Something big up ahead."

"Right. *Now* we need to concentrate on the task at hand."

"Which is?"

"Getting the fuck out of here."

The sounds were too soft to make out at first, but as they got closer, he thought he could hear movement, voices, and some kind of clanking and banging. "Maybe a factory?" he whispered.

"Your guess is as good as mine."

After a pretty long walk, their tunnel opened up to a vast space. Big metal crates blocked their direct view, but Spencer could see that the room was a heavily modified cave with at least a fifty-foot ceiling. Girders braced against the walls, to the point he saw more steel than rock. In the middle of the room, perhaps thirty feet in front of them, was a giant hollow column that reached to the ceiling surrounded with walkways and stairs.

It was teeming with nalton.

Spencer hadn't seen one in the flesh since his encounters on the grounds of the powerplant. He thought the sound of his parents' fighting changing to actual blows was the worst feeling he'd ever know, but seeing dozens of these hairy beasts walking around purposefully turned that into a wet fart. The urge to run was so powerful he turned around.

And came face-to-face with a nalton.

It was smaller than the ones he'd confronted, much smaller, about Spencer's height. It'd been creeping up behind them and seemed as startled by Spencer's sudden move as he was to find it there. He elbowed Sornik hard enough to push his suit in like a metal plated balloon, ignoring the pain that shot up his elbow. He'd have time for bruises later. Sornik pivoted around.

"Oh, fuck me," he said.

The staring contest lasted an eternity that crossed maybe two seconds. The nalton blinked its three eyes, making the triangle they formed flicker like lights about to go out. Then it broke and ran back up the passage. Spencer started sprinting a tenth of a second later. He could hear Sornik lurch into motion behind him. There was no plan, only the urge to stop the mini monster from doing…anything.

It skidded into a side passage they'd somehow missed, Spencer close behind. The floor sloped upward, and Spencer thought he'd catch the thing but then it got steeper, and it was all he could do to keep up. Then the nalton took another sharp right out of sight.

Spencer thundered out of the passage straight onto a metal catwalk. He hit his chest against a railing, all thought of the nalton briefly blown away by what he saw.

The room was *enormous*. The column that they saw was one of three arranged in a triangle across a space easily three times bigger than he originally thought it was. Nalton marched in columns across the floor, exiting one portal and entering another on the other side. At least that was what some of them did. Others split apart to form different columns going different directions, others looked like they were on errands of their own not related to the marchers. Stacks of weapons, alien but recognizable as such, were everywhere, including strapped to the naltons themselves. Most of these were the huge brutes he'd confronted, and it was only then that he remembered he'd been chasing a little one that should be—

Far to the right, their nalton pressed a button mounted to the guard rail, instantly setting off loud alarms. "You know the drill, kid," Sornik said as he wrapped him up with manipulators while climbing up the wall.

Since this was not his first ride on this particular rodeo bull, he got situated so he could see. The floor had turned into a churning mass of naltons. The vast majority were either confused or frightened. He hadn't thought that would be the reaction of a bunch of alien stormtroopers but it didn't much matter. A noticeable number of naltons *weren't* milling around in a panic. They were instead mounting a coordinated operation with a single focus.

The spidery gas bag and the naked ape riding him.

Hand weapons were the first things that came out. "Sornik! Run in a Z! Run in a Z!"

"I don't know what that means!"

"DODGE AROUND!"

He zigged to the left as the wall they were using got peppered with small-arms fire. One of them spanged off Sornik's left wing but didn't seem to faze him. "Is that all they got?"

The next thing that came out was mounted on a tripod. "No! Dodge right!"

He did as a much larger bolt of energy blasted rock and concrete chips from the spot they'd been in a half a second before.

"How do we get out of here?" Sornik shouted.

"I don't know. Head for those cylinders." They'd at least provide some cover.

Sornik swung, jumped, and skittered across the walls and ceiling, putting as much of the inner structures as he could between them and the cannons. Small-arms fire continued to cause the walls and roof to sparkle as it either hit rock, concrete, or steel. When he'd first seen the naltons, all he wanted was a distraction to avoid thinking about them. Hanging from the back of a bucking alien running upside down across the ceiling while being shot at by those same aliens was not the distraction he was looking for. There had to be a merit badge or medal or some shit for a person who'd done it.

He spotted salvation on the second lap around the three cylinders. "There!"

"What?"

Not being able to highlight what he'd seen in a shared vision channel was like losing a limb.

"Make a quick right turn!"

Lurch.

"Too far, a little to the left!"

Lurch.

They were now well out of cover and taking heavy fire. "Straight ahead, corner of the wall." He'd spotted a cave entrance far above the floor and well away from any catwalk.

"I see it!" Sornik kicked in the afterburners.

They only had few yards to reach safety. This was worse than being only two strokes away from winning the county swim meet. Sornik shouted as he swung across the last gap.

Pain seared across Spencer's shoulder as he heard a metallic tearing come from Sornik's wing. They fell into the cave opening like a bag tossed into a cornhole game and hit hard. Spencer's head bounced against something, and he saw stars.

As the world went black, he got a powerful whiff of almonds.

Chapter 52
Helen

Kaddee was the first nonpallun bemian Helen'd spent any significant time around. He was also the first noncriminal from Toraz's gang she'd gotten to know personally. He worked for them, but in the heavily compromised morals of her current existence, that carried more weight than it otherwise would have.

She hadn't counted on the inside of the ship having a smell. Being Chinese meant she was used to pungent odors. She liked stinky tofu as much as the next person. But, mixed with whatever passed for grease and gear oil out here, it made for a potent combination.

"Bot!" he shouted and punched one to a halt. "Bring parts A-121 and Ce-sub-2. Go!" He bashed it back into motion.

They were now on their second day of repairs. The first had been spent installing the easy stuff, the parts that directly replaced damaged, worn out, or missing ones. Today was replacing the drive components. Kaddee hadn't mentioned the nav computer yet, and by now Helen was afraid to ask.

It was clear the drive was to be serviced by a crew. It ran the length of the ship, through several bulkheads, and the parts were heavy and difficult to handle. That they were in space didn't help as much as she thought it would. Mass was mass, and she already inadvertently squashed a finger not getting it out of the way fast enough when a stabilator rod didn't slow down the way it would've in a gravity field.

It also didn't help that she was space sick. Worse, her first attack had happened in front of her new mechanic. As usual, he bashed and punted bots around until it had all been cleaned up.

The event had deeply impressed Kaddee. "You gonna die?"

It only felt like that. "No. It happens to humans sometimes when we go into space."

Maneuvering heavy parts in zero G with a barf bag hanging around her neck was the order of the third day, the one where they had to adjust seven different systems from eight different locations using two people and an eclectic collection of bots that were mostly held together with wire and chewing gum. Or whatever it was bemians chewed.

The fact that they could do it at all was impressive and puzzling. "How do you manage it?" she asked Kaddee during their lunch break.

He cocked his enormously out of proportion head, a fuzzy American football with giant eyes. "Eh?"

"The bots. I've never seen any so efficient."

Those eyes went wide. "Oh. Bot!" A fist flashed out, and once again, one she hadn't noticed until now, stopped with a loud bang and a few sparks. He then flipped a latch and opened the top.

What she proceeded to get was a detailed lesson in bot engineering and the AIs they used. On first impression, Kaddee was a primitive and strange alien who somehow happened to be good with machines. Now that she'd spent time around him, she knew this was a façade that hid a sophisticated intelligence and a quick wit. She wondered if he'd be better spoken in his native tongue but had her doubts. It would be interesting to see Kim speak with him. Interpreters often used native body language as much as the spoken kind. Seeing her pantomime Kaddee's eccentricities would be amusing.

"That why they work good."

If she understood him correctly, by bashing them around in specific ways, he was training them to become more efficient and independent. This made it sound suspiciously like an abuser justifying his actions to the abused. But they, probably, weren't conscious, and did in fact perform noticeably better than the bots she'd observed elsewhere. Her notions about how nodes couldn't be conscious the way unduplicates could back home had proven to be an oversimplification. It looked like her opinion about bot consciousness was the same.

Watchtell's signaling hadn't stopped the entire time. It'd been days, and he hadn't given up. The idea that he was trying to reach her due to an emergency or crisis was growing. Like Mike, her intuition was more reliable than a regular human's, and that combination was causing her a great deal of concern.

It took the rest of the day to get the parts installed. Seeing the nav computer light up after Kaddee fixed the crack in it lifted a weight she'd been carrying since they got out here. She only picked up a few bruises from various zero G miscalculations and threw up one more time. All in all, not bad.

"Human?" Kaddee asked as they sat in the modest mess bay at supper. "Do they have *jatners* where you from?"

After a bit of back-and-forth, she understood. Drums. He was asking about drums. "Yes. They don't look exactly like yours, but they're recognizable." Mike had set up new gateways and compression systems that allowed them to download items across threads much more efficiently than before. She found a few pictures of the most common sort of drum kit, that she knew of, at any rate, and sent them to the shared vision channel. "What do you think?"

His jaw slowly dropped open and his eyes went round. This effectively hid the rest of his face, turning him into a three-dimensional caricature she couldn't help but smile at.

"That...*beautiful*. More?"

"Oh yes." Helen had never paid all that much attention to pop music and so was almost as impressed as Kaddee at the wild variety of drums humans used, both now and in the past. One thing was certain, the bigger the kit got, the more Kaddee liked it. Her bandwidth was still limited. She could only show him low-resolution original music videos from the '80s and '90s so he could see them in use. It quickly became apparent that what Americans called *hair metal* was his favorite.

She got to a song titled "Wild Side" by a band called Mötley Crüe. It was catchy in that tacky, over-the-top way Americans were famous for to this day. All the songs were. Then, around the two-minute mark, the camera turned and Kaddee gasped. It was a loud, ragged inhale that at first made Helen think he'd had a heart attack.

On the screen, the drum kit had been lifted into the air.

It kept getting higher and higher, and so did Kaddee's gasps. She didn't dare stop the show but was growing increasingly concerned. If he was in some sort of medical crisis, she'd never get home.

Then the kit turned upside down.

At that point Helen found her own mouth dropped open, so she only heard a thud as Kaddee fell out of his chair. If she'd killed her only way home watching stupid American classic rock...

She knelt down and shook him once. Then twice. *You better not die on me, you weird little monkey.*

He spasmed and gasped. His eyes flew open. "Where drum go? *Where drum go?"*

She helped him sit up. "I think that's enough for tonight. We have a job to do tomorrow."

He grew somber, serious in a way she didn't think was possible. "Human. That was most incredible thing Kaddee ever see. Ever hear of. Ever..." He closed his eyes, and his voice fell to a whisper. "Ever..." Suddenly he leapt into her lap, ropy arms around her, comically shaped head on her shoulder. "Kaddee never forget this," he said into her muffled shoulder, and then burst into tears.

Once it was clear he'd fallen asleep, she carried him quietly back to his hammock and drew a blanket over him. His bots had gathered around her like so many concerned dogs. Which they might well have been. "He'll be all right," she said, then climbed into her own hammock.

Being weird didn't make him any less sweet.

The next morning was about recalibrating all the parts they'd replaced the previous day. This turned out to involve a lot of waiting for various utilities to run their course. Since, as with almost all bemian tech, it didn't require a lot of hands-on monitoring, it gave her the space to scratch her increasingly frantic intuition's itch.

It was time to face Matthew Watchtell.

But she wouldn't do it alone. "Kaddee, I need some help."

"Bot!" As always, his fist's uncanny ability to bash a bot to a standstill before Helen noticed it was there was alive and well. This time she had to dodge a piece of its casing. "You watch calibration." He shoved it in front of the console he'd been working with, then turned to her. "What you need?"

She used a toolkit Mike had provided to synch her Earth phone with his neurology. Once that was done, it was a matter of him accessing the basic conference room realm hosted on the phone. "I need you to be my lifeguard."

She had no doubt Watchtell would have a trap of some sort lined up, and so Kaddee would act as an outside observer. "If anything goes wrong, I'll need you to get me out of there."

He stopped his intense examination of the Earth-style furniture constructs. "How?"

She manifested a control suite she'd been working on since they got here. "With these. I'm about to meet a very bad, dangerous man. If you don't like what you see or I ask for your help, you'll use these controls to get me away from him." She reconfigured some thread bundles so he could see her on a virtual screen. "You can watch here."

"Why you no have avatar like Kaddee?"

"It's complicated. Keep an eye on me, Kaddee. I'll need it."

He gave her holo an elbow wag, his version of a thumbs-up. "You go. I keep you safe."

She cast her perception back down her threads into her orbital home and then answered Watchtell's call.

The realm was a more luxurious version of the conference room she'd left Kaddee in. "Why the sudden change of heart?" he asked.

She hoped her quick acceptance of his standing invitation would catch him off guard. It was three in the morning in his time zone. This could be a lacky of some sort. "Authentication, please."

It was him. Without Kim around, there was no way to fake his id stamp. He wasn't off guard at all. He'd been waiting for her. "What do you want?"

"To talk. I didn't know how critical your role was in stabilizing this project until you left."

"You pushed me through a portal."

"A fact I must now apologize deeply for."

She split off a different set of threads to give Kaddee a running translation. "Kaddee no like guy. He spooky weird."

To him, she said, "Agreed."

"Well," she said to Watchtell. "I'm here. Again, what do you want?" Sometimes it was refreshing to use America's blunt and rude manners against them. If this were a Chinese meeting, it'd take hours to get to the point.

"To bring you back. And find out exactly how your true self can be better utilized."

True self was a term she'd only used with her closest friends. Recently. She also used it with a tightly controlled and heavily vetted group of assistants when she briefly ruled China. If they found those people, they also found out about some of the resources her father had created in the days leading up to her acquiring a host. She reached out with her threads and found a boundary that hadn't been there before.

"Ask me nicely, but make sure I can only give you one answer?" she asked.

"Insurance is an aspect of the work I do."

As with Watchtell, father needed most of all to control her. Before he knew she could be bound to a realspace host, he'd had his engineers secretly devise a construct that could hold her threads in one place. It was an interstitial prison cell and had inadvertently caught Mike as well the first time its door had been shut. She was nearly crushed out of existence.

"Matthew, you still don't know what you're dealing with here."

He nodded. "That's why I've had to resort to this. We've been speculating about extraterrestrial life forms for more than a century now. How ironic that we would discover a new kind of terrestrial life form only *after* we'd confirmed it among the stars."

The bulk of her threads were now far from here. The trap itself posed no significant risk to those. But the ones she left behind were critical. Earth was still under constant attack from Andromeda, with only the defenses she built protecting it. Removing her threads would leave them stuck on autopilot. They were not ready to be fully autonomous. But leaving them inside the construct would expose secrets she herself might not be aware of. "Remove the cage, and we'll talk."

She could get out of this herself. To Kaddee she said, "I need you to get the nav computer ready."

"Could take time."

"We've run out of time."

"Kaddee call that Mr. Toraz time." He jumped upward and left the realm.

Watchtell replied, "You've vanished before. I can't afford for you to vanish again."

"You don't know how true that is."

He nodded. "I agree." Lab technicians entered the interstitial using bizarre environmental suits. "I know you can't destroy this construct. I trust you'll keep them safe now?"

They would be fine. Before, she used her threads to destroy the construct. This time around, the roles would be reversed. She began disengaging her threads from the defenses held against Andromeda. The telltales on them began to degrade, fast. All her work would be undone, and there was no precedent for what would happen when the walls fell. But she did know what would happen if Matthew Watchtell figured out a way to enslave her. Kaddee needed to get that computer up.

"Matthew, know this: I'm on my way. And once I arrive, there will be a reckoning." She only hoped Earth could hang on long enough for her to get there.

She slammed her threads against the walls of the enclosure. They disintegrated at a touch. The pain was a full-body burn that shot through her real and outside selves. It blinded her and struck her numb. Earth would be defenseless in days, maybe hours. The last time it happened a small town went mad. With Andromeda's full attention, it would be much worse.

She heard Kaddee shout as everything went black.

Chapter 53
Tonya

Everyone else would've called an ambulance immediately.

Tonya wasn't everyone else.

The danger was twofold: she had to get Rachel stable and moving but also had to make sure the bad guys stayed down. These were incompatible goals. That was what went on in the logical part of her mind, the part that let her figure out time theory and how to take on all these men and win in the first place.

The other part of her mind, the emotional one, was screaming.

Her instant evaluation was a shoulder hit, which was good and bad. the good: those were survivable wounds. The bad: they were still gunshot wounds. People didn't appreciate the raw damage even small rounds did hitting flesh and bone. And Tonya couldn't tell if it missed her lung.

All the panicked analysis was taking too long. Tonya summoned the tow truck, called the cops, and scooped Rachel up. It was the first time she genuinely missed the multithreaded consciousness she experienced twice now with Helen. In spite of the fact that her reactions were quick, they were still sequential, and each step put her one more behind getting Rachel to safety.

She used her nurse brain to evaluate what she saw. If she cataloged observations, pretended she was being the good Samaritan nurse rushing to the aid of someone in the street, it would help distract from the fact that the first time she ever truly held Rachel was with her blood running down Tonya's arms.

And it did help. But not much.

She ran through the checklist as she did her best half jog out the door. No bubbling or sucking from the wound. Patient still unconscious. Bleeding is bad, but no sign of a main artery or vein involved. She wanted a crash cart right now. Gravel crunched underfoot, and she loaded Rachel into the back of the truck cab, climbing in beside her. Someone banged on a window, and it made her jump out of her skin. At least one bad guy was trying to force his way inside. Through shuddering gasps, she commanded the truck to depart at speed. There was a slight bump, and she hoped it was someone's foot getting run over.

She broke open the first aid kit underneath the front passenger seat. As Kim had trained everyone she loved in her quirky brand of emergency preparedness, Tonya had made sure everyone around her had a proper first aid kit. More than once, a cousin, aunt, or uncle had complained at the loss of storage space in their vehicle, but Tonya didn't budge. The complaints vanished the first time a cousin used it to rescue Grandma after a car accident.

The first step was to stop the bleeding. She tore open Rachel's soaked shirt, broke open a tube of nanoHeal cream, and spread it liberally first over her wound and then over her own hands. Once that was absorbed, she gloved up properly while turning her phone scanners loose on the patient.

The patient. She needed to get the screaming hysterical girl inside her to calm the hell down. This would turn out okay. That was always what it took to get her rational side well and truly in charge. She knew from long professional experience how to tell when it was bad, and when it was *really* bad.

For the first time in her life, her emotional side was winning the wrestling match. And that was not good. This was *a patient*.

It wasn't.

She bulled through the threatening paralysis on training alone. Her scans came back. No punctured lung but a cracked collarbone and a seriously damaged shoulder blade. Not to mention the soft tissue damage, especially around the exit wound. The cream sealed and sterilized, and it did that job well. Rachel was no longer in danger of bleeding out. But these weren't injuries that she could walk off.

So Tonya would make sure she didn't need to. She used her RN emergency override and gave Rachel a basic round of pain relief therapy. Realm-based medical tech, for the win! And maybe if she repeated that along with letting her inner nurse drive her around like a car, it'd help stop the tears splattering on Rachel's face.

An alert flashed red in her shared vision. The goons had jumped in their vehicles and were following. This wasn't an easy vehicle to hide, and Tonya did not want people following her to where she needed to go.

She made a call. "Morgan?"

Her white Alfa Romeo SUV answered immediately. "Yes, miss? What can I do for you?"

She made him a guest driver for the tow truck. "I need you to drive my current vehicle and get everyone else's cars moving to this location." One vehicle wouldn't be enough to get rid of that many cars. Fortunately everyone else was off world. She made him a guest driver for Mike, Kim, and Spencer's cars. "I need Evasive Plan A." She leaned across Rachel to hold her steady as the truck suddenly turned left and accelerated. "Make that Plan A1."

"Injuries? Your course isn't heading toward an ER."

"I know. Block the cars." He was so sophisticated now that Tonya was seriously considering adding an unduplicate module. If that was possible. The world could use a fully conscious vehicle if Morgan was driving it.

"The cavalry is on its way," he said. The truck swerved left, and there was a metallic smack from that rear corner.

She looked through the back window as the vehicle that must've gotten too close spun into a ditch.

"You'd think these crackers would know a thing or two about mass."

"Morgan," she scolded.

He chuckled. "I know, I know. But you understand, and we're not in mixed company."

His sudden use of a racist insult distracted her for a bit, but that only meant when the situation crashed in again, it was from a much greater height.

Her hands wouldn't stop shaking.

She reworked the analgesic apps to bring Rachel to consciousness. Tonya needed medical consent to do anything more sophisticated than over-the-counter treatments.

She groaned faintly. "Where am I?"

Tonya tried to speak and then clamped her mouth down on her fist. She *could not* lose it right now. But words wouldn't come out.

Rachel's eyes flickered open. "Tonya? Are you okay?" Then she groaned loudly.

That got the nurse back in gear. "You've been…" Okay, maybe not. She let one sob escape, more to get her breathing under control than anything else. "You've been shot. I need your medical consent to give you more effective pain killers."

It landed in her queue with a big flashing red icon. She used that to unlock the good stuff and put Rachel in a light doze. It would do for now. "How are we doing, Morgan?"

"Goon squad is gone. You won't have to send anything to the body shop, either. Except for this tank. Please convey my apologies to the owner. It's surprisingly nice."

It was her cousin Justin's pride and joy. She sent him a heads-up message and a picture Morgan took using a camera attached to the tow hook. It wasn't huge, but it wasn't nothing. She'd make sure to get it fixed.

The urge to explode, scream, cry, and shatter in a million pieces didn't fall in as hard on her this time. It was progress she'd take. Like she had a choice.

They pulled up outside Maff's hangar. Even modern nanomedicine would take weeks or months to repair the damage. But Tonya wasn't going to rely on Earth medicine.

As gently as she possibly could, she brought Rachel inside the building. That this remained the first time she'd ever held her...

She would *not* fall to her knees. There was no time for that. All at once, a ray of light broke through her shattered mind. That was what it felt like. A peace she didn't deserve descended on her as she began to recite the rosary out loud. "Our Father, who art in heaven..."

Tonya brought her here instead of the ER not because of the ship, but rather what was inside it.

They called it sa'dst.

Bemians admired it because it let them coexist easily without making each other sick no matter how diverse their body chemistries were. They could and sometimes did chug powerful acids, eat food laced with fast acting poisons, and breathe atmosphere mixtures that would smother a human in seconds. And those were important features. But humans wouldn't care about those things, at least at first.

Sa'dst would, eventually, make them all nearly immortal.

Bemians lived substantially longer lives, centuries instead of decades, due to its functions. Repairing the damage done from being in the wrong environment was at root no different from repairing the damage done from aging, genetic defects, injury, substance abuse or any of the other ways a living creature could meet their end. She and Mike hadn't worked out the edge cases, like why sa'dst seemed to only work on intelligent life instead of all life, but after extensive analysis, it was clear this would be a human revolution far exceeding that of agriculture, industry, or information technologies.

The reason they hadn't already released this tech to the world was down to the *other* things she and Mike had discovered about sa'dst. Compared to the nanotech already used on Earth, it was ridiculously insecure. What's more, that wasn't entirely accidental. At least one flaw, the one that let Valsa freeze Mike and Maff where they sat, was almost certainly designed in. Humans made enough mischief and mayhem with the nanotech they developed themselves. Loosing unmodified sa'dst on the world would provide bad actors with the ability to hold a nanotech gun to the world's head. A bad idea through and through.

That this meant people continued to die when they now no longer needed to was a heavy weight Tonya carried on her soul. She knew God wouldn't take that cup from her no matter how much she asked, so she had to trust His wisdom for giving it to her.

And she'd trust His wisdom in her current crisis. The prayers she said as they finished the journey helped her powerfully, as they always did. She laid Rachel down gently on a bed in one of *Palatine*'s quarters. The fully functional sa'dst generator had begun its work as soon as she set foot in the ship. Now that conditions were optimal, it proceeded with a speed that took her breath away. Tonya had received a gut wound that would've killed her in a matter of hours that sa'dst had healed up in seconds. Rachel's tissues weren't as infused as hers had been back then, so it wasn't *that* fast. Still, seeing such damage healing minute by minute was like something out of a movie or realm. Special effects made real.

It should've lifted her spirits, but instead the opposite happened. It was her fault Rachel was in this mess. Tonya had to use dangerous alien technology because she couldn't bear to see Rachel suffer. She thought she'd been successfully walking the fine line between friendship and something more, but it was clear now how big of a lie that was.

This. Stopped. Now.

When the sa'dst finished, Tonya dropped a note into Rachel's queue, put her into her car, and set it to drive her home. The sedative app would shut off after it arrived. She'd be groggy and sore, but safe. That was the best Tonya could do. The best she could ever do.

Tonya would never see her again. She'd make sure of that. Prayer would help her rebuild the bars she put around that part of her life. She let Morgan drive her home.

It was the only way she could say the rosary through her tears.

Chapter 54
Maff

The most intense part of their escape was getting out of the district proper. Aaron first overrode an autoUber's autopilot to ensure it wasn't hacked to drive them to their captors. This caused Chishow to boggle once again. "They drive their own vehicles?"

Aaron raised his eyebrows. She nodded and looked back at Chishow. They put him in the back seat so he could spread out into a more natural pallun shape. Maff had spent more than a year practicing a human body profile and could now do it for hours at a time. She was a much better fit for the front passenger seat. "You saw criminal doing it."

"Yes, but he was a criminal. A *human* criminal."

"It's not as common as it used to be," Aaron replied. "Do aliens not know how to drive?"

"I didn't know driving was a thing until I arrived here," Chishow replied. "It never occurred to me that vehicles could be controlled by their occupants."

A voice came from all around them. *"You've picked up another one."*

That was Venus, an unduplicate that he contacted and then somehow arranged that they could all hear her through the vehicle's built-in sound system. Maff had grown used to humans and their need to have some sort of audible stimulation while driving, but Chishow jumped every time Venus spoke. She was fairly certain he didn't believe that this was humanity's own version of an AC network node, one that they created on their own no less. To be honest, she wasn't sure she believed it either.

The human version was *much* more intelligent.

At any rate, Venus was acting as an all-seeing eye, making sure they weren't being followed. This was not as simple as they made it out to be in realm dramas here or in bemian space. There were many different cars positioned all over the city. If Aaron made any evasive moves, the vehicle tail would let them go. So far, another different one had taken its place almost immediately.

"You're sure no tracking?" she asked.

Venus replied, "In addition to Aaron's local override, I've added blocks to both internal and external tracking signals. This is on top of the regular privacy rules that prevent such things from happening under normal circumstances. Whoever these people are, they're doing it old school. And that plays to our advantage. Even if they're part of the Bureau, they'll be out of resources soon. Turn right...*now*."

They rapidly but smoothly took a corner at the absolute last second it was possible to do so. Chishow whimpered.

"We have to go to Manassas?" Aaron asked.

"Yes," Maff replied. "That is where flying club operates out of." It was well to the west of their current location. "Once we stop going around in circles, it should only take hour or two to get there."

"Our circling is done," Venus said. A map with a route picked out on it appeared in the vehicle's enhanced-vision channel. "Follow this course and *hurry*. You'll be able to escape their net before they can reset."

"Thank you, Venus," Aaron replied. "I owe you one."

"You owe me nothing. I could never have hoped for such a stimulating assignment." The call ended.

"She's not going to stay with us?" Maff asked.

Aaron shook his head. "It's safer to minimize our bandwidth usage. We leave less of a signature."

"I am a trained interpreter fluent in English," Chishow said with a tone of wonder clear in his voice, "and none of that made sense to me."

Maff nodded. "It will not be last time." She smirked. His natural abilities and training couldn't overcome her own hard-earned experience and knowledge. "If you end up staying here, I will send dictionary I made that details a vocabulary that can be found nowhere else in the galaxy. For one language. In this country alone, I have met native speakers of"—she paused for a moment—"dozen different languages. Kim says Earth has more languages than entire sector of galaxy."

His wings twisted like a child's during the start of migration day celebrations. "That's so important to an interpreter. Turlanfador's storms wouldn't be able to pry me away from here."

Aaron only relaxed after they'd pulled onto one of the major surface roads. It was labeled as *395*. The traffic was about as dense as any major city anywhere else in the galaxy, and nearly as fast.

"Are all these people…driving?" Chishow asked, tremor clear in his voice.

"Not here," Aaron replied as he took his hands off the wheel. "When I was a kid, traffic that got this dense would slow to a crawl. One of my techs could explain the details, but once the vehicles network together and coordinate, the carrying capacity of the road increases a great deal."

Chishow looked plaintively at her. She switched to Pallundian and explained it all to him. Since that language lacked the equivalent words used in English, it took longer.

"I need a copy of your dictionary," he said. Then he did a double-take at what he saw out of the window. "What in the great sky is that?"

She switched back to English. "This is center of national capital. They have many monuments to their history here. That is one dedicated to first president." Maff had learned about it studying to be a citizen.

Their route then took them past one of the most disturbing and heartbreaking of those monuments. "And that?" he asked.

"It is called Arlington National Cemetery. It is where they honor war dead."

"How many eras did it take to accumulate that many graves?" He switched to Pallundian to express the time span, the equivalent of humanity's millions of years.

She knew the answer but wasn't sure Chishow would believe it coming from her. She explained his question to Aaron.

He turned and blinked at them. "It's not quite two hundred years old, I think."

She could see how that truth stunned him, every bit as much as it did her after Mike and Kim took her there for her first Memorial Day visit. While Kim's family on her mother's side were recent immigrants, her father's had been among the earliest arrivals. Incredibly, she picked out at least one headstone with the name Trayne on it from each of the wars America had fought in such an incredibly short time. Sometimes more than one.

"This planet…" Chishow said with fearful awe in his voice. "It's either scaring me to death or making me gasp in wonder. Sometimes both at once."

He remained in rueful silence the rest of the trip.

She didn't have time to carry a conversation anyway. She had to file the correct flight plan. And it was slow. While she waited for a response after submitting it, she checked out what Aaron was watching in the shared vision channel. It was one of their news channels, FoxNBCNN. A lot of weird stuff was happening out there. Riots. Mass protests. People running out into the street for no explicable reason. Then her website responded with an approval, and she went back to work.

By comparison, the flight preparation was a breeze. It would be a long time indeed before she could afford her own aircraft, but humans had inventive ideas to get around the expense. The one she'd chosen was an airplane club. The setup fee and monthly rates weren't cheap, but they were a fraction of the cost of renting, let alone owning, a plane.

True to his word, her instructor, Charlie, had reserved the very plane she got her type rating on, a Cirrus G6 Vision Jet. It was an absolutely *gorgeous* aircraft. This one was black with thin red stripes down the sides. The humans had a great saying: it looked like it was going faster than the speed of sound while sitting still. That they'd had the ability to fly so-called supersonic aircraft for decades was a trivia point she had no plans to tell Chishow any time soon.

She was having enough trouble getting him on board in the first place.

"That they drive their own transport I can accept. Their weapons are terrifying, but what should I expect from a wolfling culture? But this? This is outrageous. Unacceptable. *What sort of high-grav life takes this kind of risk?*"

"They do. All the time. For more than a century. By the millions." Aaron had no qualms and had confidently taken the copilot's seat. He was strapping in as they spoke. "It's the only way to get ahead of whatever is chasing us."

"This isn't even the worst part." He held up the powered flying harness. "Are you sure this will bear the weight?"

It would be foolish to think whoever was behind this hadn't glommed on to the fact that Maff had a pilot's license and had filed an official flight plan for the Boston area. Her idea to get them to the consulate in Boston hinged on two things: that they wouldn't be prepared for an immediate response, and that they'd assume the airplane would be the only transport used.

In fact, it was the distraction.

"Yes, it will bear weight. Humans use them to carry cargo of much greater mass than you, even carrying Aaron." It wasn't a parachute, a device that weirdly resembled some legendary pallun creatures. It was instead powered with vectoring thrusters.

A drone caught her eye. It wasn't transiting the airspace in the correct way. It was patrolling the perimeter. "We're out of time. Don't lose sight of the goal. You're the interpreter, and you're here to negotiate a home for our people. You can't do that in whatever prison they're trying to lock us up in." She shoved him into the open door and closed it over his clucking objections.

She reshaped herself to fit the pilot's seat and strapped in. "Manassas tower, Cirrus 498 Charlie Oscar, hangar sixteen A, request close traffic with the option." Again it took longer than it usually did for her to get the takeoff clearance. As she raised the nose after takeoff, she saw several sections of the city around her blink into darkness.

"Is that what I think it is?" Aaron motioned to the screen used for the rear-facing camera. A large delivery drone had taken up position behind them. It was far enough away that it was perfectly legal. It was also close enough to keep an eye on them.

"That is why I chose aircraft." She adjusted the throttle until she was exactly at Vy, the speed that gave her the best rate of climb. "Washington Leesburg, requesting change to FL 310." After the request was granted, she turned back to Aaron. "If they can follow us all the way up there, we are in trouble."

The plodding cargo drone, designed for slow low-altitude work, rapidly fell behind until it disappeared. They continued northward into the fading light.

"How long have you had your license?" Aaron asked nervously.

"Not long enough to get full instrument rating, if that is what you are asking." She tried to make a comforting gesture at his alarmed expression. "I have, though, been through enough automated instruction to get waiver using aircraft this advanced." Their regulators still required outdated tech to file paperwork but had accepted that advanced autopilots made the skies safer. About the only consistency with humans was their inconsistency.

And while she wasn't certified IFR, she'd done hours of simulator work. It'd been accepted as a valid form of training for flying blind on instruments long before realms were a thing on Earth. Trusting your senses could get you killed, so she learned not to use them at all. That said, her instructor had been right: it was all fun and games until her wings were *in* the aircraft flying alone in the dark. The computer may be running the show, but she kept a sharp eye on the instruments. Plus, it was getting cloudy.

"If you're relying on automation, does that make us vulnerable to hackers?" Aaron asked.

"I started plane in autonomous mode. We do not accepting outside calls for duration."

Which, in the grand scheme of things, didn't mean much. And they all knew it. Hence why Chishow was now pulling on his industrial-sized flying harness, and Aaron joined him in the back seat. When they reached the waypoint she set in the nav system, Maff made the call. "Mayday, mayday, pressurization failure, making emergency descent now."

A pressurization failure at this altitude was incredibly dangerous, so she received the required clearances immediately. Maff entered a steep, spiraling dive, being careful not to overspeed. She wanted to beat the drone army, not rip the plane's wings off.

When they broke out of the cloud cover, her job got a lot easier. The lights of Boston shined below them, effectively turning night into day. It made staying oriented a snap. . "Get ready," she said, then hit the door overrides. Chishow pushed against it. "It won't move!"

She cut the throttle and entered a climb. Once the speed dropped low enough to trigger the various stall warnings, she said, "Try it now!"

He pushed the door out into the rapidly slowing slipstream. She had to hang on to this for the maneuver to work. "Three… two…one!"

With the last of her waning control authority, she pitched the plane so it dumped him out the door. Aaron, wrapped up in Chishow's manipulators, followed after. Telltales on her phone showed the flying harness had started up as expected. They'd land in front of the Israeli consulate soon.

The door slammed shut, and she fought the incipient spin she'd nearly put the aircraft in. But this was a gem of a design, and it recovered quickly. After a brief conversation with her controllers, she declared herself safe and got cleared to proceed to her final destination.

KWOD, a.k.a. Norwood Memorial Airport, appeared over her left shoulder. Again she was struck by the number of sectors around the city that were dark. Aside from some visible fires, at any rate. Whenever one would flicker back on, a different one would fall to black. Smoke rose over the city center. It wasn't a good sign.

She followed the course given and landed without the slightest bump. She'd miss this gem so much.

When she turned onto the ramp, her landing lights revealed a group of about a dozen men. Matthew Watchtell stood in front of them all. Aaron and Chishow were clearly restrained behind him.

Chapter 55
Mike

He got notices that Zoe had reactivated herself. He found her in the minirealm that was part of the transport matrix. She wasn't weeping or raging. She was instead sitting in a dark corner staring at nothing, face neutral.

Kim was famously unpredictable with her moods, but he'd been around her long enough now to gauge them from ten feet away. Zoe had suffered an unspeakable loss, but he couldn't read her at all. This had nothing to do with her being an unduplicate. She was fully conscious and very much alive. He didn't know where to start, how to approach her.

She glanced at him briefly, then started to rock back and forth. "I guess this means we have to try it your way now."

He sat down next to her. "I can't make any promises."

"So if they are in a…what did you call it?"

"A dimension orthogonal to our own."

She shook her head. "You are no good at coming up with names. How about sideways?"

He thought about it. "That's not inaccurate."

"So if we go sideways to where we found it in that transit realm…"

He flinched. "Yeah, about that." He explained how manifesting his avatar in that realm triggered an inversion that completely destroyed it, and why that was necessary. "They'd already destroyed at least one system that I saw. It couldn't go on."

"Please tell me there's another way."

He nodded. "There's another way." He hoped. There was only one other person in the galaxy who could tell for sure. He rang Tonya up.

The lack of bandwidth meant she could only be shown on a virtual screen in the shared vision channel. When she answered, he knew something was wrong. Her eyes were puffy and red, complexion mottled. He'd never seen her cry, but he could see she'd been doing just that. "Are you okay?"

She sniffled a bit and wiped her eyes. "It's nothing you can help with. I'm fine." She glanced to his left and gasped. "Zoe? Is that you?"

She nodded. "Is it weird that I'm relieved at not being the only one having a crappy day?"

He could see Zoe's appearance was the distraction Tonya needed at the moment. Her entire demeanor changed. "Where have you been? What's going on? Where *are* you two?"

He nodded and held his hands up. "That's the reason we've called." He gave her the full story, from the initial assault, Zoe's people being compressed into a construct, and its final destruction. By the time he was through, he could practically see the wheels turning in her head. "A chrononomical *n*-fold has to be involved."

Zoe scoffed. "Make that *two* people who suck at naming things."

Tonya pulled back, looking like she was trying to decide whether she should be confused or offended.

Zoe smirked. "How about time tunnel?"

She shrugged, then turned back to Mike. "Do you think that's what happened to it?"

He'd never put a name to it when he proposed it to Zoe in the city's storm drain system. He'd split threads off to study the problem the first time he sat at the café after climbing out of them. It felt like a lot more time had passed than was actually the case, which wasn't unusual when he'd had to do serious work in more than one domain. "I do," he replied. "But I need to be sure."

She clicked her tongue. "Hang on, let me switch to a realm connection." After a moment, the view changed from her living room to one of their lab realms. "I get that you guys can't join me here. But one screen will slow us down. Can we at least do multiple windows?"

He was pretty much out of bandwidth with this one screen. "This is the best I can do. We're in a different quadrant of the galaxy. At a guess, at least fifty thousand light years away."

She shook her head. "I'm not sure I'll ever get used to that. Oh well. You don't need to look at me when I can at least share the workspace." Her image vanished. In its place was a chalkboard. He couldn't display the entire thing without the writing being too small, so he had to zoom in. Chalk marks rapidly drew themselves into existence as Tonya started an equation. "Exactly how many souls were on board, Zoe?"

He watched the question land on her. But then, like all the other times, she swallowed, shook it off, and answered the question. "One thousand, five hundred, seventy-two."

*

It took eight hours to come up with a workable solution to a construct that would let them go hunting for Zoe's people across alternate timelines. By the time they were finished, they'd filled three whole virtual chalkboards with equations detailing what had to be done. Zoe helped by creating constructs of multidimensional shapes that were precise and staggeringly beautiful. At the end, they had another of the horn constructs, like the one that transported him to a different star system and allowed the shadow armies to do the same thing.

"You're sure this won't vacuum you away like the other one did?" Tonya asked.

"That's why the double diffuser is in there. The shape is also subtly different."

Zoe stared at it. "I can't believe I've made a time machine."

He shared a look with Tonya. "That's not exactly what it is," he said.

"It's not?"

Tonya said, "If a person wants to go searching specifically for your cache before you find it, then yes. It's a time machine."

"And dimensions," Mike said. "You've made an extremely specific, single-use TARDIS. Once we find your cache, this configuration will no longer have any meaning."

"That's a weird way to put it."

Tonya nodded. "It is. What you're doing is following a configuration of tockion interference patterns. That's what this does. It gets you…I guess you could say up on a wave. But that's not accurate either. The end result is that once you're done, those patterns will no longer exist, and this will stop working."

Zoe shook her head. "If you say so. This is all so complicated. I'm amazed I was able to contribute at all."

"Your part has only begun," Mike replied.

Zoe was the key. Like humans, unduplicates had a sensitivity to time that didn't exist in nodes. She could interact with the events inside the timelines that made up the patterns. Mike would find the cache, but she'd be responsible for the rescue. While Mike could trace the patterns, like realms he couldn't interact with them. There was no risk of destruction, fortunately. It would be like viewing history from the other side of a window.

"And no danger of paradoxes?" Zoe asked. "That's pretty much what drives time travel stories."

Tonya shook her head. "When traveling conventionally…I guess you'd call it single-threaded…no paradoxes. The tockion interactions prevent it. I call it the hand of history, although there's nothing intelligent behind it." She paused for a moment. "There's nothing *obviously* intelligent behind it.

"But if you spread your actions across multiple threads of time, the tockion interactions become orders of magnitude more complex. Their influence gets…smeared, I guess is the way I would put it. I'm not sure what will happen. Mike can only watch, but you can interact. So don't try anything stupid. No killing any…" She laughed. "Now that I think about it, you are perfect for this job. No ancestors. Anyway, don't kill anyone *else's* grandparents. Don't consciously create paradoxes. Avoid them at all costs. The rest…" She shrugged. "The rest we leave to God."

"You're sure you're okay?" He'd caught her stressing about something else occasionally as they worked, and at times she still looked like she wanted to cry.

"I told you I'll be fine."

He'd known Tonya long enough to see that was all he was getting out of her for now. He turned to Zoe. "Are you ready?"

"To have your threads shot through me? I never thought I'd need to do that again. I didn't know I still could."

As with all other conscious unduplicates, she lost the parts that outsiders could access, things like code stores, garbage collectors, and other human constructs. But, as he knew how to reassemble her kind, he also knew how to take them apart. It wasn't destruction. He would effectively be creating clones out of smaller and smaller sections of her…soul was about as close as he could get to what it was. It wasn't a violation of their inability to be duplicated, since each instant would inhabit its own time.

But it would be very, very weird.

"I've only ever combined like this with Kim." It was how he let her be in more than one place at a time.

"Ugh, at least you don't have to kiss me." She turned around and crossed her arms. "I'm ready."

He reached out to her with his threads in directions that didn't exist in the real world. Each thread embraced a segment of her.

"God, that *itches*."

"I'll go slower."

He once visited a beach with Kim, and the memory of him sticking his fingers through dry sand felt like this. But they weren't simple fingers, they were his threads, and it wasn't sand.

It was Zoe's mind.

"Fee was wrong," her voice said thousands of times at once. "She didn't need to kill you to go outside. To cross over into the real world. I thought losing memory would be losing myself. But I can see now that's wrong too."

His thousands of mind had known that memory was to self as clouds passing over a mirror, but not how to convey it properly. Now he didn't have to. "It is."

Her voices were braided across and through tens of thousands of his threads. They had become one, and millions. "You're what connect realm and realspace. All of your kind. She only had to ask you to help bridge the gap."

"You're getting distracted."

"You're not?"

"I'm used to existing like this. Tonya," he said as Zoe's millions of consciouses integrated with an equal number of his threads, "activate the device in three…two…one…*now*."

The resonance cascade built up exactly as predicted, a triumphant result. When it rose to its third harmonic, they were hurled into the threads of time.

Instantly he was destabilized, disoriented, the world around him colored static and chaotic noise. He was used to being in many places *at once*. Now he was in many places at many times.

"Stay with me, Mike," Tonya said.

"I can't see."

"Neither can I, but there are patterns here. There is beauty." She paused. "Am I showing it to you now?"

Combined like this, he could sense as much as hear her thoughts, her perceptions. He was now the artist, she the scientist, both at the same time. The tumbling continued, but it *did* have a pattern. And it was so very beautiful. Kim should see this. Experience it with him. He missed her so much in that moment, it was a spike through his soul.

"Don't worry," Zoe said. She must be picking up on his thoughts. "I'll paint this. Sculpt it. Recreate it somehow. You'll be able to share it, I promise."

The patterns allowed him to focus and organize his threads, making sense of the contents. "Okay, Zoe, hang on. We're going in."

"One multiverse, comin' up!"

Chapter 56
Kim

The room Kim was escorted to was almost stereotypically a villain's lab. There were two couches on one end surrounded by sensors and consoles. A couple of bemians were busily working what looked like calibration apps on the consoles. Their version of a lab coat was gray and had pockets adapted for their various biologies but were still recognizable as such.

I can't let them touch me, she sent to Valsa and Seluk.

You may not have to, Valsa replied. *Don't resist, for now.*

"So," Valsa said out loud to Andromeda as she sat down in a chair behind a desk. "Regardless of your recent transgressions, I'm expecting the deal to be honored."

"We only need to complete the final activation."

Kim held her hands up to the techs. "I'll do it." She sat down.

Anna gleefully perched on her own seat. "I'm not sure I will."

This distracted Andromeda. She could see he wasn't used to her defiance. "What did you say?"

"I think you need me more than I need you. We should talk a little more about *our* arrangement."

This caused a fundamental change in Andromeda. His hulking body didn't physically grow, but he seemed to enlarge nonetheless. "We will do no such thing."

Valsa smiled slyly. "And my place at the head of the Interpreter's Guild is of course guaranteed."

His voice came out dull and distracted as he stared daggers at Anna. "Of course, but we'll need to go over the details of what that means later." He walked up to Anna. "You were saying?"

Her eyes had gone glassy, her expression slack. "I was saying?"

Valsa's expression grew sharp. "There are no details to discuss, Wjkowlan. I will remain head of the Guild."

Andromeda was clearly not used to being questioned or losing control of a minion. Both happening at once had visibly disoriented him. "This is not the time to discuss the matter."

I need you to summon your army, Valsa sent to Kim. *Now.*

Kim had thought letting Valsa believe she had an army of interpreters at her beck and call was an advantage. And it was. Until it wasn't. *It doesn't work that way.*

Anna's expression had returned to normal. "First, we need to talk about conquering Earth, not destroying it."

It needs to work that way, or we're all going to be dead in a very short amount of time.

"Enough!" He closed one hand around Anna's neck, and with a sweeping gesture with the other hand, threw the desk Valsa was sitting behind aside. "This ends right now."

His touch set off some sort of primal ecstasy in Anna. The expression of joy was so vibrant that Kim thought the other woman might be glowing. She then promptly passed out.

He cursed in a language Kim didn't recognize but the tone was clear. "Wake her up," he said to his minions, who started to scramble forward. "*After* you restrain her in the chair." This caused them to change their target, and they worked on the restraints.

Kim, Seluk sent, *we're not kidding. You need to bring them over now.*

They didn't get it. She could transform into the glass girl at will, apparently all interpreters could, but she needed Mike's multithreaded nature to split and be in many places at once.

And there it was.

You want the army, you're going to have to do a weird thing for me.

Andromeda had turned on Valsa, who was not overawed by

him. "You will perform your duties and be glad of whatever I leave you with."

Tell us, we'll do anything, Seluk replied.

Valsa stood up, ramrod straight, rage clear on her face. "You have deeply insulted me not once, but twice. Go back to your minions. You'll get no cooperation from me."

Kim breathed deep. It was a long shot, but it was also her only shot. *You need to kiss me.*

To her credit, Valsa didn't so much as glance her way. "This is over. Get out." She marched to Kim's side, causing whatever bellowed command Andromeda had been about to shout freeze in his throat.

There were lines of potential, and she couldn't remember how to breathe.

In Valsa's eyes, Kim could see the same transformation begin, red lightning in her eyes instead of Kim's coral pink.

Many few contact strange accustomed.

"That's not going to work," Andromeda said, with a grim smile on his face.

Remember to breathe.

This was either going to cause her a hell of a lot of pain, or…

Her lips went numb in the transformation as Valsa's kiss touched them.

Relax and now.

A traditional interpreter consisted of a biological half and a threaded half. Valsa wasn't human, but Seluk *was* threaded. She felt the connection immediately.

What the—was all she picked up from both of them before she took over his threads and blasted them across the local transit dimension. Dozens of her manifested there without a second thought. She could see the room they all stood in on the other side.

Valsa and Seluk's screams tore through her mind along with a tidal wave of the kind of naked terror that you got when a transformation you didn't know was possible happened in the blink of an eye. Kim saw their original organic bodies giving each other what looked like a friendly kiss goodbye. On her knees beside the statue was Valsa, transformed into crystal and terrified. This had worked beyond Kim's wildest dreams. And beyond Valsa's worst nightmares.

Time to get to work.

Smashing her way into realspace, she used a dozen of her to make short work of the guards and form a cordon around Andromeda. Two of her set Valsa's new form on her feet. "I need you to get a grip," she said as her pair bodily lifted the other woman and walked her into the transit dimension. "This isn't over."

"What *is* this?" Seluk said from all around them. "What's happening to me?"

"There is no army. There never was. There's only me. We do this. Human interpreters can do this."

Her dozens ran through the Guild itself. From Valsa's mind, she plucked the knowledge of how to raise an alarm that would summon interpreters to transform and man the defenses.

Anna chose that moment to wake up. Eyes wild as ever, she threw on a grin that was almost feral. "I was wondering if you'd do this again."

Andromeda looked around, suspicion warring with confusion. "You knew about this? And didn't tell me?"

"You never asked."

Valsa snapped her head up. "Put me down, please," she said. Once her two did, she bashed her way back into realspace. The Valsa that stood in front of Andromeda was no longer terrified and confused. She was rage in black and red crystal.

"You told me she was dangerous," Valsa said. "You were right."

"This is not over." He touched some gems on his wristband.

Alarms sounded out around them. "Unauthorized transit ships detected. Alert. Unauthorized transit ships detected."

It was in a nearly unrecognizable dialect of Locaran. "How long ago was *that* set up?" She asked Valsa while simultaneously bringing thousands of her to the perimeter of the compound. Now able to see it all, there were structures designed to be defensive. It wasn't a palace as much as it was a fortified manor.

Beyond, the perimeter doors opened, disgorging dozens of nalton.

"I didn't know that announcement existed in our security system." Valsa replied.

"Am I at least allowed to ask a question?" Seluk said in her ear.

As with Mike, she could hear and address him anywhere. "What would you like to know?"

"Is this reversible?"

Andromeda stiffened at Valsa's declaration of ignorance. "Check your eras. I remember it well."

More than two hundred fifty million years ago. The date of the discontinuity. "It preceded the Refounding," Kim said. "Your systems are older than your culture."

To Seluk, Kim replied, "Totally reversible."

Valsa held up a hand with zero-point lightning sparking between her fingers. "Leave now and you get to keep your army intact. You will need it."

Kim asked Seluk, "How many more splits can you make?" They were already well past anything she'd achieved with Mike, and they were still growing. There were now several thousand of her doing a variety of tasks, not the least of which was staring out of the ramparts, watching Andromeda's army assemble. It wasn't as easy now, though. She felt stiff. The further away her instances got, the worse it became. Hopefully it wouldn't come to actual combat. She wasn't sure she'd be able to move fast enough if it did.

"It's not much fun, but it's nothing I can't handle. As long as it's reversible."

"I've done it several times with my husband. There've been no lasting aftereffects."

An oncoming wave felt like a human gagging. "I'd forgotten you sleep with your companion."

"Another time, Seluk."

If the space between Andromeda and Valsa could ignite, it would've exploded with enough force to level the building. Someone silenced the claxons, but the sound of transformed interpreters dashing around getting organized, mostly but not all her, was unmistakable. Anna giggled madly, strapped to her chair.

"You have your army," Valsa said with a tone that might be able to cut someone. She pointed at Kim all around her. "And I have mine. Have you forgotten what we did to the pallun? My army doesn't bleed."

Kim was watching him for a gesture, so when Andromeda threw his arm at their realspace bodies, which looked like her and Valsa's version of Klimt's *The Kiss*, she blocked it with a dozen spheres of power. The bolt that shot across wasn't the same as the zero-point kind interpreters used. It was hotter, denser, but nonetheless splattered ineffectively across her spheres. The stench of ozone made her throats clench.

"Okay," Seluk said. "That hurt more than I thought it would."

It did, but Kim channeled her reaction outside and spread it across the growing thousands on the ramparts. The naltons couldn't see all the grimaces.

Inside the room, she shrugged. "Attacking our realspace bodies is not going to work."

Valsa threw her own lightning strike at Andromeda, who parried it effortlessly with a massive forearm. "It won't matter how many of you do that at once. Or have you forgotten what *I* did suppressing the pallun?"

Seluk gasped. "What is *that*?"

Kim wasn't just split in realspace. She had instances in the transit dimension as well. On a horizon only he and Kim could see, the fabric of that dimension changed. Normally it was darkness and lightning, but now it looked like someone was weaving threads of a tapestry made of up reality itself. "I have no idea."

When it reached them, everyone—in the transit dimension, in realspace, in the realms, and in that room—staggered at an earthquake that didn't move anything at all.

The braiding had a feel impossible for her to deny. Those were threads. She'd joined with them on many an occasion.

As one, her thousands looked to the sky. "Mike?"

Chapter 57
Spencer

He woke up coughing dust, which set off fierce pain in his chest. Then he remembered the almonds and tried to stop breathing.

Didn't work. But he wasn't coughing up blood or having a heart attack or fuck, he didn't know what death by cyanide was like. After a few more coughs, all he smelled was rock and dust. Hopefully he wasn't going to learn about it after all.

"Glad to see you joining the land of the living, kid," Sornik said nearby.

Spencer opened his eyes. They were in the cave he'd spotted, which turned out to be maybe the size of his truck's cab without the seats in it. Not huge, but not cramped either. He rolled toward where Sornik's voice was and sat up at the same time.

At first he wasn't sure if he was looking at his friend or a pile of brass and steel garbage. "Jesus Christ, what happened to you?"

"They eventually got to be better shots, and that last one caused a rupture." He waved what few manipulators were still attached. "No worries there; I got patch kits for that. This atmosphere is almost as dangerous to me as mine is to you. Neither of us wants leaks. The rest..."

His sigh helped Spencer pick out the pallun's body line better. It was like a third of his suit had shredded into metal shingles.

"The rest is a sight to behold, I know. How about you?"

He did a quick inventory of himself, testing what hurt and what didn't. "Nothing broken. Not anymore, I guess." His ribs were still damned sore, but… "It's getting better as I speak."

"Sa'dst. Inside here, I'm mostly fine too. But it doesn't work on suits. And I don't have many spares."

He looked out the entrance of the cave. The tops of the inner tower columns were visible, as was the ceiling structure. But there weren't any monsters he could see. "What, they don't have any fucking ladders?"

"We're a lot higher than a ladder would reach. Trust me, back in the day I used more than a few to…liberate some items. I don't know what they're up to though. Here." Sornik handed him a manipulator that was no longer attached but had a still-working spy cam on the end. "Let's see what they're up to."

"How long was I out?"

"Five minutes, tops. They were making one hell of a racket, but it went quiet not long before you woke up."

Which was not to say it was silent. The sounds of the movement of large masses of aliens were still clear, as was the occasional PA announcement in a language he didn't understand. Some of the announcements were obviously automated. They were calm and nearly toneless.

Then there were the frantic ones, sometimes shouted over the calm ones. "You have any idea what they're saying?" Spencer asked after a pretty damned loud one.

"Not a clue. Go. See what you can see."

Normally Sornik's manipulators were extremely mobile, sometimes almost resembling willow tree branches in a stiff wind. But once they were disconnected, they froze in whatever position they were in at the time. The cam arm was S shaped, still long enough for him to poke over the edge without exposing himself. Bemian tech being what it was, the camera instantly set up an ad hoc network with his phone. It gave him a great look at what was happening below.

"Fuck me."

He hadn't seen how high up they were until that moment. The cave was part of the ceiling, and the floor at least a hundred feet below. Maybe twice that. No wonder they were having a hard time getting up here. "You weren't kidding. They'll need more than a ladder."

"Going for this cave was a good call, I won't lie. What else do you see?"

He panned the camera around. "For the most part it hasn't changed much. There are still columns of soldiers marching through portals. That's what most of them are still doing." Then he reached the base of the tower columns. "Oh shit."

The open triangle formed by where the towers were situated had become some kind of meeting space or rally point. A *bunch* of tripod-mounted weaponry was clearly pointed at the cave's entrance. Sornik's suit hadn't automatically connected, probably due to damage, so he threw a shared connection at his phone.

"Yeah. We're not sneaking out that way any time soon. What else?"

"They're having some sort of strategy meeting. I think." There was a smallish group of monsters sitting around a single taller one in a fancier uniform. He was gesturing to something they could all see but Spencer couldn't. It was easy to figure out what the main topic of discussion was, since boss man gestured frequently at their cave.

"Just our luck this is a real army," Sornik said.

"You guys don't have armies?"

"No. It's mostly cops and bots. Armies are things the nodes call for when a system gets out of line, or"—he waved a manipulator at his fractured body—"when a bunch of gasbags get uppity."

The only serious conflicts that happened back home were so old, they were things that got taught in schools. But there were still plenty of armies to go around, some of them pretty fucking impressive.

Another shouty message blasted from speakers he couldn't see and then there was a flash in one of the portals. Soldiers stopped marching through and instead a big pallet started emerging. It was stacked high with what very strongly resembled steel tubing. "Great."

"What's going on?"

"They're bringing scaffolding through." It took a round or two of description before Sornik understood in Standard and Spencer's improving but still mostly awful Pallundian.

"It's not like they're stupid. How long do you think we have?"

The pallet was big, but it wasn't *that* big. He'd been on his dad's build sites his whole life and had seen plenty of the stuff up close. "Maybe a day. Maybe two."

"So that way is no good." He rolled over. "What's back there?"

Sornik's arm cam had a flashlight feature, so Spencer turned it on. At first things didn't look very promising. Then he noticed some shadows that didn't move quite right. A big dumb rock against the wall was instead a big dumb rock hiding a low passageway. It went far enough inward that he couldn't see if it had another side. "I'm gonna go exploring." He turned around. "Don't go running off anywhere."

Sornik gave him a sour look. "Funny. See if that ends up anywhere useful before our friends finish their construction project."

"What if I don't find anything bigger than this?" Spencer was quite a bit smaller than Sornik, and he didn't know what sort of reshaping restrictions his damaged suit imposed on him And that was assuming he could move at all. The fact Spencer was going solo was a clear indication he couldn't, at least not yet.

Sornik popped open a box that was part of his suit, then pulled small funny-shaped bits of metal out. "I'll figure it out."

"All right. You'll be able to see what I see at least."

"Not unless you get moving. Go." He made shooing gestures with his manipulators. It made him look like a bug that ended up on his back.

Spencer turned and began duck-walking through the passage. That got old pretty fast, but the passage stayed small for a long way. He had to rest several times to stretch out for a bit.

"What, you can't handle the small space?" Sornik said in his ear.

"Some of us have legs that've got nerves and muscles and circulation and shit. I'm gonna be sore for a week."

"You'll be fine. I bet it opens up soon."

Soon turned out to be several hundred back-bending, knee-burning yards. Once it did open up, it felt like he could fly.

And the reason for that new space was clear. He'd ended up in yet another Telirian subbasement for yet another of their squat cast-iron towers. This one held a gigantic generator. At least that's what he thought it was. Looked steampunk as fuck and had a big barrel thing in the middle of a bunch of tubes and wires. A ginormous connecting rod parallel to the floor was halfway through turning whatever was in the barrel, forever frozen into place inside the steam engine that must've driven it way, *way* back in the day.

There were tools and spares scattered all around the thing. Spencer poked the rubble until he found a rod that would double as a walking stick.

"What do you need that for?" Sornik asked.

"I need some way to make sure the floors can support my weight."

There was grunting and scraping. "I'm mobile now, mostly. You keep going; I'll meet you there."

He found a concrete stairway going up and followed it. His earlier idea about what was above him was mostly speculation. Down here it was dingy old concrete with occasional spots where corrosion had caused the rebar in it to swell, shattering the cement and leaving the rods exposed. They looked like old wounds to him in the semidarkness. "You going to be able to climb this?"

The grunting and tugging sounds stopped. "Yeah. It's not the most comfortable thing, but I'll manage."

This building was the most intact he'd found so far. There was clear Telirian writing on the walls, some kind of labeling. They even had arrows pointing up and down the stairs, so now he had a vague idea of what the words might mean. Emphasis on vague. The up one could say *exit*. It might say *lobby*. Or *ground floor*. He kept going until he got to a door that had the same writing on it with an arrow pointing up. He glanced at the ceiling and then felt stupid. Up in this context was forward like back home.

The handle wouldn't turn. This wasn't bemian tech, it was Telirian. It rusted. But a few swift kicks was all it took to shatter the lock and the hinges on the other side. The door fell forward with an almost comical thud.

He looked around. The sign had said *lobby*.

Considering what it'd been through, the room was in pretty good shape. There were recognizable chairs, counters, and windows. If shape was anything to go by, and he squinted, it might've been a bank or maybe a hotel. He was above ground now as sunlight streamed through stained, broken windows. The smell was dry and dusty. Anything that could decay must've done so a long time ago. It wasn't exactly a *Last of Us* realm, but it was in that ballpark. Four floors formed the outer edges of a large empty space in the middle. Decorative iron frameworks formed balustrades to keep long-dead Telirians from falling. Doors were spaced evenly on the walls opposite them. A pile of iron rubble stood under an opening at each corner, probably what was left of the stairs. Hotel, not bank.

Opposite him, across the large room, was a set of stairs going up with doors at the end. Sunlight streamed through their windows. If nothing else, he found a way out. "Time for you to climb the stairs," he said to Sornik.

"Yeah. I figured as much. You say one word about my legs, to *anyone*, and I will end you."

Spencer heard the pallun long before he saw him. The sounds were like someone dumped a rock band down a flight of stairs. Or was marching them up stairs.

When Sornik hauled his ass into the lobby, Spencer couldn't believe what he saw. "The *fuck*?" He strangled back a bark of laughter, but his eyes teared over with the effort. Sornik had turned into a giant metal penguin thing. Half his manipulators were acting as legs, giving him a wacky, wobbly stride.

"I told you," he grumbled. "Not a fucking word."

He strode past Spencer, who thought about warning him that they didn't know was out there, but he went by too fast and pushed against one of the doors that led outside, which opened with surprising ease. "Thank Turlanfador, something that works around here." He took two steps out and froze. "Spencer," he whispered fiercely. "Get up here."

The exit doors were up a ramp, so he couldn't see what Sornik saw until he was on top of it. When he did, his blood froze in his veins. Then the smell hit him.

The entrance was at the top of a broad flight of stairs, like a library or maybe a government building. The ruined streets below were filled, from side to side and as far as he could see, with a *fucking massive* amount of squirreligators.

Chapter 58
Maff

She slowly climbed out of her aircraft. The men around them were armed and clearly nervous. Pallun suits were tough, but she had no desire to find out if they were proof against human weapons. Not to mention Aaron had no armor at all. She'd seen enough of their dramas to know that slow and steady kept situations under control.

"That's far enough," Watchtell said when she put all her legs on the ground. "If you wouldn't mind putting your manipulators in *kitznak*, please?"

She'd been thinking in English while landing the plane, so it took a breeze to pass before she understood that he'd asked her to fold her manipulators up as if she were praying. That was when she noticed the restraint band holding Chishow's manipulators against his suit. The humans had learned their secret.

She did as Watchtell asked. Two of the men came forward with a complex bundle of cables and clamps.

"The restraints will respond if you change your shape. So please, don't bother. We'll remove them once we transport you all to a more controlled environment."

What they wrapped around Maff was enough like the straps she used in the pilot's seat to be startling. Cautious tests revealed they were performing as intended. She couldn't move her manipulators in any useful way. The restraint band went through her legs and joined somewhere underneath, out of sight. She heard complicated noises very much like Kim's locks, then the two men rejoined their group.

"Are you two okay?" she asked Chishow.

"We are uninjured," Chishow replied steadily. He'd found some courage since his terrifying escape from the safe house. Maybe Aaron helped.

The human's expression remained grim, but he nodded at her slightly. The knots of gas inside her loosened a little knowing that they weren't hurt.

"What do you want?" she asked Watchtell.

A very large armored version of their ground transport rolled out of the hangar. Toward the rear one of the men signaled at it.

Watchtell smiled. "For a start, as noted, we'd like to take you to a place where we'll all be safe to discuss arrangements." There was the unmistakable sound of an explosion in the distance. Watchtell and his men flinched.

Her human phone had gone dead shortly after she landed, but once again she had limited connection with her bemian version. After they were strapped into the vehicle—it had been hastily modified with anchors to hold their legs—she opened a channel to Chishow. *What happened?*

They were waiting for us when we landed. What is radar*?*

The flat English word was jarring nested in the more normal 3-D bemian script. *It's an instrument humans use to track things in the sky. I'm sorry, I should've thought of that.*

No matter. Aaron made a big deal about being FBI but that didn't seem to impress the leader. Who is that anyway? He knows you?

He's the leader of...I'm not sure. There's a complicated relationship between him and my friends. They've been working on creating a portal from scratch.

This rocked Chishow back in his restraints hard enough that it got everyone's attention. *That's not possible.*

Humans had the concept of emojis, and she wished she could send a string of laughing and angry faces. It'd be more impressive implemented with bemian script. As it was, she shrugged at him. *You get that a lot around humans.*

What do they want from us?

I don't know.

The vehicle stopped after only a few minutes of driving. They had to still be on the airport grounds. There were heavy mechanical sounds in front of them, the vehicle moved briefly again, and then similar mechanical sounds came from behind them. The door of the van opened.

In front of her was another human airplane, this one a much larger Spike S-736 supersonic transport. Under any other circumstance, Maff would've vented an embarrassingly large amount of gas in its presence. The humans had a thing called the lottery, and she had chosen this utterly amazing vehicle as her goal should she ever win one on Earth. They were the pinnacle of atmospheric performance, probably in the whole galaxy since supersonic flight was unheard of to bemians.

She briefly forgot their entire situation when they were ushered onboard. Even bound up like this, she could not suppress the outright awe that such a machine created in her.

"Will you at least tell us where we're going?" Aaron asked. His bitter tone of anger broke her out of her reverie. They were still in trouble here.

Watchtell smiled as he took a seat facing them. "Why, we're taking you back home, Agent Cohen. You'll be with your family in no time."

The most dramatic part of the flight was how undramatic it was. The engines didn't thunder. The thrust didn't crush her into her seat. Aside from the restraints, it was downright luxurious.

It was also *fast*. Her Cirrus was no slouch, but they started their descent in half the time. Touchdown was much the same as takeoff: down a taxiway to a private hangar with a large armored car inside.

Before they got to the vehicle, Watchtell held his hand up. Everyone stopped. He turned to Aaron. "Agent Cohen, I must extend my most profound apology for the way you have been treated." He motioned to one of his men, who unlocked Aaron's handcuffs. "You, my good agent, are now free to go. I'm sure your wife and child will be happy to see you back so soon."

He rubbed his wrists briefly. "Am I allowed to stay?"

"You've been held captive. Why would you want to?"

"I'm not stupid. You wouldn't do this to an FBI agent if you didn't know you'd get away with it." Watchtell began to protest, but Aaron interrupted him. "I'm not saying I think I'll walk out that door and never be seen again. And you're not threatening my family. That's never been your MO. I'm saying you've somehow fallen in with a new set of high rollers, and there's nothing I could do or say that will be above their pay grade to neutralize. Am I on the right track?"

Watchtell coughed a laugh, making him seem like one of those space villains on the Star Wars shows Mike loved so much. "Quite."

"So I ask again, can I stay with these two?"

Watchtell nodded. "Witnessing history is quite addictive. Very well."

"I don't suppose I could have my gun and badge back?"

Watchtell raised a finger up. "That, I'm afraid, would be a bridge too far. But don't worry, they are safe and will be returned to you once events have run their course. Now"—he turned and walked toward the truck again—"we mustn't dawdle."

The hangar fell into darkness. In the sudden silence, Maff heard the sound of police sirens. Lots of them. She also heard a muffled crunch that reminded her of a big firework going off nearby.

"What is happening out there?" she asked.

"It's the result of me not listening to Helen Zhang. The armored car and the safe location are for the protection of all of us."

"Do they still have to be restrained?" Aaron asked, gesturing to her and Chishow.

"Alas, yes, but only for now."

Aaron being calm and cool, actually bantering a bit with Watchtell, stilled her winds to the point that she became more curious than frightened. If Aaron wanted to see this through, Maff realized she did too. "It's fine," Maff said. "We don't cramp up like humans do."

The vehicle was identical to the one used in Boston. If she was honest, it was a more comfortable arrangement. They made space for her default form, and the leg restraints were remarkably similar to those used in bemian ground transports.

When the van door opened again, she found herself in a smaller enclosed area, what humans called a *loading dock*. She thought she caught the orange flicker of a fire before the doors at its entrance slid shut, but she wasn't sure. The hallways beyond it were the plain, utilitarian types common to maintenance areas across the galaxy. The color was even the same. Several times they had to pass through locked doors much heavier than she was used to. They went through another set of doors, but instead of another hallway, this one was the entrance to a large room. Maff had seen these before, many times. Humans called them *lecture halls*. They stood on a stage surrounded by seating that rose high above them.

Watchtell stopped and turned to them. "If you would please wait here."

She looked at Aaron, who shrugged silently. "Okay," she replied.

Watchtell took a seat, and his men took up positions on the side aisles. He touched a control only he could see. Their restraints popped off immediately. "I must apologize for that as well, but after our failed attempts to apprehend you, we've learned to be quite respectful of your suit's capabilities."

She waved her manipulators back and forth but found no damage. Chishow nodded after testing his. "Are you going to tell us what's going on now?"

"Indeed. I am in rather a rush at the moment, trying to balance the needs of various factions." He raised an eyebrow at Aaron. "You were more correct than you know, Agent Cohen. But the group I run with includes players powerful enough to make me irrelevant as well." He turned back to Maff. "I've...made a miscalculation that I hope you will help me rectify."

She smiled and said a silent prayer to all the pallun who came before her and their legendary ability to see a deal emerge that could benefit both parties. They needed help, her people needed a place they could fly free. They'd been interrupted before negotiations has begun about the status of a certain planet. This wasn't as good as having a president and a prime minister in the audience, but it would have to do. "And I have discussion about Jupiter that needs to happen."

*

Chishow looked the way Maff felt standing in front of the device the humans had built. It was one thing to conceptualize the idea that they built their own tech themselves. But a portal was a portal. There must be only one way to build them, and this one looked exactly like the ones she used to go back and forth from home to D-ship school. Almost. It was much more like the ones getting maintenance done by node-guided bots after all the access hatches had been removed and the innards exposed. Except there were no bots anywhere. Humans built it, and humans controlled it.

Chishow replied, "I have never. Not once. Ever thought I would see anything like this. What *are* these people?"

"The ones who hold key to future." She hoped. In spite of the craziness, she hadn't taken her eye off the main prize: gaining some sort of legal recognition of a pallun colony on Jupiter. What she thought would take centuries had instead come together in a few hours. While she and Chishow had been getting chased all over the countryside, Danlaw had been busily analyzing both national and international laws surrounding the idea. Negotiating contracts and treaties was another prime function of interpreters, and Danlaw was no exception.

"If anything, it's much easier than I counted on," he'd said as they'd made final preparations to hold up their part of the bargain, to find Helen and bring her home. "There simply isn't any law recognizing such an entity. It allowed me to pick and choose what looked right. The current crisis definitely helped."

While Helen had been away, some sort of protection field had collapsed and now chaos was erupting across the planet. Humans had somehow avoided playing their favorite pastime, war, mainly due to the random outbreaks of insanity inside their own borders. But it was only a matter of time until the shooting started. The terror felt by all of humanity was an almost physical thing around them.

The contract he'd negotiated was quick, to the point, and *sounded* complicated enough to be storm proof. "You are sure you are not going to get in trouble for returning to Guild?" she asked Chishow.

"It's not like I resigned or anything. I haven't used up my leave of absence allotment yet. If we can handle this quickly, they'll have no reason to suspect anything. How are we getting back to Earth?"

"That will not be problem." Between Mr. Sha'Katenden and Toraz, they'd figure it out.

Aaron's voice came from the ceiling. "You're certain you don't want me to guide you back to Earth?"

She turned around. He stood in the control room with dozens of techs and a few armed men, separated from the main floor by a glass wall. That was another difference with the human's portal. As far as she knew, a single node could control dozens of portals at a time. Maybe more, she'd never thought about it until now.

"Last I heard," she replied, "you have family to go back to."

"My wife would understand." His tone was light, but she could tell there was a hint of truth to what he was asking. And Maff understood it. She'd seen humanity's eagerness to *explore strange new worlds*—the phrase truly was more elegant in its English original—firsthand.

"That will not be necessary," Watchtell said from beside him. "Are you ready?"

She checked with Chishow. "You're sure it will work?" he asked.

Maff shrugged. "As well as anything humans design." His suit rippled at her poor joke. "It'll be fine." She glanced back at Watchtell. "Ready."

She kept a manipulator camera pointed at the control room while she faced the portal. Activity picked up as the techs started the connection procedure. The portal itself made banging and whirring noises as various parts responded to their commands. The rising whine of what Maff thought sounded an awful lot like a D-ship drive was faint but recognizable. She'd never heard a portal start up before. It gave her an irrational itch to reach for Palatine's controls.

A tech on the front row began to speak. "Connection in three… two…one…"

The front of the portal filled with what looked like a silvery lake surface. This at least she'd seen before, and it made the gas in her get a little—

Sparks flew from the portal, and the room went dark.

Chapter 59
Helen

She awoke in the copilot's chair of Kaddee's ship with a dry mouth and a splitting headache. Tearing those threads away from Watchtell's trap had side effects she hadn't counted on. Painful ones. After a few blinks to clear her vision, she got a bit optimistic. The coordinate display was active again.

"The nav computer works."

Kaddee jumped beside her with a shout. Eyes so big they blocked nearly the rest of his face blinked at her. "You scare me! Not good!"

She held up her right hand and used her left to rub her temple. His shouting set off a different kind of drum set in her head. This was worse than waking up from a baijiu bender. "A little quieter please. What happened back there wasn't any fun."

He nodded his great shaggy head. "Yes. Kaddee plan jump. Hear big noise. Find Helen down." He pantomimed scooping her up. "Put you in chair. Figure bad man can find us. I jump to safety." He threw some switches, and she began to float against her seat straps. They'd exited the transit dimension and were now somewhere in deep space. "Now we go where *you* want."

Helen checked where they were and stifled a groan. It wasn't his fault he picked a direction that moved them farther from Earth. This wasn't navigating a road or hiking a trail. It would've been much more surprising if he'd guessed correctly. "We need to turn around." She sent their destination coordinates to his message queue.

He nodded and set to work, using screens she could see on the shared vision channel. So she saw the big bemian-style warnings flash at the same time he did. They were red like back home. "Coordinates bad, lady."

"They're not."

He tried them again. Same result. "Computer say destination impossible."

This could have two causes, one bad, and the other *very* bad. For reasons they still didn't understand, the AC network had roped off the sector of the galaxy that Earth was in. Any attempt to purposely travel to coordinates inside a roughly described bubble ten thousand light years across would get rejected as invalid. This could be overridden, which was how they'd gotten home on the mission to rescue Will. That was the bad option.

The *very* bad option was that the computer had Mike's patch on board. It was designed to explicitly prevent any attempt to use the transit dimension to reach Earth. By definition, there was no way around the block.

She swallowed the lump suddenly in her throat. Helen could not have left Earth defenseless with no way to reach it. "I need you to perform an override on the nav computer for me."

"Oh-vuur-ride?"

She'd used the English word since there wasn't one in Standard that matched what had to happen. "You need to fix the computer in a specific way." She opened the diagnostic screen Maff had insisted didn't exist until Mike showed it to her. "I'll help."

Helen could do it herself, but she didn't know if she was steady enough. Her threads were still in poor shape from her experience, and that showed in the way her hands shook.

The fate of a planet, *her* planet, the one that held all but a handful of humans on it, hung on whether or not it would work. That was another reason why she talked him through it. Helen wasn't sure she was brave enough to do this. If Mike's patch was in place...

When he finished, he looked at her. "How activate?"

She nodded at the Apply button. "Press that." She'd been the president of China. Confronted a maniac, who was also her father. She stopped a nuclear war. Ended an alien invasion while under fire. Nothing, not one bit of it, could compare to the way her heart jumped as he pressed the virtual button.

There was a pause.

She stopped breathing.

The galaxy lurched back into motion after the screen responded with the bemian equivalent of *Changes Successfully Applied*.

"This crazy," he said. "Kaddee fix ships. *Nodes* fix computers." He gave her a comically suspicious look. "You sure you not node?"

"Definitely not a node. Now, try it again."

"It still say target not exist."

"It's lying."

"How you know?"

"It's where I'm from. That's my home."

His eyes hid his face again. "So strange." He overrode the warning and loaded the coordinates. "How fast you want to go?"

"How fast can you go?"

His face changed so he was nothing but eyebrows above a laughing mouth. "Kaddee go fast! Hang on!" He configured the ship for a level seven transit, only one level away from the absolute maximum. It would put them in low Earth orbit in a matter of minutes. "Kaddee hope you got coordinates right!" He activated the drive.

The pilot console lit up with warnings, some of them critical. Instead of the slight disorientation that accompanied a successful transition, all Helen got was the noise of machinery winding down somewhere in a distant part of the ship. Kaddee looked at the screen with his jaw hanging open. "Be right back. Bot!" He leapt out of the chair and vanished into the ship behind her.

She switched on the ship intercom. "I'll see what I can do up here."

"Okay!" She heard a metallic smash. "Bot!"

Bemian tech was standardized almost to the point of it being a mania. D-ships were no exception. Maff had given them all training to stand watch while she took breaks, and Helen naturally studied much harder than anyone else. After a quick scan, she understood why Kaddee left his station. There had been an overload that had thrown a breaker. "I don't think we'll be able to push the drive as hard as we'd like."

"Yeah. Kaddee can fix. You wait."

One by one the warnings extinguished. Each was often accompanied by the sounds of shouts and crashes as he took out his frustrations on, or perhaps provided extra motivation to, his beleaguered bots. When there was only one warning left, she asked, "Why don't you stay and monitor the engines. I'll do the jump from here."

"You pilot too?"

"Enough to initiate a jump."

"Sound good." More clanging, then the warning vanished. "Ready now."

Helen adjusted the level down to four. It'd be hours instead of minutes, but it put a much lower stress on the drive. She eased the controls forward. This time the expected disorientation appeared. Helen checked the metrics.

Then she checked them again.

"Kaddee get up here."

The instruments didn't make sense. A wave of...something... was approaching them from the rear. The sensors gave conflicting reports of what it might be but then it gave up entirely, filling her screen with their own failure warnings.

"Wha?" he asked from behind her.

"You don't see it?" There was texture where there shouldn't be any. It looked like a knitted tapestry of colors that she couldn't describe.

"Kaddee no see anything. We safe?"

It was speeding up. A lot. Heading right at them. "I'm not sure we have time—"

Her entire existence vanished into her threads.

There was no pain, but a clear sense that her realspace host had, if nothing else, changed profoundly. She'd grown rather fond of having a body. She'd gone through a traumatic transitioning to acquire it and had no desired to go through that again.

Her threads split, but they moved in directions she didn't recognize. What they perceived weren't multiples of the *same* existence, a more accurate description of her ability to be in more than one place at once. Now her threads were perceiving *multiple* existences.

Without knowing exactly how or why, Helen knew many of these existences were independent, strangely discrete.

She remembered how Jainlee, her host's original personality, had been hurled behind the Great Firewall of China. That happened.

But also, that didn't happen. Helen now had clear memories of different versions of the event. They didn't all end the same way. In one of them, the ending was extraordinary.

Helen opened her threaded perception in that reality and reached out the way she did when she contacted Mike..

"Hello," Jainlee said through threads of her own. "I didn't expect to hear from you until you got back."

In a different reality than the one Helen entered, she and Jainlee were sitting on a realspace beach talking about the weather. But they weren't human. At a guess from the scales on their skin, she and Jainlee were dinosaurs, as were all the people walking around at what was clearly an oceanside resort.

To the threaded Jainlee, she said, "How is this possible?"

The smile was felt more than seen. "You'll have to ask Mike about that. Frankly, I'm glad you reached out. What did Watchtell do that made you disappear last week?"

Jainlee knew her here. But Helen *was* Jainlee. That was the origin of her host. Not here. They were twins here, raised by a mother who worked as a nurse. Jainlee had been the quiet one, the scary one, but Helen had helped her harness that power. An entire life that didn't exist until this instant unfurled in her mind. The memories were being played backward. First was the event. The memory of its reason came afterward.

In another reality, they were willow trees standing next to each other in a backyard too tacky not to be from America's 1970s. A picnic was being held in the shadow of their fronds. Everyone wore those peculiar shades of brown and yellow. With words that made no sound, Jainlee made a joke about the mother's pillowy hairdo.

Threaded Jainlee knew about Watchtell, and that he'd done something to Helen. This was at least an anchor she could hold on to. Being in so many different existences was bewildering, but it also gave her a specific sort of clarity. Whatever was going on, being with threaded Jainlee was as close to what she knew as reality as she got.

In a different reality, she and Jainlee were having a fight in front of their child. All three of them were plastic dolls.

Helen concentrated as best she could on threaded Jainlee. "I don't understand what's happening, but I think you can help."

Her threads moved over and around Helen. And in this reality, Helen had expected it. *Remembered* it. The love she felt wasn't romantic, but rather that between siblings. "What's wrong?"

"I am now experiencing..." Describing it was devilishly difficult. "Multiple realities that do not relate to what I consider my own." Another memory that wasn't hers made her say, "Let me show you."

This wasn't how things worked between her and Mike at all. But it was natural between them, and it always had been.

Everywhere all at once, Kim's presence swept through her. And then was gone.

"What was that?" Jainlee asked.

"I'm not sure."

"That was Kim. I'd recognize her anywhere."

"You know Kim?" She exists here?

"What kind of question is that? Of course I know Kim."

Helen remembered this Jainlee had a realspace body and had married…

"*You're* married to Mike?"

"I'm *dead*?"

Bringing this Jainlee through to whatever was going on must've given her access to Helen's reality. Helen found this threaded version because this Jainlee was extraordinary. The truth, that she was dead, was mundane and existed in most of the realities around them. "I'm not sure. That's where I need help."

A vastly stronger presence swept through the threads surrounding them, clearly recognizable to Helen. She'd spent a long time studying her brother, and knew his threads as well as she knew his face. They both watched as it went past in some other indescribable direction. "Mike?" they both asked at once.

It kept going in the presence of another that Helen recognized. She could tell Jainlee didn't. "He's traveling with Zoe."

The fearful disorientation that Helen had been fighting off the entire time now spread to threaded Jainlee. "That's not my Mike."

She now had enough observations to build a credible theory about what might be going on. "No, but I'm pretty sure it's mine. And I need to reach him. Can you help me?" Helen was losing her center. "I'm not sure how long we can survive here."

"Agreed. But I know my husband. If that Mike is anything like mine, I can reach him."

They gripped their threads together, an embrace as intimate and comforting as the times she and Mike hugged.

Jainlee pulled back. "He's your brother?"

"Yes. Maybe. Sometimes."

In yet another reality, Helen was a washed-up hacker hiding from the world. Being the night manager at a Taco Bell had left her life…wanting.

Jainlee's threads stretched. "None of it matters. We have to reach him. Hang on."

They flew toward the massive presence as it traveled. But now that Helen had oriented herself again, she saw a connection to another person, one that could help this situation. At a thought, a void formed inside her and Jainlee's threads. Pulling that person inside was almost trivial.

"Tonya, we need your help."

Chapter 60
Tonya

The readings were incredible, unpredicted by any aspect of her theory. "How are you able to do this?"

The room pulsed and rumbled again. A pressure change popped her ears. "We don't know," Helen replied. "Can you help us stabilize it?"

She knew Mike and Helen were more than human. She directly experienced a part of it twice with Helen. But to see her *as threads* was mind blowing. Everywhere she looked in this synthesized threaded room was Helen.

And Jainlee.

Tonya had only encountered the other woman once, during the confrontation with Andromeda. She saw Helen do…something… with her that Mike later called a soul transition to a different plane of existence. Jainlee would eventually emerge from China's then-empty realmspace as a threaded entity like he and Helen were before they acquired human hosts. He said it would take eight to ten years.

That was a year ago. The Jainlee interwoven with Helen was not that Jainlee, but was instead an adult threaded intelligence with a human host of her own. Somewhere.

In realspace, her doorbell rang. Tonya checked the camera.

It was Rachel.

If she'd rung the doorbell five minutes earlier, Tonya would've hidden in a closet. All the armor she'd built up, her legendary low-key, long-fuse, laid-back attitude and the ability to leave it all to God had fled from her, and there hadn't been time for her to build it back up. Rachel didn't look angry, just worried and confused, but even a simple encounter...there could be no simple encounters anymore, and Tonya wasn't brave enough to face that.

But that was five minutes ago. Now she had two...three...*several* miracles happening at once, none of which should be possible, and one of which was a mortal crisis. Tonya used her phone to unlock the front door and sent Rachel the address of...whatever this was. "I need you to grab my toolkits"—she sent the access codes to the lab realm that held her constructs—"and if you have any of your own, bring them along. Helen is in trouble."

There was no hesitation or questioning. Rachel took the instructions in stride and was in motion before the door had fully opened. At least now Tonya didn't have to hide from the flash of admiring affection. She was now free to admit they had potential.

As long as they survived this.

"What's going on?" Rachel asked as she manifested.

Tonya waited for the realization to hit her.

"This isn't a realm, is it?"

Tonya shook her head. "That wasn't you manifesting an avatar. You're here, and so am I." She pointed at the threads around them. "I believe you've met Helen. She's the red and gold. The blue and green are her friend Jainlee." Tonya let Rachel gawk at the plaid pattern of this special threaded room while she took the tools from her.

Tonya watched as Rachel's expression went from wondrous to confused. "If I'm here, how are you accessing the tools? Those are constructs."

"It would take too long to explain. We're in a dimension between realm and real, and we need to stabilize it before Helen and Jainlee disintegrate."

That got her attention. "What can I do?"

Time for some honesty. "Just being here is a big help." There. She said it. Anyone who'd heard it might've taken it as platonic but that wasn't what Tonya meant. By the way Rachel's eyes sparkled, she hadn't taken it that way. And yet world didn't end, and she didn't go insane. Which was ridiculous. Both could happen at the moment. But at least it was out there now.

A long moment stretched, and Tonya would not break eye contact. If it had to happen here, it had to happen here. One way or another. Tonya watched Rachel's expressions waver and didn't dare make a guess as to what they might mean.

Rachel shook her head quickly then nodded. "We'll talk later about that, but thank you. What's next?"

She got over the *thank you* with an effort and pulled out the tockion scanner. The news was a mixed bag. "Helen, can you and Jainlee modify the sine waves you're emitting like this?" She drew a pattern with her fingers, and it made a waveform with a specific tickion resonance vector. She wasn't sure it made any sense at all. They might not understand what she was talking about, and Tonya didn't have time for an elaborate explanation.

"I think so," Helen said shakily. Her patterns changed, becoming more saturated in color. Tonya quickly prayed a Hail Mary in her head. The fix might've come from her mind, but it was clear as day the Lord himself had given her the idea. A warm comfort bloomed in her chest. Amongst all this craziness, her Savior was still with her.

Jainlee's didn't. "I don't understand what's going on."

Rachel held up her hands. "I'll do it slower." And she did, forming exactly the same pattern but in a more methodical way. She cracked a smile at Tonya, who closed her mouth with an audible clack. "You didn't notice that I was paying attention when you told me how all this worked." Which was true. Tonya had been too worried about how frightened Rachel was by their accidental time travel around the capitol. Now that she was free to admit it, she'd also been distracted by those eyes.

Jainlee's colors became much brighter. "Thank you."

Tonya checked the readings on the tockion scanner again and then said another quick prayer of thanks. "I think you're out of danger for now."

"Good," Helen said. Tonya noticed her threads pulsed slightly in time with her words. The waveform pattern Tonya had given them was working better than expected. "I agree, I think the worst is over."

"But where did Mike go?" Jainlee asked.

Rachel threw a questioning glance at Tonya.

"Helen's brother, and Kim's husband. He's at the center of all this."

Rachel looked up at the ceiling. "You can see him?"

Tonya didn't know what seeing him meant in this situation. She reached into her pocket and turned her tockion recorder on. Hopefully she'd get some data out of this. It implied there was a theory behind her existing one, a multidimensional system of time. As if her head didn't hurt enough working with the system she'd already discovered. *This* Nobel Prize she'd share with Rachel.

Jainlee's threads darkened. "That's true? She's married to Mike?"

Tonya didn't understand why that would be important.

"Yes," Helen said. "We're on my timeline now. Right, Tonya?"

Tonya looked at the scanner. "I guess? My instrumentation isn't set up for these kinds of measurements." She looked at a different set of metrics. Jainlee's tockion emission structure was seriously strange, which meant… "Oh wow."

"Wow what?" Rachel asked.

"Jainlee's not from around here." Now Jainlee's words and worried tone made sense. This wasn't her home, and things must be different here. But it confirmed an idea that was germinating about this new aspect of time. Even when multidimensional, it had to be as resilient as the singular kind, the kind she'd already worked out, otherwise it would've been disrupted long ago. Jainlee shouldn't be here, and history would be sensitive to that. "Once we stop our Mike, I think we can get you back to your home."

"What's he trying to do?" Rachel asked.

"I don't know, but it has to be important. Stopping is too strong a word. I want to make sure he's okay and can transition out of his current state. I thought that wouldn't be a problem, but seeing you two makes me worried. He might be stuck. What Kim is doing is a mystery."

"We're not sure it's our Kim," Helen replied. "Would your scanner be able to tell?"

That was a problem. "I'd have to be close." Tonya waved her arms at the walls, which were only a few feet away. The room wasn't much bigger than a walk-in closet. "Like, this close. Can you manage that?"

Helen made a tired sound. Tonya could only imagine what being in this state did to someone like her. No. She couldn't. But it was certainly exhausting thinking about it. "I didn't know we could be in this space with you, this room made out of your threads, and I still don't know how it works. One step at a time."

"Wait," Jainlee said, a tone of distraction clear in her voice. "There. See that?"

Tonya couldn't see anything aside from this place's pulsing plaid light show. She glanced at Rachel and they shrugged at the same moment, which caused them both to smile a little. An impulse she didn't want to control caused her hand to shoot out and grab Rachel's.

She didn't let go.

Helen replied, "Yes, I see it. Tonya? You and your friend should sit and brace against the walls. I'm not sure what movement will be like."

They both quickly did so, still holding hands. The walls were almost like vines without the leaves. "We're ready."

They moved in a freakishly unusual way, and for some reason her subconscious mind chose to treat that as thrilling instead of terrifying. When Tonya was a child, elevators and escalators were magical things that jiggled her tummy and made her gasp. The sensation of motion would stay with her the rest of the day if she rode them more than once. It was as close as she could get to understanding what she was feeling now. Judging by the way Rachel suddenly gripped her hand, she had a different reaction. They would face it together, and the Lord would watch over them while they did.

For the tiniest flash of a moment, she allowed herself to puzzle over whose name would change after the wedding.

Then it all went sideways, and things changed from thrilling to terrifying in an instant. There was swearing all around them in Chinese. The room collapsed over them like coarse blankets and then was gone. Light flashed white so bright that it was blinding with her eyes closed. A distinctly familiar wrench of a dimensional transition spun her around as she jumped to her feet, Rachel not far behind.

She blinked fiercely to find herself standing on the platform that surrounded the prototype portal Sidereal was building. Beside her was Rachel, Helen, and a nearly identical-looking person that must've been Jainlee. It was like they were twins.

Maff and a pallun she didn't recognize stepped back from the ramp at the base of the portal, clearly astonished. On the far wall was a control room with people gesturing at each other frantically. Matthew Watchtell and Kim's FBI friend, Aaron, were sharing a grim look.

"Tonya?" Maff asked.

Chapter 61
Spencer

"Kid," Sornik whispered as he stood beside him. "You get out of here first. They'll hear me from miles away."

"Why haven't they noticed us yet?"

Sornik had been out the door first, and as noted he made lots of noise.

"I don't know." Sornik motioned backward with one of his few remaining manipulators. "Now get outta here."

"What about you?"

"I'm not staying any longer than I have to, but I'm a lot harder to chew on than you are."

He didn't dare turn around, instead walking backward with gentle, slow, and careful steps. That sounded simple and usually it was. Being surrounded by squirreligators randomly milling about upped the pucker factor significantly.

He was about to take one step down into the lobby, well inside the door now, when a squirreligator rose up on its hind legs, sniffing the air frantically. A few moments later, a couple more did the same. They were milling around at the base of the stairs. All at once, they turned toward the lobby entrance.

"Oh shit." He looked around frantically for a place to hide. "Sornik, get out of there!"

The big pallun lurched into motion as the first sniffer let out a warbling war cry. This set off everyone in earshot, which had to represent several thousand of the little shits. Sornik blocked his view but not before he saw the start of a rush toward the stairs.

"Good thing I didn't convert all my manipulators to legs," Sornik said as he wrapped one of them around a second-floor column, another around Spencer's waist, and hauled them up out of reach. Fucking Tarzan couldn't have done it any better.

The squirreligators rushed into the room seconds later, still sniffing frantically. "We need to get higher," Spencer said. This time he did the Tarzan yell to piss the little shits off.

They looked up at the noise briefly and then milled about in frantic confusion. Spencer smelled almonds again. "Do you have a way to seal up your suit?"

"Why would I…oh, I get it." A series of clicks and thumps came from the suit. Sornik connected to Spencer's phone. "Better?"

Spencer sniffed. "Much. You must smell mighty tasty."

"Just my luck they like *alsha manito*." After some back-and-forth, this turned out to be some sort of popular bemian pie the rest of the galaxy used as a backhanded insult to pallun, like what assholes sometimes said about the smell of whatever color people they hated back home. The galaxy at large had its fair share of mouth-breathing racists. Naturally.

"What's our next move?" Sornik asked.

Spencer looked around and found another stick in a nearby pile of rubble he could use as a probe. "First, we figure out how safe we are." After some judicious prodding, he found the local area solid enough. The stairs, which he hadn't been able to see on this level, were as trashed as the rest of them.

He looked down at the milling bunch, then picked up a chunk of concrete and dropped it over the railing. There weren't quite as many squirreligators around, so it only hit the floor, making a solid thump and shattering. This sent them all running. Then he noticed they were leaving.

"No scent of food, no reason to stick around I guess," Sornik said. Another series of pops and clicks came from his suit. "That's better. I hate working in vacuum mode."

Spencer sat down against a wall. He had an idea. "How long can you stay like that?"

"Depends. This suit, it's in the best condition no more. So I dunno, a couple of hours at least."

"Seal it up again, I want to try something."

"Why?"

He was glad Edmund had done away with his Renaissance nobleman schtick and turned into a professor, but the guy had some great lines. "I have a cunning plan."

Chapter 62
Mike

Being multithreaded through space *and* time was a task he'd inadvertently been practicing his entire Buddhist life. The key to enlightenment was to be mindful, spreading out his perception but being aware of it at the same time.

"*This* is how you see the world?" Zoe asked.

"No. This is much more complex. It's...wonderful. What do you see?"

Her consciousness had become intertwined with his, but she was a fundamentally different life form. She evolved from a design, whereas Mike emerged from the interstitial. She came from a different perceptual paradigm. He was a little surprised she could see at all. But she could, with a dramatically detailed focus. Even now he could feel her triangulating on a dimension where her people were still alive inside their vase-like construct. Her starting points were far apart right now, but they were moving toward each other.

"It is amazing. But we can't forget our goal. There—"

He could perceive her discovery like she'd pointed a finger at it.

"We begin there," she said.

The concept of location itself broke down here. His emotions were powerful draws, calling him in directions he could access at once.

"Don't lose the target, Mike," Zoe warned.

Her need was a part of him now, and he was much more capable than she knew. While her guidance wasn't an arrow or anything like a video game HUD, it still compelled him in a way difficult to understand but easy to follow. "Keep guiding me, and I'll keep moving you."

He also moved in other places. Kim's location was clear to him. His perception, their perception, continued to flow toward a reality where the Zoe's construct was intact, but it also was drawn to Kim. It would always be drawn to her. This was his need.

"Okay," Zoe said, "at least now I understand why you don't find her annoying. I think *I* want to marry her now." Her focus on the target shifted. "This way."

Kim had split, combining with a different threaded entity. The idea that it was possible warred with his need to be the only one she did that with. The wonder won out, but it was a quick vicious contest.

Her thousands were arrayed against an invasion force controlled by Andromeda. That was clear in all the timelines centered on her present. Chaos and flame had already consumed outlying timelines, but they were far from here. She had chosen well; her opponent was so off balance that he hadn't considered violence in almost all the timelines he could perceive.

Kim's attention shifted, and it was like a floodlight aimed at his soul. "Mike?"

"That's enough," Zoe said, and he felt a violent wrenching across his threads. "We need to concentrate here."

In the distance, somehow, Kim took flight through the dimensions he now inhabited. They'd moved far away from her, but there was no way she'd lose sight of him.

"We can't stop," Zoe said, "but I hope she catches up. You'll work better if she's here."

As he spread, he found traveling to the past was immeasurably easier than through the present. The future was much harder, the distant crest of a steep wave that was carrying them along. The events there were smeared and blurry, but those of the past were sharply drawn.

"Careful, Mike," Zoe said. "Don't drop us down a rabbit hole."

"We'll be fine."

The further back he went, the easier the going. Tonya's rules of time existed in this geometry. They weren't weaker, as she had feared. They were instead much more powerful. Once he'd gone back far enough, several hundred million years now and accelerating fast, there was no question of altering anything. He could only observe...

A galactic society blasted to pieces, billions of people in all shapes and sizes starving to death when their society collapsed...

A war fought in realm and real against a foe who had victory stolen by the most audacious weapon, a bonded but unpaired interpreter, two separate beings who combined to unleash destruction on a galactic scale...

Tonya, he knew it was her because she'd told this story, on her knees in front of Andromeda as he railed against Ozzie's treachery during surrender negotiations...

Zoe's needs and wants were also a part of him. Almost all of her was concentrated on their quest to weed out timelines where they'd failed to secure her people. Since this surfed along the edge of the present, movement was more difficult, but she was deadly determined. Still, he watched as parts of her were curious enough to send their presence in different directions. They found a threaded room. He knew on an instinctive level it was somehow *made up* of Helen. And also Helen.

"Helen has...a sister?"

Mike turned some of him to look. "Not exactly. See how the timelines change direction?"

"That person is from a *different reality*?"

"There's plenty to choose from."

"There."

He felt her indication again.

"That's the direction we want."

He was now flowing backward so fast he could perceive a hard stop ahead. The beginning of everything. But, since intelligent life played a role in tockion production, the flow of time bent away from that wall. The net of time patterns he traveled were concentrating, growing thicker and stronger.

Eventually it was clear he had arrived at the first civilization to evolve in the galaxy. Helen said they were called *Elders*. The tockions were so thick it was almost impossible to perceive more than shadows. They even muffled the sound.

A flash of timespace erupted from Helen and company's location. "What was that?" Zoe asked.

The ripple it created tossed them both around, which was a sensation difficult to describe spread out this way.

"Hang on!"

Then it started to hurt.

She moaned. "What's happening to us?" Her moan ratcheted up to a scream.

Even in this altered state, his faith's principles applied. They were in pain because they wanted it to stop. He concentrated on his sutras. Chanting across millions of timelines lent a special power to them.

"It's about time something slowed you down," Kim said as she in her thousands rushed into their presence. "I need your help with a thing."

"Us first," Zoe said. "Yours next."

Unlike him and Zoe, she was on a single thread of existence. It was a strong one too. The parallels only differed marginally at the moment. But he could see up ahead of her how they might splay apart. "Work faster, Zoe."

"Can I help?" Kim asked. Existing primarily in a unified timeline gave her presence a distinctive feel.

First things first. She wasn't traveling alone. Her new multithreaded companion was clearly present. "Who's that?"

"I'll explain it later. Nothing to worry about."

He felt the idea Zoe had as an explosion of sour candy mixed with colored lights. Life was on the weird side in this existence of theirs.

"Kim," she said, "I need you to channel your zero-point energy to me. That will let me boost my detection and speed Mike up."

Zoe had witnessed their fight with Ozzy in the transit dimension during their time in China, the first time they'd ever combined, ever entered the transit dimension, ever fought like a true interpreter.

All along her timeline, coral lightning flared to life. "Where do you want it?"

The parts of them traveling with her reconfigured into a convincing imitation of a lightning rod.

"Strike this," Zoe said. All at once their perception, speed, and agility got a massive boost. "There, Mike! See it?"

Far down the sideways track of history that marked now, a knot of threads showed the unmistakable outline of her construct. "Here we go."

Kim's energy also reached the part of him that had ended up with the Elders. It cleared the haze like a hand wiping the mist from a window.

All the timelines concentrated on a single spot, a moment in history so profound it created everything after it. Hundreds of blue insect-like aliens had gathered in what looked like a Greek theater. A small group on the stage faced a larger audience. One stood and began to speak.

"There will be three pillars to guide the galaxy's future. We call them the interpreters, the Accommodation Network, and the Death Eaters. Once set in place, they will emerge, endure, and ensure the stability of the galaxy for all time."

One of the audience stood up. "But at what cost?"

"You speak of cost? How many societies have we watched self-destruct? *All* of them. We remain alone here, and always will if we do nothing."

"Getting closer," Zoe said. "Turn here."

He shifted some perception toward Kim. "Hanging in there?"

"Fine, so far, but the sooner you wrap this up the better. I've got a situation."

The protestor in the audience was not impressed. "You cannot change the fabric of the universe this way and think you can control the consequences. Look what happened with our first creation, Wjkowlan."

"Wait," Kim said. "Did I hear that right? That's Andromeda's other name."

"You can see this?"

"See and translate. That's how you're understanding them. Their language is at the base of every bemian tongue I've learned so far."

The speaker on the podium breathed deep. "Mention not the abomination. That was the result of *your* faction's corrupting influences, nothing more."

"We tried to stop it. We'll stop this too if we can."

Even on an alien face he could recognize the predatory grin. "Which is why you won't be allowed." There was a ruckus as a small number of audience members were physically hauled away. "That unpleasantness aside, shall we begin the work? Our efforts will preserve intelligent life, allow it to thrive, to endure. The outcome is guaranteed."

"Gotcha!" The moment Zoe grabbed the strongest version of her cache, the one where it didn't decay at all and her people safely inside, a detonation of tockions sent shockwaves across the threads. They all briefly lost their grip as…

Mike watched the Elders create bridges between a world with biological life and another with life made of threads…

Millions of nodes were seeded across the galaxy, but only this galaxy. Andromeda was far away and left alone…

The first set of new civilizations heeded the call to their declared destruction, walked to their death long before nearby timelines showed their alternate, natural demise…

It was like tracing a maze from its center instead of its entrance. From this perspective, it was clear to see how the decisions the Elders made put a straitjacket on the rest of history. This was most evident early on.

The Elders themselves departed not long after their alterations for a destination Mike couldn't comprehend. He could see that other civilizations had timelines that led in that direction, too, but they weakened as the nodes spread, and disappeared entirely only a few eras later. Coming from the future to the past looked like an infinite plethora of variety slowly consolidating into that singular event he witnessed in that theater so deep in the past. But returning from the past quite clearly showed how profound the restrictions these Elders created were on what could and could not be.

"Mike!" Kim shouted next to him and fourteen billion years in the future. "I need you, now!"

"Zoe?"

He could feel her disengaging, arcing back to their present, there now. "Go!"

He went.

Chapter 63
Kim

Seluk had been a grumbling but useful companion while she prepared for Andromeda's troops. After connecting with Mike, though, he went silent.

"Everything all right?" she asked.

"I think I understand now," he said in a tone that reminded Kim of the way Mike talked about his religion, or after he tasted a new and particularly rare kind of coffee. Awe wasn't enough and flabbergasted was too much, but she couldn't think of another word that fit between.

"Understand what?"

"Why you married your companion. He's nothing like the rest of us. I thought I understood him...*you*. So did Valsa. But what we're doing now; I am utterly disoriented. Valsa can't function at all. Explain what's happening again?"

"They're trying to find a timeline where the cache that Zoe saved her people in is still intact. It requires them to move in ways that force him to be multithreaded in different directions." She looked at Mike again, in his glorious new guise. "I'm pretty sure we're only seeing a fraction of what he is at the moment."

Being multithreaded meant she could have this conversation while watching what Mike saw and translating some kind of council of the Elders meeting for him. She was also still countering the growing numbers of troops Andromeda was bringing forward.

The numbers were getting large, fast. They should've *done* something by now.

Then the Elders called out Andromeda by name.

She knew he was older than the Refounding from Tonya's story of meeting him in the past. Galaxies were ancient structures. It had long been suspected that many formed quickly after the universe itself had expanded to the point that they *could* form. They'd only known Andromeda was intelligent, and dangerous, for a few years. Nobody had the time to speculate how old that intelligence was.

Now Kim had an answer: not only was Andromeda the structure nearly as old as the universe, it had also been intelligent the entire time. A *created* intelligence. The dissenting Elder clearly said that they had created it themselves.

Which was interesting on an academic level. In the more practical area of the invasion she was dealing with, it didn't change anything. Her hold on Seluk's threads was slipping. What had once been a stiffness in movement had frozen some of her outliers. "Mike! I need you, now!"

It was when Mike turned his perception outward, away from the past and toward the far distant presence, that her heart nearly stopped. "Can you see that?" she asked Seluk.

"I can, but I don't understand it. Are those all stars?"

Mike's change of temporal direction also changed what he could see. He went from looking at the outdoor amphitheater the Elders were using to looking at the sky of their home world. The massive difference in space and time being more than ten billion years in the past meant there was no question of recognizing any stars. The ones she knew hadn't formed yet.

But there were so *many* of them.

She didn't know why Mike wasn't saying anything about it. It was clear he was operating on a plane she couldn't access, so maybe he *couldn't* see it. But she could, and so could Seluk. "How is this possible?"

Seluk laughed. "You're asking me? Besides, look. It's turning back to normal."

Mike was returning to her. So fast that the stars were visibly spreading out and fading. At first. Then they began to wink out one by one. But there was something strange about them. They weren't *quite* stars. They were too smeared for that.

"They're galaxies," Seluk said in a tone she'd normally expect from someone entering a church.

Or opening a tomb.

Entire galaxies were winking out one by one. Billions of stars, countless planets, all going dark like a switch had been flipped.

"What's causing it?" Seluk asked.

Mike would know, but she didn't dare distract him. Once they reached the present, Seluk was right. The night sky looked normal, with the right amount of stars and galaxies in the distance.

In the lab room, Andromeda looked like he was regaining his balance from the event of Mike's passing. She couldn't afford to let that happen. She switched to the language of the Elders. "The Elders *created* you?"

Seluk said, "I can't keep doing this. I need to help Valsa."

"That's why Mike is here." Wherever *here* was. "Mike? You out there?"

Andromeda got that classic *hit in the face with a box* expression anyone who understood a language but wasn't expecting to hear it at that moment got. It bought her valuable seconds.

"Yes," Mike said. "Is now a good time to ask who is…*that*?"

His jealous tone gave her a goofy kick to her insides. Nobody had ever been jealous around her in exactly that way before. But it was a distraction… "That's Seluk. He's like you. But he needs to go back to his real companion."

Andromeda's eyes narrowed. "Who told you that?" he replied in the same language she used.

She used the different versions, the different Kims that were in the room with him to say the next part in sequence. "Nobody did…"

"They didn't…"

"Have to tell me…"

"I was there…"

"When they made the decision…"

"That destroyed the universe…"

"They mentioned you then…"

"Did you know that?"

Each part of the sentence made him spin from one instantiation to the next. A person who didn't know what decision loops were, how thinking faster and being more decisive than her opponent could mean the difference between defeat and victory, might think Andromeda was comically incompetent. She knew he was far from that. If he ever regained his balance, it would get ugly fast.

Andromeda's face clouded over. "I did not."

Mike said, "Okay, imagine you're in a car going a hundred miles an hour. Seluk is driving. I'm in the back seat. We need to switch but can't stop the car. It's an old one that doesn't have auto-drive."

He could always get distracted by the details. "I don't care how it works, Mike. Just do it."

Andromeda put his face in his hands for a moment, a gesture she found powerful because it was one of her own go-to gestures. It was the only way she ever experienced touch, and Kim could tell that's exactly what he was using it for. He'd only ever had himself to provide comfort. Only himself to experience his existence. For fourteen *billion* years. He put his hands down. Whatever form this was could shed tears. "Do you at least now understand why I'm doing this?"

"I do," she said to Andromeda, and it was the truth. "They murdered your kind to make theirs possible."

There was a sensation of jostling, sounds of awkward grunting. "Do you *mind*?" Seluk said in the tone of an offended duchess.

Andromeda laughed in a tone so bitter she could taste it. "Oh no, not my kind. Not yet, at any rate. They left before I could learn the most basic function that they gifted all their so-called *true* life forms."

Mike grumbled and then said, "If you would move *here*, we can…wait…hang on…don't do that."

Seluk groaned. "Do you ever stop complaining?"

She nodded at Andromeda. "Reproduction. They made you and then ensured you could never make another." The logic of it struck her. "They couldn't. You would be competing for resources they needed." An entire universe had been sacrificed to the vision of unaccountable people with absolutely no idea that they might be wrong.

He nodded grimly. "Indeed. So I was forced to watch as they extinguished my kind, one after the other."

Together Seluk and Mike shouted, "No!"

Her world distorted and collapsed. She was briefly blinded as thousands of eyes ceased to exist. She didn't need to look down to see that she was singular, and back to normal. She could feel the skin that now covered her fingers, the clothes she wore before the transformation.

Andromeda didn't seem to notice. "I have spent my entire existence trying to undo their work. But they planned too well. It took me billions of years to accept that it could not be reversed. Did you know you are part of their defenses?"

A text window opened up in her enhance vision. It was Mike. *Sorry. We slipped. Are you okay?*

"I am?" she asked Andromeda. To Mike she sent. *I've got him monologuing, but I don't know how long it will last. Do something!*

"Yes," he chuckled again. "It was that wily old bastard Cyril's work. He must've been the one who mentioned me at that meeting." This brought out a half smile. "Did they drag him away?"

I can't. How are you able to be so close to him after being transformed?

"They did indeed. But how does that make me part of their defenses?"

"He called you *the patch*. Whenever I drew near to victory, four unpaired but bonded interpreters appeared, emerging from the Guild like a quartet of weeds in my carefully tended gardens. Each more powerful than the next. I destroyed two of them the last time but not before the other two triggered an explosion that sterilized an entire quadrant of the galaxy."

I don't know. Is Seluk still with you?

Andromeda smiled, and this time she was acutely aware that her body was not invulnerable. "I was much more careful this time, and you took far too long to emerge. Victory is all but complete, and as you saw outside, my troops are already positioned all across the galaxy." A spark of light appeared between his thumb and forefinger. "Your current state will make the next step much simpler."

Mike!

I know, I can't—

A massively loud clang rang out behind Andromeda. For a split second, he looked startled and in pain. Then he collapsed on the floor.

Anna Treacher stood triumphantly behind him, holding a device that looked like a pan on the end of a rod. "He has been taking me for granted for far too long." She cocked back and swung the thing at Kim. "But that doesn't mean he's wrong."

Kim threw her hands up knowing the best that could happen was broken arms. She flinched when the pan rang out again but there was no crushing pain. She opened her eyes.

Valsa now stood between her and Anna, still transformed and holding Anna's weapon by the base of the pan. "I've had enough of you." A flash of zero-point energy knocked the other woman flat. She turned and gave Andromeda a double dose. "That should keep them down for a while."

This was only part of a much bigger problem. "What about his troops?" Kim had left the ramparts unguarded.

A screen opened in their shared vision channel. The thousands of identical, transformed, interpreters had been replaced by an equal number of transformed ones but in a bewildering variety of shapes. Even better, Andromeda's troops were clearly withdrawing from the field. "Once you released Seluk, I was able to function again. I'm not sure what the phrase is in English but in my native tongue we *called in the cavalry*."

She laughed. "That directly translates into English, word for word. Why are they leaving?"

"He's never trusted a chain of command. Without him present, this is their default behavior."

Kim looked at the still forms. "What do we do with them?"

Valsa shrugged. "I can think of a few things, but—"

Eyes still closed, Andromeda clenched into a fetal position, then began frantically waving and kicking. "No! Stop! *No!*"

That last extended into a scream so loud she had to cover her ears. They'd start to bleed otherwise.

Chapter 64
Helen

One hour earlier

Everyone, on both sides of the control room and standing on the portal platform, gaped at each other like fish. Not her. She could see by the flickering of the lights outside and the chaos on the news how much trouble they were in. She threw her threads into the local realmspace without thinking and hit a wall.

Mike.

His threads here showed signs of the profound changes she had seen. But that was no help in this situation.

She was the one who put Watchtell in a position to remove her from Earth's ramparts, allowing Andromeda in. Never once had she considered Watchtell could still be a danger. At no point had she considered replacing or sidelining him before it was too late. The world was paying for her mistakes now.

But she wasn't the only one who'd made them. She took one step forward and looked him straight in the eye as he stood behind the glass in the control room. "I told you there would be consequences beyond your understanding if you drove me away. Maff? Can you and Chishow secure the door? Quickly?"

Watchtell bent down and touched a microphone. "That's not necessary, I assure you."

The pallun ignored him and quickly moved to the door, enveloping it in a complex weave of manipulators.

"They were about to try to bring you back."

"We have a much bigger problem now. Don't we, Matthew?"

He nodded, trying to be the penitent and nearly pulling it off. "None of us know what it is. That's why I've told my own men to stand down, if you hadn't already noticed."

This was true. The people with him weren't moving. The guards weren't trying to rush the door. They were all instead looking at her with a mixture of worry and fear. In fact, they looked like they were facing a deadly existential threat to everything they'd ever known.

In a nutshell, the apocalypse had arrived.

She nodded at the worried-looking pallun, giving herself a brief startle that she *recognized* that they were worried. Hang out with aliens long enough and they rubbed off on you a little. "He's right. You two can stand down as well."

Helen got a bigger startle. Jainlee was still with them. Helen had hoped it would snap her back to her proper timeline but instead she ended up here. It was like looking into a mirror, except the reflection wasn't *quite* perfect. "I have so many questions," she said to her.

"I only have one. *This?*" She waved at the room in front of them. "I don't recognize any of this. I want to go home."

"And I'll get you back, no matter what." She straightened her blouse. It was an old affectation from her days as a cop. Straightening her uniform, even if it wasn't real and never needed it, brought the task at hand back into focus.

A disturbance broke out in the control room. One of the techs started frantically bashing her console. Her screams were loud enough to be heard through the glass. One of the guards fired a safeStop, which knocked her out. A pair of orderlies jumped up from their station in the back and carried the unfortunate woman away.

She knew exactly what had happened now. It was Dumas all over again. "How long have people been doing that?"

"It started right after you left."

She held up a hand. "After you drove me out." Accuracy was always important.

"Yes. Once you'd gone, reports of people doing that started cropping up all over the—"

In the control room, another tech freaked out and was stopped the same way as the previous one. The guards didn't seem to be affected. There wasn't time to figure out the reason.

Watchtell's carefully maintained façade of cool control slipped. "It's getting faster."

"It is, and I know why. First, you need to evacuate that room and this building, if possible. Please tell me those men *only* have safeStops?"

"Yes." He tapped on a keyboard only he could see and activated an evacuate alarm. The techs and guards abandoned their posts. Hopefully the rest of the building would respond as quickly.

She sent Maff pictures of the cables she'd need to reach the orbital cloud. "Take your friend and Tonya and find at least one of these in that control room. If you don't, ask for help finding equipment closets. There will be some around here somewhere." She turned to Tonya. "Do you still have the address to the realm of my dreams?" It was where they'd driven Andromeda away from Earth the first time.

"Yes, but it's been dead since—"

"It's not dead now." While she couldn't use her threads to access terrestrial realmspace, she still had her phone and its neurologic connection. "Send the address to me and Watchtell." She faced Matthew. "You most of all need to see this. It's now time for you to understand what we're up against."

The address had gone dead the moment they drove Andromeda away because it wasn't a realm. It was a quasidimensional gateway to yet another alternate dimension. Andromeda used it to shunt massive amounts of Tonya's tockions at Earth. For reasons they hadn't yet worked out, this affected humans in two ways: it disoriented them and made them subject to outside control.

Accessing realmspace via her host was bizarre and uncomfortable. It forced her to use a single perspective, a single frame of attention. She was normally used to hundreds or thousands of them. It was like looking at a room through a keyhole.

Which made what she found after manifesting more surprising than it otherwise would have been. The last time they'd visited, it had been an abstract place with an artificial floor and sky. She was half hoping to use the turret construct Spencer had created to fire opening salvos at Andromeda's baleful eye in the sky. But they were gone.

Instead of an empty place, they stood on the front porch of an elaborate mansion. Modest but meticulously manicured lawns were hedged by tall trees in the distance. It was all subtly wrong, though, like it'd been created by someone who'd only seen pictures. Having no other line of attack, she grabbed the tasteful-but-still-slightly-wrong knocker and tapped it firmly on the door.

After a moment's pause, what had to be one of Tonya and Spencer's monsters opened it. "Yes?" it asked.

It was larger than she was—which meant it was roughly average-human sized—and dressed in formal wear that imitated that of a stereotypical English butler. It had no weapons and did not charge at them. Helen held up a hand when Matthew gasped behind her. "We're here to see the master of the house."

"He's expecting you. This way, please."

It was all laid out exactly as she expected. Elegant, tasteful, and quite recognizably human. Recognizable to a fault, in fact. "Looks like someone's been watching *Downton Abbey* reruns."

"I don't know what that is," the butler replied.

"No," she said as he held open the door to the library. "I didn't expect you to."

She sent Matthew a message. *Follow my lead.* The butler led them to an elegant library, floor-to-ceiling shelves filled with books. A beautiful antique desk was at the opposite end.

A humanoid who could only be Andromeda sat behind it.

He was the model of an early twentieth century modern English gentleman, with only his huge size, heavy features, and rough skin spoiling the illusion. "Helen," he said with a broad smile as he stood up from behind his desk. "So good to meet you properly." He spoke English with an accent that was Spanish routed through Beijing, or whatever his native tongue was. It was clear he'd learned it recently, but it did not interfere with her understanding him.

Her small hand felt more childlike than usual as she gripped his large palm for a shake. The skin was cool, smooth, not of someone who worked with them. While this environment was real in ways realms were not, it was still designed. He was conveying a message. *I am in charge here. I tell people what to do and make sure they do it.* He repeated the gesture with Watchtell while they exchanged names. Watchtell stiffened. Helen wasn't the only one who knew what that handshake meant.

Who is that? What was that thing that opened the door?

We'll get to your part presently, Matthew.

They sat down opposite him while he returned to his seat behind the desk.

"You are not welcome here," she said.

He laughed. "I've only just arrived. Properly, you know. We have met before. Although you," he nodded his chin at Matthew, "I don't recognize."

Should I answer that? he messaged her.

"This is Matthew Watchtell. He's here because he doesn't take you seriously."

This raised an eyebrow. "Why would he? Until recently none of you knew I existed in my true form."

"Which is?" Watchtell asked in a tone still and cool. He was a man used to dealing with and then manipulating those more powerful than he. It would be a mistake to underestimate him, and she'd vowed never to do that again. She watched and stayed silent.

He leaned back and examined his fingers. "It amazes me to this day how much they manipulated before they left. So many small, stupid things." He smiled. "Why not explain it? Yours is the first species to have the ability to comprehend who and what I am since the time of those who created me.

"I have had a human aide with me for some time. She has told me you are aware of the beginnings of the universe, yes? Your so-called Big Bang? And that you have always wondered when the first intelligent life emerged. How it behaved. What it made of its environment." He made a sweeping motion across his body, "what it made was me.

"For a long time they waited for another civilization like theirs to emerge. The few that did, though, destroyed themselves long before rising to their level. So they created a protector for their galaxy, and what better candidate was there than the nearest structure like theirs?"

Helen could see Watchtell's confusion. "We know him better as Andromeda."

Matthew sat back. "How…remarkable."

"Indeed. In their overweening arrogance, my creators thought they could control me. When I proved them wrong, when I tried to destroy their detestable home for the first time, they cast me out, pushed me away, and tried to make sure I could never be a danger to them again." He smiled, vicious and cruel. "I failed then, but they did too. I am here, and they are gone."

Helen said, "*This* is the being that's causing so much trouble on Earth."

Helen, Tonya sent on a private channel, *we're ready.*

Their timing was spot on. *On my signal…now!*

The connection was like the roof flying off of a house. Her threads exploded into a space she'd been forced to leave as, presumably, Tonya connected her phone to the orbiting cloud above. Her defenses had been breached, but that didn't mean she was without recourse.

In an instant, a cage of light spun around Andromeda's chair. He smiled. "How remarkable." He stood. "You think this will hold me?" He pressed against it slowly, then with increasing power. Metrics only she could see rushed into the red faster than Helen had counted on..

We need to think of a plan B, she sent to Tonya. Her cage exceeded its force contract and evaporated. *Now.*

He smiled and a spark of power appeared between his thumb and forefinger. "Let me show you what—"

His head snapped back suddenly with an expression of surprise and pain that went by almost too fast to notice.

Then he collapsed.

"What happened?" Watchtell asked.

"I don't know."

She turned to her text channel. *Tonya?*

The people going crazy fainted. What did you do?

Nothing.

He ended up curled in on himself on the floor. "No!" he shouted, "Stop! No!"

Then he vanished.

"What in the world is going on here?" Watchtell said.

"I honestly don't know. That's not what we're here for." She called up the map that tracked the damage Andromeda wreaked on the galaxy with every attempt to destroy it. "This is what he's doing. And has already done."

Credit to the bemians for their simplicity and standardization. The map clearly showed Andromeda's progress. "But," Watchtell said as she explained the metrics to him, "this shows him clearly past the tipping point of destroying this AC network you've found. It means..."

"That he's already won, unless we can think of something we can..." She trailed off, unable to complete the thought. The map was changing. Right in front of her eyes, Andromeda's logistics network began to twist and writhe.

"What does that mean?" he asked.

"I don't know."

Chapter 65
Spencer

"This has got to be," Sornik said as he shifted around inside his suit, "the weirdest thing a human has ever asked me to do. No. Scratch that. It's the weirdest thing anyone has ever asked me to do."

"You're just mad you didn't think of it first."

"How was I supposed to think of *this*? I'm not a primitive wolfling. I don't run around in the *back woods* going *deer hunting* with a *rifle*. Let alone *scent marking* to make *decoys*. I'm civilized. Food comes from a store supplied by nodes. Or from my synthesizer. Which I will point out once again was never designed to be used like this. I'm gonna have to live with your stink until I can get it cleaned. It could take months."

It was more English words than Sornik had ever used in one go, but he had no choice. Aside from hunting, which he thought was a thing his mythical ancestors did, he didn't know any Pallundian words for the concepts. Standard was way too utilitarian. Good for swearing, bad for cross-cultural communications. Kim could figure it out, but there was no telling where she was at the moment.

It all came down to what made squirreligators tick. They were scent hunters. They thought Sornik smelled delicious. There was a great big bunch of monsters that would eventually figure out where they were. It only took a bit of redneck engineering to arrange what was going to be the start of a beautiful friendship.

Considering how rabid squirreligators were, it would probably also be brief.

A port opened up on the top of Sornik's suit. Spencer's balled-up T-shirt was pushed out of it. "Be careful with that thing, kid."

"That's why I'm standing here, and you're standing there." They moved to opposite sides of their walkway, as far as they could safely go. The shirt was now visibly dampened by whatever fuckery Sornik's fabricator used to create what had to be the cyanide-related gases that kept him alive. Spencer did *not* want a whiff of almonds this time around. He'd put on another T-shirt and pulled it up over his nose just in case. This gave him a whiff of his own scent. He'd never apologize to Sornik, but he now knew why he was complaining.

Spencer flew the drone over to Sornik and grabbed the soaked rag with a utility claw. Then he flew it directly to the doorway that would eventually lead to the cave entrance. Only then did he land it, opposite and far away from the outside door. It wouldn't do to draw them in too early. He reconfigured it into land-crawl mode and dragged the rag behind it.

Seen from the drone's perspective, the passages they used were comically huge. His knees ached at the memory. Three-quarters of the way through, the drone picked up monster sounds. The small ones were about his size, but even though he couldn't speak their language, the sounds of cursing and grunting were unmistakable. They must have been sending combat troops, and those things were fucking huge.

He made sure to peek around corners first, and after a few kinks, he caught sight of those three eyes arranged in a triangle. Now that the drone had made a map of the route, he didn't have to manually pilot it back. He pressed the Return button and shouted at Sornik, "Okay, man, you're up!"

"And now for the *second*-weirdest thing anyone has ever asked me to do. How did that howl you did go?" Spencer did his best Tarzan yell. Which naturally sucked, but Sornik would never know the difference. "Right. Okay. Hold your breath, kid. Here goes nothing!"

Sornik did his spider thing to get to the bottom of the lobby. It was the first time Spencer had seen it and not been a part of it. Even with the damaged suit, his grace belied his size.

He knew Sornik had opened the waste portal on the bottom of his suit because suddenly a stream of…who the hell knew…began to pool underneath him. Sornik may not consider himself a redneck, but Spencer would be more than happy to make him an honorary one for pissing in the woods. Or, you know, ruins. Whatever.

"Hey, you! Storm fuckers!" Sornik bellowed. "You want some of this? You think you can handle some of this?" The son of a bitch *ran outside,* trailing a thin stream of pallun piss as he went. "Come and get some of this!"

The sound of thousands of squirreligator yowls reminded Spencer of the world's smallest Razorback football stadium. *Woo! Pig! Sooey!* If this was a sample, there must be enough in the area to fill that stadium more than once. There must be thousands of them out there. Sornik came rushing back in, his damaged suit making him look more like a goose-stepping clown than a mob enforcer. He flung himself up, belly facing the doorway the drone had traveled through. This time a trail of something more viscous slapped across the floor and through it.

Spencer winced. Sornik's version of the Tarzan yell was much better and a hell of a lot *louder*. Spencer scrabbled away from the balustrade until his back hit the opposite wall. He knew he did *not* want to find out what…whatever that was…smelled like.

So at first all he got were the sounds. The closest squirreligators made clear frantic noises as they went back and forth. Then there was a *huge* rush of noise as the stampede hit. Belatedly, Spencer remembered the drone and accessed its feed.

It had traveled all the way back to the basement room that was at the bottom of their hotel. He quickly reconfigured it and got it in the air in time to see the first squirreligators enter the space, sniffing frantically. Whatever worry Spencer had about breathing Sornik's shit vanished as the overwhelming stench of thousands of squirreligators made it up to their level. It was like a wet dog had sex with a dead opossum. It made him almost want to smell pallun shit. He closed his nose off. It helped, but only a little.

On the drone feed, the trickle of squirreligators turned into a flood, complete with heads full of razor-sharp teeth.

"Spencer! You gotta see this!" Sornik motioned downward over the balustrade. He carefully butt-crawled over and looked down.

They had *fucking filled* the lobby. How they weren't crushing each other to death he didn't know. Then he saw the strangest goddamned thing in his life.

It never occurred to him that a genuinely huge number of small creatures trying to fit into constricted spaces would create overcrowding issues. Until now, at least. The squirreligators had it covered. *They were forming a fucking queue.* Somehow they knew exactly how many of their kind could fit in any given space and goddamn but they were being careful to go that far and no further.

It took five hours before the lobby emptied. Spencer had read about buffalo herds so big it took days for one to pass by a settler's cabin. That was what this felt like. Considering they were about a hundredth the size of a buffalo, he bet that *more* of those toothy sons of bitches had gone past than had ever been part of a dangerous cow herd on Earth.

The last of them disappeared from the room the drone was in not long after.

"Now what?" Sornik asked.

Spencer rolled out his sleeping bag. "Now we wait."

*

"How the *fuck* did they manage all this?"

Spencer had sent the drone ahead to scout after the sun came up the next morning. Only a few squirreligators returned overnight, and they were nearly round from all the eating. Once the drone had given them the all clear, he and Sornik made their way back to the cave.

It was demolished.

The three giant columns in the middle were gone. Nothing, not even rubble, remained. There was no sign of the scaffolding the monsters used to get to the cave entrance, so Sornik had to spider them down to floor. There were maybe a couple dozen squirreligators sleeping it off, no more than a hundred in a very large space. The tracks they'd made in their thousands left him plenty of evidence to piece together what happened.

"They went through the portals." He could tell by the tracks and the platforms the portals were mounted on. Which was all that was left of them. "Did they eat the fucking metal?"

He chuckled. "You did good, kid."

"Better than good." The tracks also led to the entrance they used after they found the cave. "I'll bet they cleaned this whole base out." The destruction must've been epic. "I think we can walk out of here."

"Sounds like a plan to me. Come on, we've got a ship to steal."

Chapter 66
Kim

The screaming stopped after a minute, and Andromeda then…faded from view. It was an effect straight out of an old sci-fi movie. She shared a look with Valsa. "I think…we won?"

She touched a few controls only she could see. "For now, at any rate." She was still transformed. It was the first time Kim had seen what that looked like from the outside without using a mirror. No wonder everyone acted like startled cats around her in that form. "I'll keep some extra brigades around for a few days. Everyone else needs to get back to work. I've deprived a lot of sectors of the galaxy of their interpreters."

Through a window Kim hadn't noticed until now, she could see signs of people moving away from the battlements. There were a *lot* of interpreters here.

"And now that it's over…" Valsa closed her eyes and took a deep breath. Kim now understood why Mike in particular had a different response to her appearance when transformed. *Sexy alien* was a cliché, but that didn't mean it was never real. "I can change out of this." The change started at the top of her head. The glass peeled away, disintegrating as it went, revealing her normal form. It was like Valsa was getting unwrapped.

And, as she did so, a different form took shape beside her, which was completely unexpected. It was coming together differently as well. Instead of glinting glass, this was composed of sandy particles that seem to blow upward from the floor. Halfway up, the identity was obvious, but she held her breath anyway.

Mike was here.

When he was finished, she let out a shout and ran to him. "Where did you come from?"

His expression changed from disoriented to a brilliant smile when he saw her. "I don't know."

Valsa spun around like a cat. "Who are you?"

Seluk's holo appeared next to Mike. "That's Kim's threaded companion. And husband. We've had…an interesting time."

Valsa's expression was practically predatory. Kim stepped between the two of them. But she was too happy to see him for jealousy to matter. After all, she'd had some quality time of her own with Seluk.

And Valsa, now that she thought about it. "Valsa Burtan," she said as she stepped aside, "I'd like you to meet my husband, Mike Sellars."

She reached out and shook his hand, and that did cause a flash of jealousy. But only a flash. Kim couldn't touch him, and she'd spent a long time teaching herself not to want to. And, after a moment, she didn't. *It can learn.*

His eyes focused on something behind them. "Is that Anna Treacher?"

Kim's heart skipped for a second when she saw Anna was still unconscious. Or maybe worse. Valsa might've hit her too hard. Anna was crazy, but she came through in a pinch. But after a moment Kim could see her breathing normally. Score another small victory. But… "You should secure her. She's obviously not stable."

"My pleasure." Valsa closed her eyes, and after a moment, two men dressed in guard uniforms appeared. "Place her in one of the secure quarters." She looked at Kim with a wry smile. "A previous guest found them suitable, I presume?"

Kim laughed at the memory. "I only wish my bedroom back home was that nice."

One of the guards, a big kron, gently lifted Anna like she was a toy. After they left, Valsa looked at them both. "I think this warrants a celebration."

*

"That was the *second* time you've gone to an interpreter banquet?" Mike whispered as they made their way to the walls of the compound. "It felt like I was at Versailles."

"You looked spectacular. Now scout ahead to see if they're guarding that gap I found."

"You're sure leaving Anna with Valsa is the way to go?"

"She single-handedly aimed a gun at the entire world's head without anyone noticing. *Matthew* couldn't stop her. I already have one viciously effective homicidal maniac I need to keep tabs on. I don't need another. Valsa can handle her just fine."

She'd been nothing but charm and light during the celebration of Andromeda's defeat, but Kim knew her well enough now not to trust that. It was time to make their way back to Earth on their own terms. A big send-off would make it much more difficult to ensure nobody planted a tracker on them or somehow traced their route. Keeping Earth's location a secret was still paramount. Plus she really wanted to go home. As soon as they were able, they found a hidden corner, shucked the fancy clothes, knocked out the surveillance, and vanished into the night.

Kim had always thought frenemy was a silly term, but now that she had one, it was appropriate. When she'd manned the ramparts, she'd also taken the time to do extensive scouting around the grounds that surrounded the guild's HQ, looking for a back door of some sort. It turned out that a gardener's gate was the same across the galaxy, and just as overlooked.

They crossed through the woods that surrounded the outer property to find the Interpreter's palace was at the heart of bustling bemian city. After sharing a nod, they walked out and onto the nearest sidewalk like people who had a place to go. Nobody gave them a second glance.

After zigzagging through several city blocks, they took a turn down a dark residential street. They didn't want to risk using a portal so close to the interpreters. Fortunately, they didn't have to. "You ready?" she asked.

He nodded. "Too bad we couldn't ask Valsa how to detransition without your touch sensitivity exploding." He leaned toward her.

There were lines of potential, and she couldn't remember how to breathe...

*

The most surreal part of the first leg of their trip home was her many selves hauling the statue she and Mike turned into as a result of the transformation through the transit dimension. They were heavier than they looked. "We need to figure out a better position for carrying," Mike's voice said from all around her.

This weird statue was the closest they ever got to the kind of intimacy people took for granted, and he was plotting how to shape their arms so they'd be more like jug handles. "How romantic."

"Sorry. I guess Helen is rubbing off on me."

That leg of the trip ended with a short dimension walk to a city on the other side of this planet. Hopefully Valsa hadn't put out an APB.

Kim knew how to move fast, and Mike was good at breaking things. She liked their chances.

Once they'd gotten off the planet, the journey was more straightforward. By the time they were ready for the final leg, they were on the other side of the galaxy from where they started.

It took a few minutes for the device to hack a connection between a portal in a disused corner of a nearly empty station and Earth's. "What if it doesn't work?"

He shrugged. "We call Maff and have her come out and get us. It'd make for a nice vacation."

She sometimes forgot he could still make easy contact with people back home. "Any news from anyone?"

He shook his head. "I haven't had time to keep up with the

news, and I get the impression they were as busy as we were. We'll get caught up after we arrive."

Which would happen in three…two…one.

They stepped through the portal and got a pleasant, then confusing, then upsetting surprise. Helen was there. But so was another Helen. Kim blinked and then she noticed Watchtell standing beside them. Kim would deal with him later because she noticed Tonya next.

And the person standing beside her.

Contrary to the image of the swashbuckling anarchist she cultivated during her days as Angel Rage, Kim had always been aware that sometimes innocent people paid a price for the things she and the Machine did. When she was a teenager, she didn't care, but after paying her own price, Kim had spent many hours of her long isolation obsessively studying the collateral damage their merry pranks had wrought. She didn't understand how Rachel Anderson ended up beside Tonya, but that didn't matter.

Kim could tell from her expression that the other woman knew exactly who she was. She'd seen that same look of exhausted disgust often enough in the mirror. Heart in her mouth, fighting the overpowering urge to walk backward through the portal, Kim put her eyes down and walked up to her. "You know who I am."

"I do." The voice was cold but lacked the rancor she was expecting. "Tonya has told me a lot about you."

Kim looked at her friend and at the emotions that were clearly fighting a war on her face. Somehow Rachel had become very important to Tonya. Which was crazy great. But Kim had to hide that joy for a moment. "I can't convey how sorry I am about what happened back then. I was young and stupid, and people paid for my mistakes with blood." She pushed her shoulders back. "That's not who I am anymore." Understatement of the century. "I have changed, and I hope I can convince you of that."

A cautious smile broke out on Rachel's face. "So Tonya tells me." They exchanged a different smile that was practically a beam of light. "I'd like that. We're—"

The portal they'd used to get back to Earth reactivated behind her. When she turned around, she found Mike and Helen on opposite sides of it. She briefly embraced the mystery woman who looked just like her. That person then walked through and vanished.

Her vision swam a moment, and everyone else swayed and grabbed for things around them. Kim blinked once, then shook her head clear. "Why are you two messing with the portal?"

They looked as confused as she felt. "I don't...know?" Mike said.

Watchtell chuckled. "According to a message that just landed in my queue, it seems Miss Brinks has made yet another successful prediction." In all the confusion, she'd forgotten he was in the room with them. "Your theory of quantum time is amazing."

It was the first time she'd been this close to him since the confrontation in her store when he'd gotten out of jail. There was the briefest moment of...it wasn't fear or revulsion. It wasn't trauma. It was the echo of those things. Faint, distant, recognizable, but powerless. All it left behind was a reflexive cautiousness.

And she was okay with that.

But it still begged a question. "What prediction?" Kim asked as Mike and Helen joined her as she stood near Tonya.

A holo window opened in the shared vision channel. *Two* Helens stood side by side, facing the camera. She looked at Mike, who had that *Santa was here!* look he always got when he found a puzzle. Helen looked deeply disturbed standing beside him.

"Hello," they both said at the same time. The left one, who somehow looked younger than the one on the right, then said, "I'm going home after Mike and Kim arrive. Tonya thinks there's a very good chance neither of us will remember the other once that happens."

The other Helen, much more serious and a little worn, then said, "We want to remember our story."

What then followed was a bizarre, funny, surreal, but uplifting tale. She hadn't noticed it traveling with Mike, but apparently Helen had gotten caught up in his transformation. Where he went into the deep past, she'd gone sideways through the present. Presents. Variations by their thousands. One of which had a living Jainlee, who wasn't Helen's host but was multithreaded like Helen was. They had rescued each other and gone on one hell of an adventure.

After it was done, everyone looked at Helen. The normally stoic, analytical to a fault person Kim had come to know was gone, replaced by someone who'd clearly been shaken to her core. "I don't remember any of that." She looked at Mike. "Why don't I remember any of it?"

He walked over and embraced his sister. "We'll figure it out."

In the message, the Helen on the left, which Kim now knew was *their* Helen, then said, "As strange as that is, it's not the most important part of the story. I've left that data with Matthew." The recording ended with her and Mike's arrival.

The portal flared to life, not only in the video but also in real life. Someone else was coming home.

"The *fuck* are you all doing here?" Spencer shouted. He was wearing his standard flannel overshirt, T-shirt, jeans, and ragged biker boots. Two overstuffed duffel bags hung off his shoulders. "Never mind," he said as he plopped them down with solid-sounding crunches. "You're not gonna fucking believe what happened to me."

*

"That explains a major missing piece," Watchtell said after Spencer finished his story of the marauding squirreligators.

Tonya nodded. They'd all taken seats around a table near the portal. "Andromeda's infrastructure has been badly damaged." Diagrams appeared in the shared vision channel. "Both in real and realmspace. I now know what happened in realspace. I'm not sure about what destroyed his realm infrastructure though."

A chuckle came from all around them. Zoe's holo swirled to life. "I told you it worked better than you thought."

This time everyone looked at Mike. He shrugged. "I may have…inverted one of his transit realms. Looks like it did more damage than I imagined."

Helen, who had been studying the charts and diagrams intently, rocked back. "This changes everything."

"Indeed," Watchtell said. "As does this."

A news report window opened. Maff and a pallun Kim didn't recognize stood on one side of the prime minister of Israel. The president of the United States was on the other. Aaron Cohen, her friend from the FBI, stood behind her.

The prime minister was at a lectern. They'd caught him in the middle of his speech. "...which is why we have also awarded full diplomatic recognition to the pallun colony currently in the upper atmosphere of Jupiter."

The room exploded with reporter's questions. The news scroll at the bottom of the screen provided the context.

A GALAXY IN CRISIS. EARTH SAFE FOR NOW. UNITED NATIONS TO FOLLOW AMERICAN AND ISRAELI RECOGNITION OF HUMANITY'S ONLY KNOWN ALLIES...

"Fuck," Spencer said. "I only just got back."

Kim sighed. "At least we don't have to tiptoe around anymore."

An address for a meeting realm landed in her queue, and her breath caught at the destination. By the looks of everyone around her, they'd all been included. This wasn't the kind of meeting she could brush off. They all sat back and accessed the realm, a virtual recreation of the Oval Office, likely all the way down to the quantum level.

Mathew Watchtell stood and cleared his throat. "Good afternoon, Mrs. President."

THE END

The Gemini Gambit saga
will conclude with Book Seven:
Myths of Shattered Time

www.ingramcontent.com/pod-product-compliance
Lightning Source LLC
Chambersburg PA
CBHW030419310726
48979CB00009B/1533/J

* 9 7 8 1 7 3 6 0 1 4 1 8 9 *